THE GIRL AND THE GLIM

Special thanks to JP Jordan,
Reka Kovacs, Jessica Doll, Elle Power,
Brett Bean, Oatley Academy, and the Peg Bar.

 **@IDWpublishing**
IDWpublishing.com

LETTERS BY:
Hassan Otsmane-Elhaou

EDITED BY:
Zac Boone with Chase W. Marotz

DESIGNED BY:
Nathan Widick

ISBN: 978-1-68405-741-2   25 24 23 22   1 2 3 4

Nachie Marsham, Publisher
Blake Kobashigawa, SVP Sales, Marketing & Strategy
Tara McCrillis, VP Publishing Operations
Anna Morrow, VP Marketing & Publicity
Alex Hargett, VP Sales
Mark Doyle, Editorial Director, Originals
Lauren LePera, Managing Editor
Greg Gustin, Sr. Director, Content Strategy
Joe Hughes, Director, Talent Relations
Keith Davidsen, Director, Marketing & PR
Topher Alford, Sr. Digital Marketing Manager
Patrick O'Connell, Sr. Manager, Direct Market Sales
Shauna Monteforte, Sr. Director of Manufacturing Operations
Greg Foreman, Director DTC Sales & Operations
Nathan Widick, Sr. Art Director, Head of Design
Neil Uyetake, Sr. Art Director, Design & Production
Shawn Lee, Art Director, Design & Production
Jack Rivera, Art Director, Marketing

Ted Adams and Robbie Robbins, IDW Founders

For international rights, contact licensing@idwpublishing.com

THE GIRL AND THE GLIM

Created, Written, and Illustrated by
India Swift

Colors by
Michael Doig

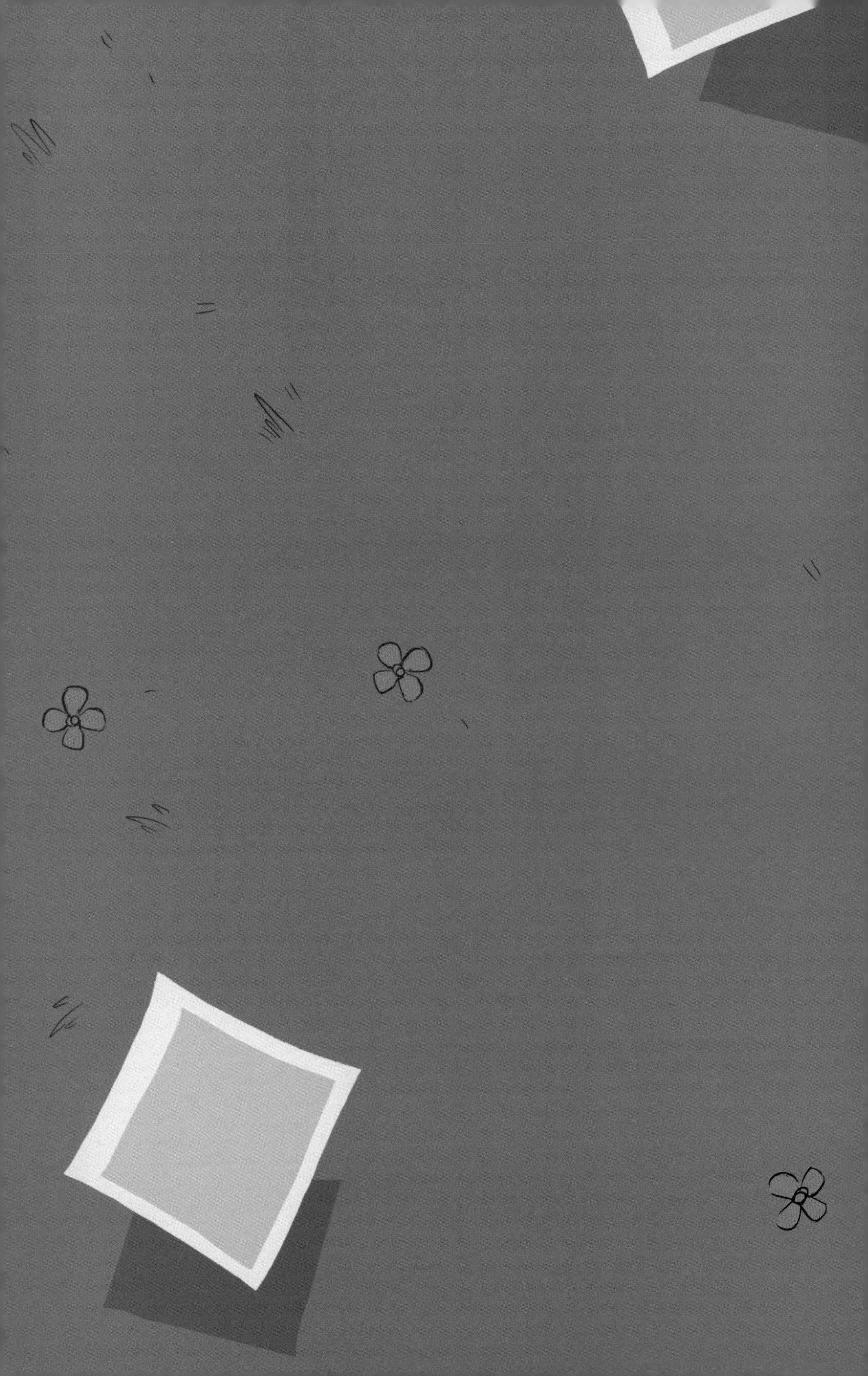

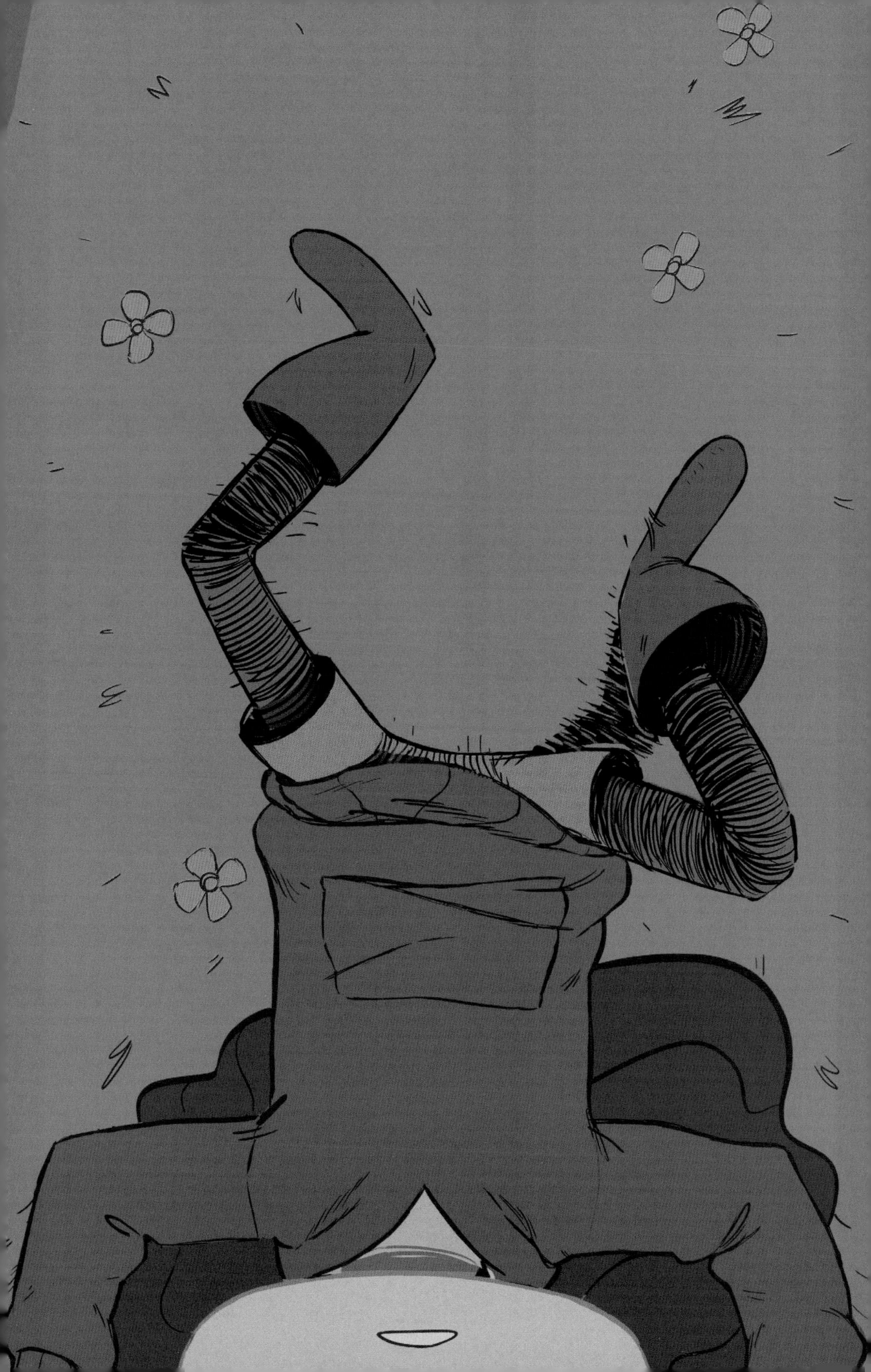

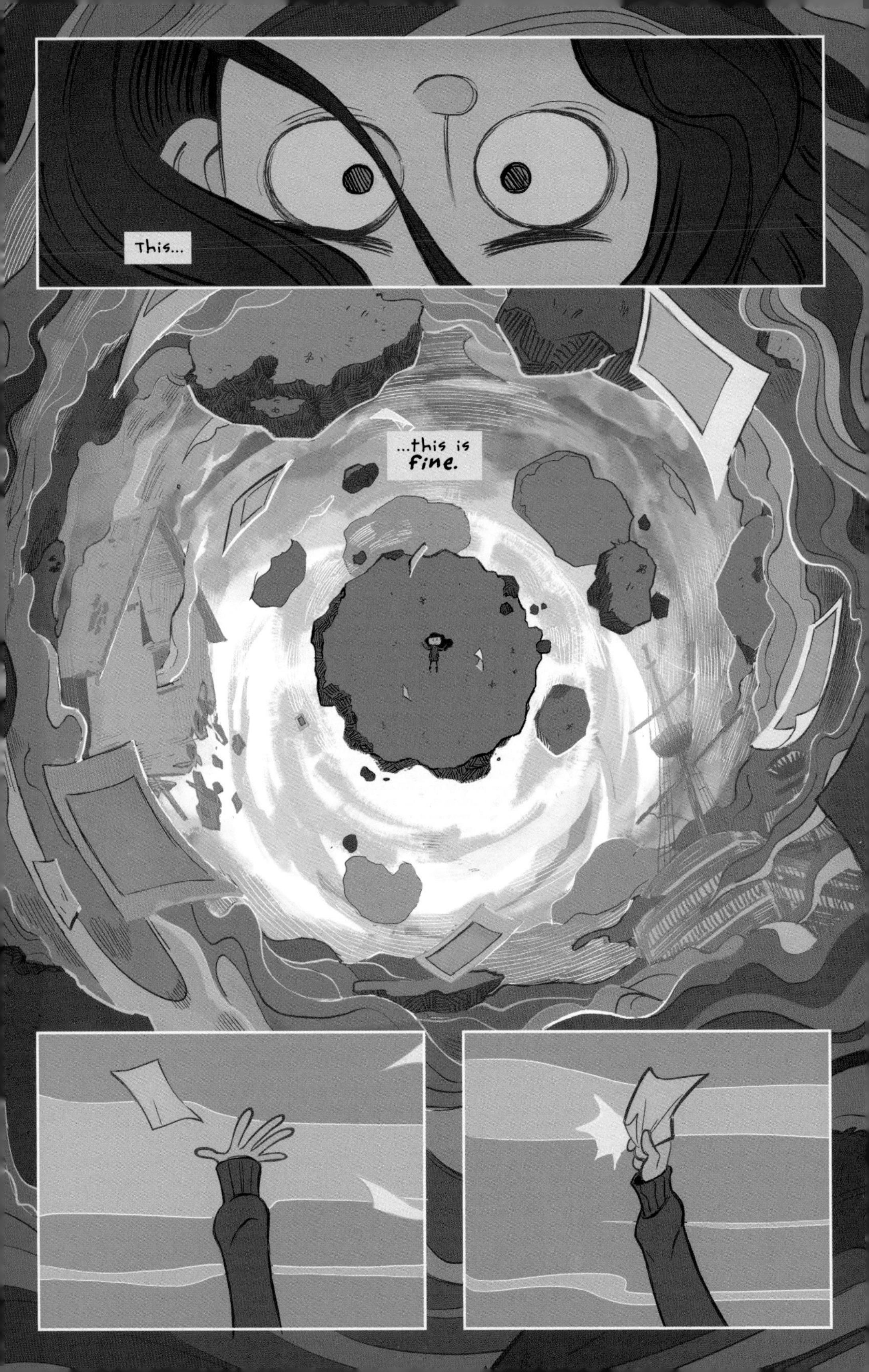
This...
...this is fine.

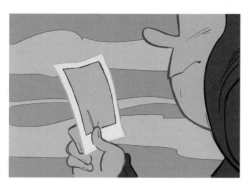

After all,
everyone would
be better off...

...if...

...I...

...just...

...disappeare

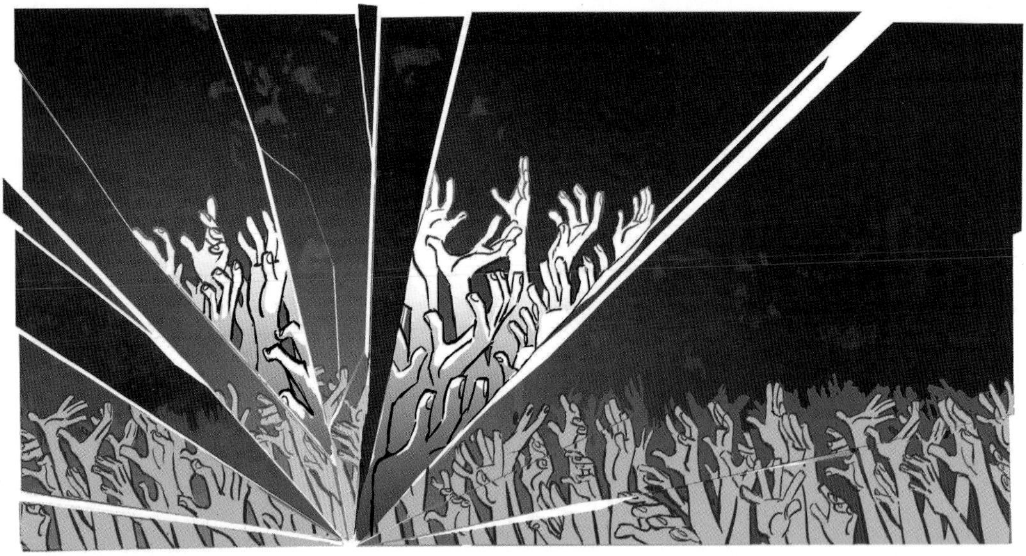

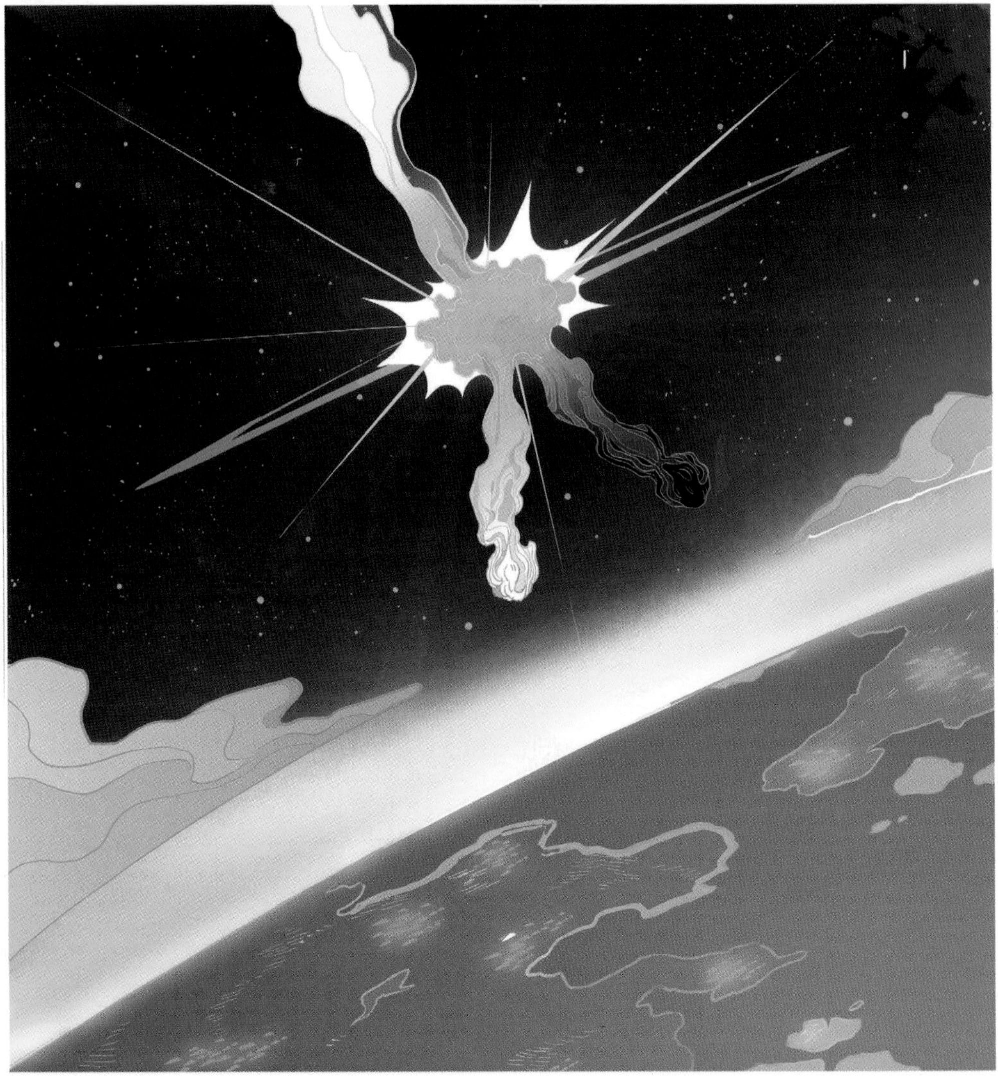

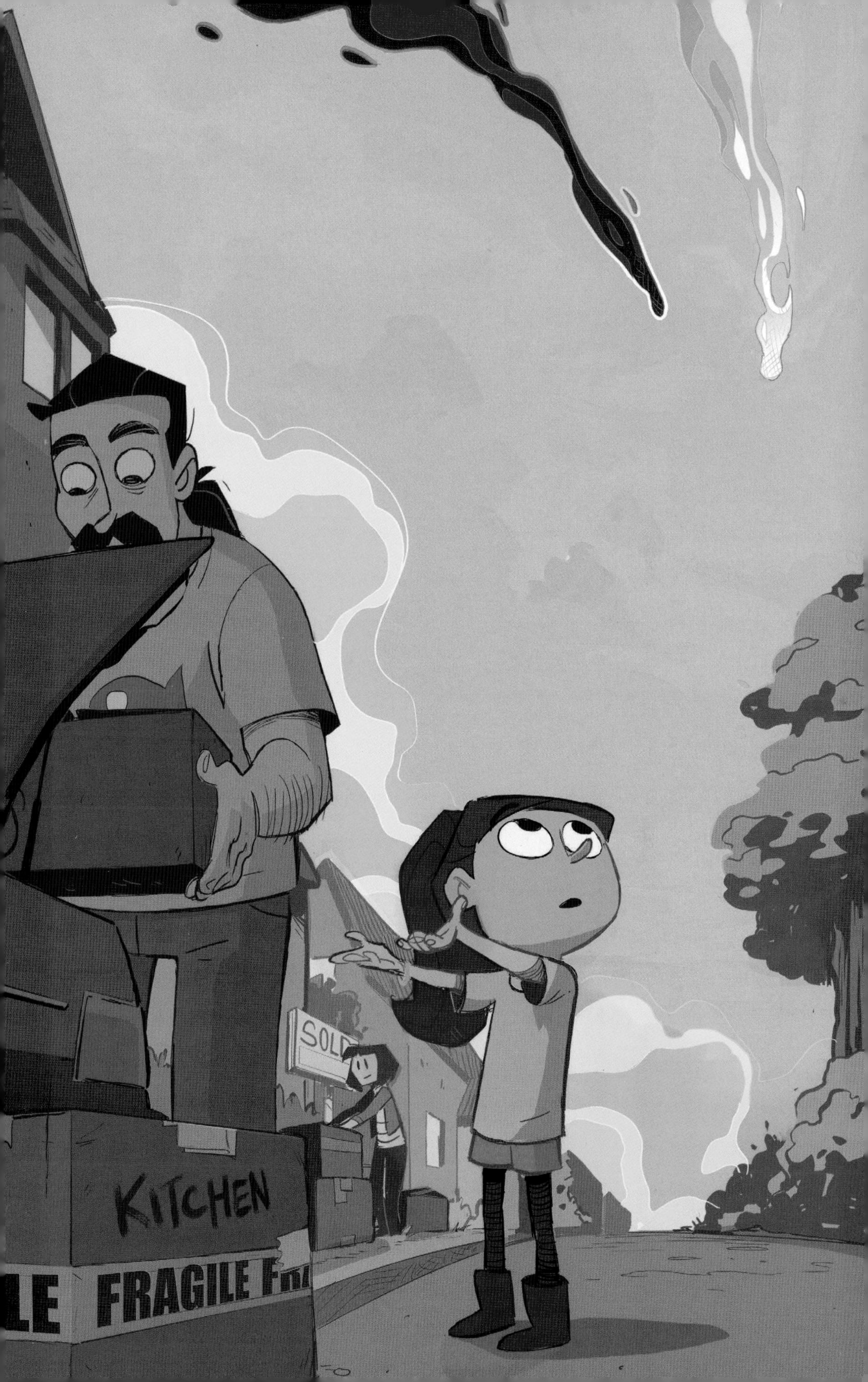
SOLD
KITCHEN
LE FRAGILE FR

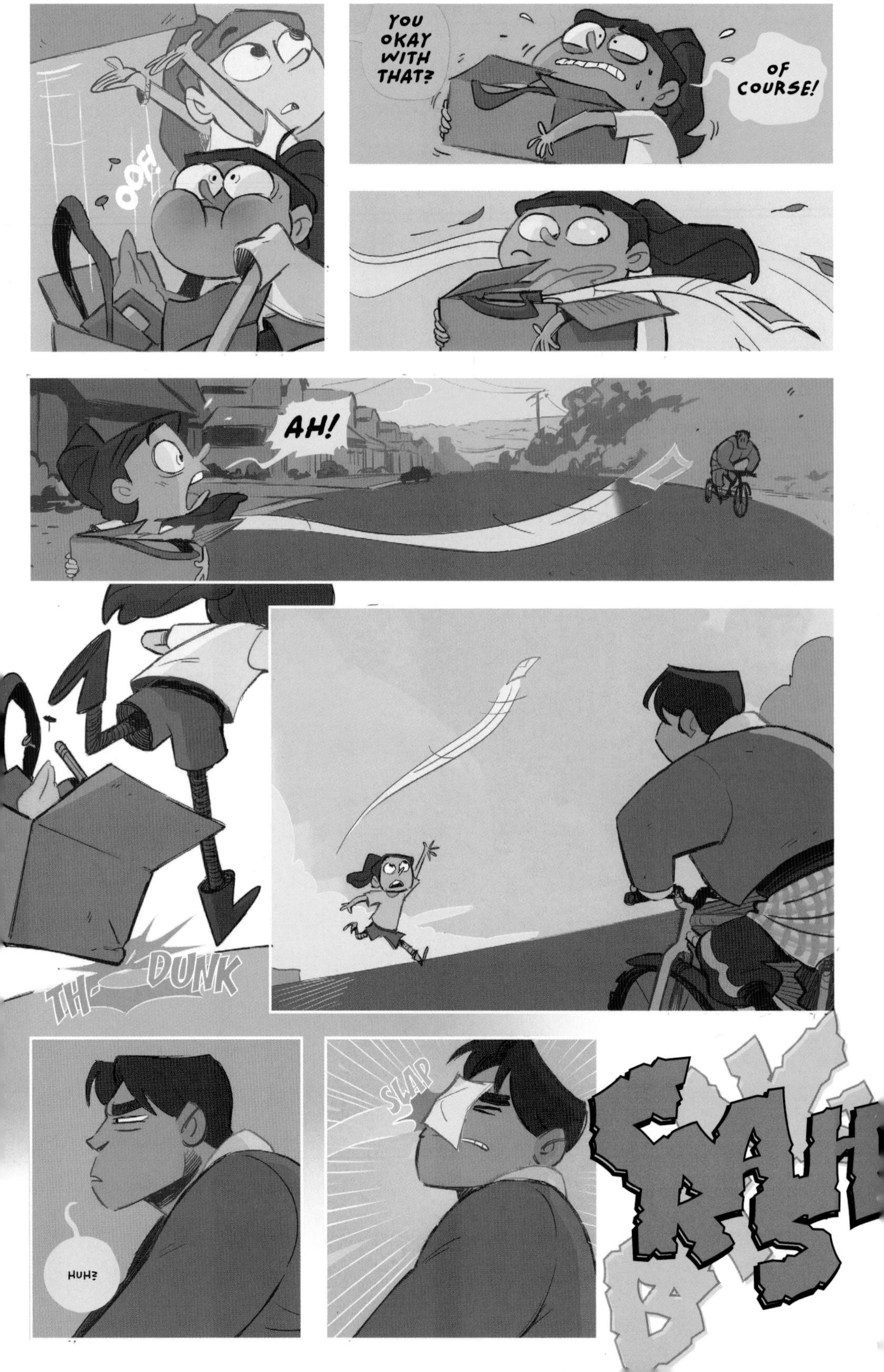
OOF!
YOU OKAY WITH THAT?
OF COURSE!
AH!
TH-DUNK
HUH?
SLAP
CRASH

AH!

Ehhhhhhhhh...

UGHH...

OH MY GOSH!

I'M SO SORRY, ARE YOU HURT? CAN YOU STAND? R... OUR JACKET TOO! IS IT RUINED? I, ...TO, IT WAS ...ACCIDENT! DO Y... ...OR? IS YOUR... BROKEN? IT'... ...YOU...HOULD I G... ...CAN... DID Y...

DON'T WORRY ABOUT IT. I'LL PATCH OVER IT OR SOMETHING.

WHU--?

...

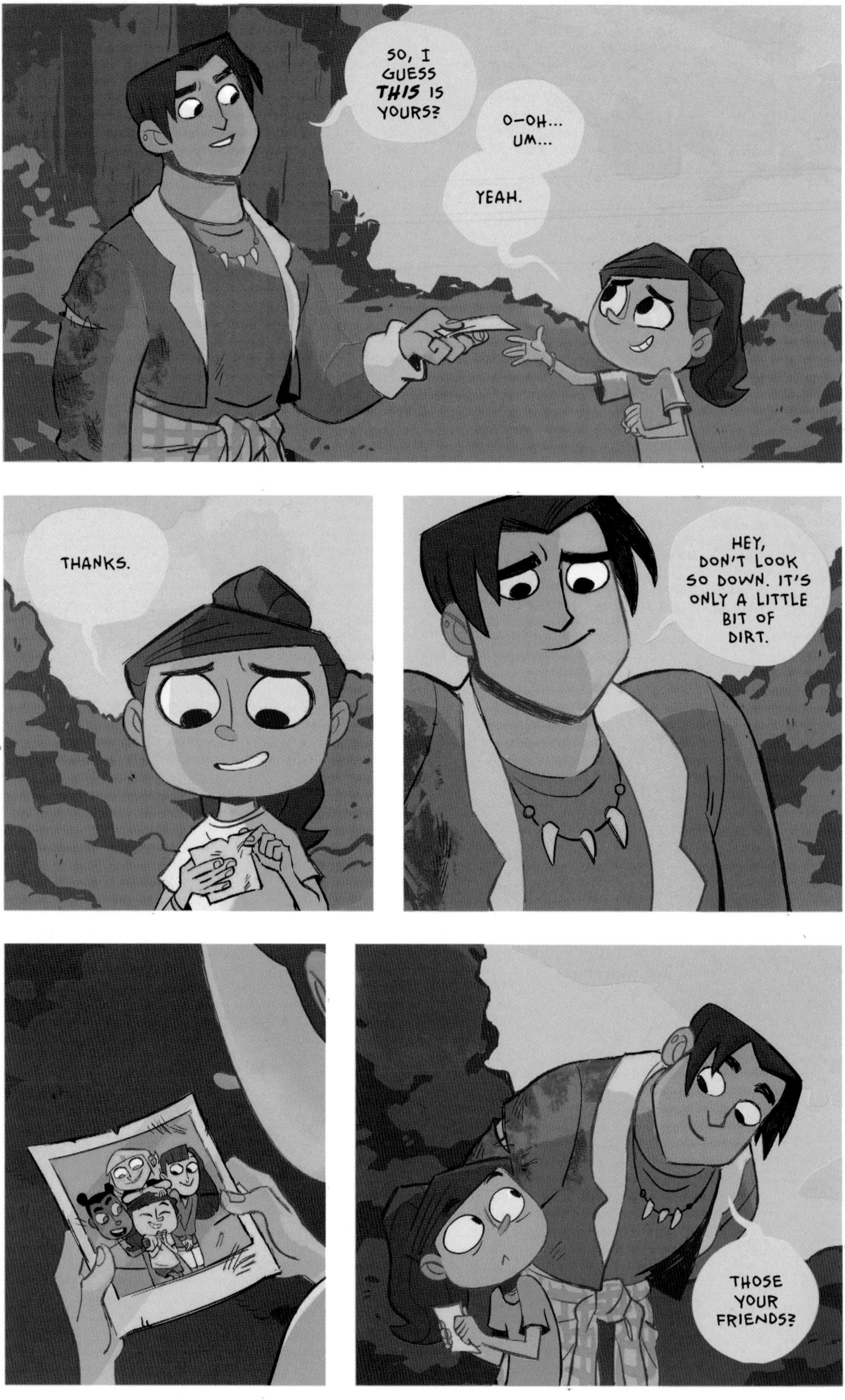
SO, I GUESS *THIS* IS YOURS?
O-OH... UM...
YEAH.
THANKS.
HEY, DON'T LOOK SO DOWN. IT'S ONLY A LITTLE BIT OF DIRT.
THOSE YOUR FRIENDS?

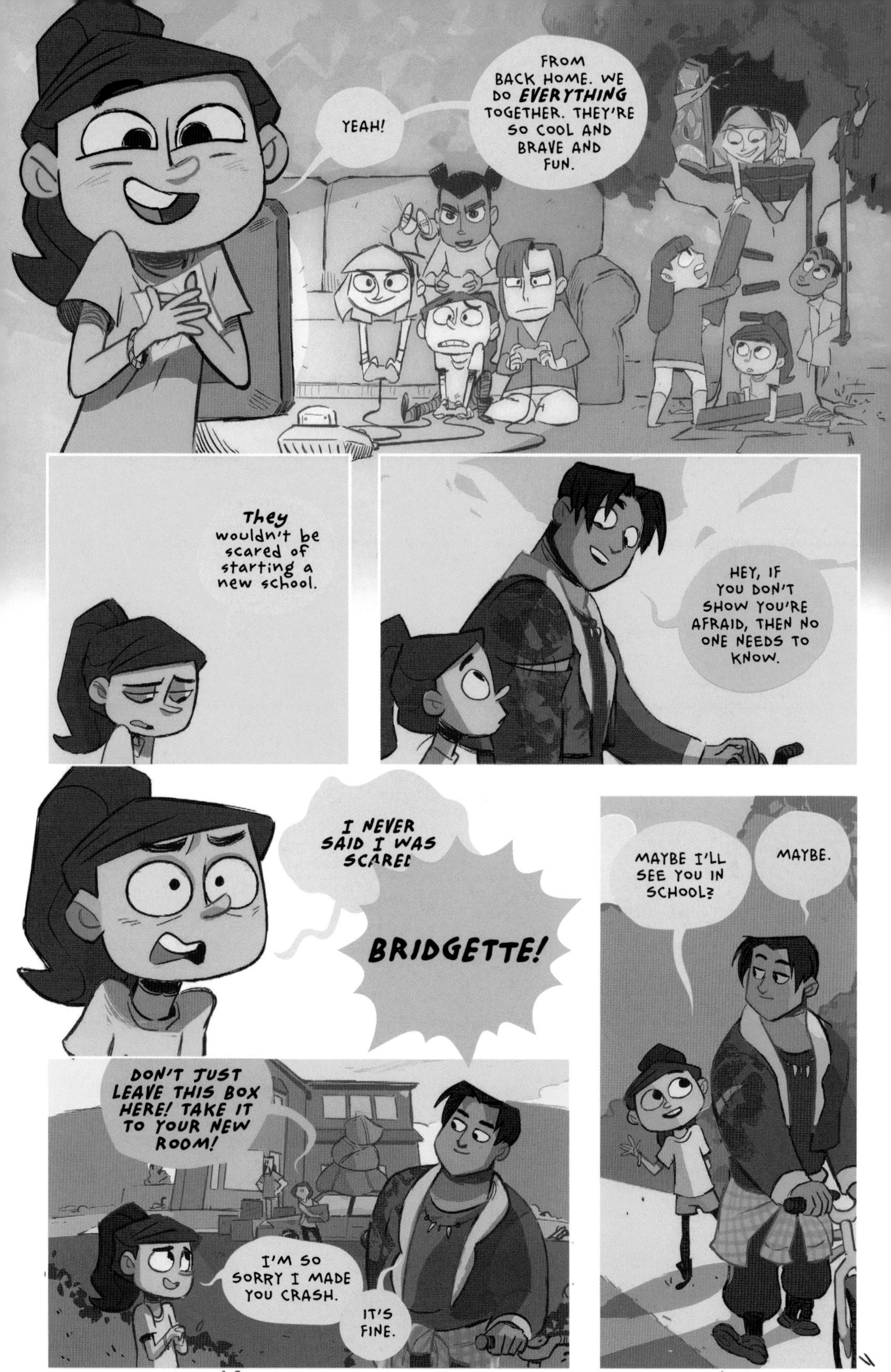
YEAH!
FROM BACK HOME. WE DO EVERYTHING TOGETHER. THEY'RE SO COOL AND BRAVE AND FUN.
They wouldn't be scared of starting a new school.
HEY, IF YOU DON'T SHOW YOU'RE AFRAID, THEN NO ONE NEEDS TO KNOW.
I NEVER SAID I WAS SCARED
BRIDGETTE!
DON'T JUST LEAVE THIS BOX HERE! TAKE IT TO YOUR NEW ROOM!
I'M SO SORRY I MADE YOU CRASH.
IT'S FINE.
MAYBE I'LL SEE YOU IN SCHOOL?
MAYBE.

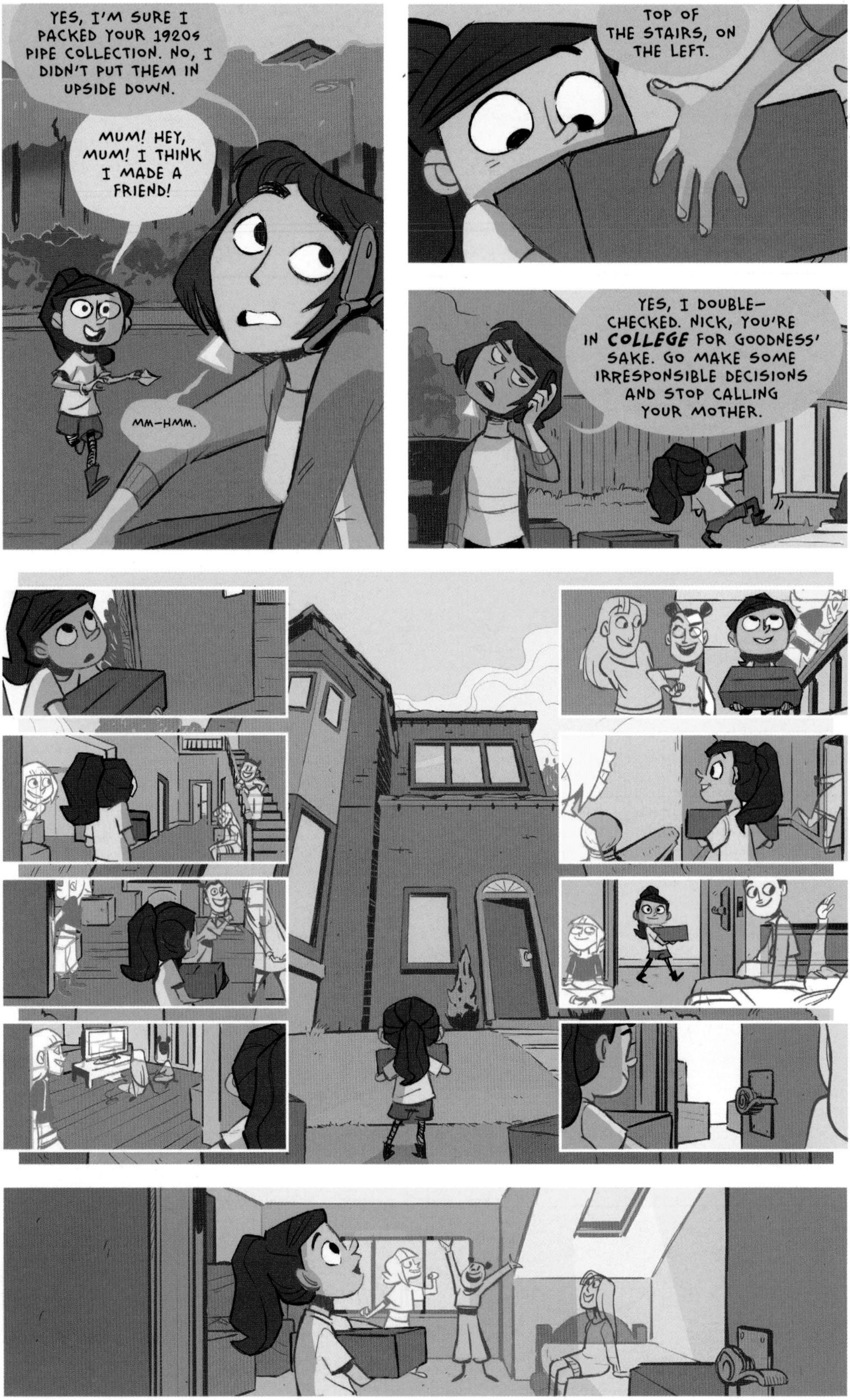

YES, I'M SURE I PACKED YOUR 1920s PIPE COLLECTION. NO, I DIDN'T PUT THEM IN UPSIDE DOWN.
MUM! HEY, MUM! I THINK I MADE A FRIEND!
MM-HMM.
TOP OF THE STAIRS, ON THE LEFT.
YES, I DOUBLE-CHECKED. NICK, YOU'RE IN COLLEGE FOR GOODNESS' SAKE. GO MAKE SOME IRRESPONSIBLE DECISIONS AND STOP CALLING YOUR MOTHER.

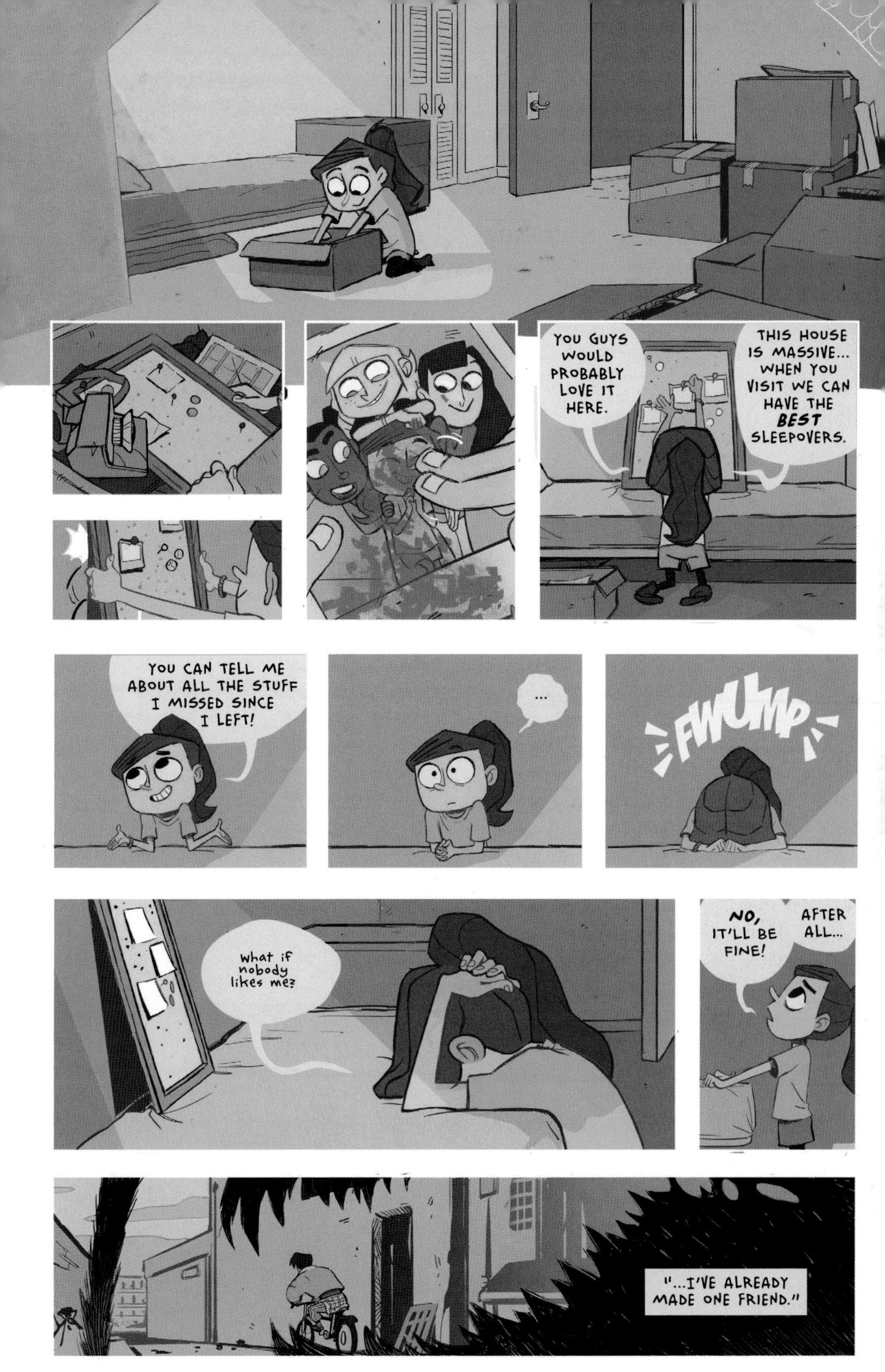
YOU GUYS WOULD PROBABLY LOVE IT HERE.
THIS HOUSE IS MASSIVE... WHEN YOU VISIT WE CAN HAVE THE BEST SLEEPOVERS.
YOU CAN TELL ME ABOUT ALL THE STUFF I MISSED SINCE I LEFT!
...
FWUMP
What if nobody likes me?
NO, IT'LL BE FINE!
AFTER ALL...
"...I'VE ALREADY MADE ONE FRIEND."

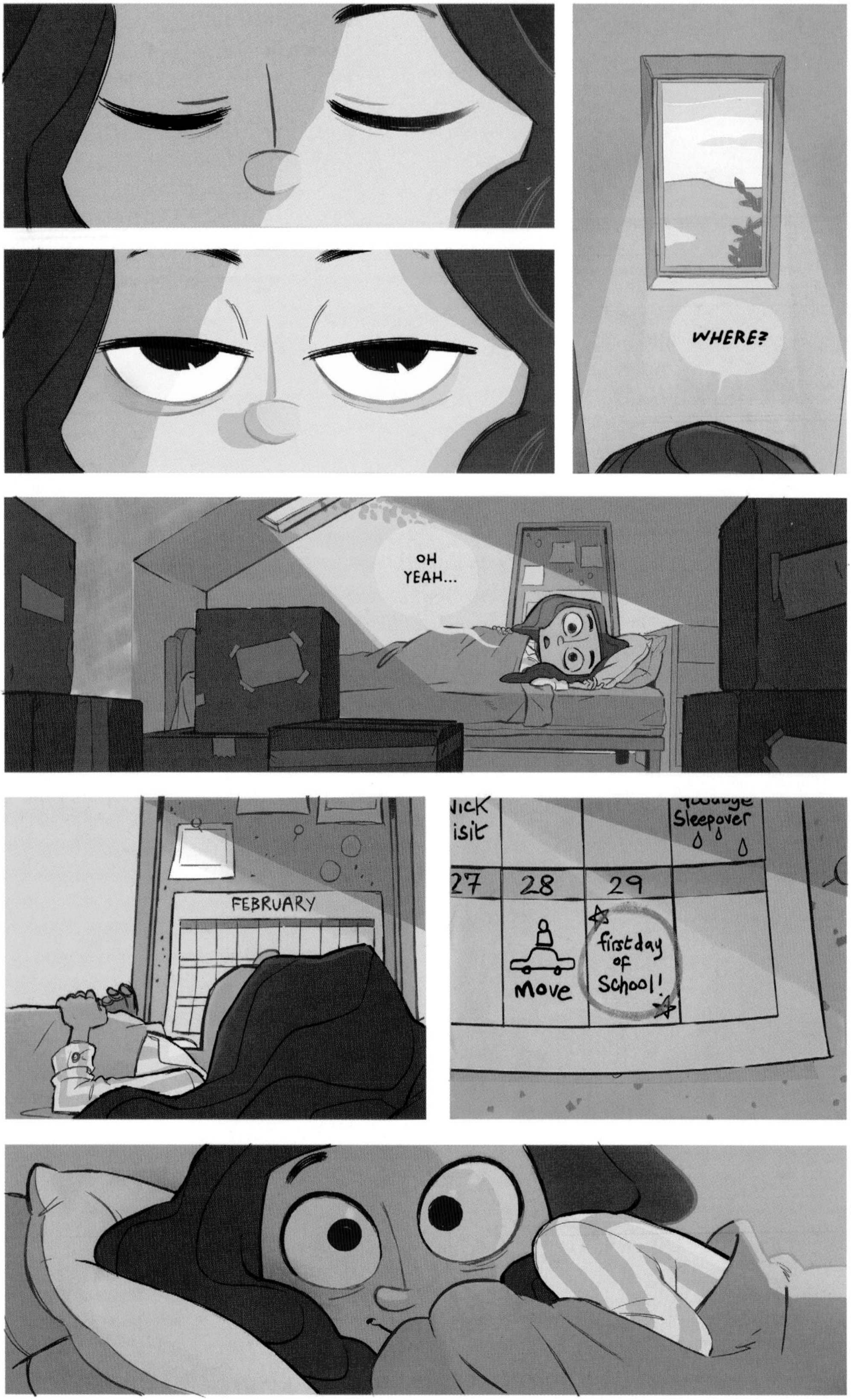
WHERE?
OH YEAH...
FEBRUARY
Sleepover
27
28
29
Move
first day of School!

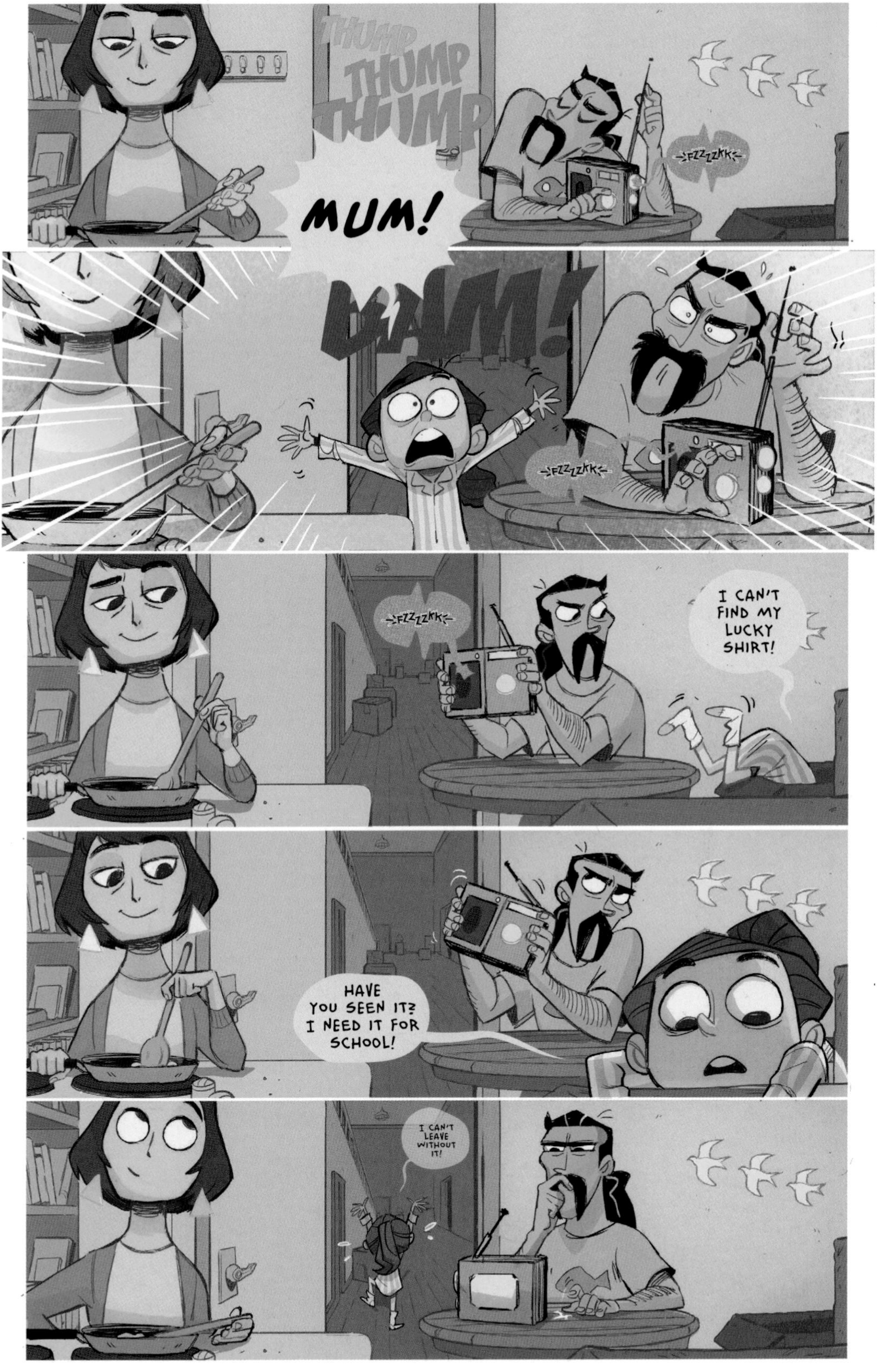
THUMP
THUMP
THUMP
-FZZZZKK-
MUM!
BLAM!
-FZZZZKK-
-FZZZZKK-
I CAN'T FIND MY LUCKY SHIRT!
HAVE YOU SEEN IT? I NEED IT FOR SCHOOL!
I CAN'T LEAVE WITHOUT IT!

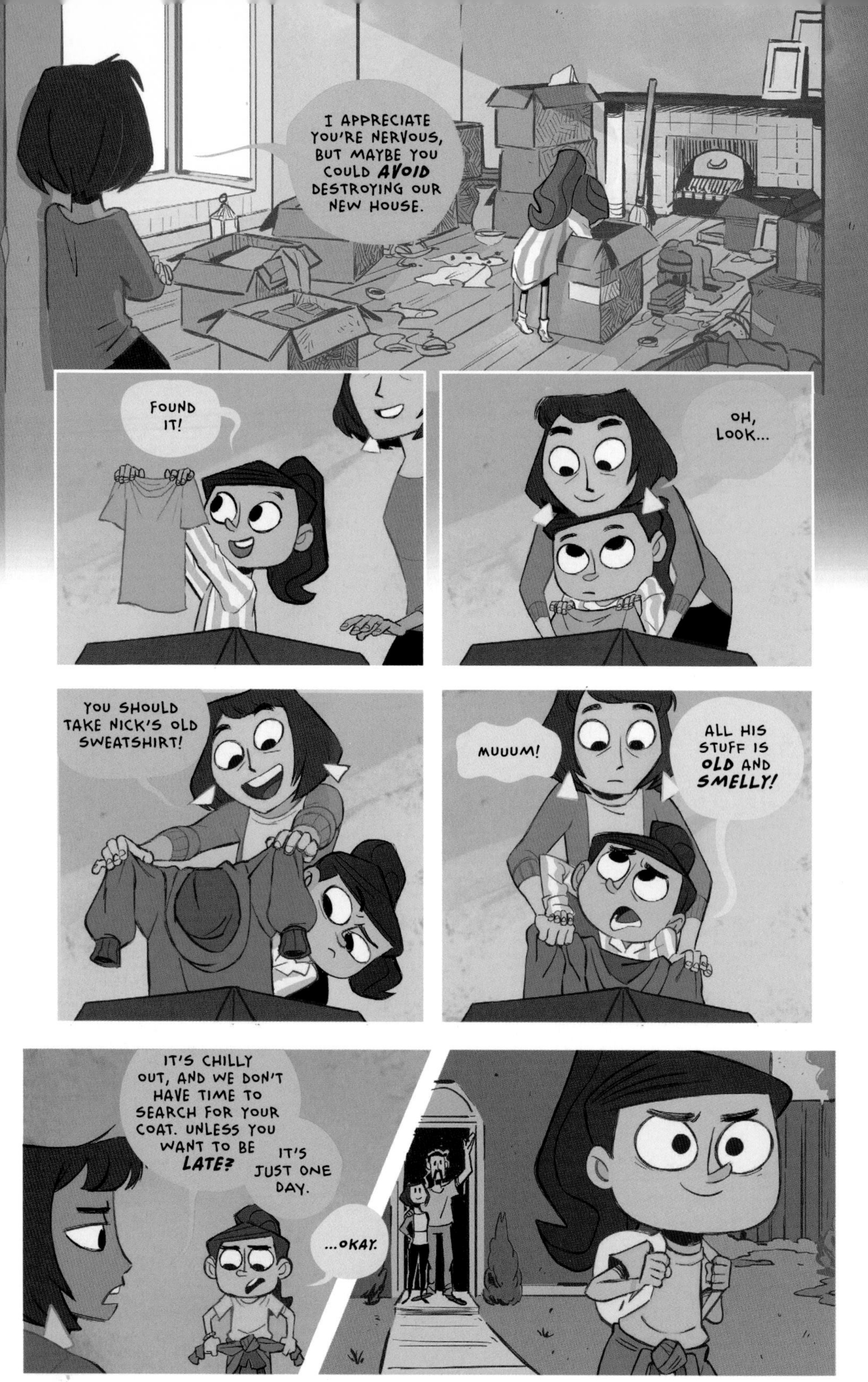
I APPRECIATE YOU'RE NERVOUS, BUT MAYBE YOU COULD AVOID DESTROYING OUR NEW HOUSE.
FOUND IT!
OH, LOOK...
YOU SHOULD TAKE NICK'S OLD SWEATSHIRT!
MUUUM!
ALL HIS STUFF IS OLD AND SMELLY!
IT'S CHILLY OUT, AND WE DON'T HAVE TIME TO SEARCH FOR YOUR COAT. UNLESS YOU WANT TO BE LATE?
IT'S JUST ONE DAY.
...OKAY.

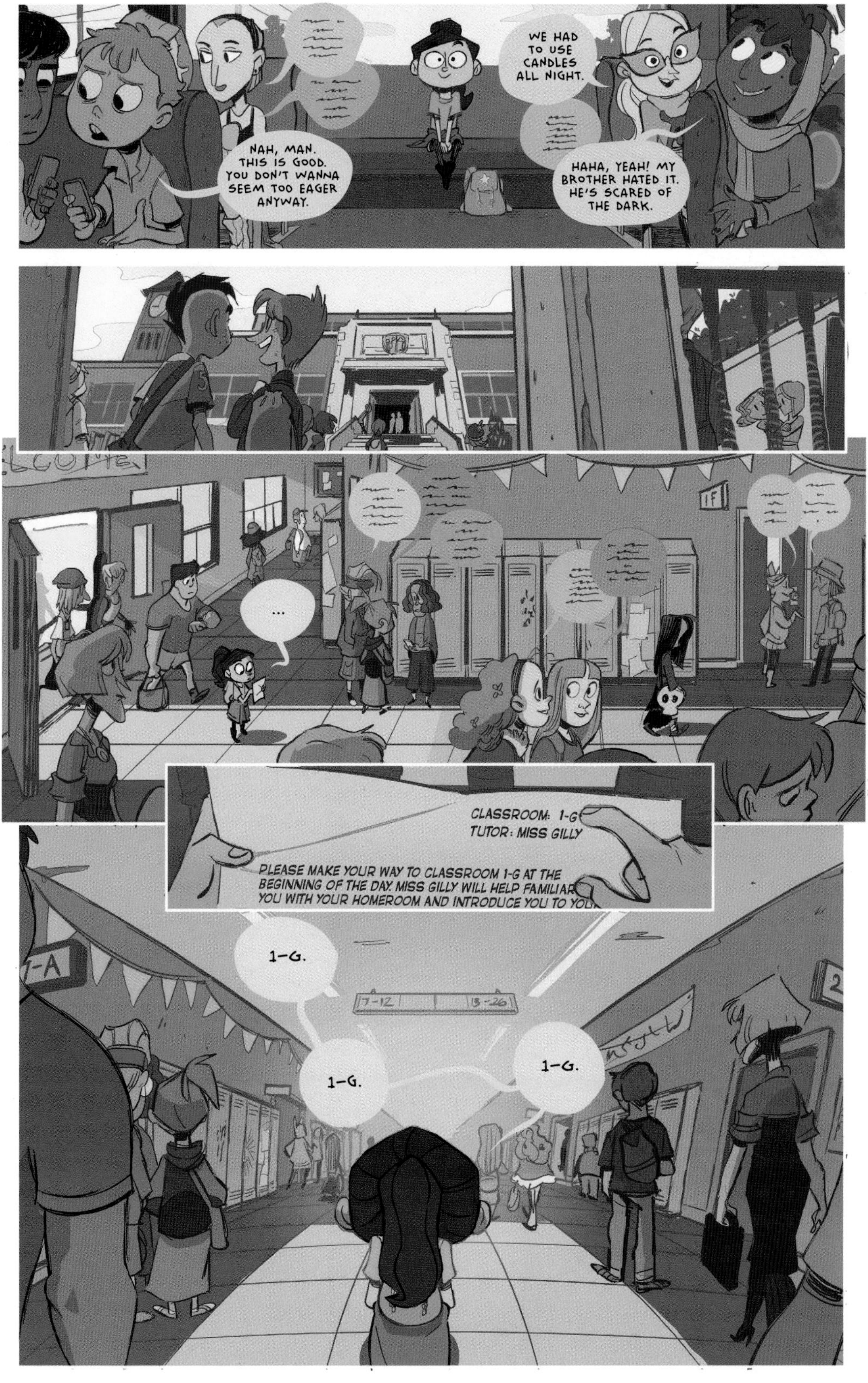
NAH, MAN. THIS IS GOOD. YOU DON'T WANNA SEEM TOO EAGER ANYWAY.
WE HAD TO USE CANDLES ALL NIGHT.
HAHA, YEAH! MY BROTHER HATED IT. HE'S SCARED OF THE DARK.
...
CLASSROOM: 1-G
TUTOR: MISS GILLY
PLEASE MAKE YOUR WAY TO CLASSROOM 1-G AT THE BEGINNING OF THE DAY. MISS GILLY WILL HELP FAMILIAR
YOU WITH YOUR HOMEROOM AND INTRODUCE YOU TO YOU
1-G.
7-12
13-26
1-G.
1-G.

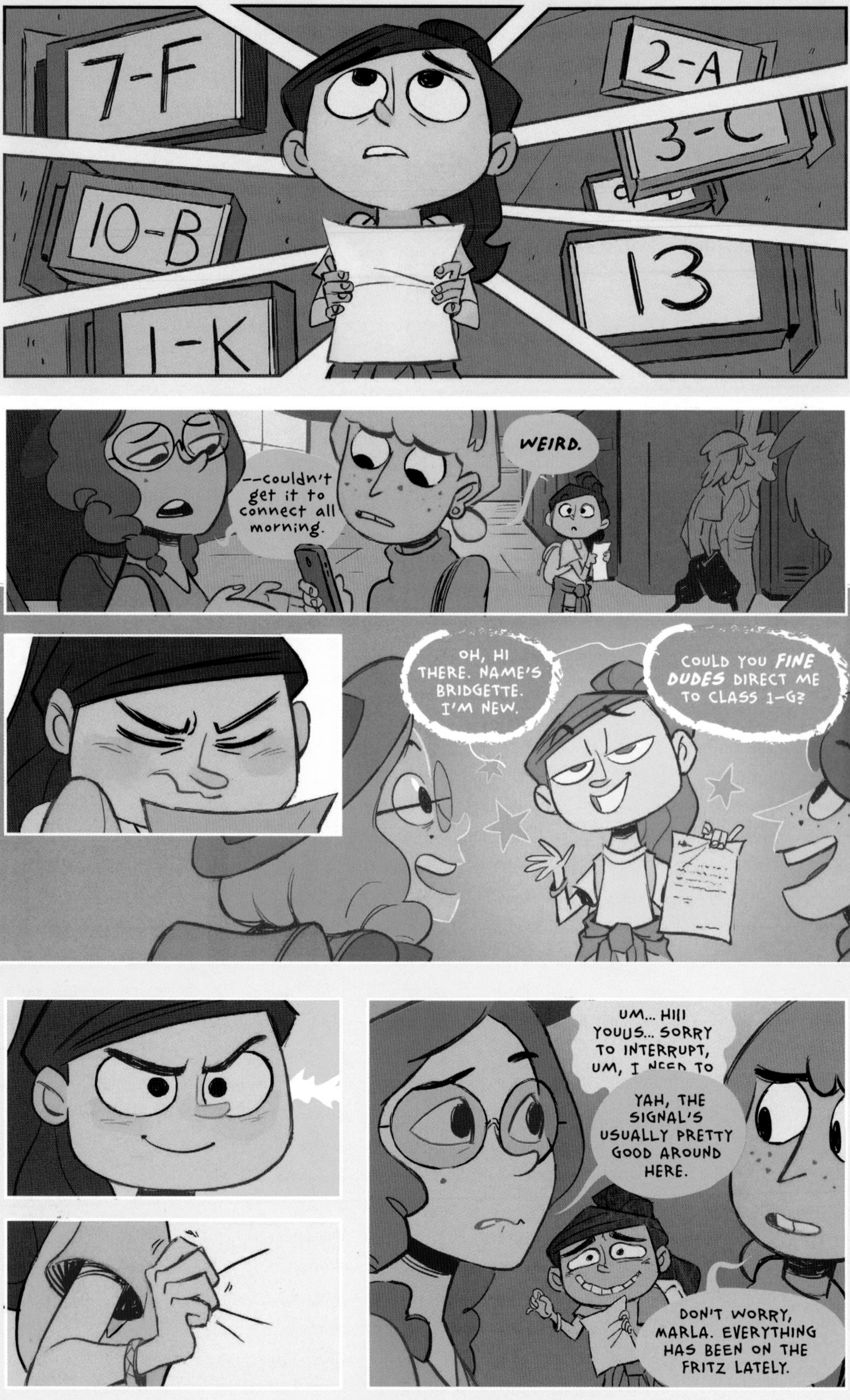
7-F
2-A
3-C
10-B
13
1-K
--couldn't get it to connect all morning.
WEIRD.
OH, HI THERE. NAME'S BRIDGETTE. I'M NEW.
COULD YOU FINE DUDES DIRECT ME TO CLASS 1-G?
UM... HI!! YOUUS... SORRY TO INTERRUPT, UM, I NEED TO
YAH, THE SIGNAL'S USUALLY PRETTY GOOD AROUND HERE.
DON'T WORRY, MARLA. EVERYTHING HAS BEEN ON THE FRITZ LATELY.

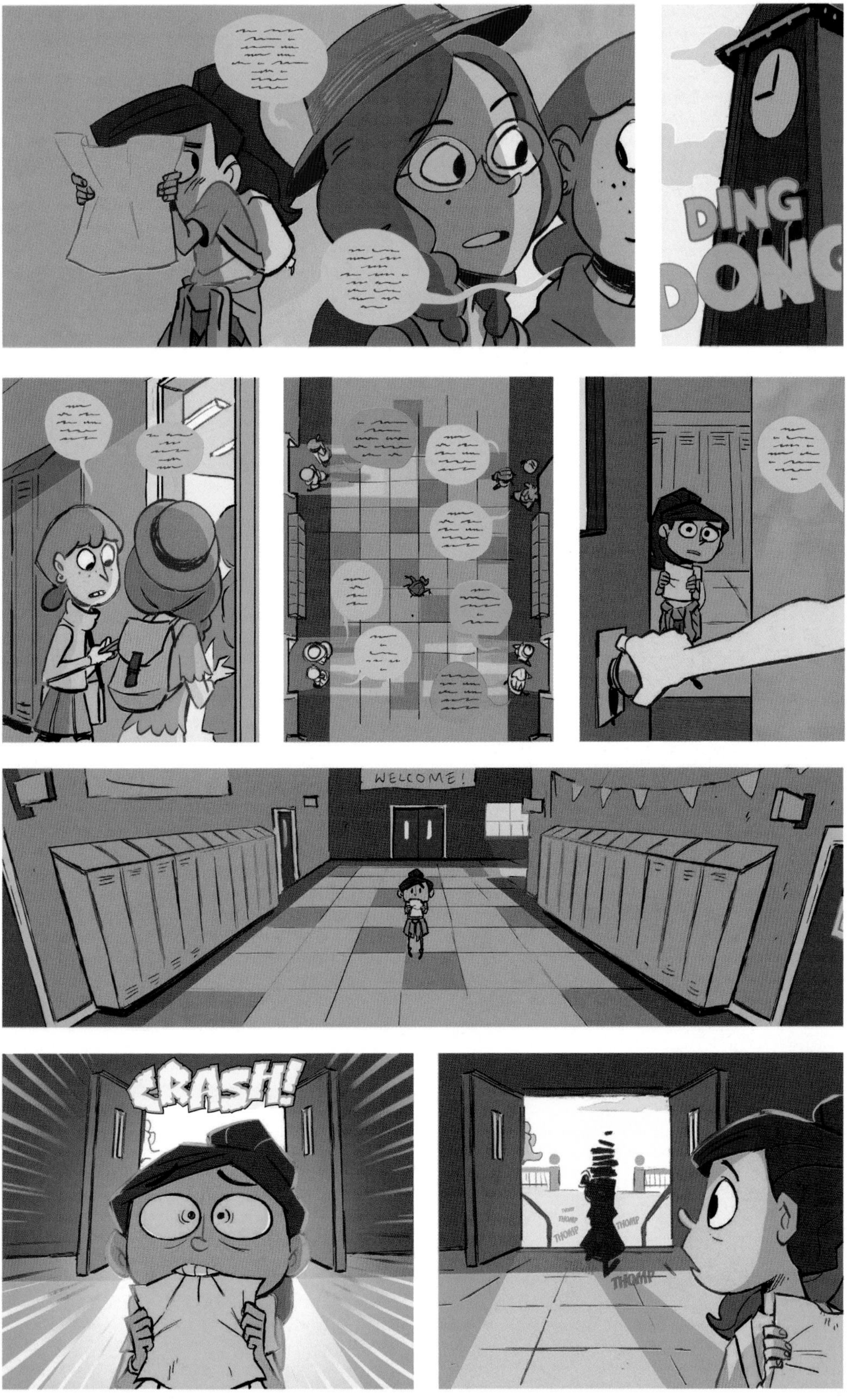
DING
DONG
WELCOME!
CRASH!
THOMP
THOMP
THOMP
THOMP
THOMP

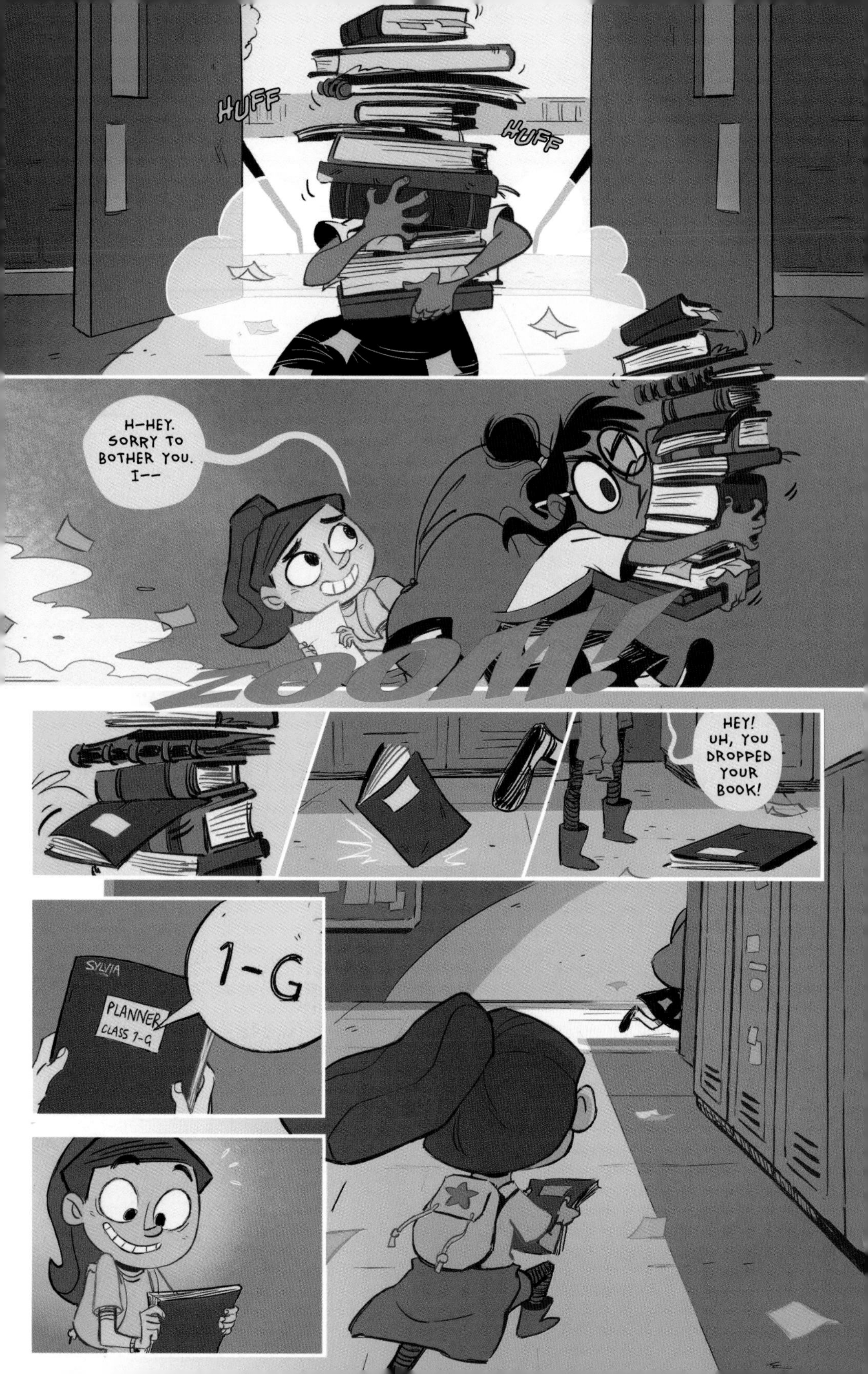

HUFF
HUFF
H-HEY. SORRY TO BOTHER YOU. I--
ZOOM!
HEY! UH, YOU DROPPED YOUR BOOK!
SYLVIA
PLANNER CLASS 1-G
1-G

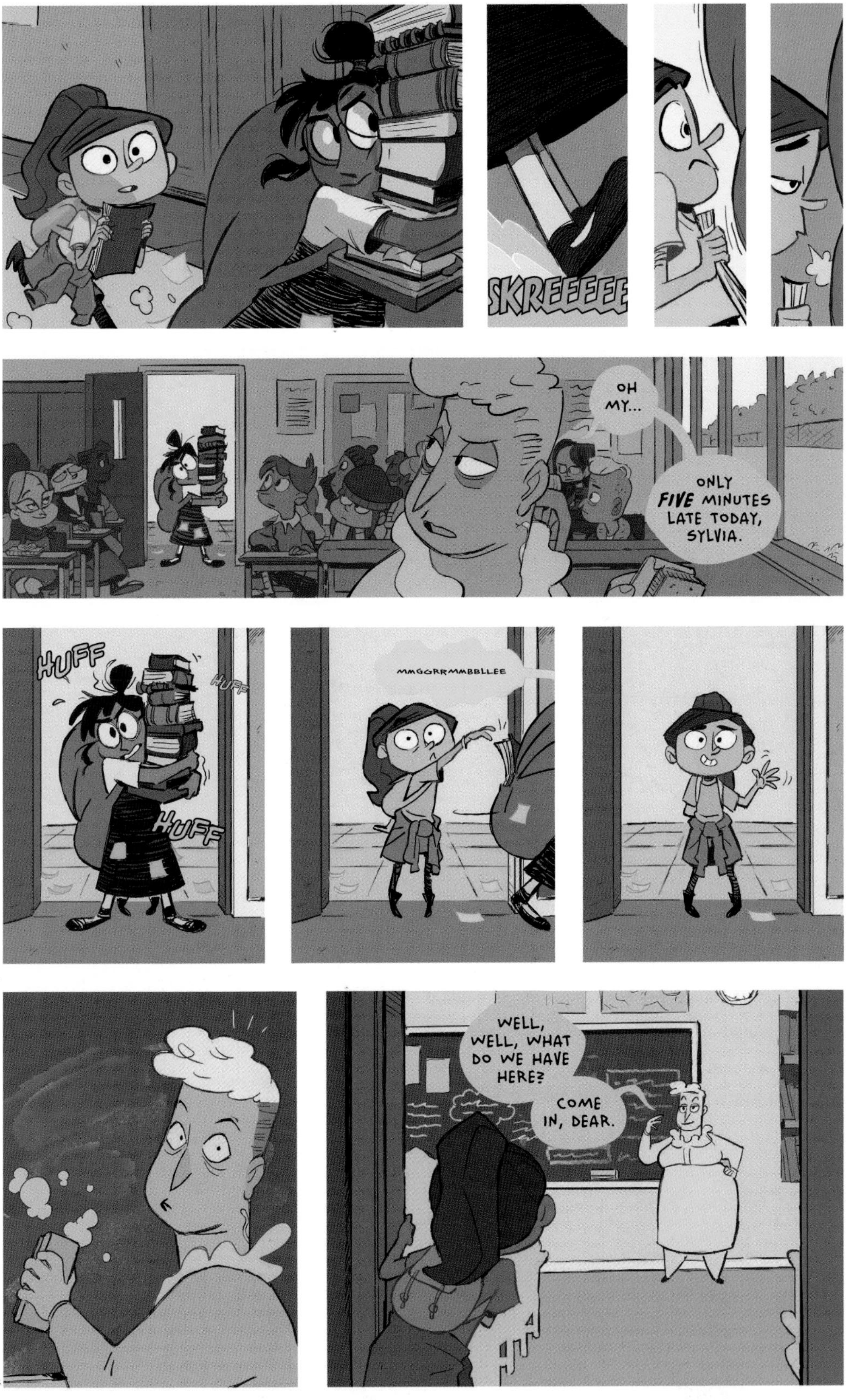
SKREEEEEE
OH MY...
ONLY FIVE MINUTES LATE TODAY, SYLVIA.
HUFF
HUFF
HUFF
MMGGRRMMBBLLEE
WELL, WELL, WHAT DO WE HAVE HERE?
COME IN, DEAR.

WE HAVE A *NEW* STUDENT STARTING TODAY!

WHY DON'T YOU WRITE YOUR NAME ON THE BOARD FOR US?

TAKE NOTES
ASK OPEN ENDED QUE
RASE YOUR
DISCUSSION DISAGREE

HOMEWO

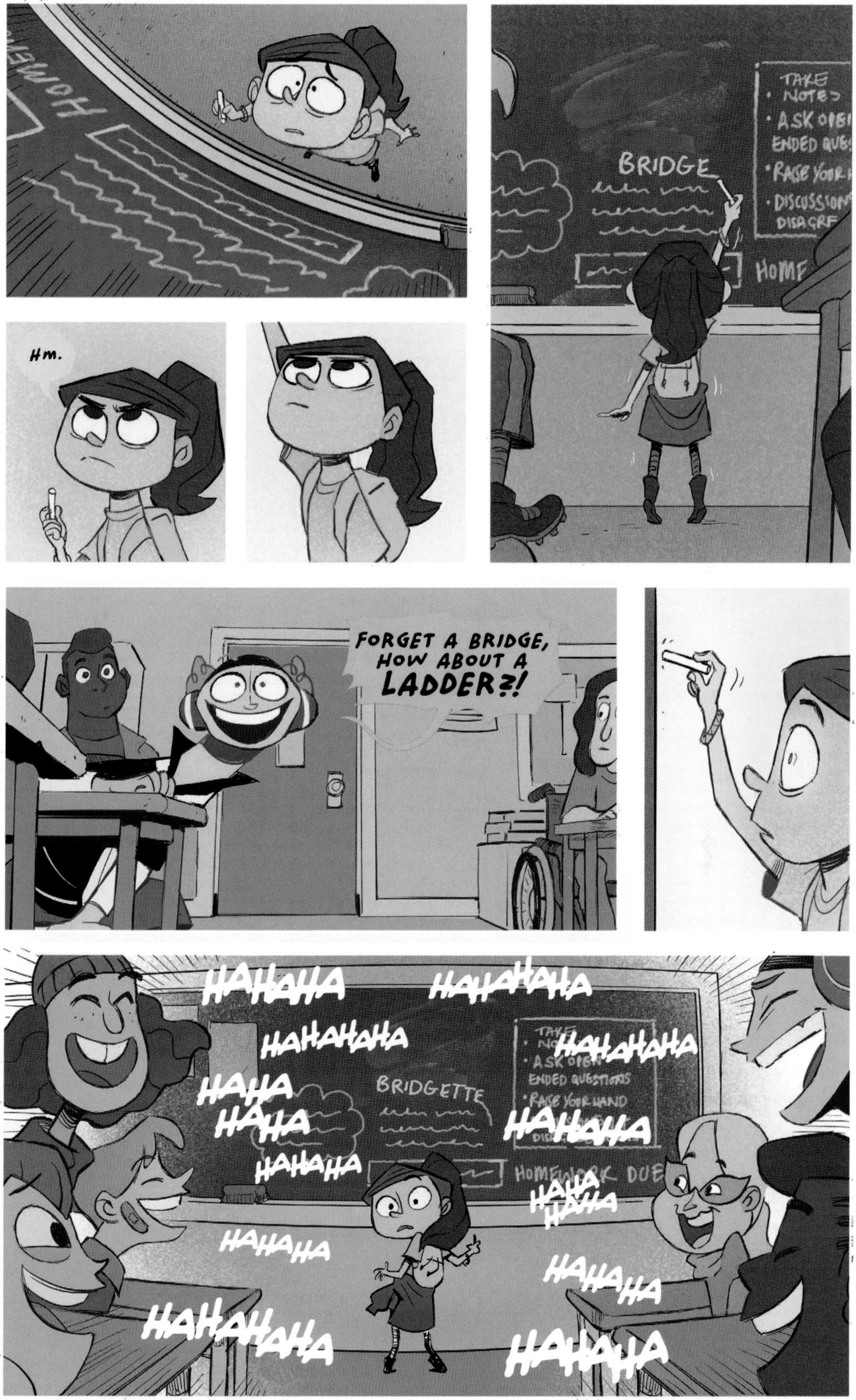
HOMEW
TAKE NOTES
• ASK OPEN ENDED QUES
• RAISE YOUR H
• DISCUSSIONS DISAGRE
BRIDGE
HOME
Hm.
FORGET A BRIDGE, HOW ABOUT A LADDER?!
HAHAHA
HAHAHAHA
HAHAHAHA
HAHAHAHA
HAHA
HAHA
HAHAHA
BRIDGETTE
ENDED QUESTIONS
RAISE YOUR HAND
HOMEWORK DUE
HAHAHAHA
HAHAHA
HAHAHA
HAHAHA
HAHAHAHA
HAHAHA

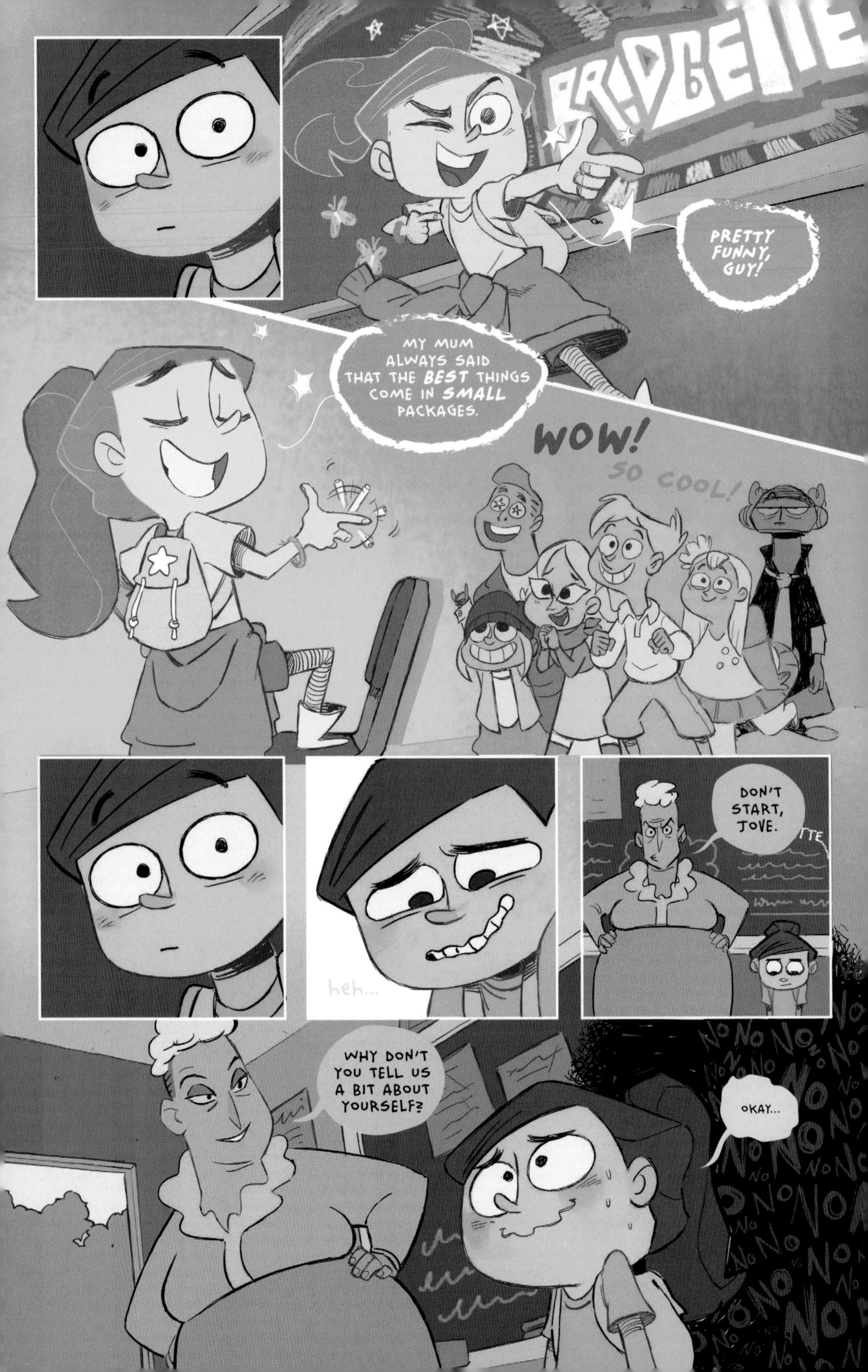
PRETTY FUNNY, GUY!
MY MUM ALWAYS SAID THAT THE **BEST** THINGS COME IN **SMALL** PACKAGES.
WOW!
SO COOL!
heh...
DON'T START, JOVE.
WHY DON'T YOU TELL US A BIT ABOUT YOURSELF?
OKAY...

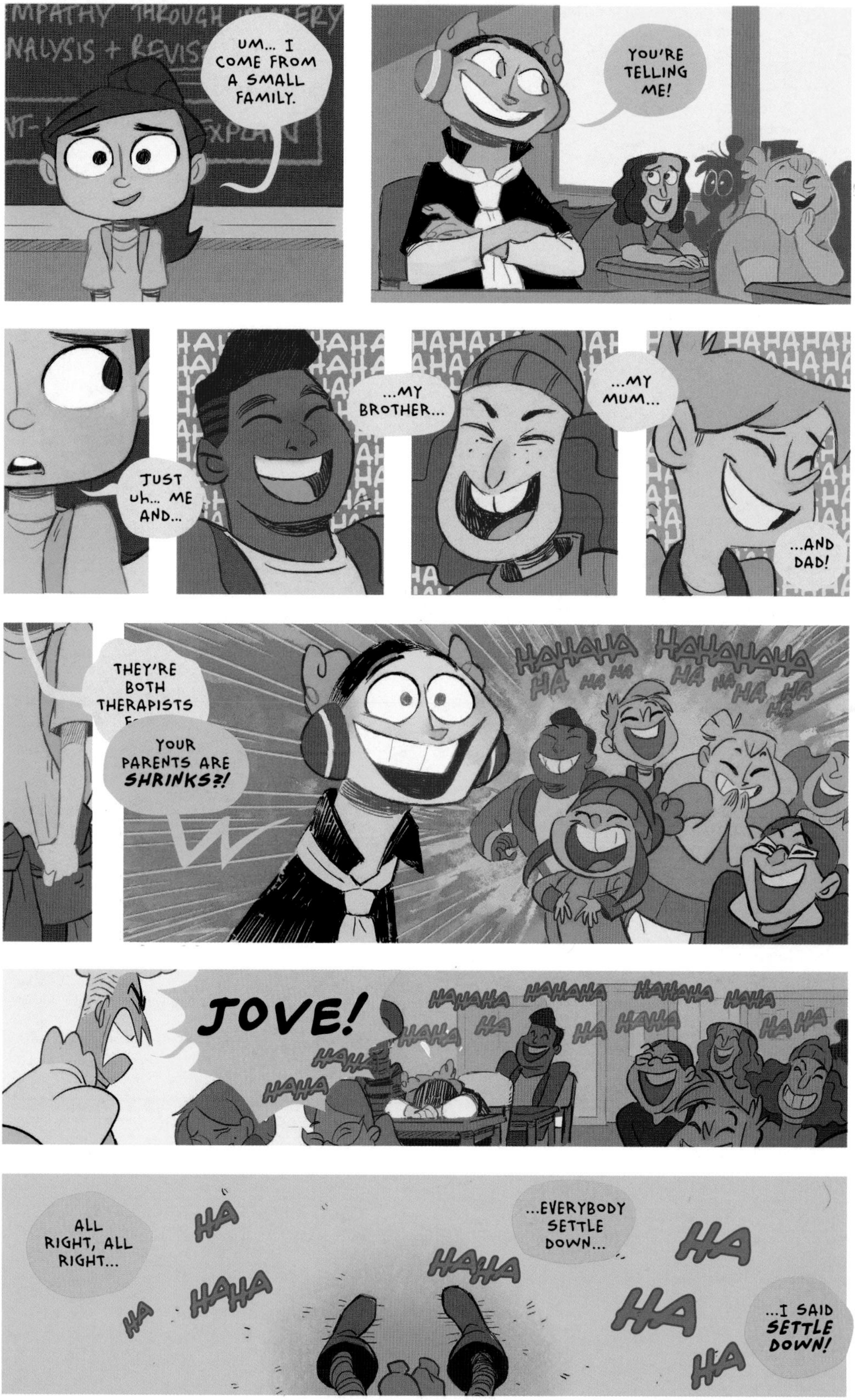
EMPATHY THROUGH IMAGERY
ANALYSIS + REVIS
EXPLAIN
UM... I COME FROM A SMALL FAMILY.
YOU'RE TELLING ME!
JUST uh... ME AND...
...MY BROTHER...
...MY MUM...
...AND DAD!
HAHAHA
THEY'RE BOTH THERAPISTS
YOUR PARENTS ARE SHRINKS?!
HAHAHA HAHAHAHA HA HA HA HA HA HA HA
JOVE!
HAHAHA HAHAHA HAHAHAHA HAHA HAHA HA HA HAHA HAHA HAHA
ALL RIGHT, ALL RIGHT...
HA
...EVERYBODY SETTLE DOWN...
HA
HAHAHA
HA HAHA
HA
HA
...I SAID SETTLE DOWN!

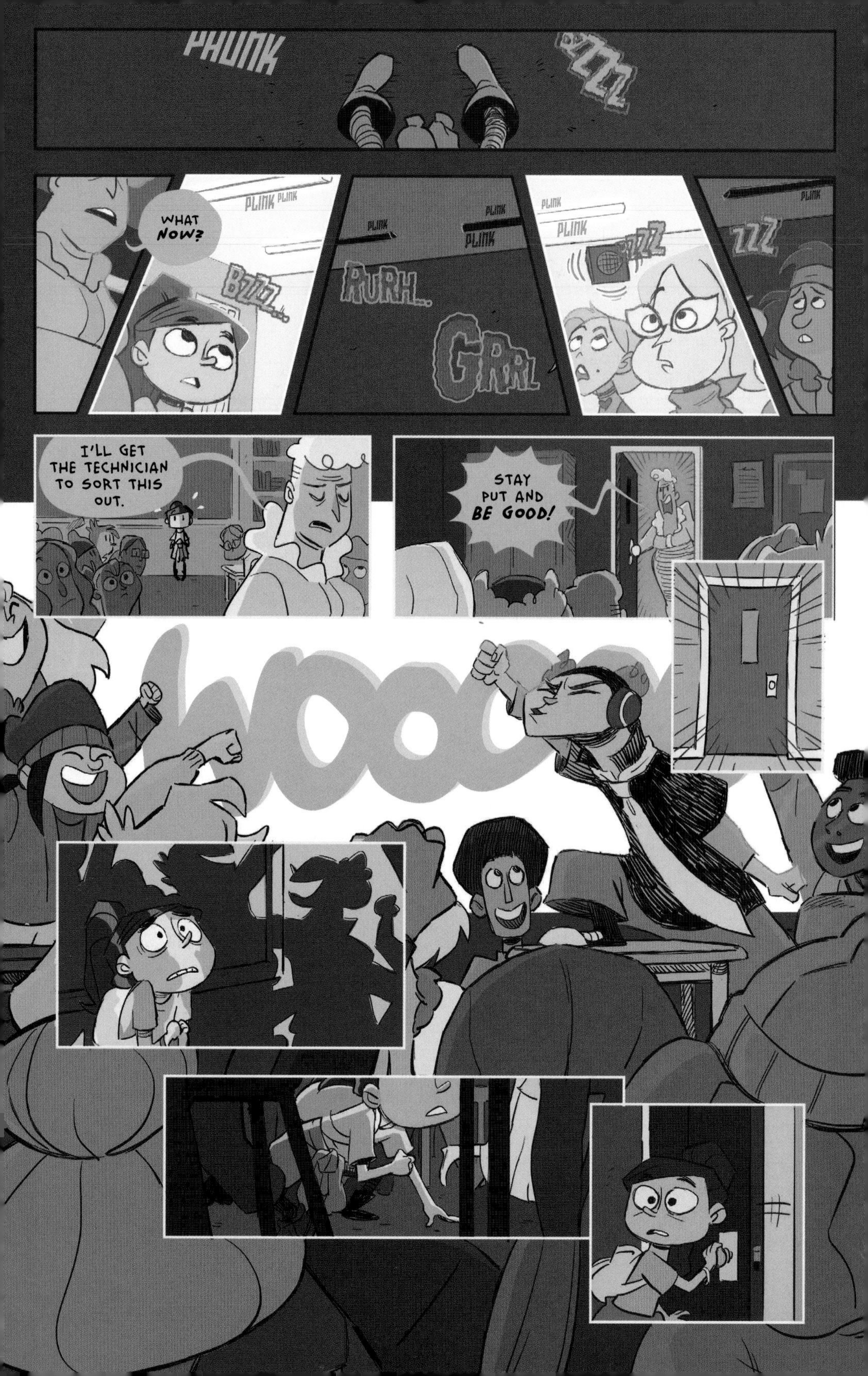
PHUNK
BZZZ
PLINK PLINK
WHAT NOW?
BZZZ...
PLINK
PLINK
PLINK
RURH...
GRRRL
PLINK
PLINK
ZZZ
ZZZ
PLINK
I'LL GET THE TECHNICIAN TO SORT THIS OUT.
STAY PUT AND BE GOOD!

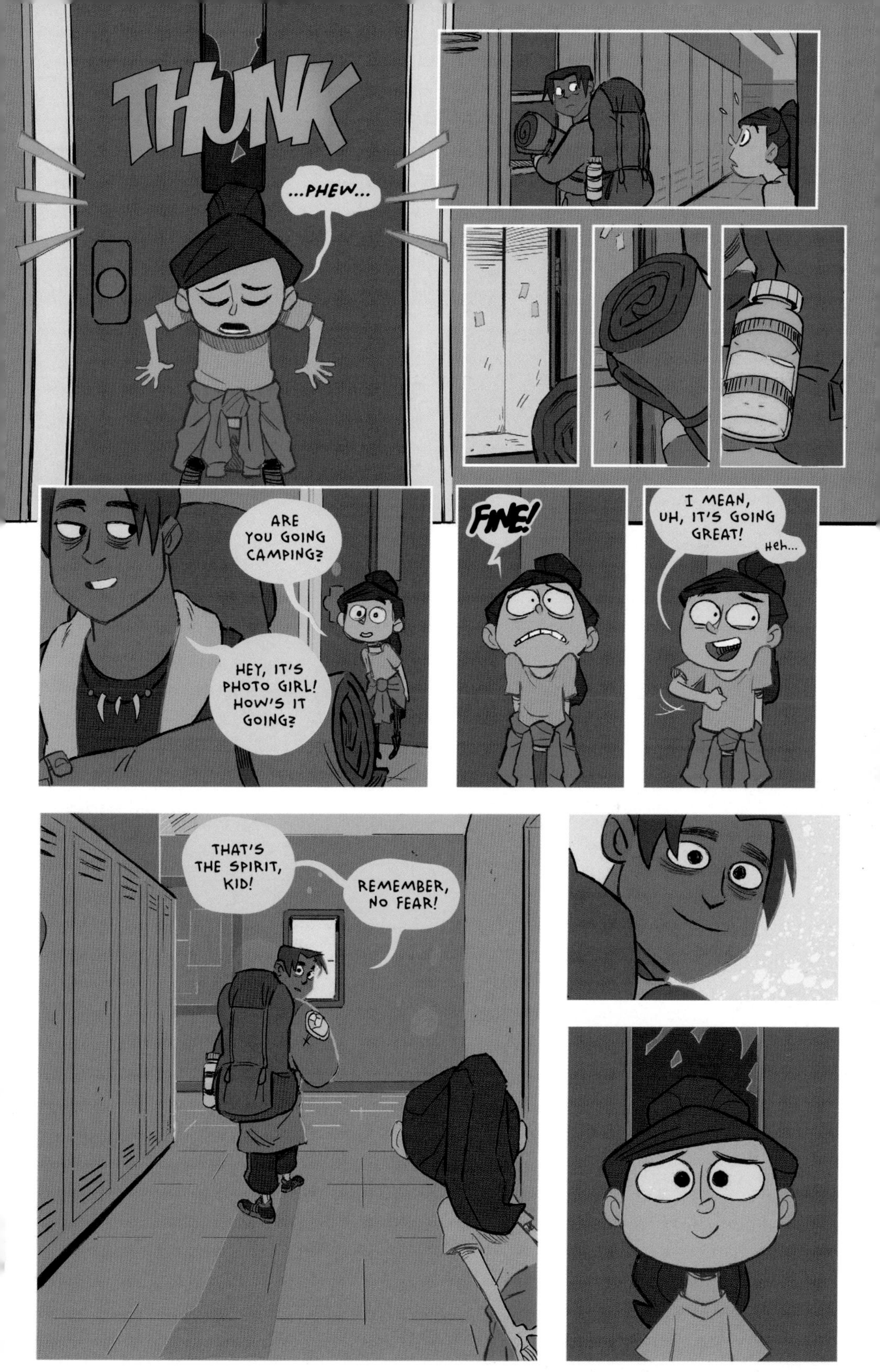
THUNK
...PHEW...
ARE YOU GOING CAMPING?
HEY, IT'S PHOTO GIRL! HOW'S IT GOING?
FINE!
I MEAN, UH, IT'S GOING GREAT!
Heh...
THAT'S THE SPIRIT, KID!
REMEMBER, NO FEAR!

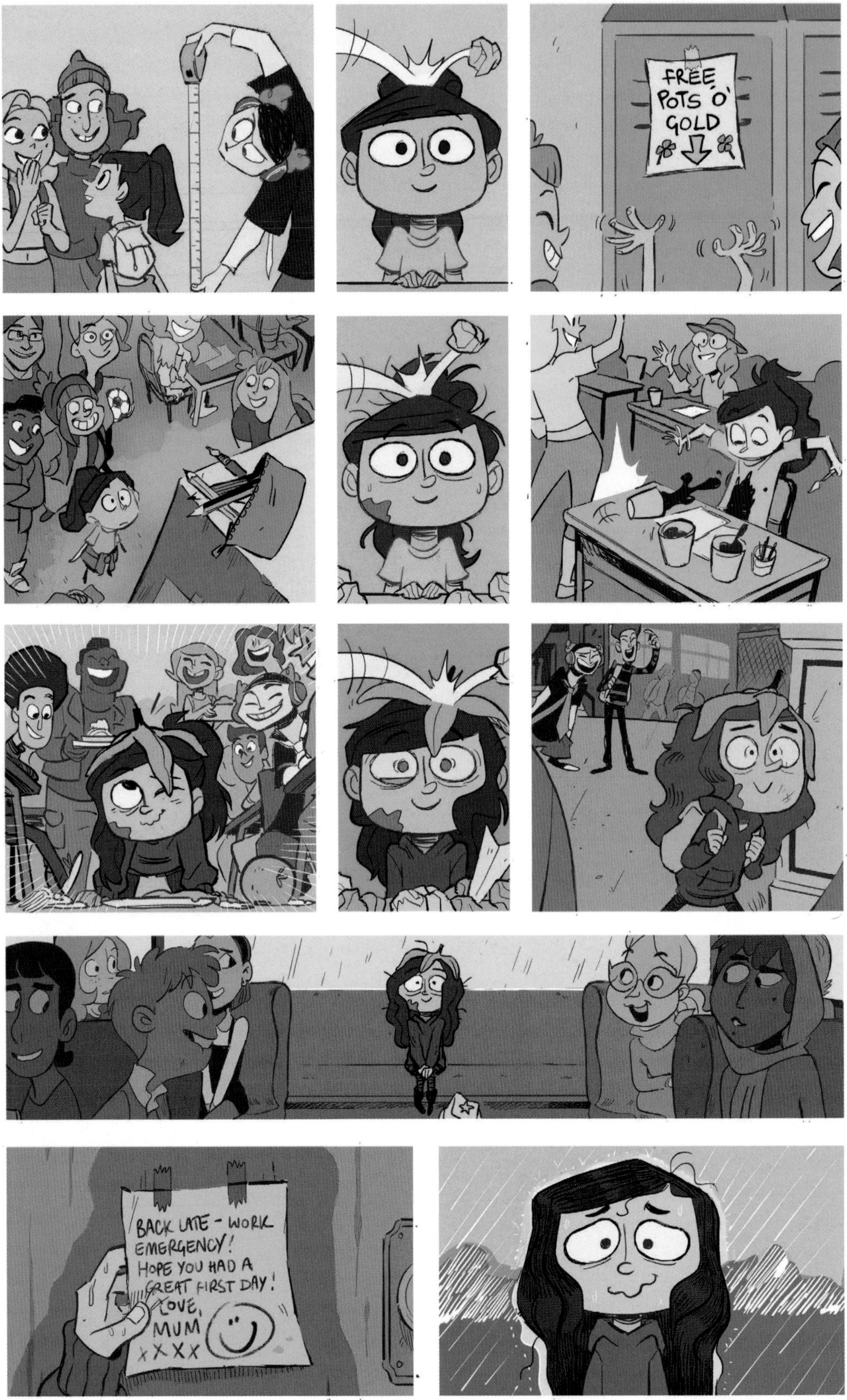
FREE POTS 'O' GOLD
BACK LATE - WORK EMERGENCY! HOPE YOU HAD A GREAT FIRST DAY! LOVE, MUM XXXX

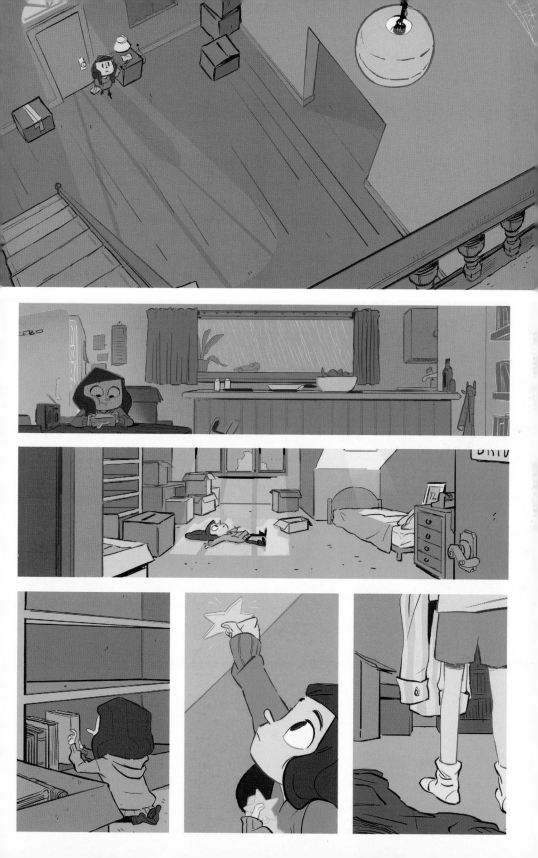

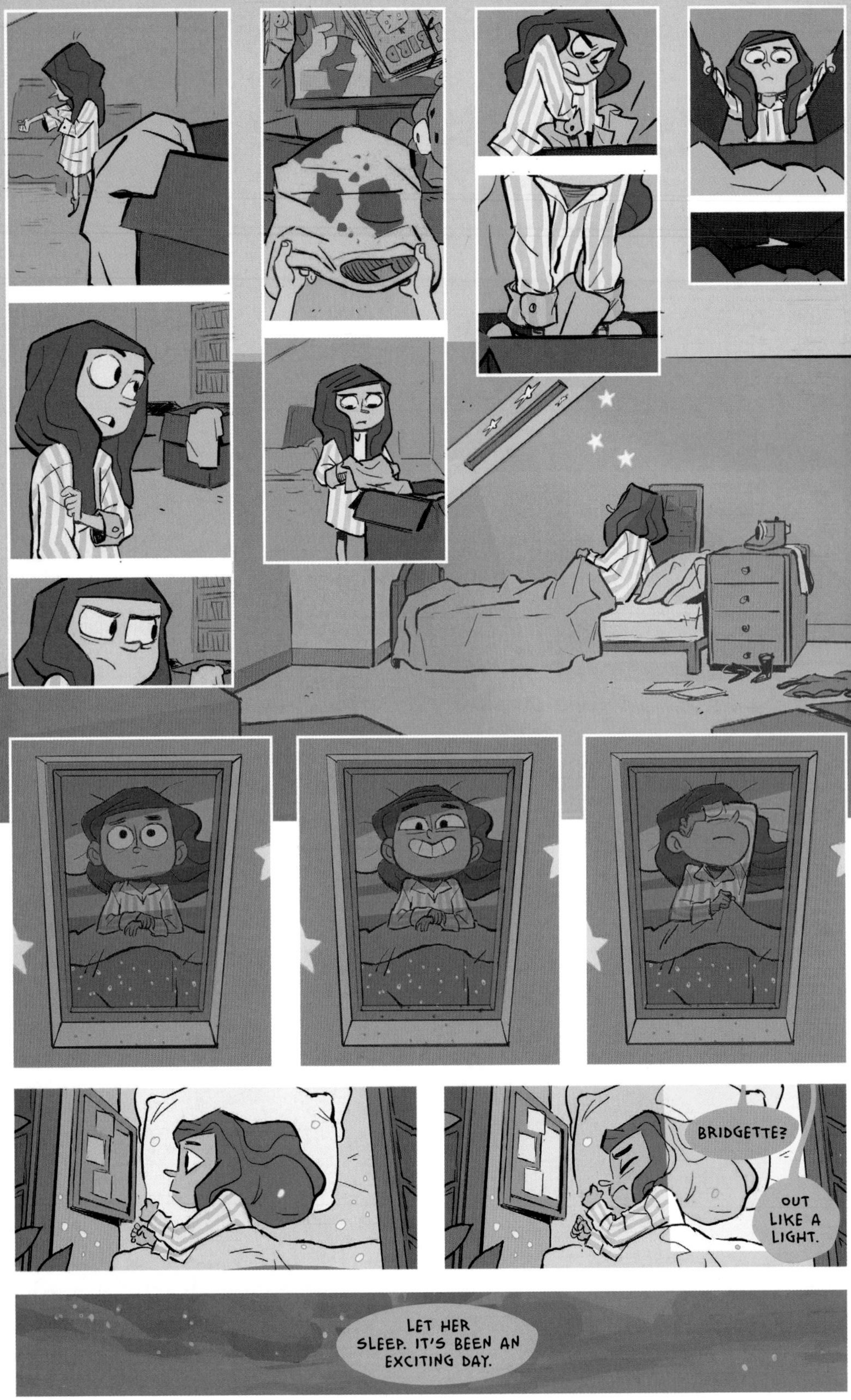
BRIDGETTE?
OUT LIKE A LIGHT.
LET HER SLEEP. IT'S BEEN AN EXCITING DAY.

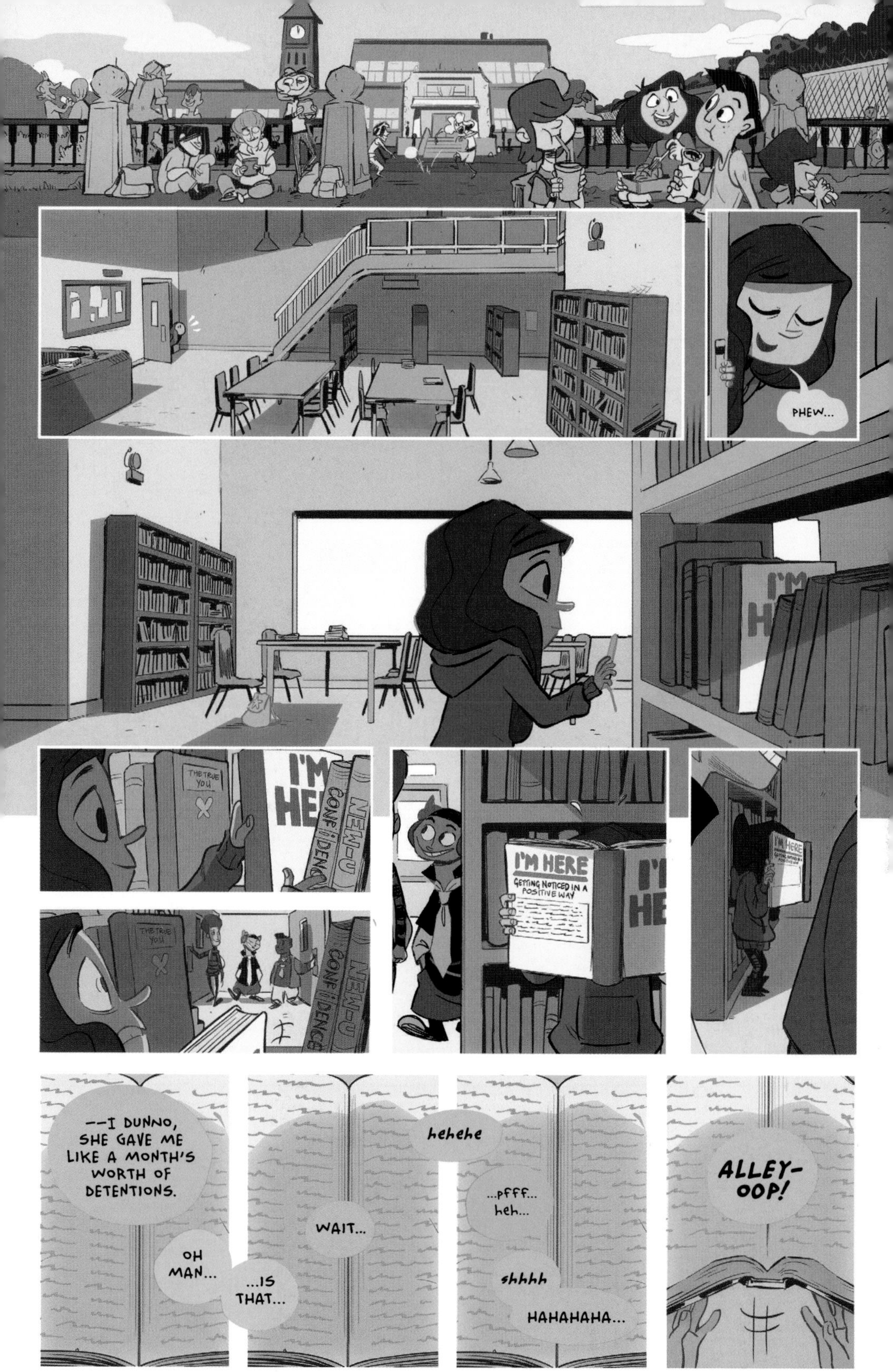
PHEW...
I'M HERE
THE TRUE YOU
CONFIDENCE
NEW-U
I'M HERE
GETTING NOTICED IN A POSITIVE WAY
--I DUNNO, SHE GAVE ME LIKE A MONTH'S WORTH OF DETENTIONS.
OH MAN...
...IS THAT...
WAIT...
hehehe
...pfff... heh...
shhhh
HAHAHAHA...
ALLEY-OOP!

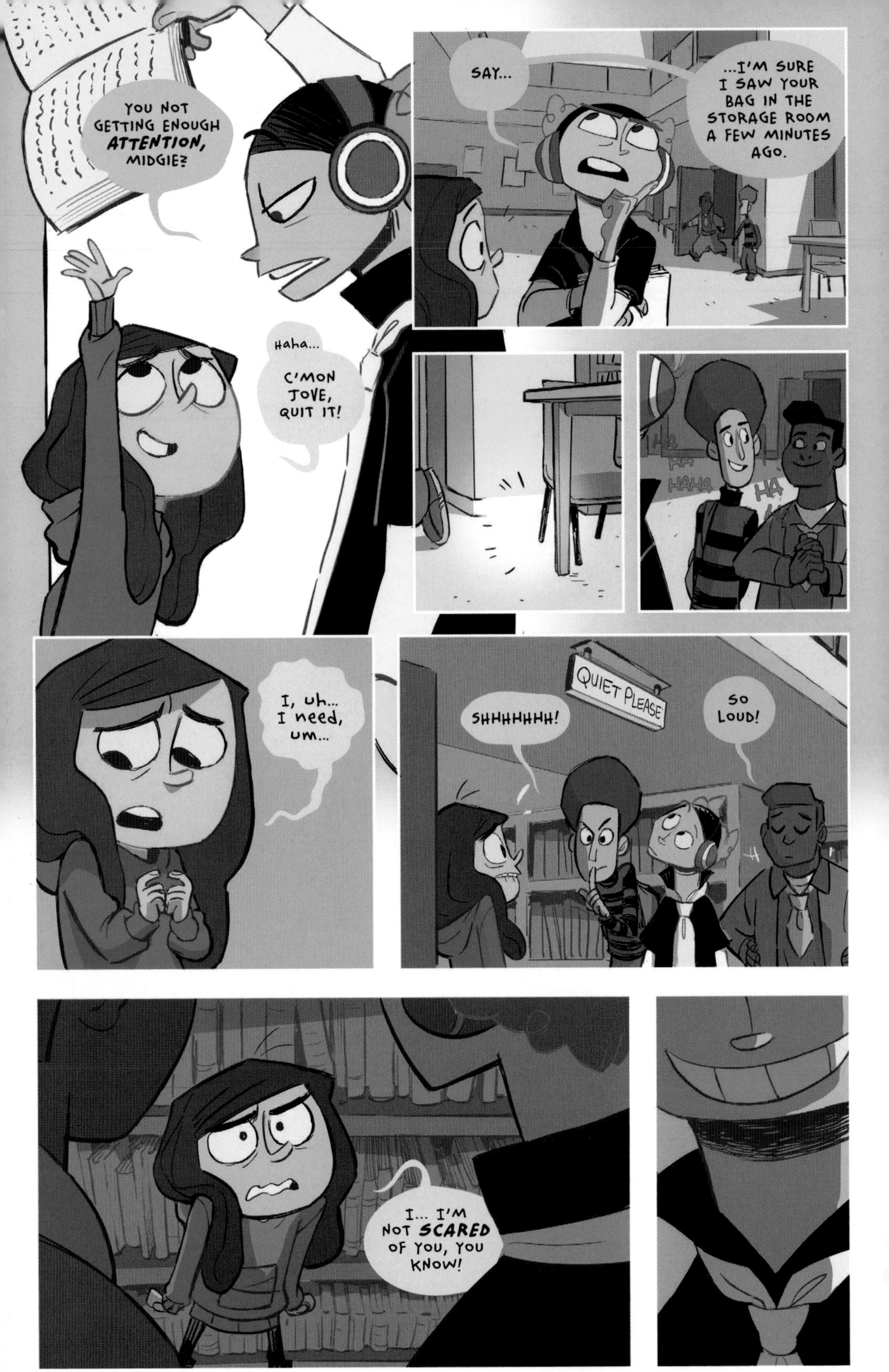
YOU NOT GETTING ENOUGH ATTENTION, MIDGIE?
Haha...
C'MON JOVE, QUIT IT!
SAY...
...I'M SURE I SAW YOUR BAG IN THE STORAGE ROOM A FEW MINUTES AGO.
HA
HA
HAHA
HA
I, uh... I need, um...
QUIET PLEASE
SHHHHHHH!
SO LOUD!
I... I'M NOT SCARED OF YOU, YOU KNOW!

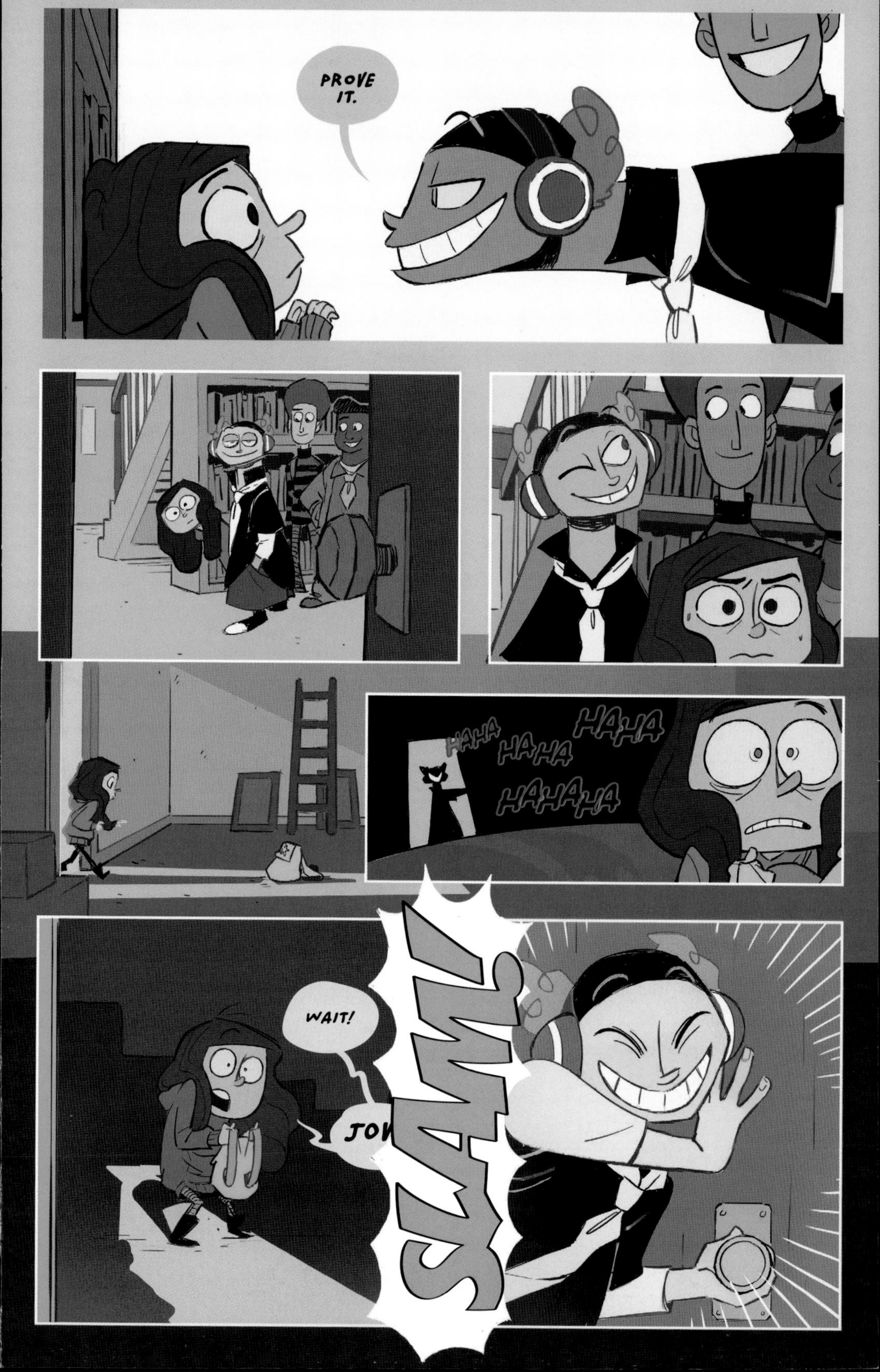
PROVE IT.
HAHA
HAHA
HAHA
HAHAHA
WAIT!
JOW
SLAM!

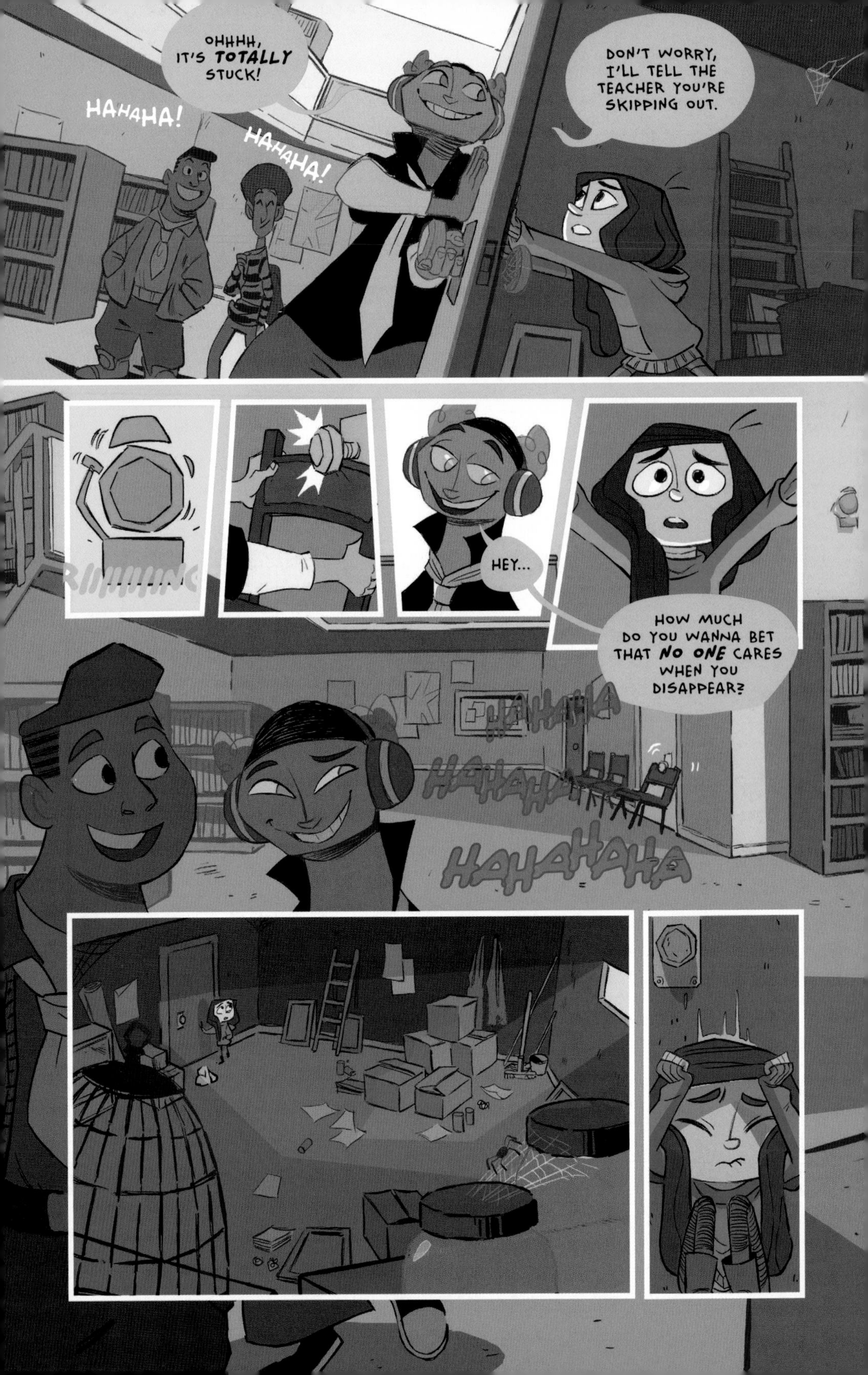
OHHHH, IT'S TOTALLY STUCK!
HAHAHA!
HAHAHA!
DON'T WORRY, I'LL TELL THE TEACHER YOU'RE SKIPPING OUT.
RINNNNG
HEY...
HOW MUCH DO YOU WANNA BET THAT NO ONE CARES WHEN YOU DISAPPEAR?
HAHAHA
HAHAHAHA
HAHAHAHA

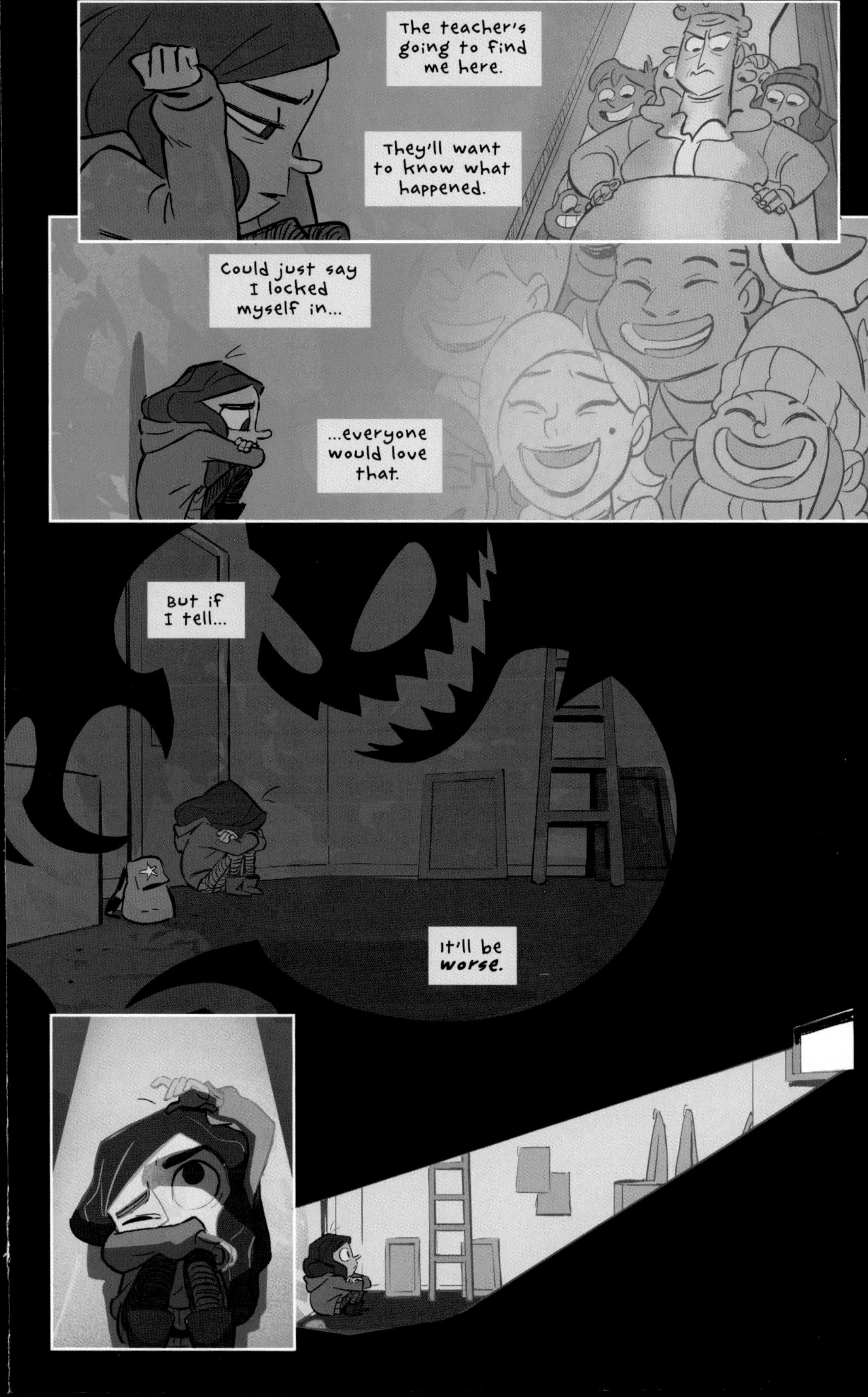
The teacher's going to find me here.
They'll want to know what happened.
Could just say I locked myself in...
...everyone would love that.
But if I tell...
It'll be **worse.**

FWUMP

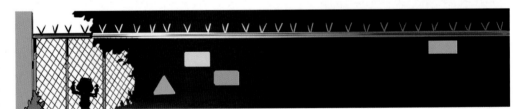

THIS *SHOULD* LEAD ROUND TO THE FRONT OF THE SCHOOL.

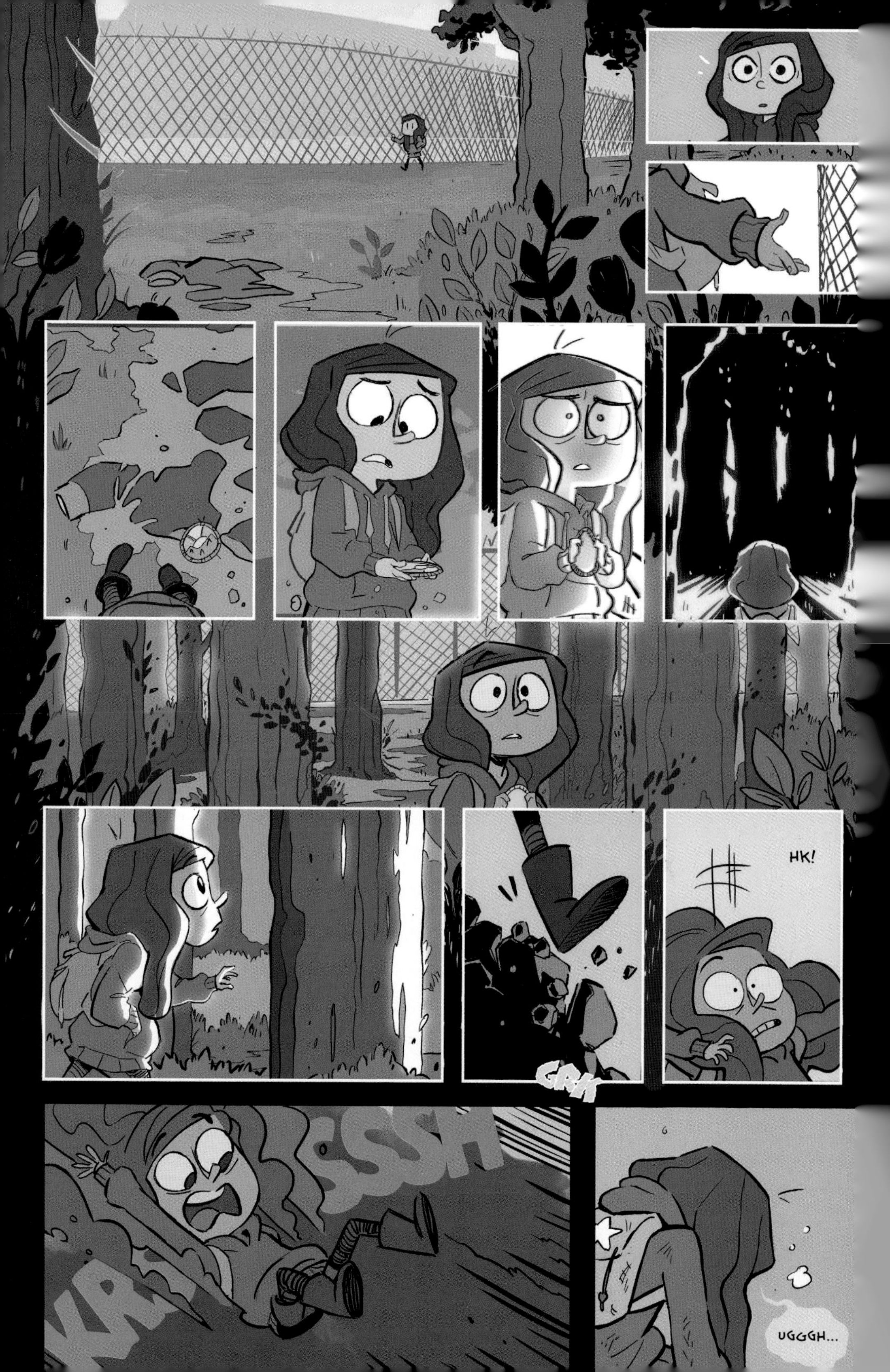
HK!
GRK
KR
SSSH
UGGGH...

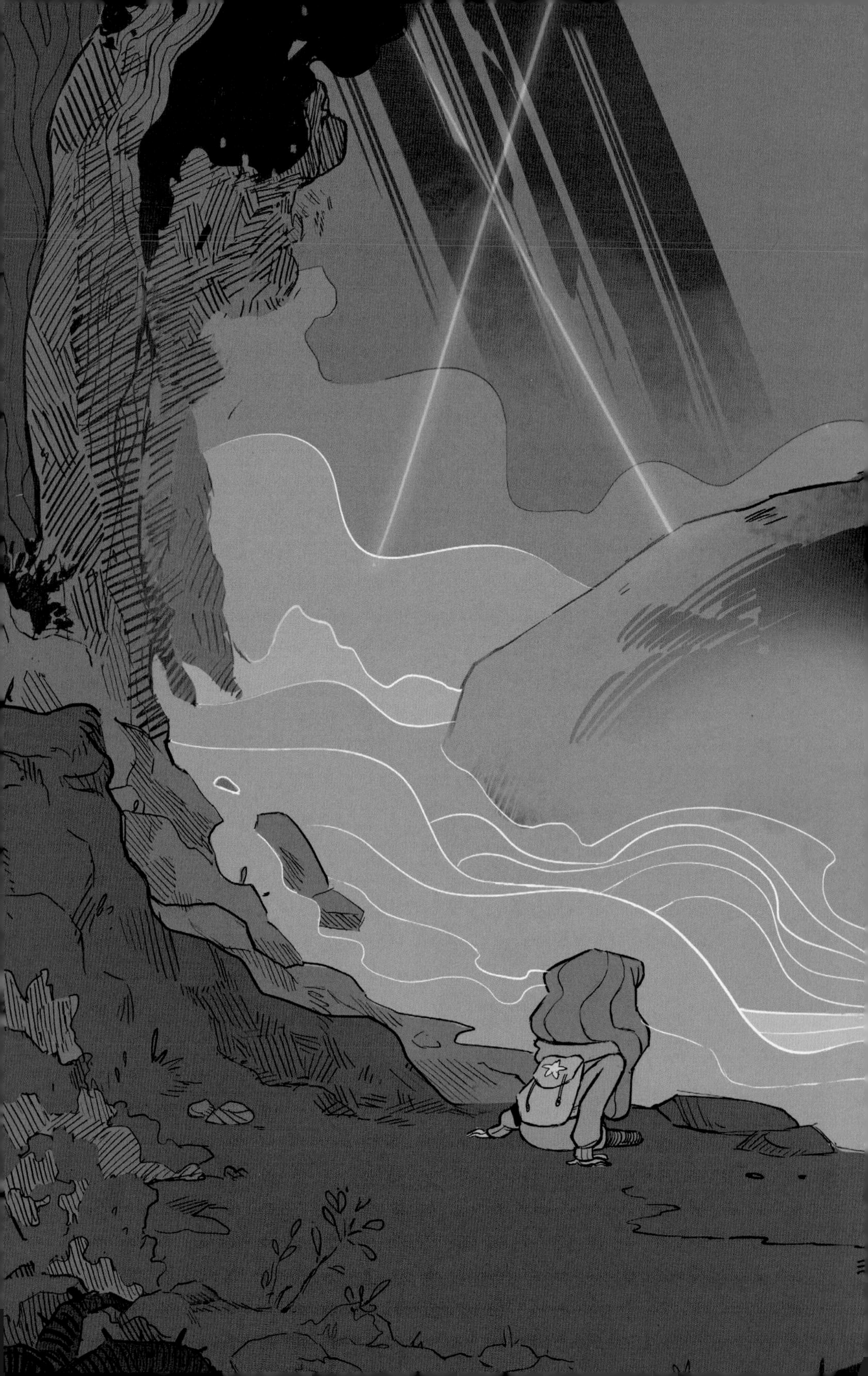

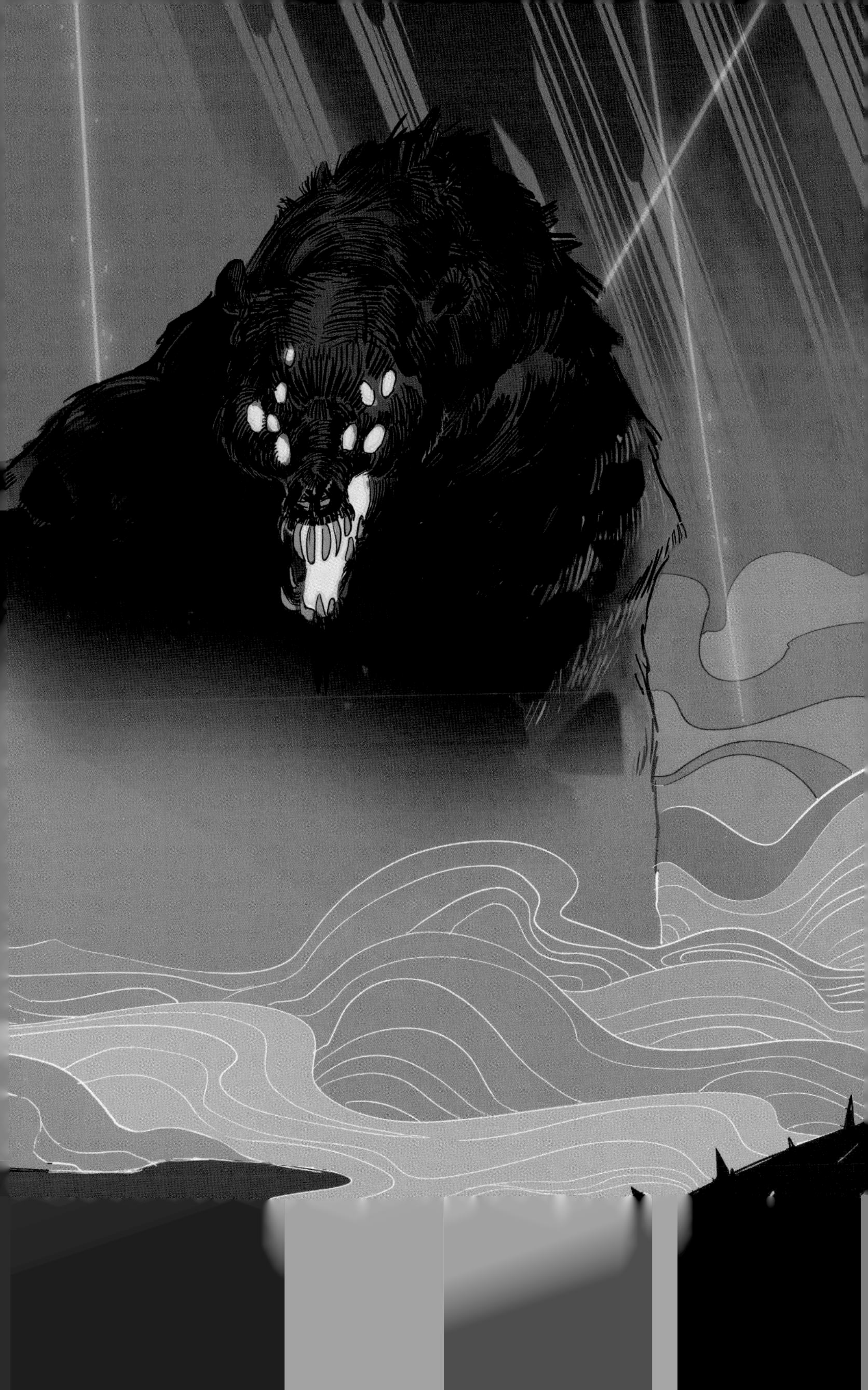

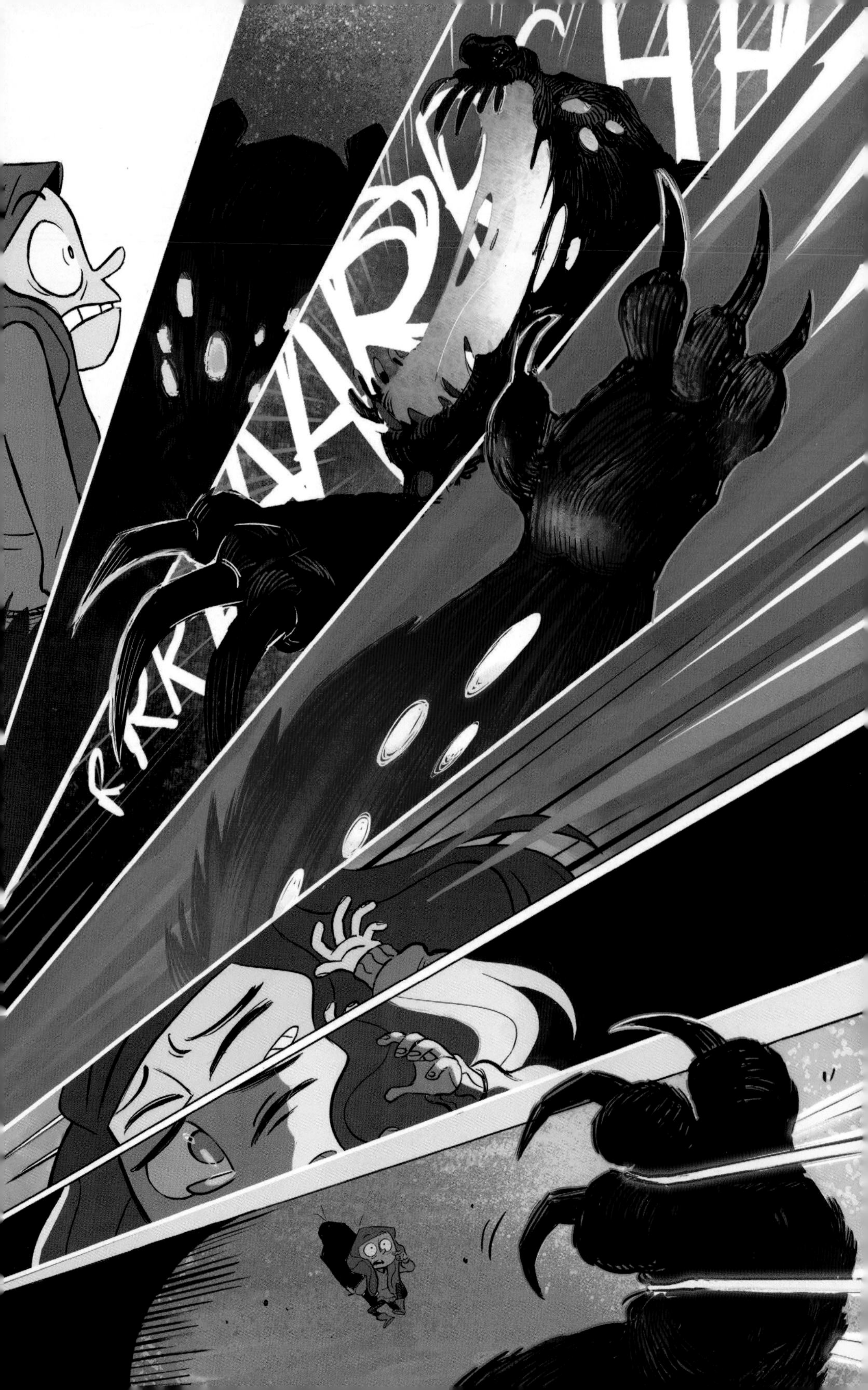

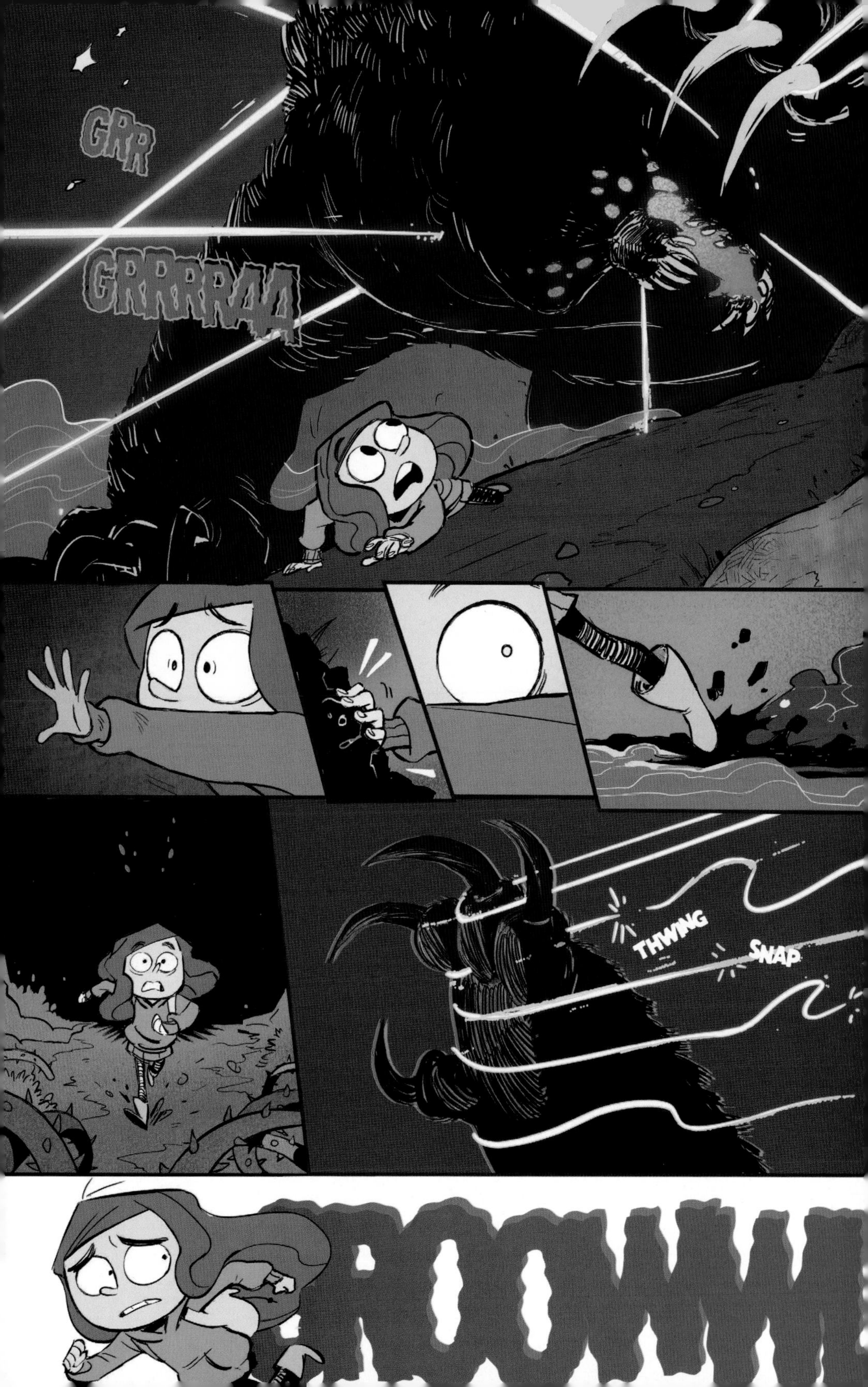
GRR
GRRRRAAA
THWING
SNAP

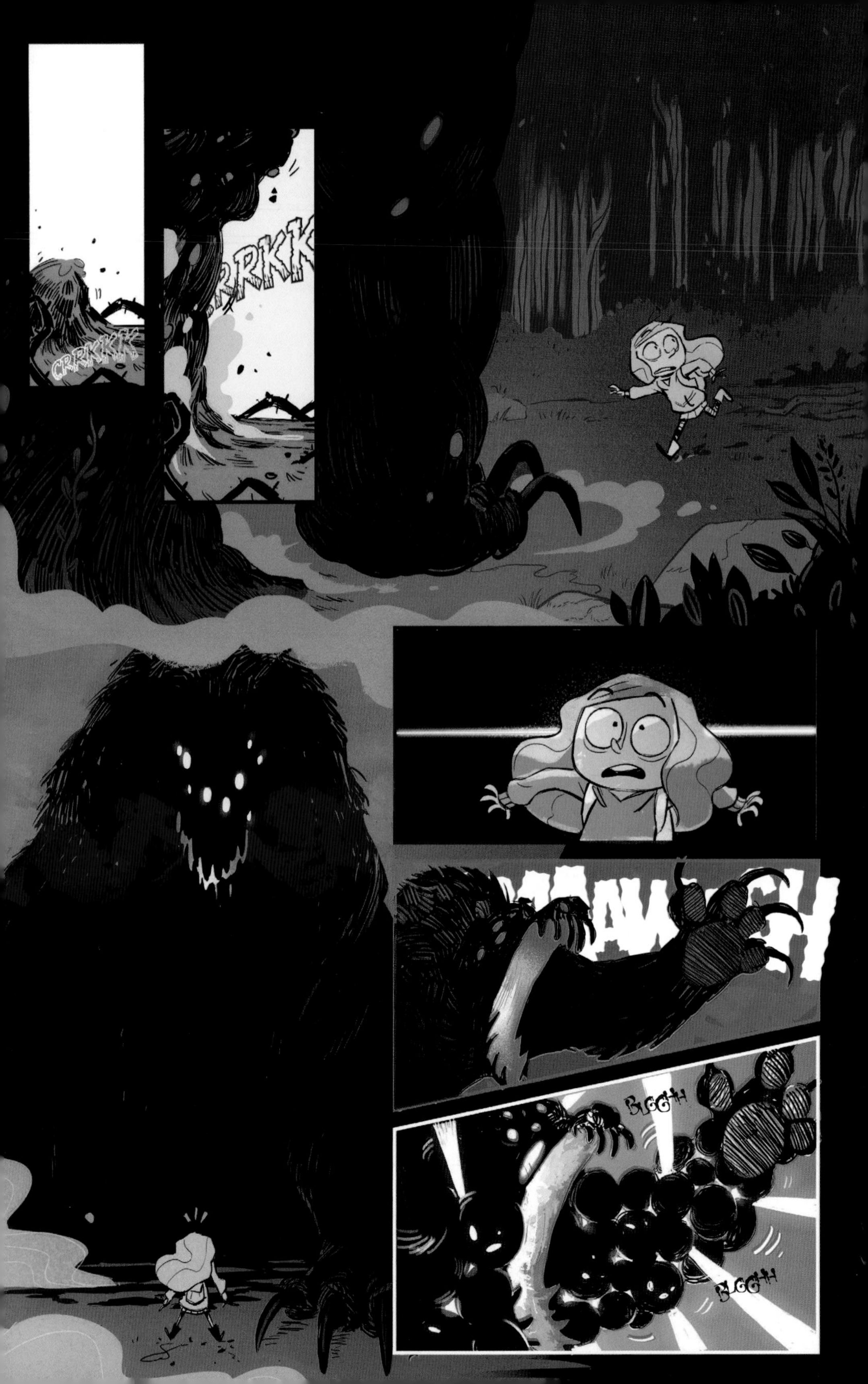
CRRKKK
CRRKK
BLGGHH
BLGGHH

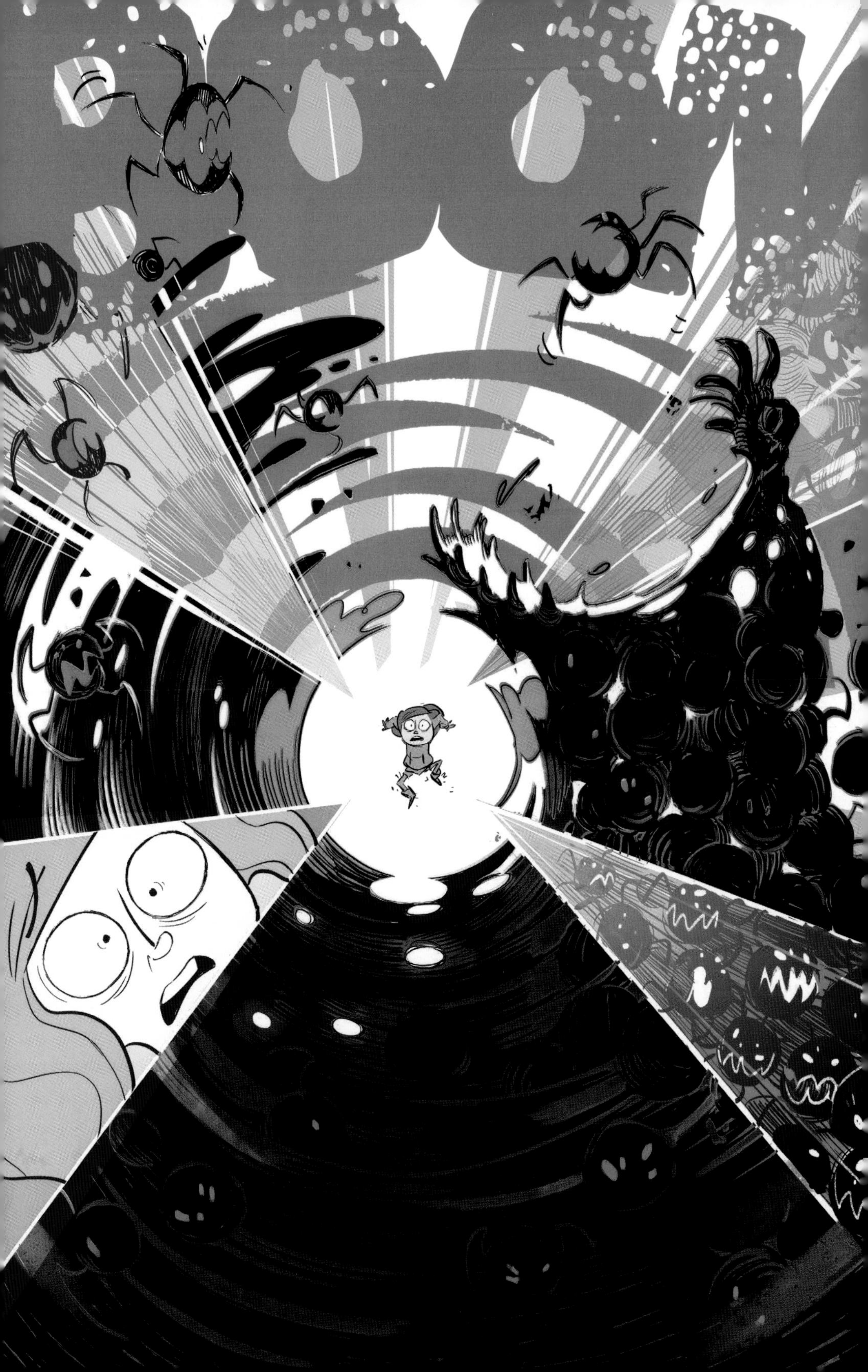

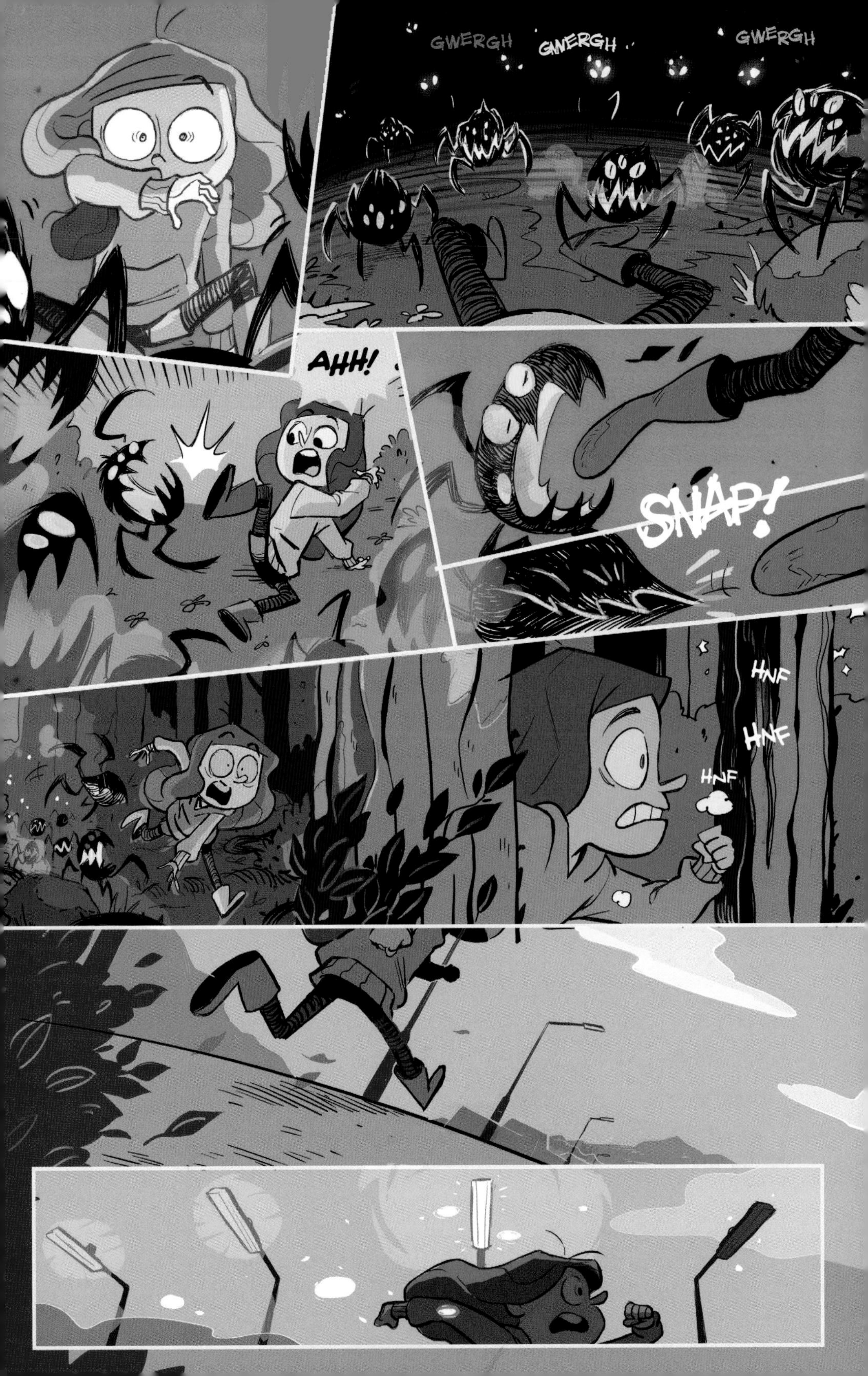
GWERGH
GWERGH
GWERGH
AHH!
SNAP!
HNF
HNF
HNF

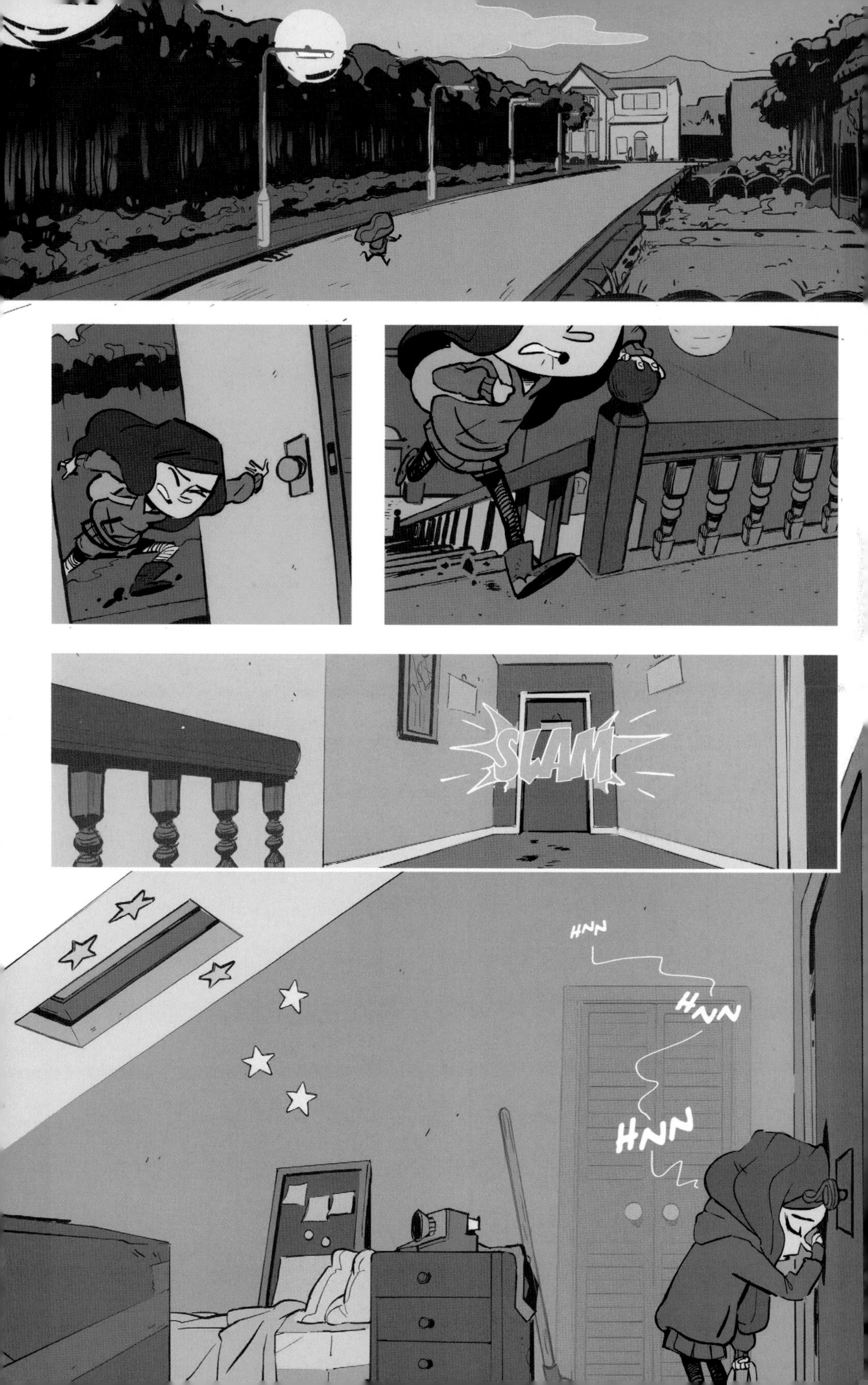
SLAM
HNN
HNN
HNN

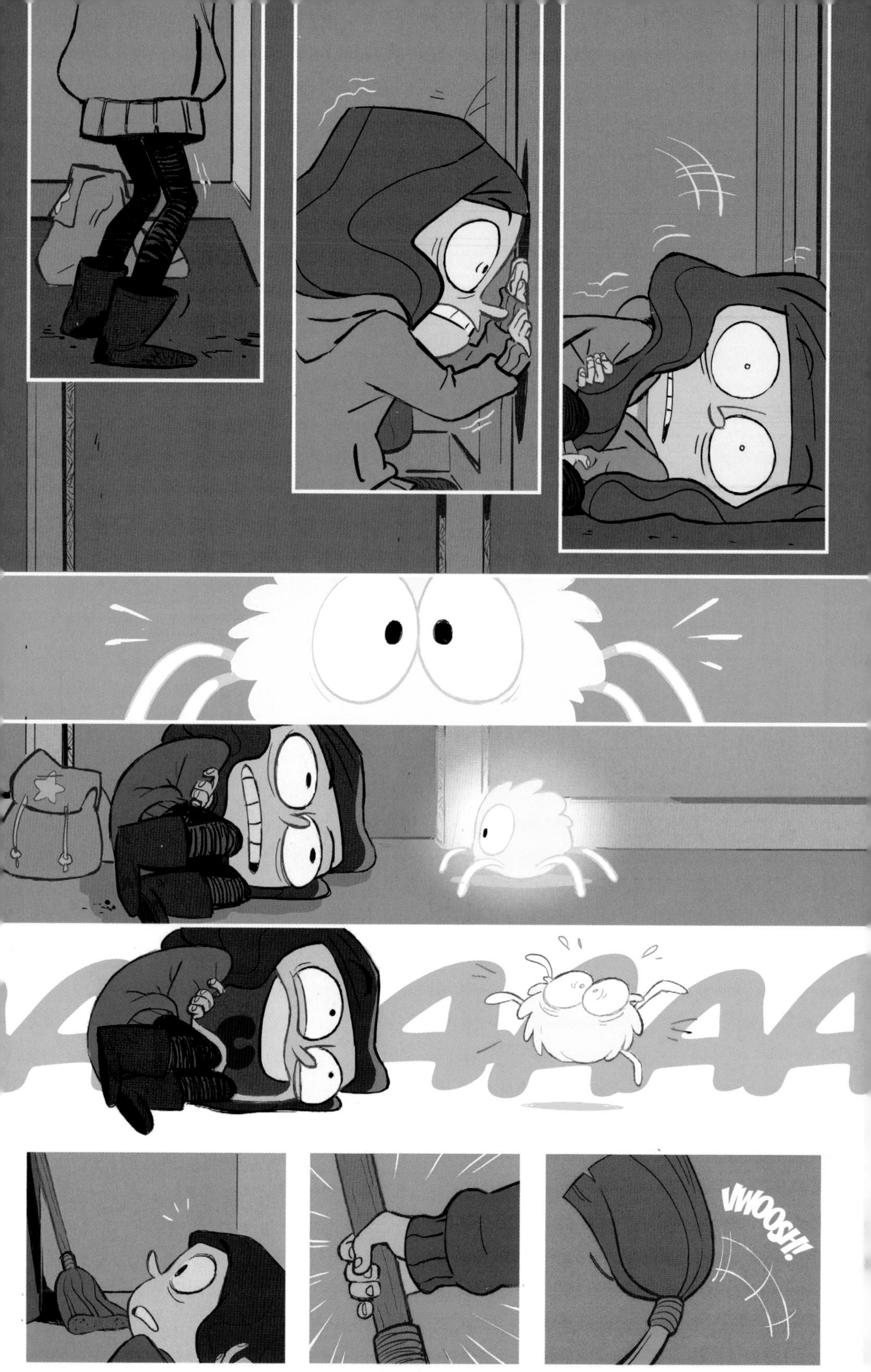
VWOOSH!!

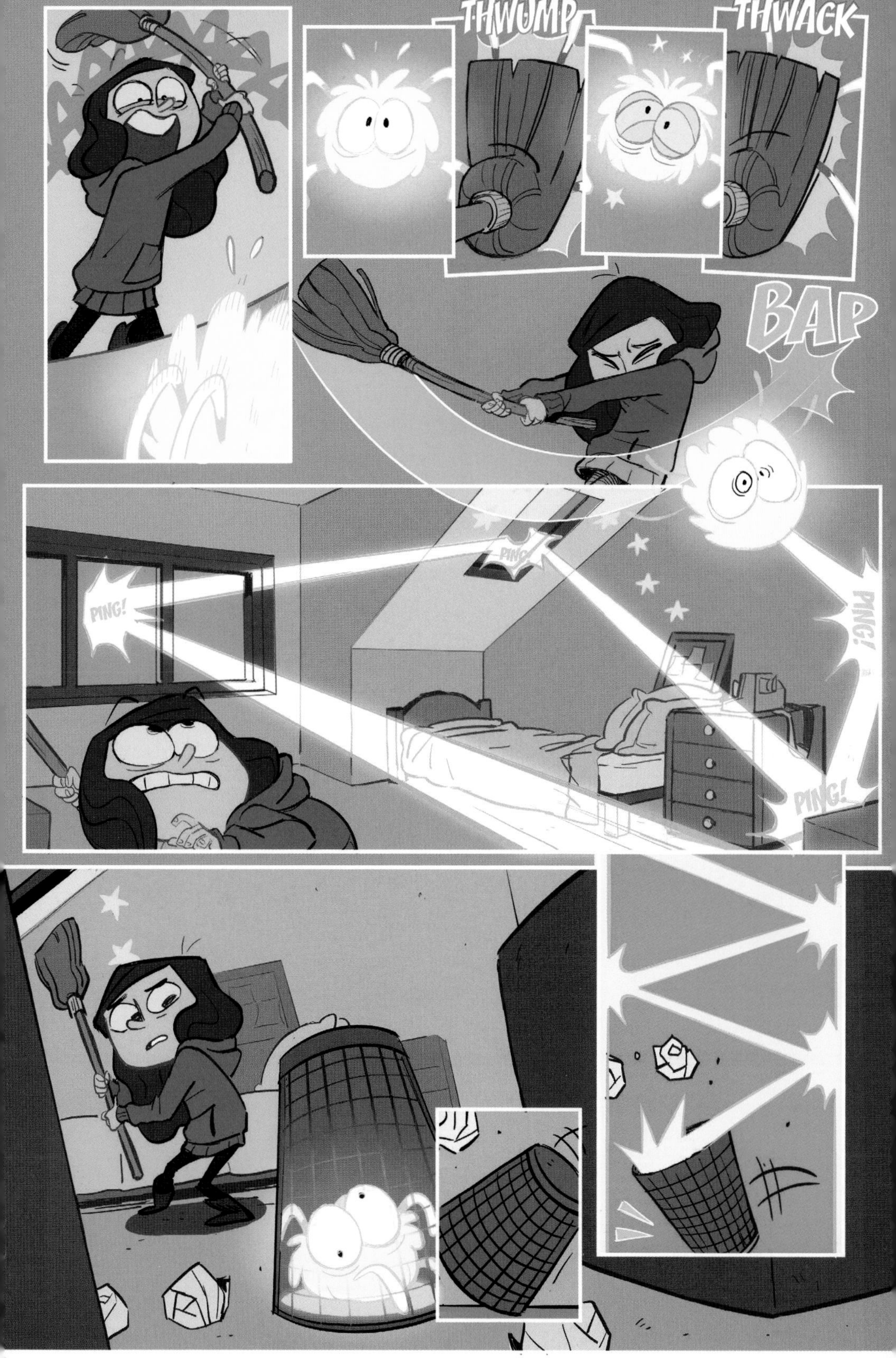
THWUMP
THWACK
BAP
PING!
PING!
PING!
PING!

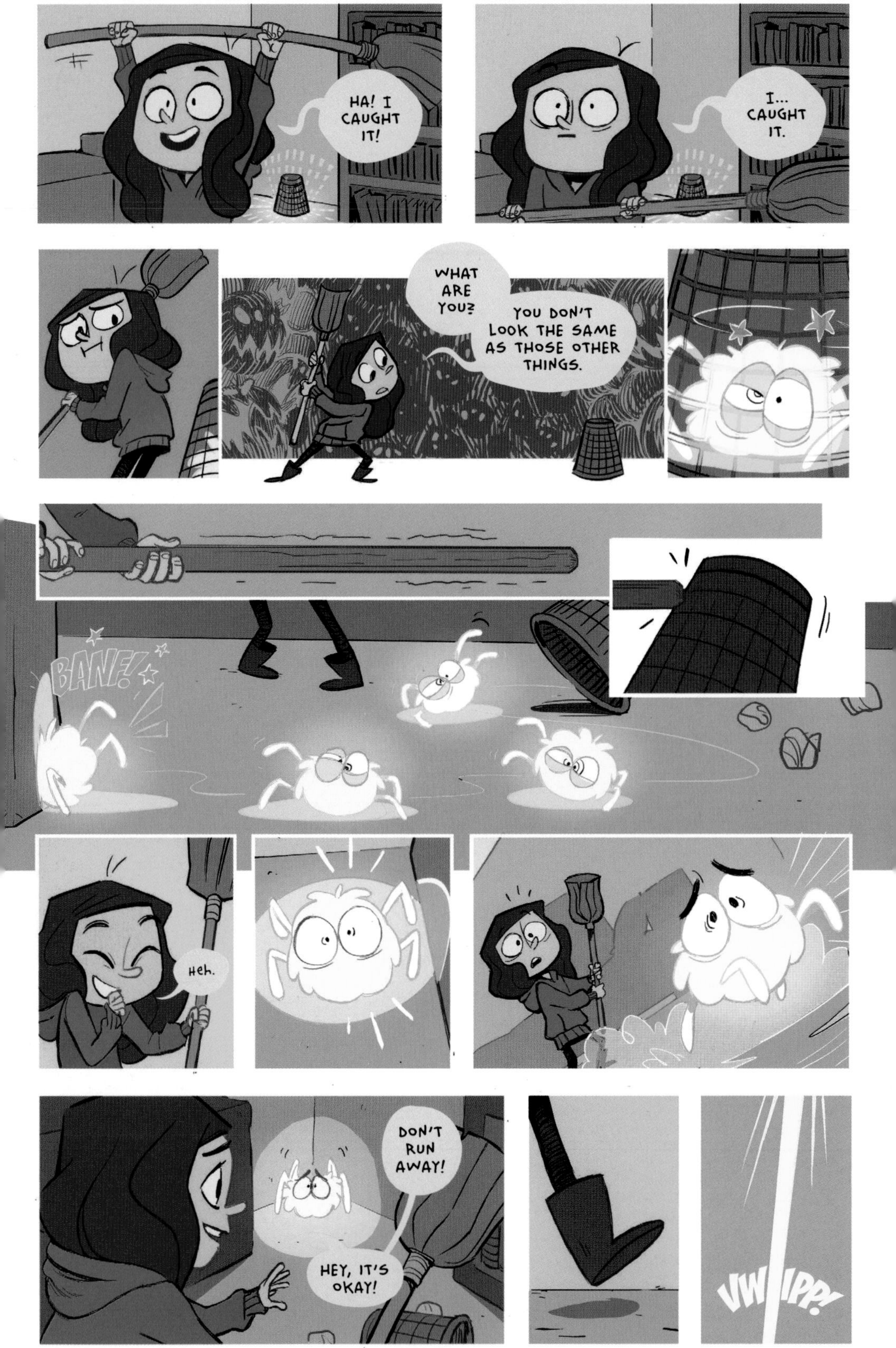
HA! I CAUGHT IT!
I... CAUGHT IT.
WHAT ARE YOU?
YOU DON'T LOOK THE SAME AS THOSE OTHER THINGS.
BANF!
Heh.
DON'T RUN AWAY!
HEY, IT'S OKAY!
VWIPP!

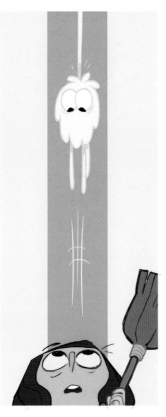

woah...

oh!

...

OH C'MON! I'M SORRY I BROOMED YOU, OKAY?!

THIS IS CRAZY!

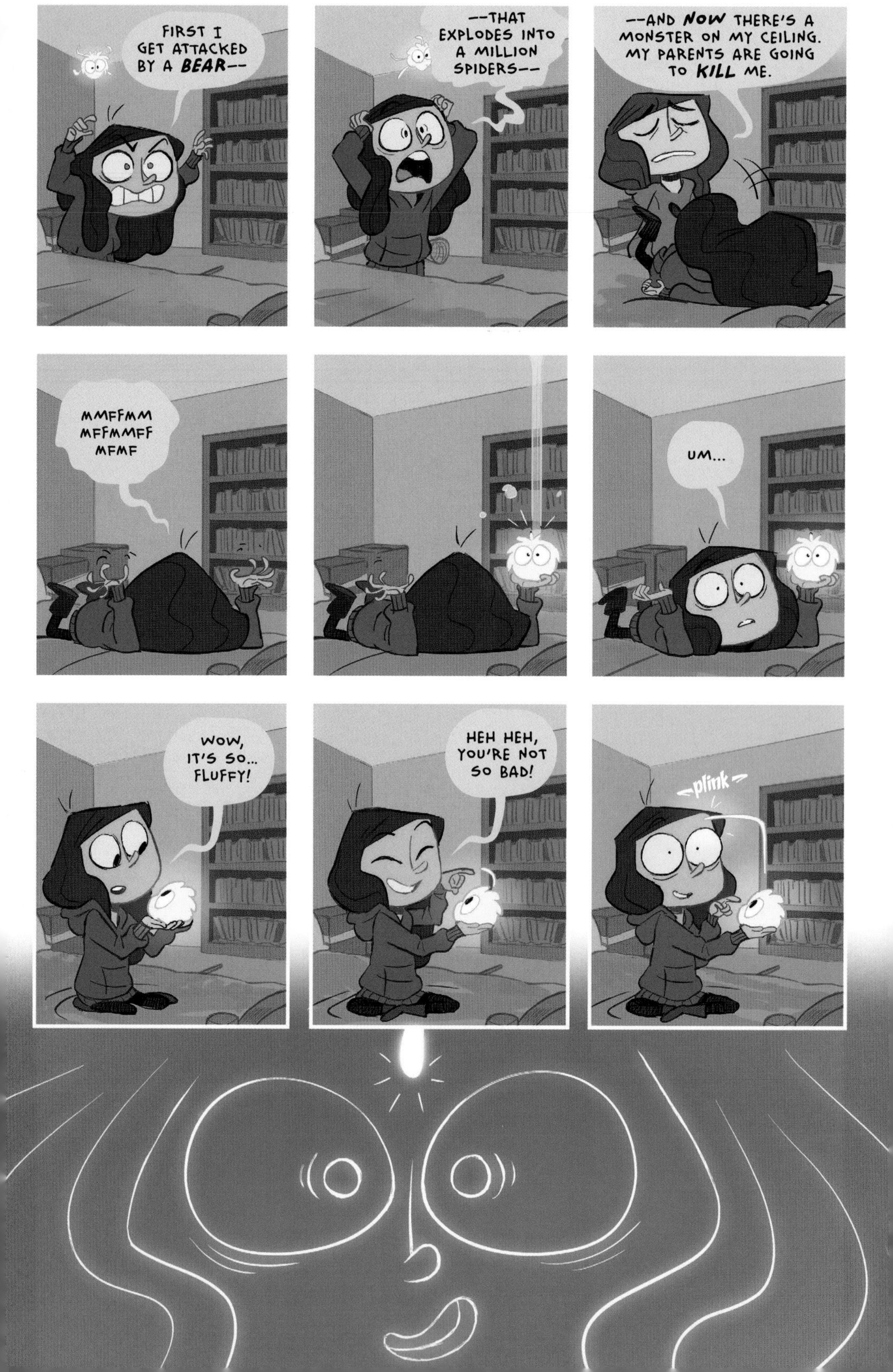
FIRST I GET ATTACKED BY A BEAR--
--THAT EXPLODES INTO A MILLION SPIDERS--
--AND NOW THERE'S A MONSTER ON MY CEILING. MY PARENTS ARE GOING TO KILL ME.
MMFFMM MFFMMFF MFMF
UM...
WOW, IT'S SO... FLUFFY!
HEH HEH, YOU'RE NOT SO BAD!
plink

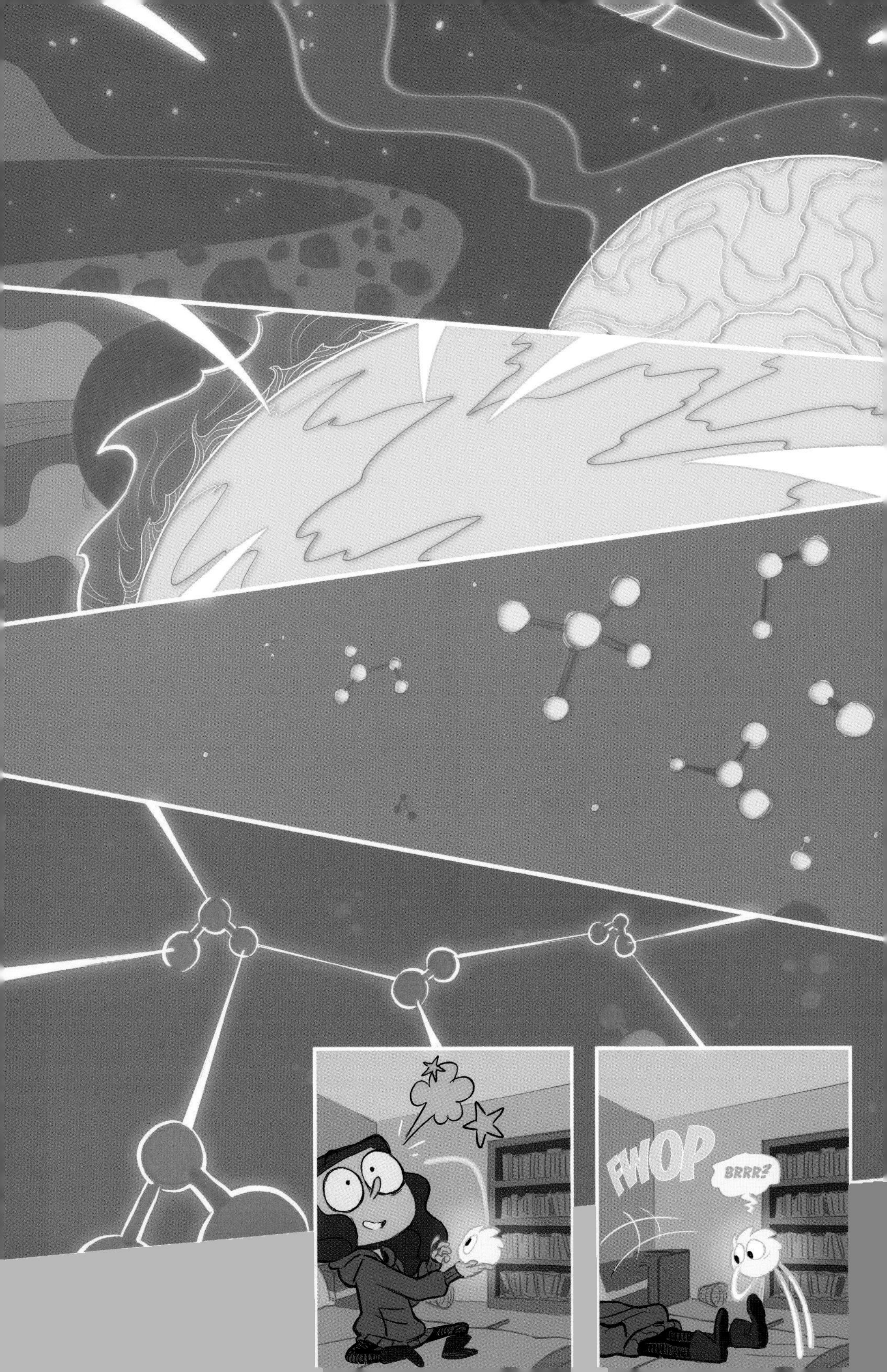
FWOP
BRRR?

✳Gasp✳

WHAT A
WEIRD—

—dream?

THAT
WAS ALL
REAL?

BUT THAT
MEANS...

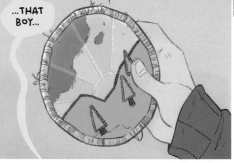

...THAT
BOY...

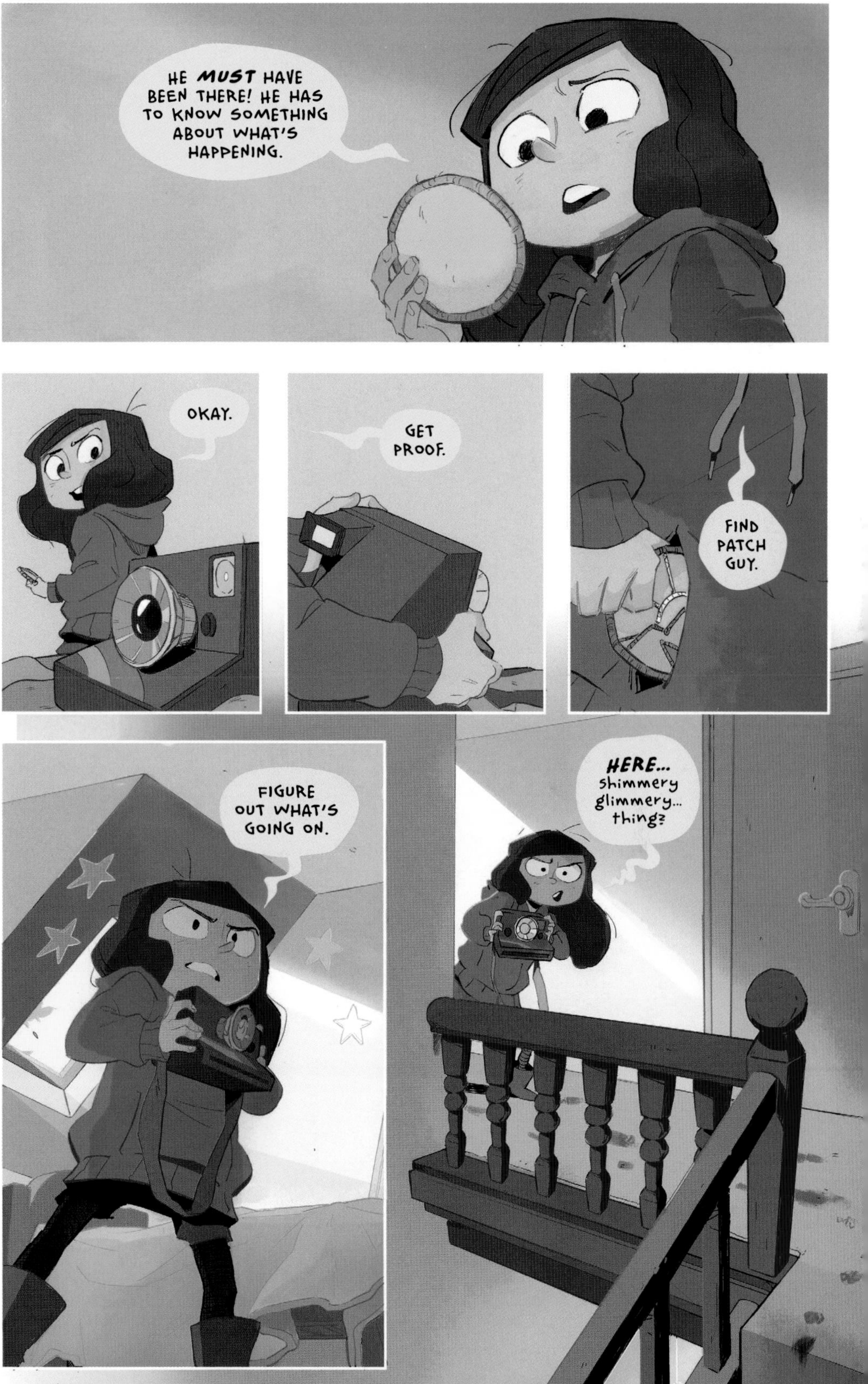
HE MUST HAVE BEEN THERE! HE HAS TO KNOW SOMETHING ABOUT WHAT'S HAPPENING.
OKAY.
GET PROOF.
FIND PATCH GUY.
FIGURE OUT WHAT'S GOING ON.
HERE... shimmery glimmery... thing?

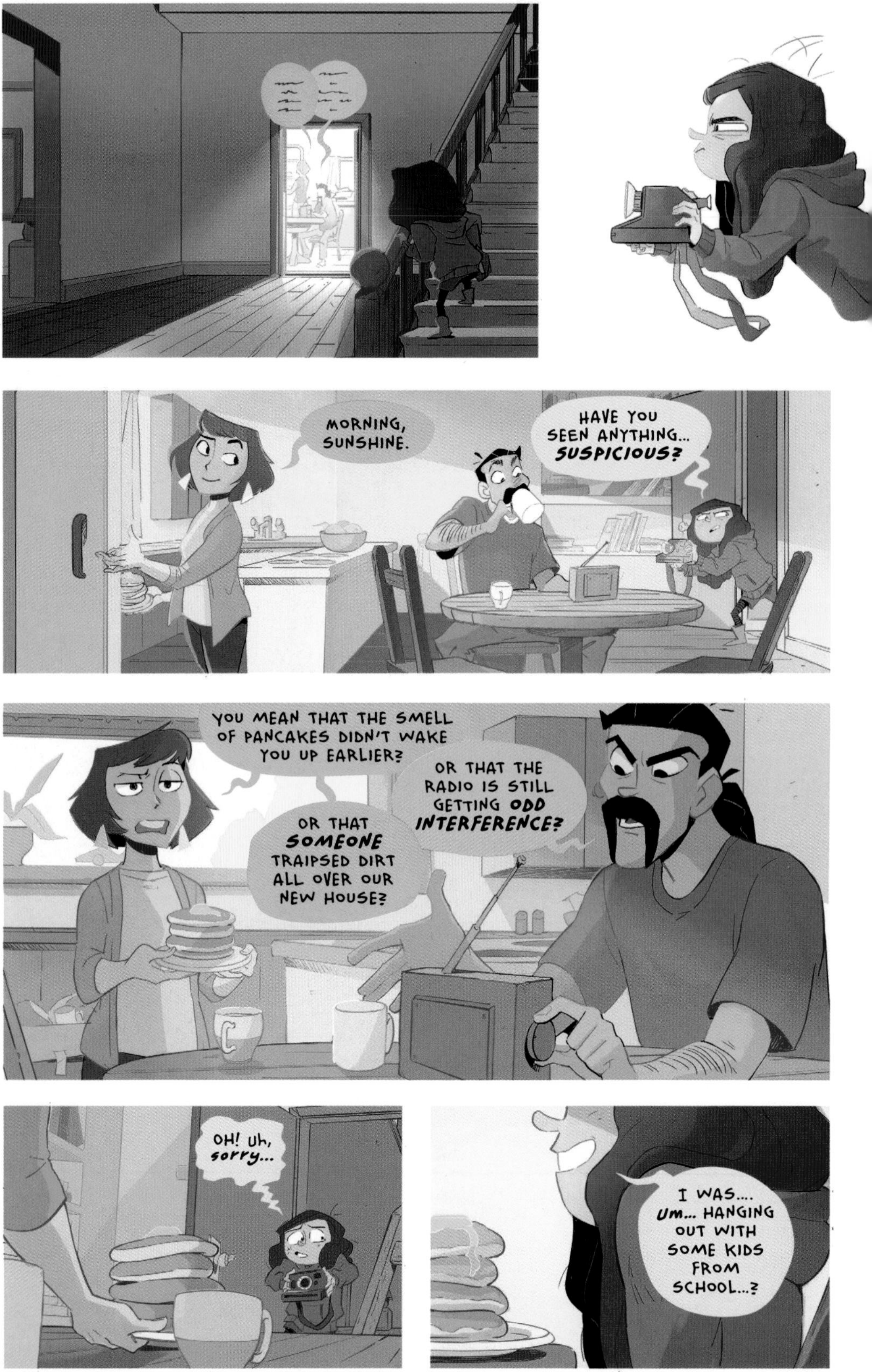
MORNING, SUNSHINE.
HAVE YOU SEEN ANYTHING... SUSPICIOUS?
YOU MEAN THAT THE SMELL OF PANCAKES DIDN'T WAKE YOU UP EARLIER?
OR THAT THE RADIO IS STILL GETTING ODD INTERFERENCE?
OR THAT SOMEONE TRAIPSED DIRT ALL OVER OUR NEW HOUSE?
OH! Uh, sorry...
I WAS.... UM... HANGING OUT WITH SOME KIDS FROM SCHOOL...?

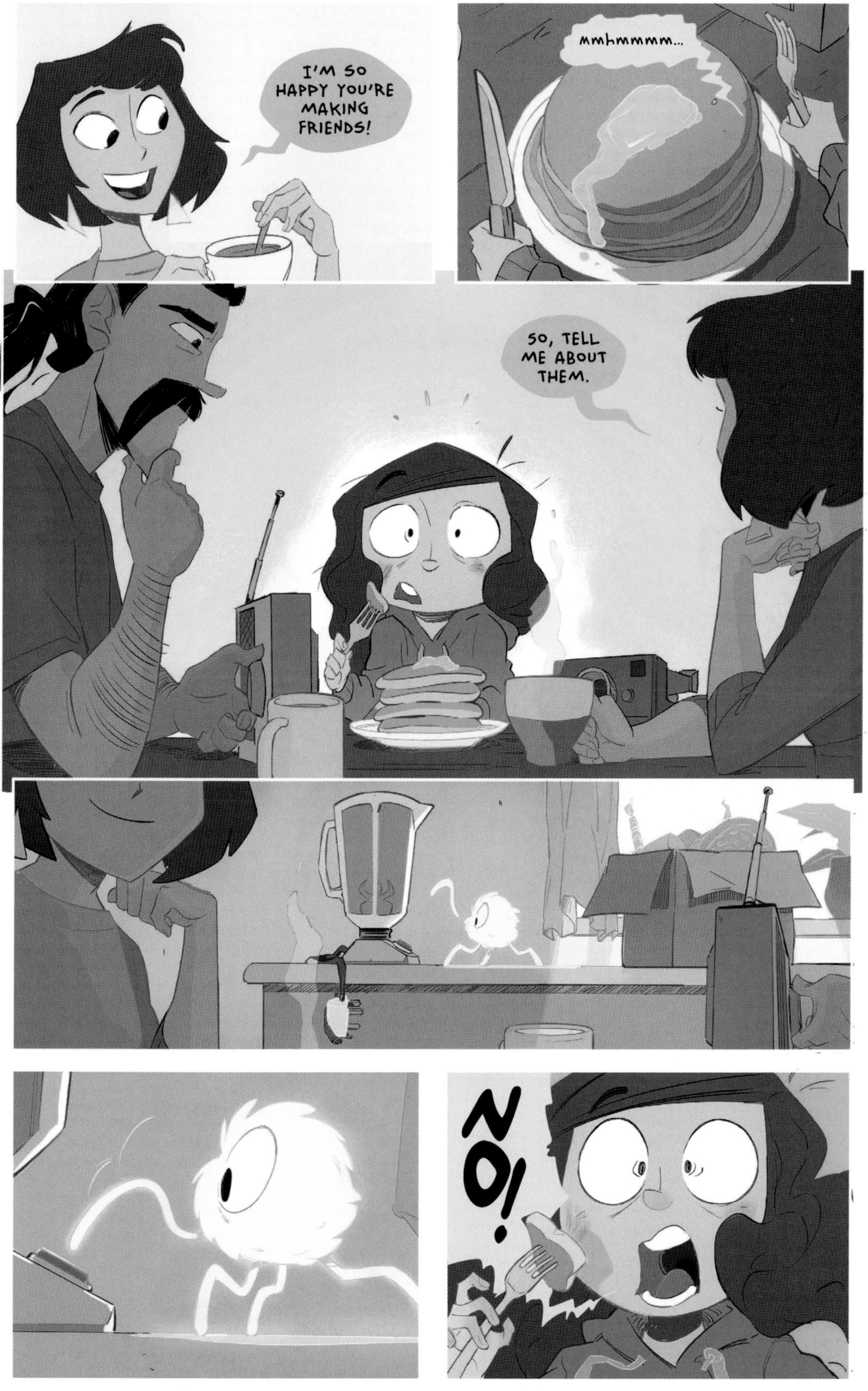
I'M SO HAPPY YOU'RE MAKING FRIENDS!
mmhmmmm...
SO, TELL ME ABOUT THEM.
NO!

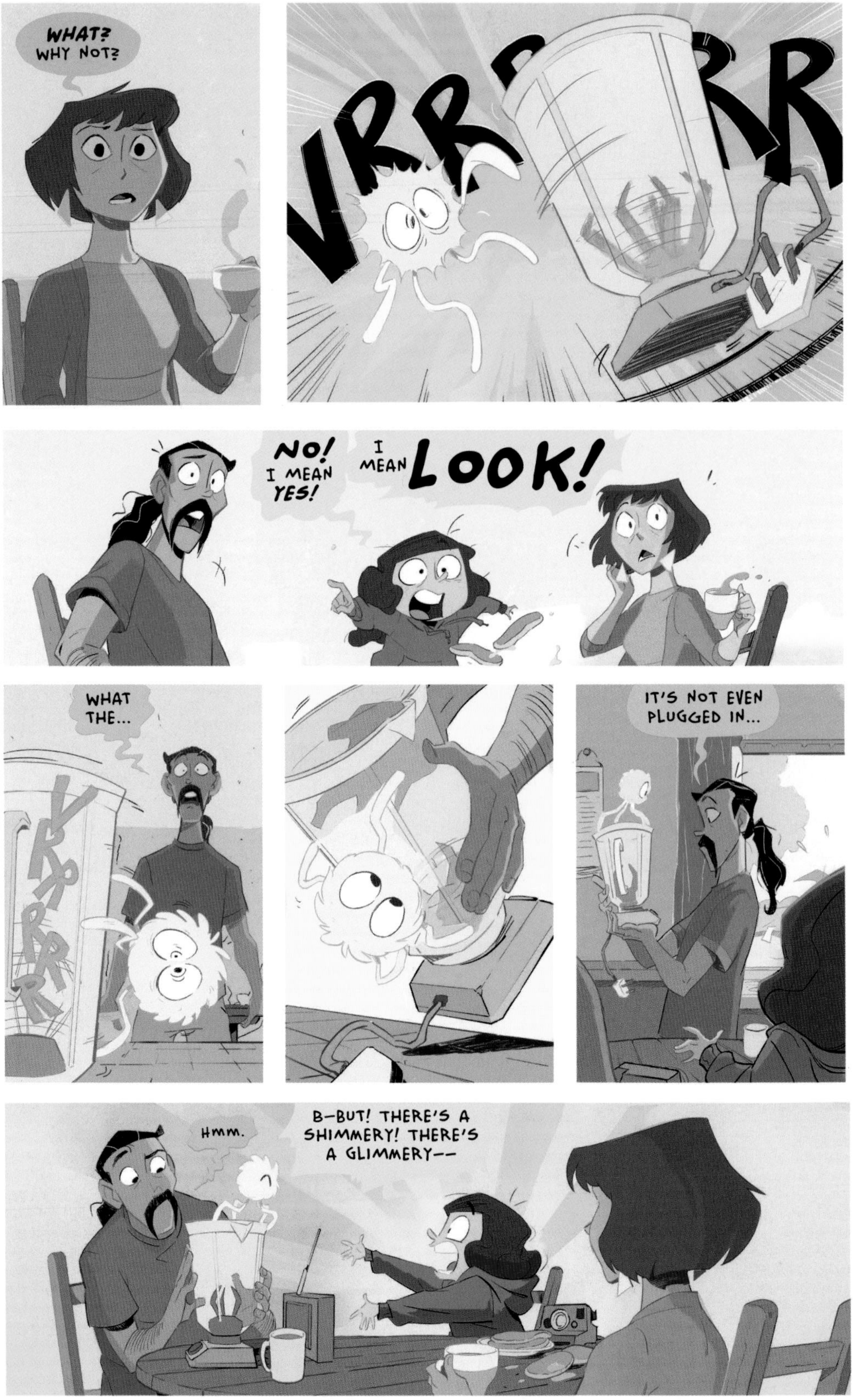
WHAT? WHY NOT?
VRRRRR
NO! I MEAN YES!
I MEAN LOOK!
WHAT THE...
VRRRR
IT'S NOT EVEN PLUGGED IN...
HMM.
B-BUT! THERE'S A SHIMMERY! THERE'S A GLIMMERY--

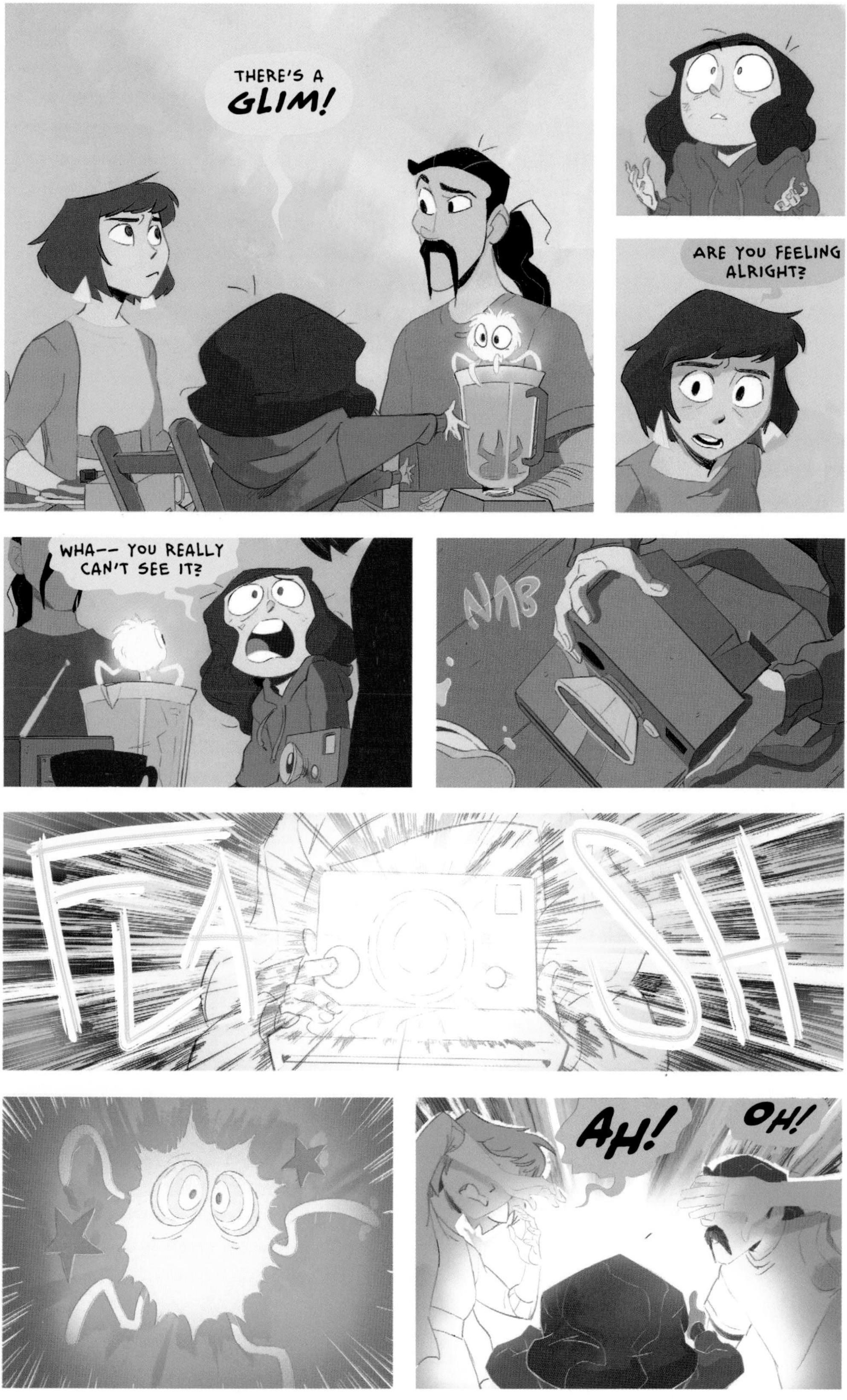
THERE'S A GLIM!
ARE YOU FEELING ALRIGHT?
WHA-- YOU REALLY CAN'T SEE IT?
NAB
FLASH
AH!
OH!

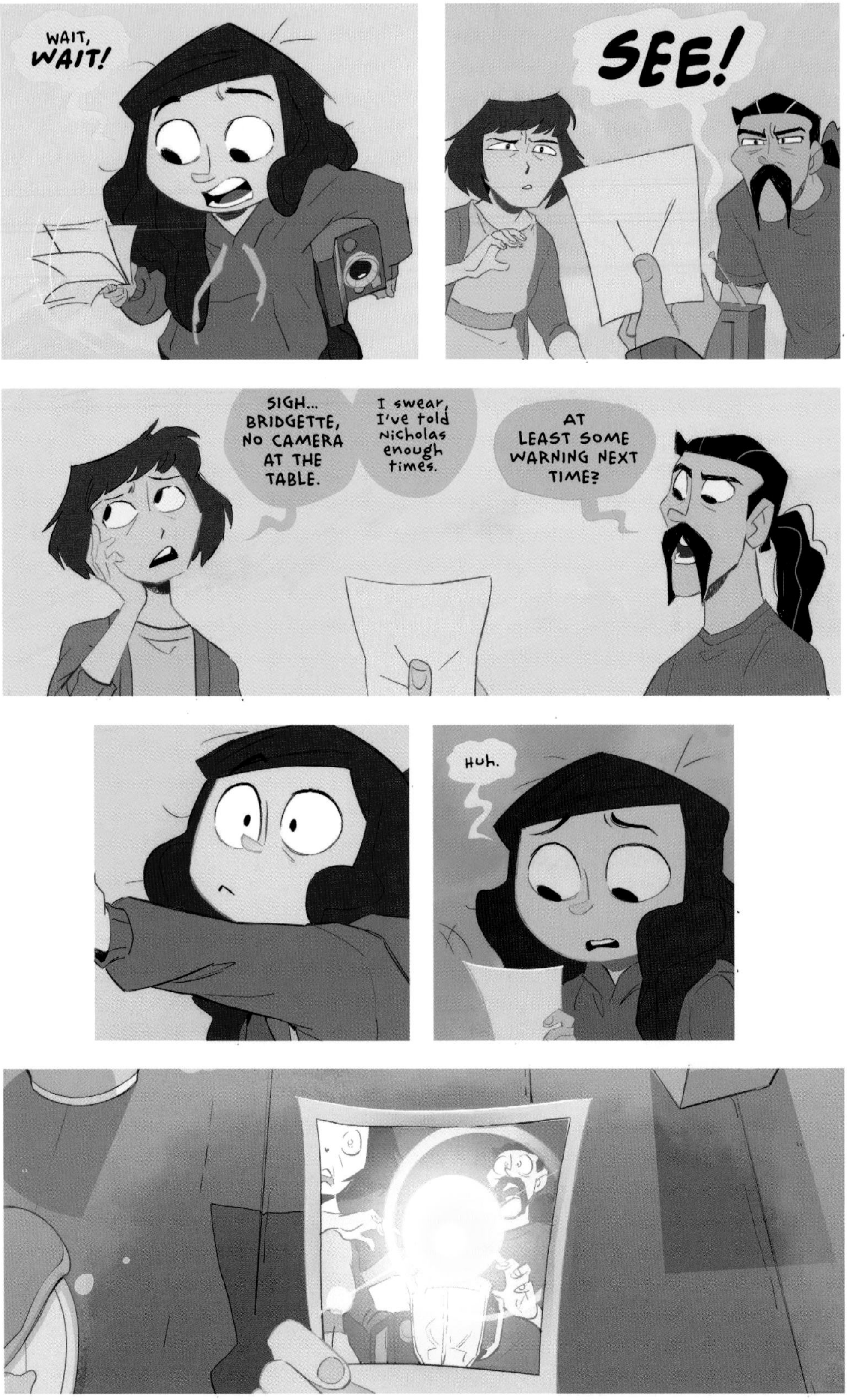
WAIT, WAIT!
SEE!
SIGH... BRIDGETTE, NO CAMERA AT THE TABLE.
I swear, I've told Nicholas enough times.
AT LEAST SOME WARNING NEXT TIME?
Huh.

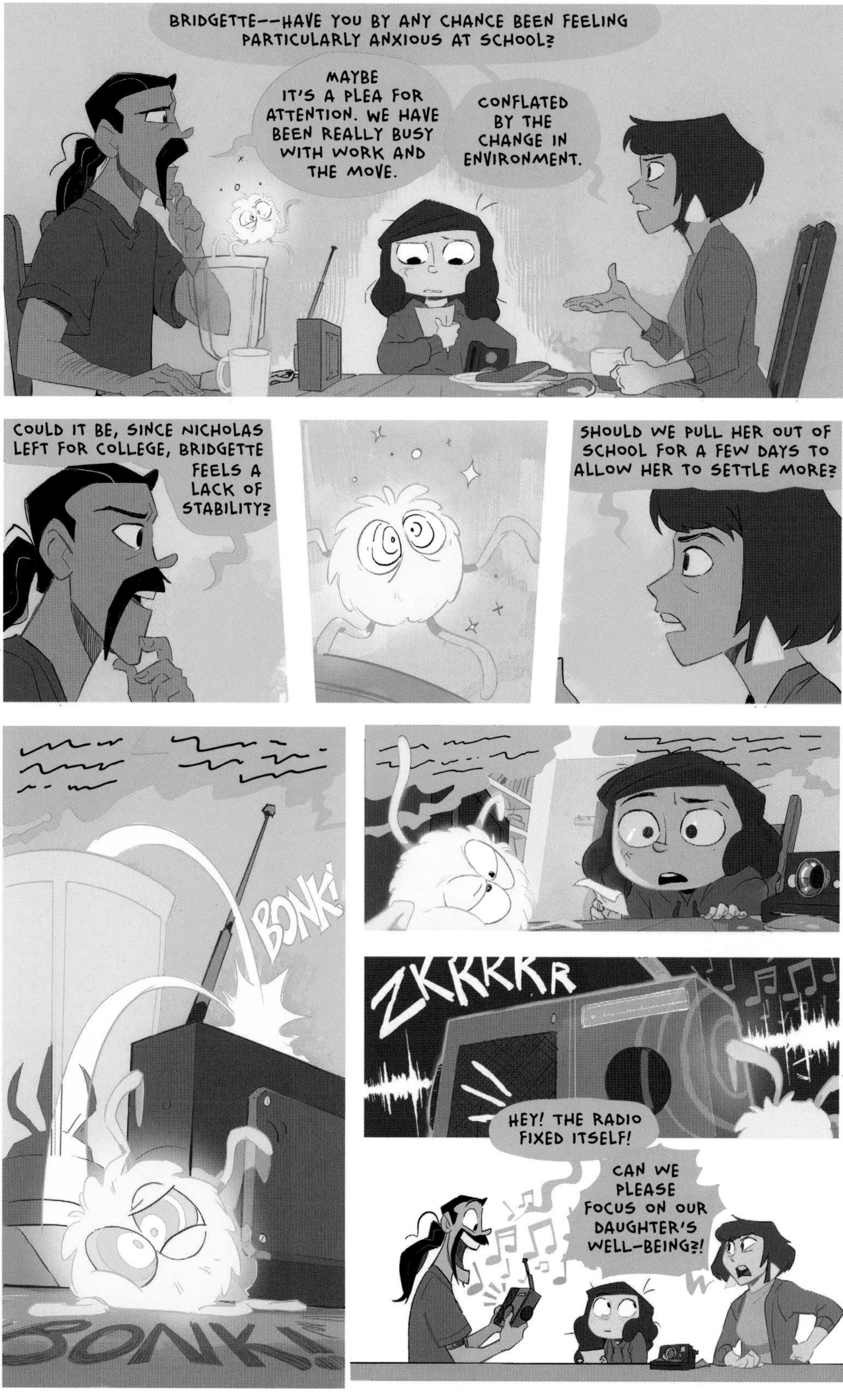

BRIDGETTE--HAVE YOU BY ANY CHANCE BEEN FEELING PARTICULARLY ANXIOUS AT SCHOOL?
MAYBE IT'S A PLEA FOR ATTENTION. WE HAVE BEEN REALLY BUSY WITH WORK AND THE MOVE.
CONFLATED BY THE CHANGE IN ENVIRONMENT.
COULD IT BE, SINCE NICHOLAS LEFT FOR COLLEGE, BRIDGETTE FEELS A LACK OF STABILITY?
SHOULD WE PULL HER OUT OF SCHOOL FOR A FEW DAYS TO ALLOW HER TO SETTLE MORE?
BONK!
BONK!
ZKRKKR
HEY! THE RADIO FIXED ITSELF!
CAN WE PLEASE FOCUS ON OUR DAUGHTER'S WELL-BEING?!

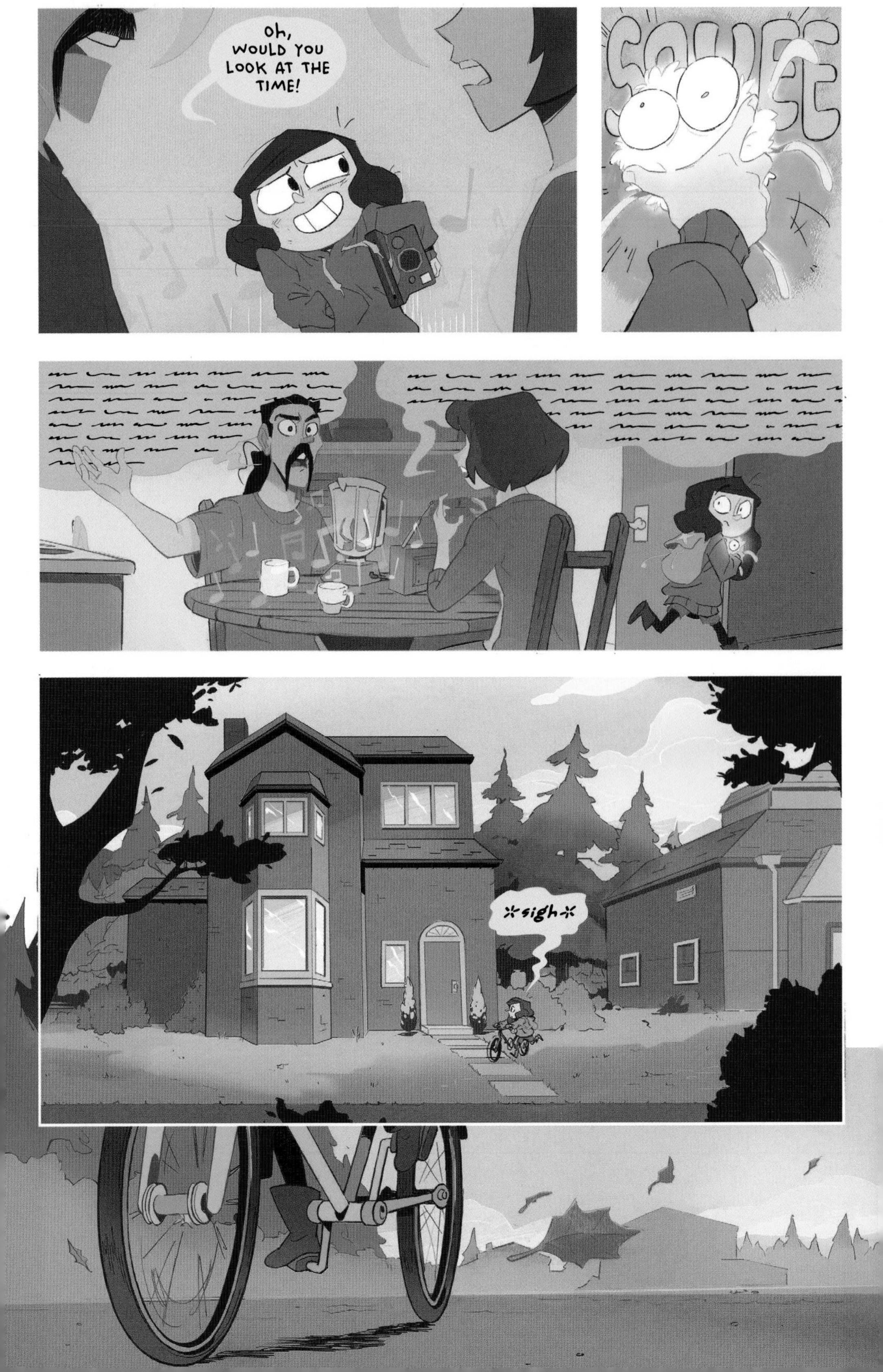
Oh, WOULD YOU LOOK AT THE TIME!
sigh

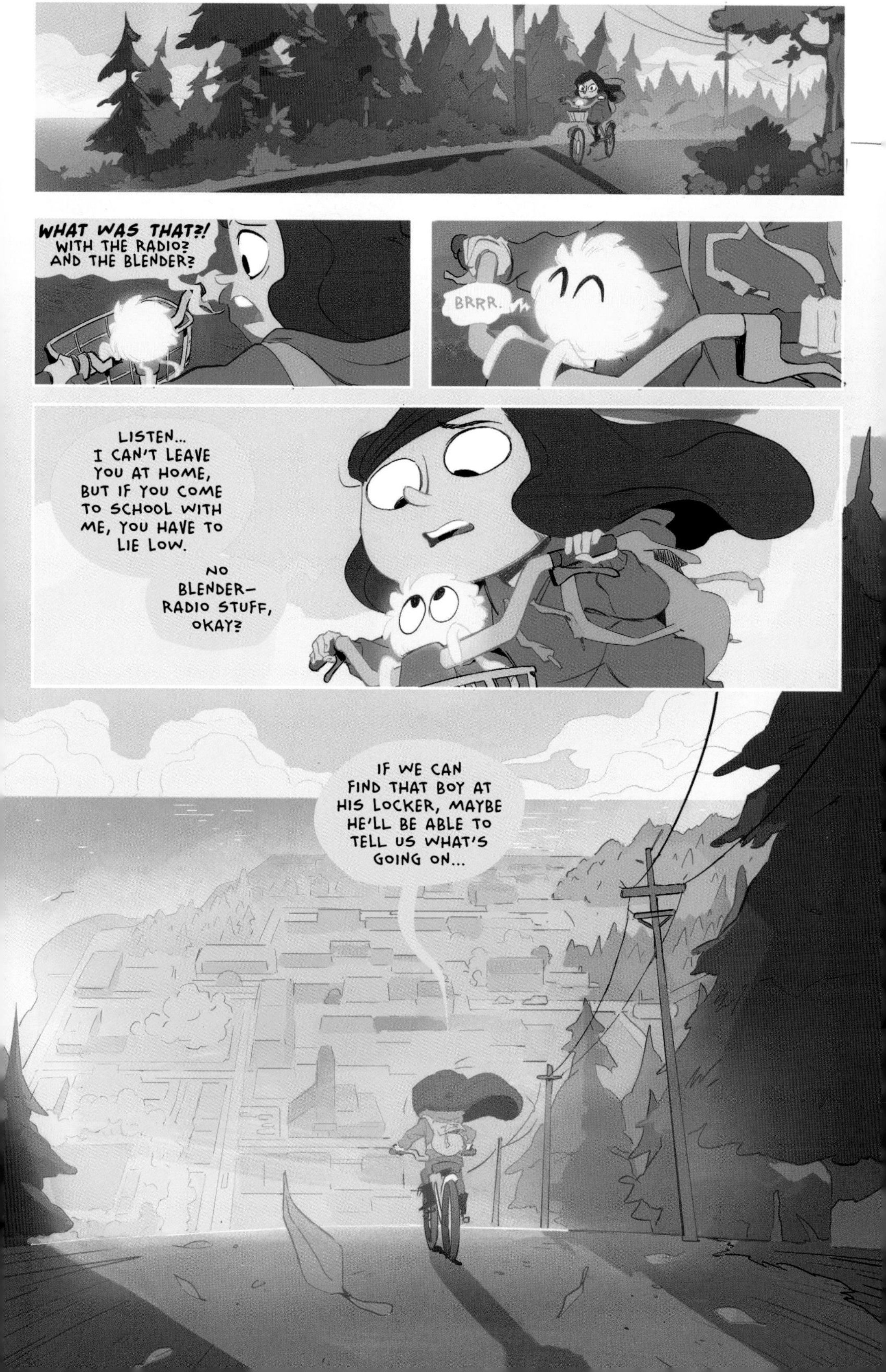
WHAT WAS THAT?! WITH THE RADIO? AND THE BLENDER?
BRRR.
LISTEN... I CAN'T LEAVE YOU AT HOME, BUT IF YOU COME TO SCHOOL WITH ME, YOU HAVE TO LIE LOW.
NO BLENDER-RADIO STUFF, OKAY?
IF WE CAN FIND THAT BOY AT HIS LOCKER, MAYBE HE'LL BE ABLE TO TELL US WHAT'S GOING ON...

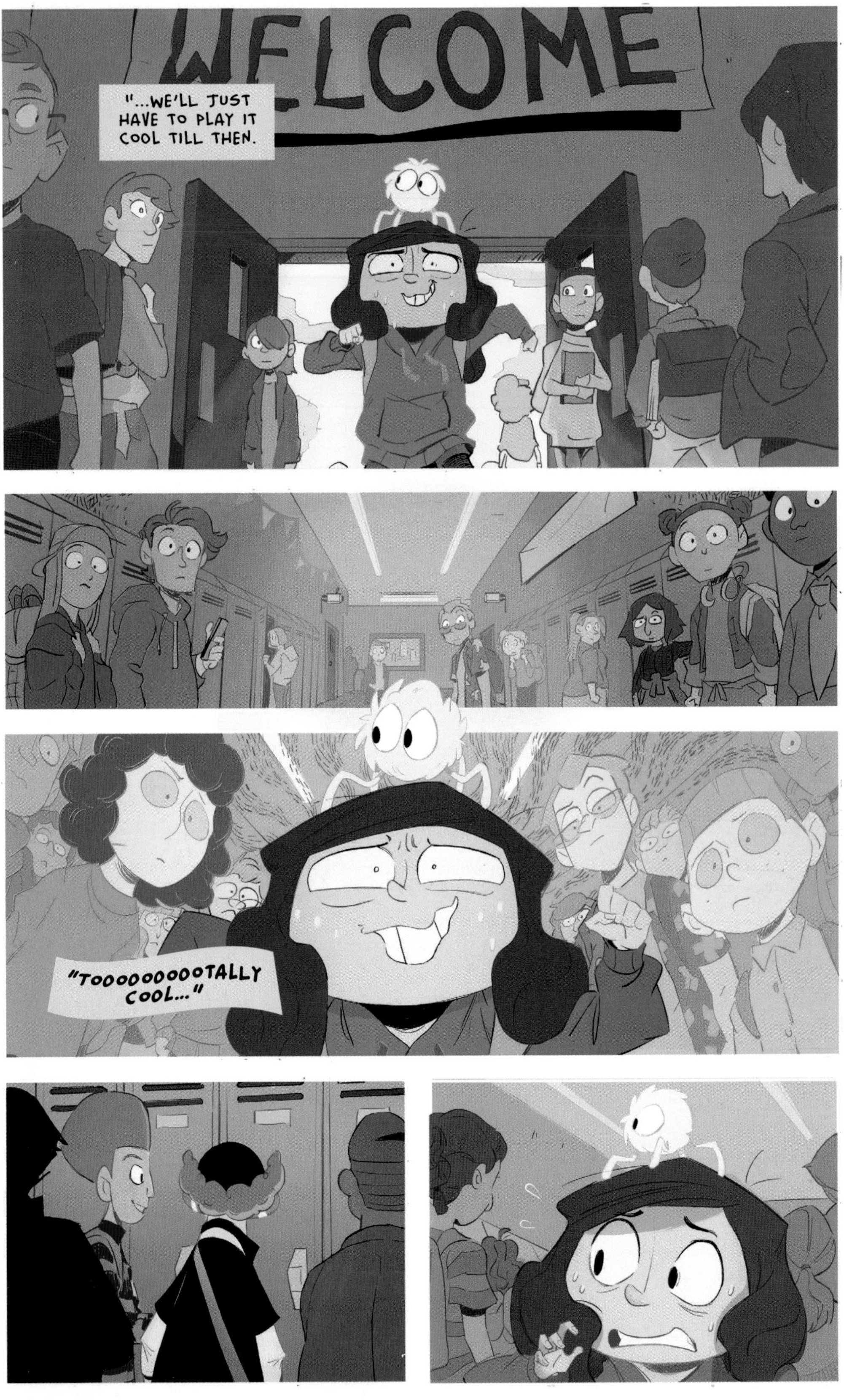
WELCOME
"...WE'LL JUST HAVE TO PLAY IT COOL TILL THEN.
"TOOOOOOOOOTALLY COOL..."

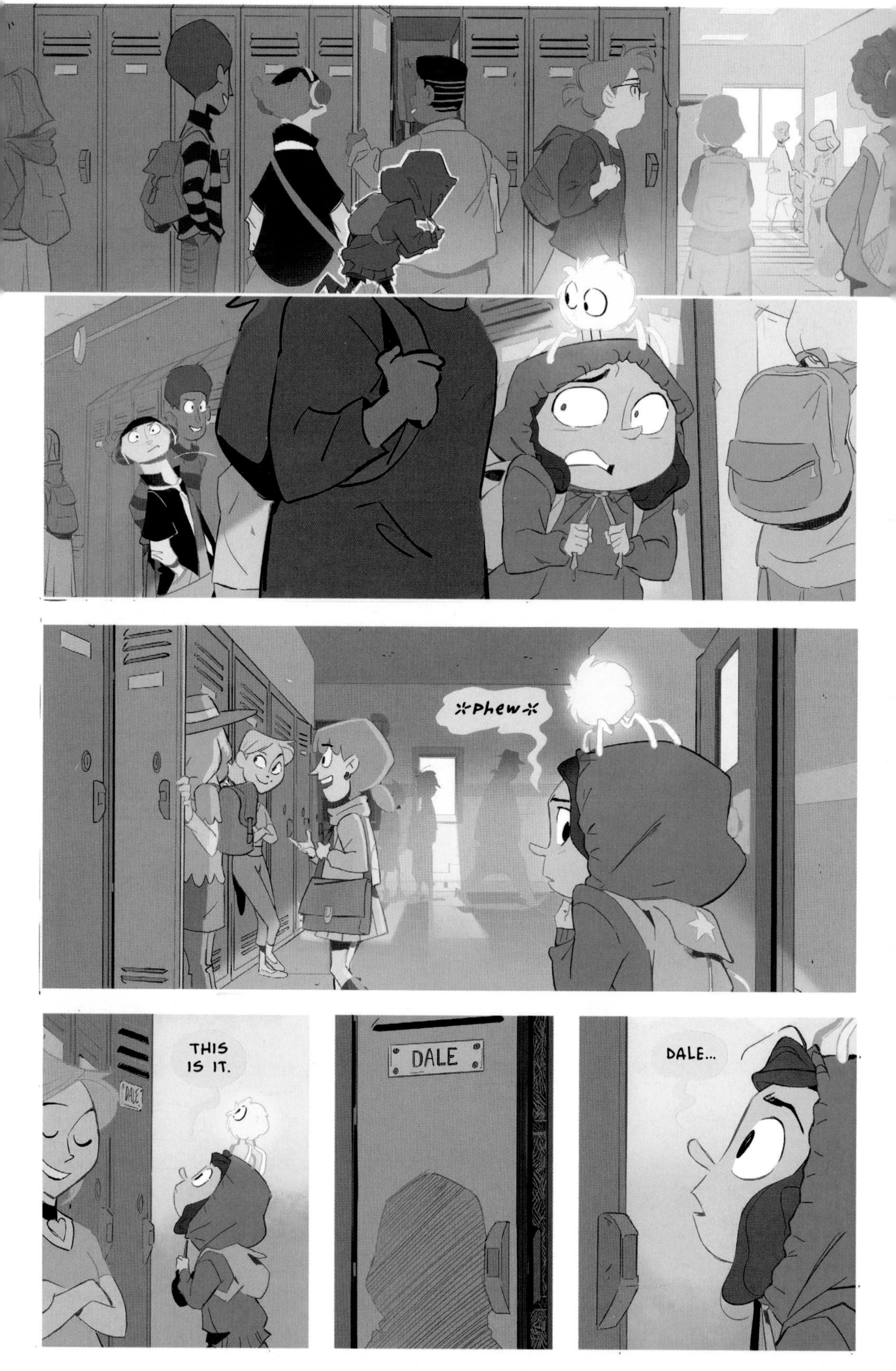
Phew
THIS IS IT.
DALE
DALE
DALE...

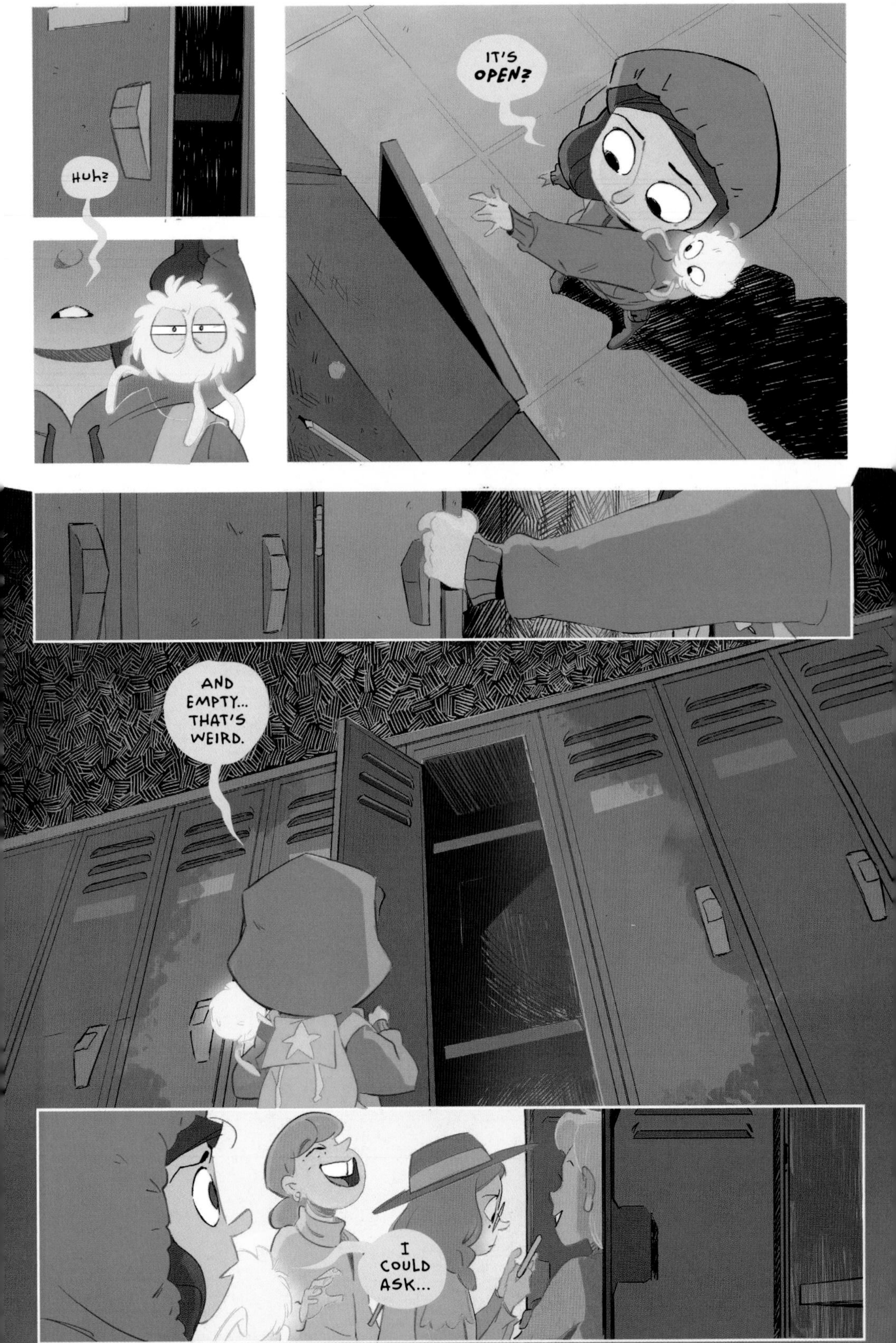
HUH?
IT'S OPEN?
AND EMPTY... THAT'S WEIRD.
I COULD ASK...

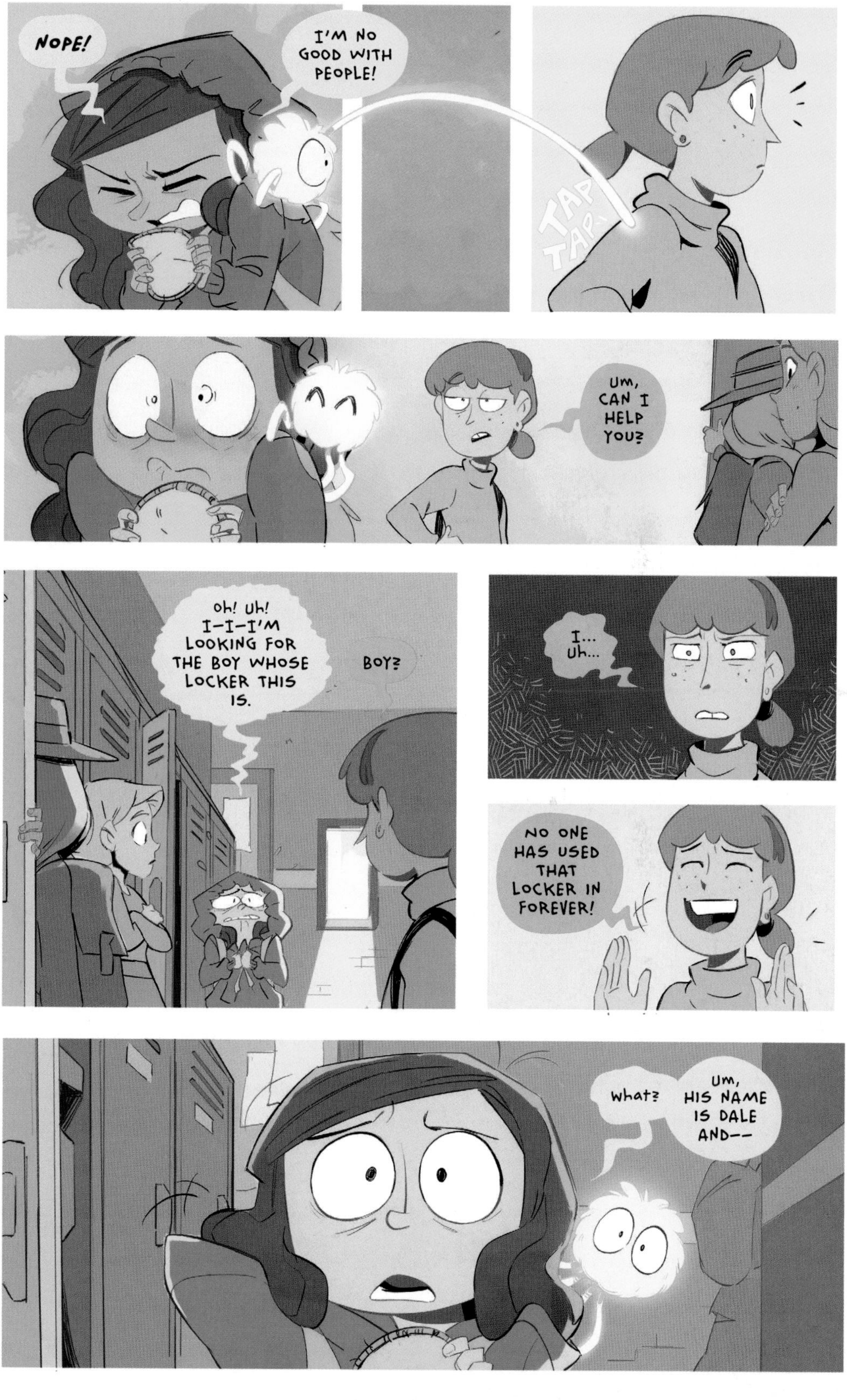
NOPE!
I'M NO GOOD WITH PEOPLE!
TAP TAP
UM, CAN I HELP YOU?
OH! UH! I-I-I'M LOOKING FOR THE BOY WHOSE LOCKER THIS IS.
BOY?
I... UH...
NO ONE HAS USED THAT LOCKER IN FOREVER!
WHAT?
UM, HIS NAME IS DALE AND--

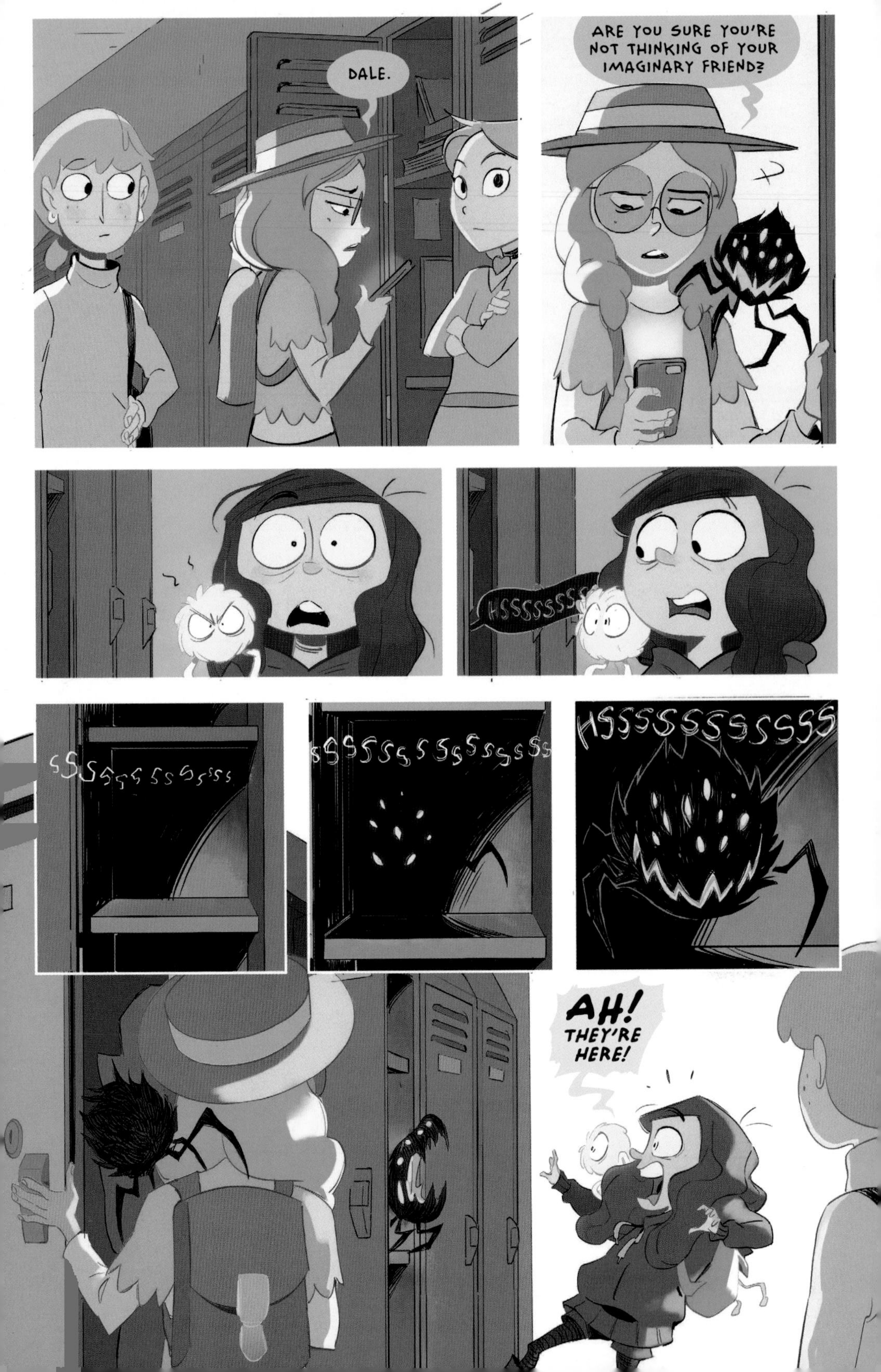
DALE.
ARE YOU SURE YOU'RE NOT THINKING OF YOUR IMAGINARY FRIEND?
HSSSSSSSS
SSSSSSSSSSSSS
SSSSSSSSSSSSSSSSSS
HSSSSSSSSSSSSS
AH! THEY'RE HERE!

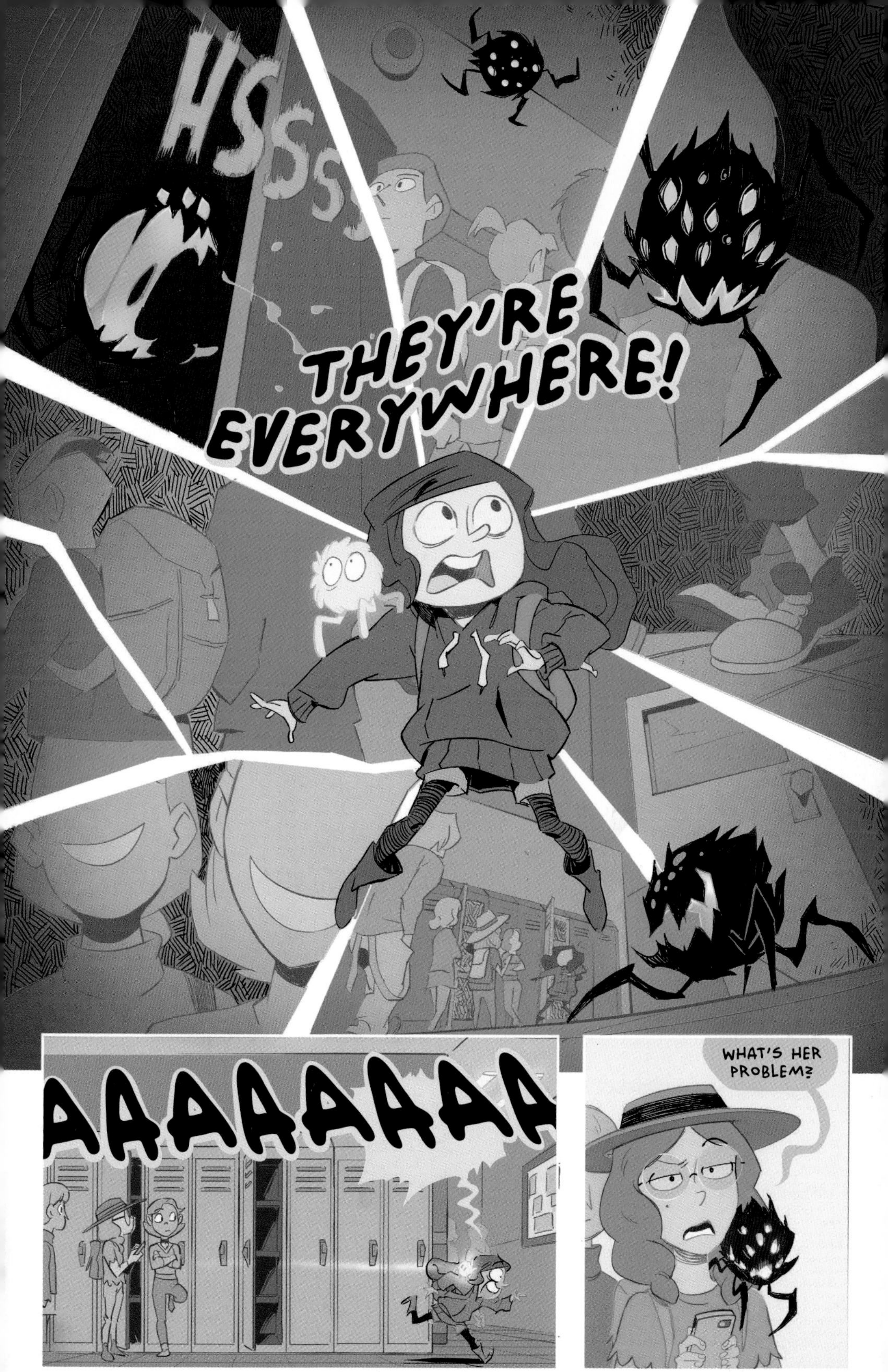
HSSSS
THEY'RE EVERYWHERE!
AAAAAAAA
WHAT'S HER PROBLEM?

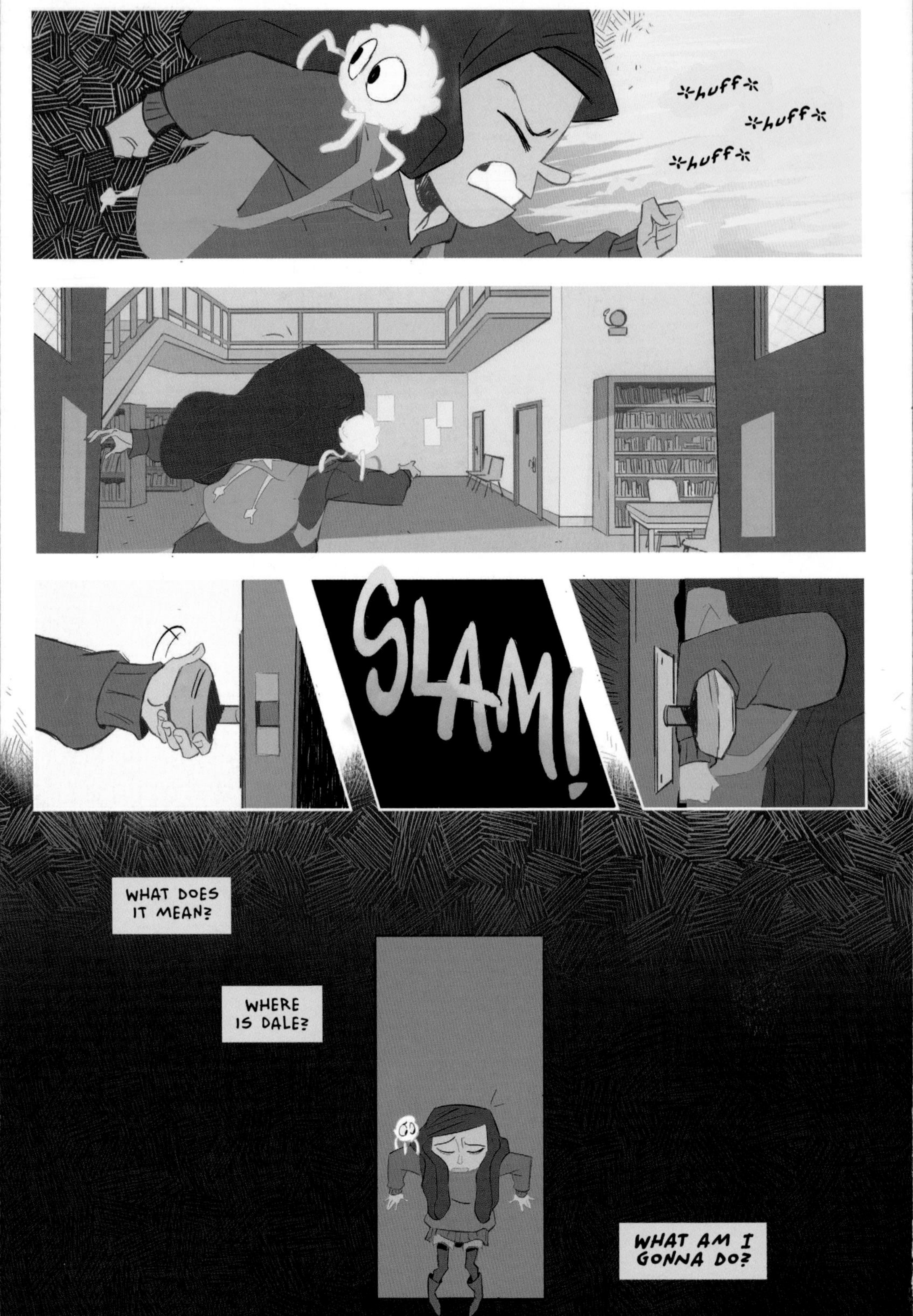

huff
huff
huff
SLAM!
WHAT DOES IT MEAN?
WHERE IS DALE?
WHAT AM I GONNA DO?

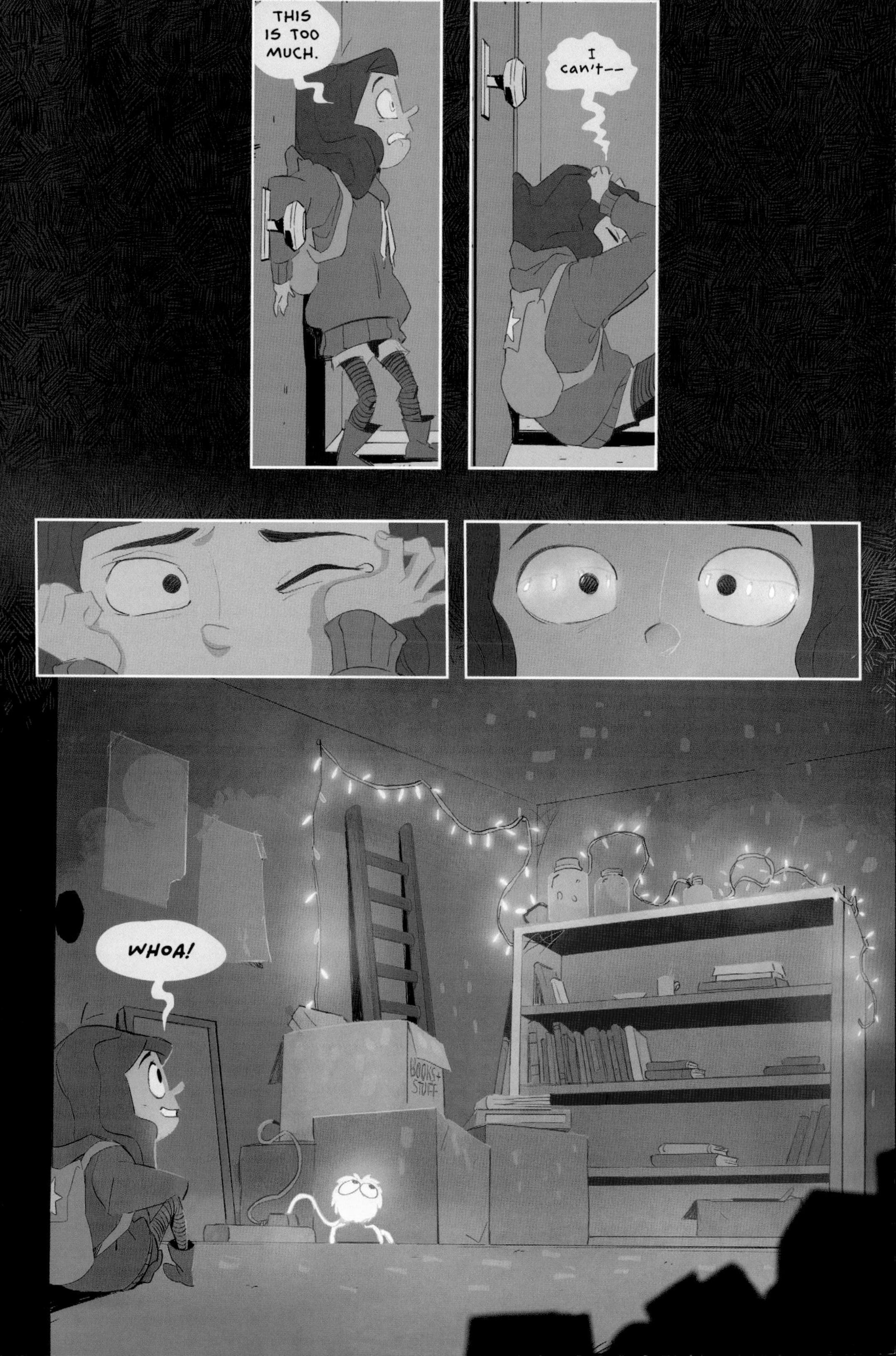
THIS IS TOO MUCH.
I can't--
WHOA!
BOOKS + STUFF

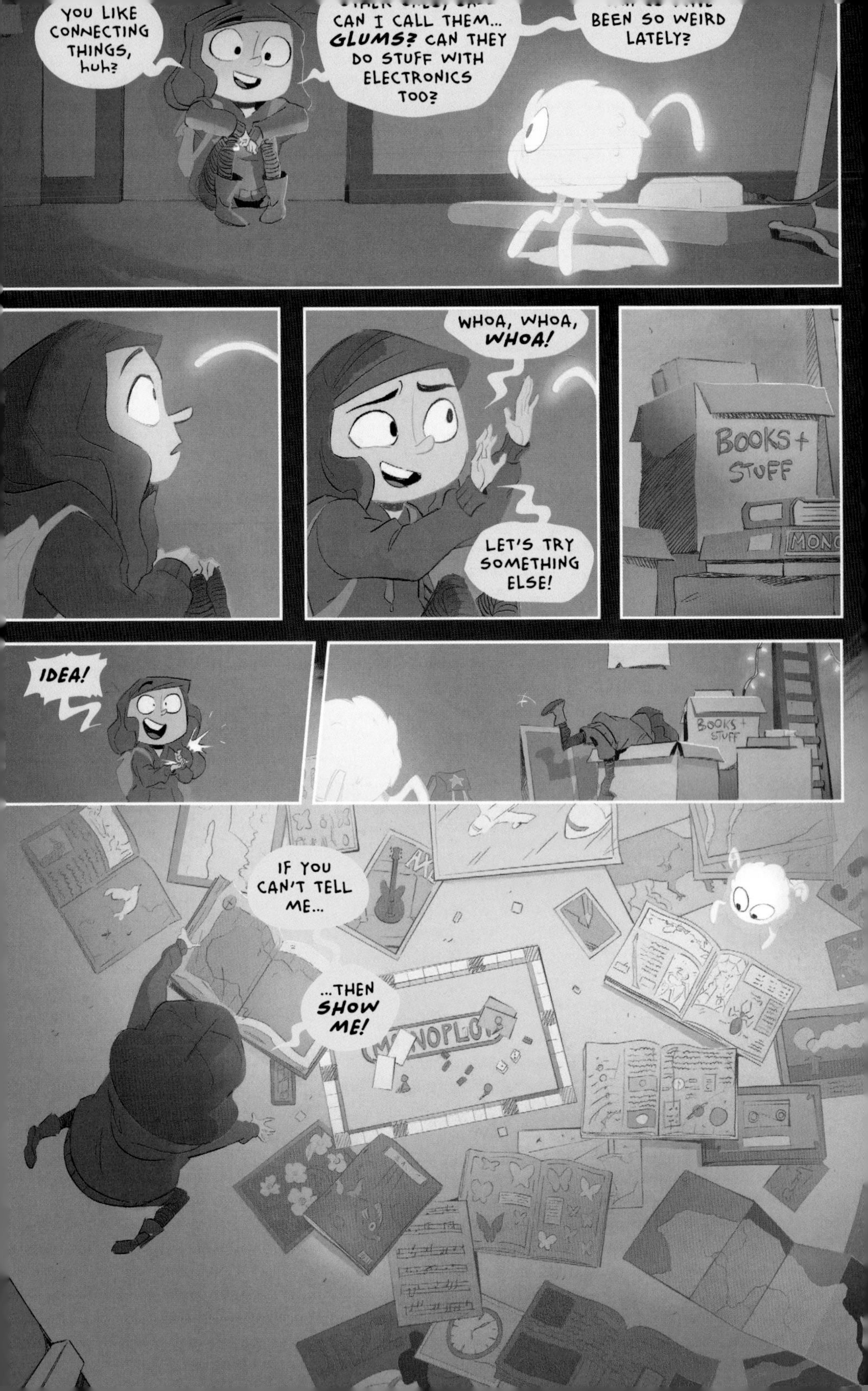
YOU LIKE CONNECTING THINGS, huh?
CAN I CALL THEM... **GLUMS?** CAN THEY DO STUFF WITH ELECTRONICS TOO?
BEEN SO WEIRD LATELY?
WHOA, WHOA, **WHOA!**
LET'S TRY SOMETHING ELSE!
BOOKS + STUFF
MONO
IDEA!
BOOKS + STUFF
IF YOU CAN'T TELL ME...
...THEN **SHOW ME!**

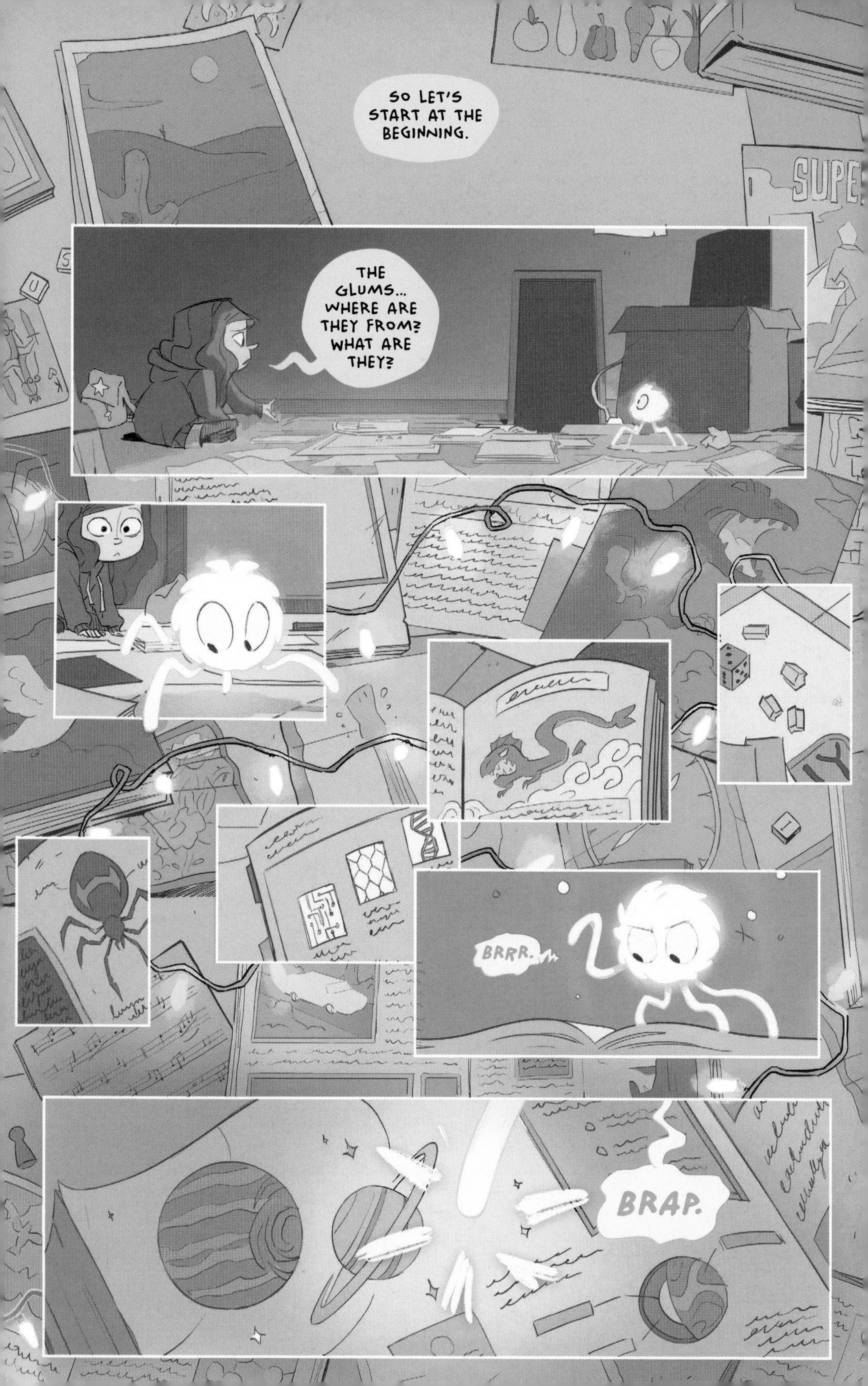
SO LET'S START AT THE BEGINNING.
THE GLUMS... WHERE ARE THEY FROM? WHAT ARE THEY?
BRRR.
BRAP.

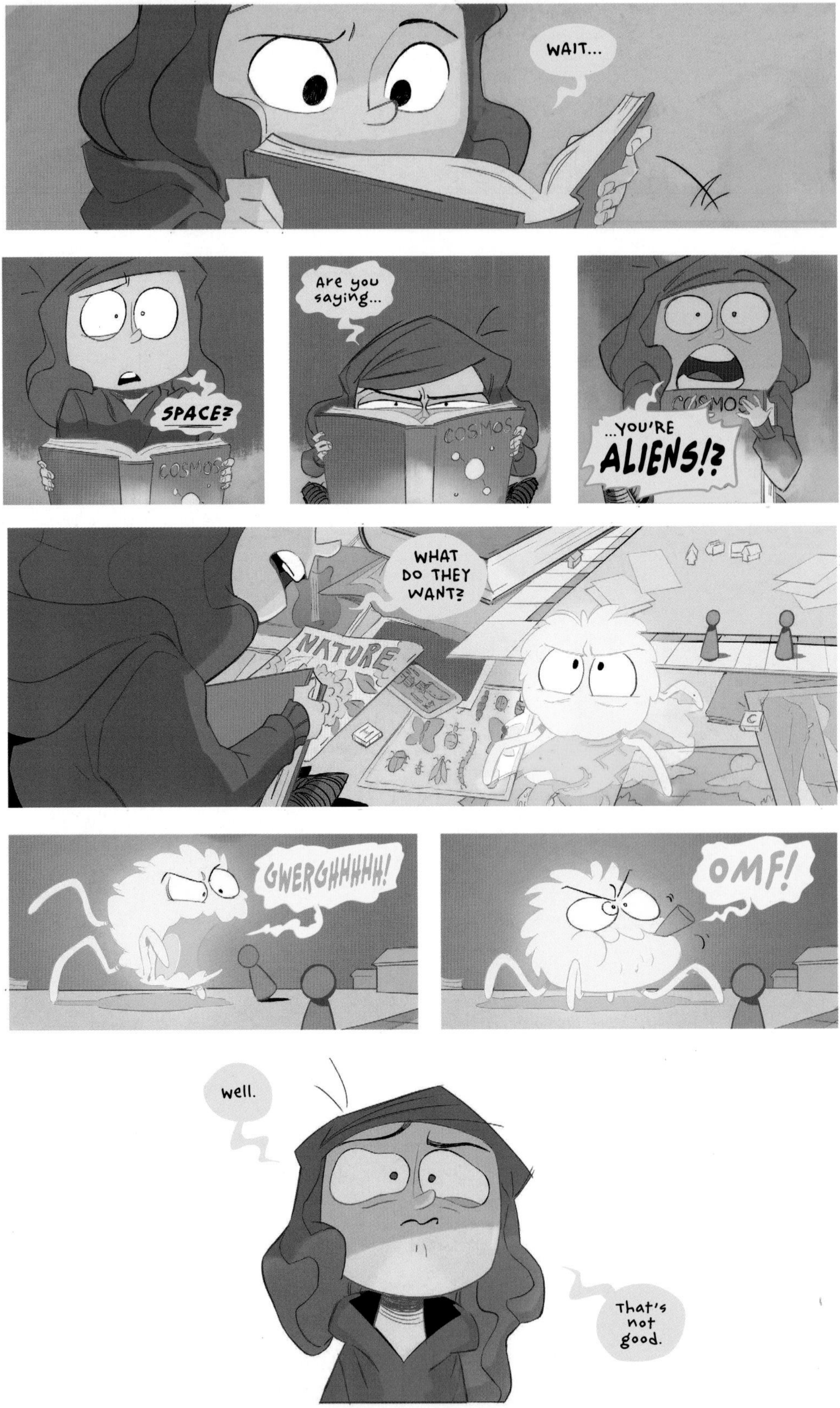
WAIT...
SPACE?
Are you saying...
...YOU'RE ALIENS!?
COSMOS
WHAT DO THEY WANT?
NATURE
GWERGHHHHH!
OMF!
Well.
That's not good.

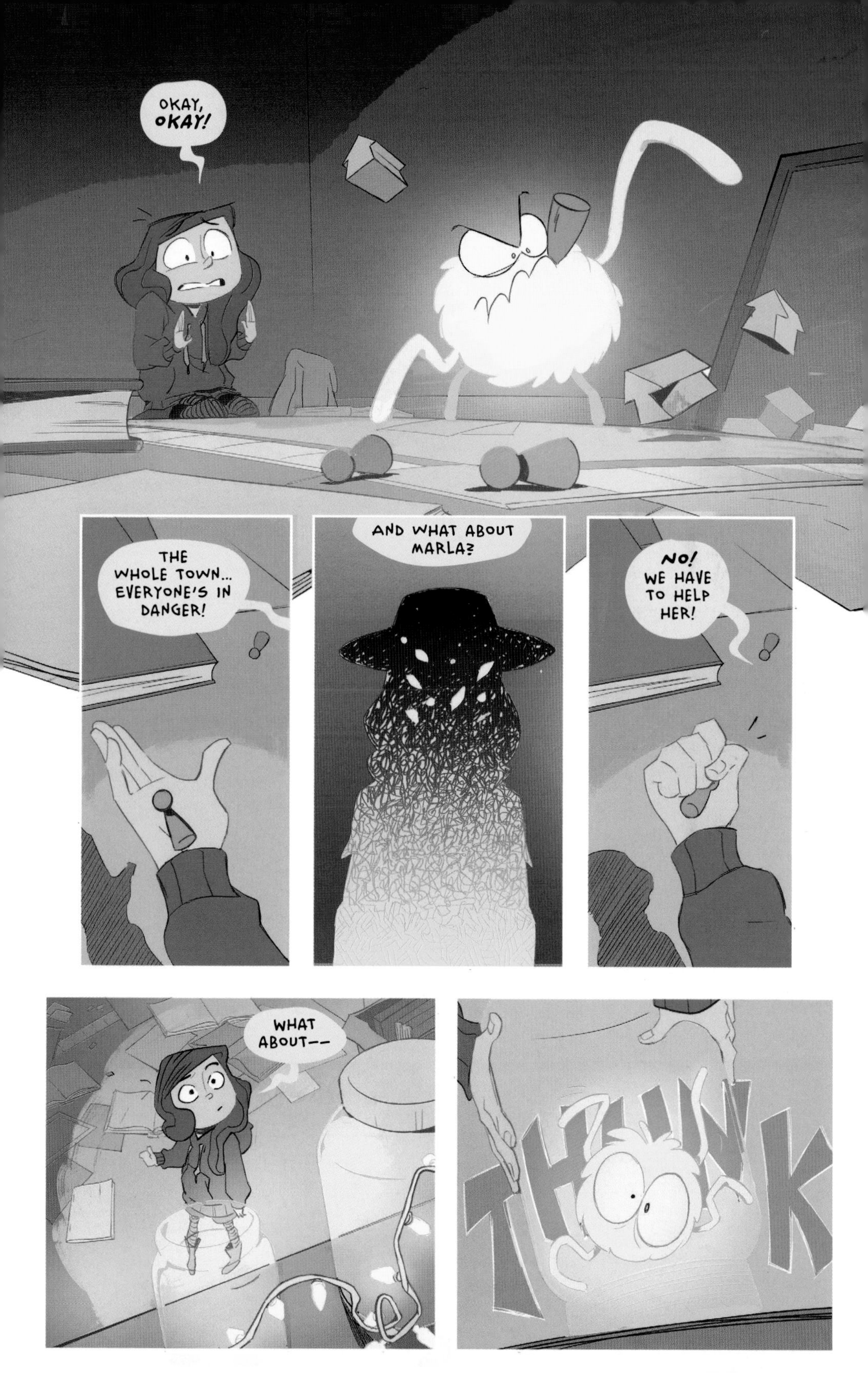
OKAY, **OKAY!**
THE WHOLE TOWN... EVERYONE'S IN DANGER!
AND WHAT ABOUT MARLA?
NO! WE HAVE TO HELP HER!
WHAT ABOUT--
THUNK

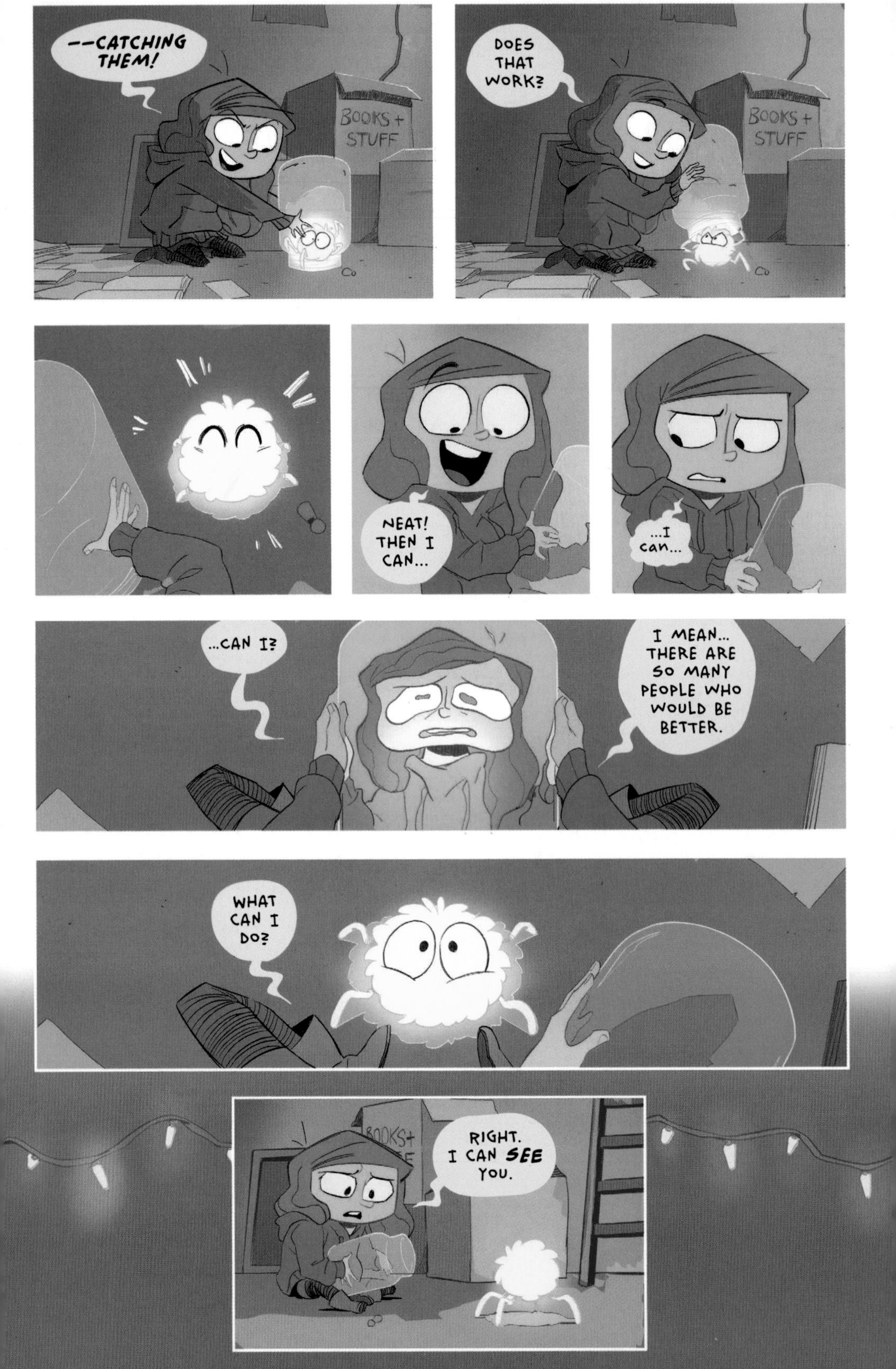
--CATCHING THEM!
BOOKS + STUFF
DOES THAT WORK?
BOOKS + STUFF
NEAT! THEN I CAN...
...I can...
...CAN I?
I MEAN... THERE ARE SO MANY PEOPLE WHO WOULD BE BETTER.
WHAT CAN I DO?
RIGHT. I CAN **SEE** YOU.

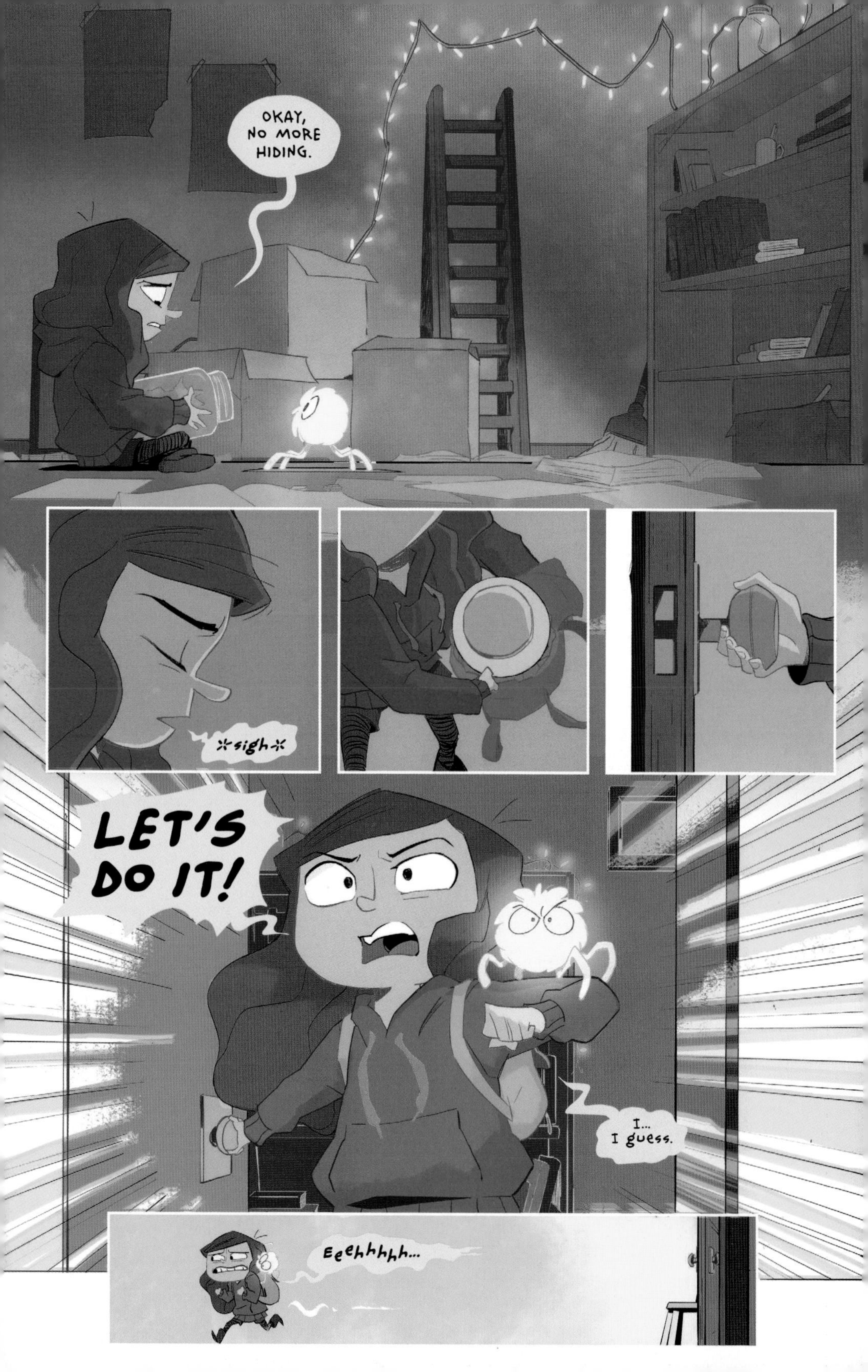
OKAY, NO MORE HIDING.
sigh
LET'S DO IT!
I... I guess.
Eeehhhhh...

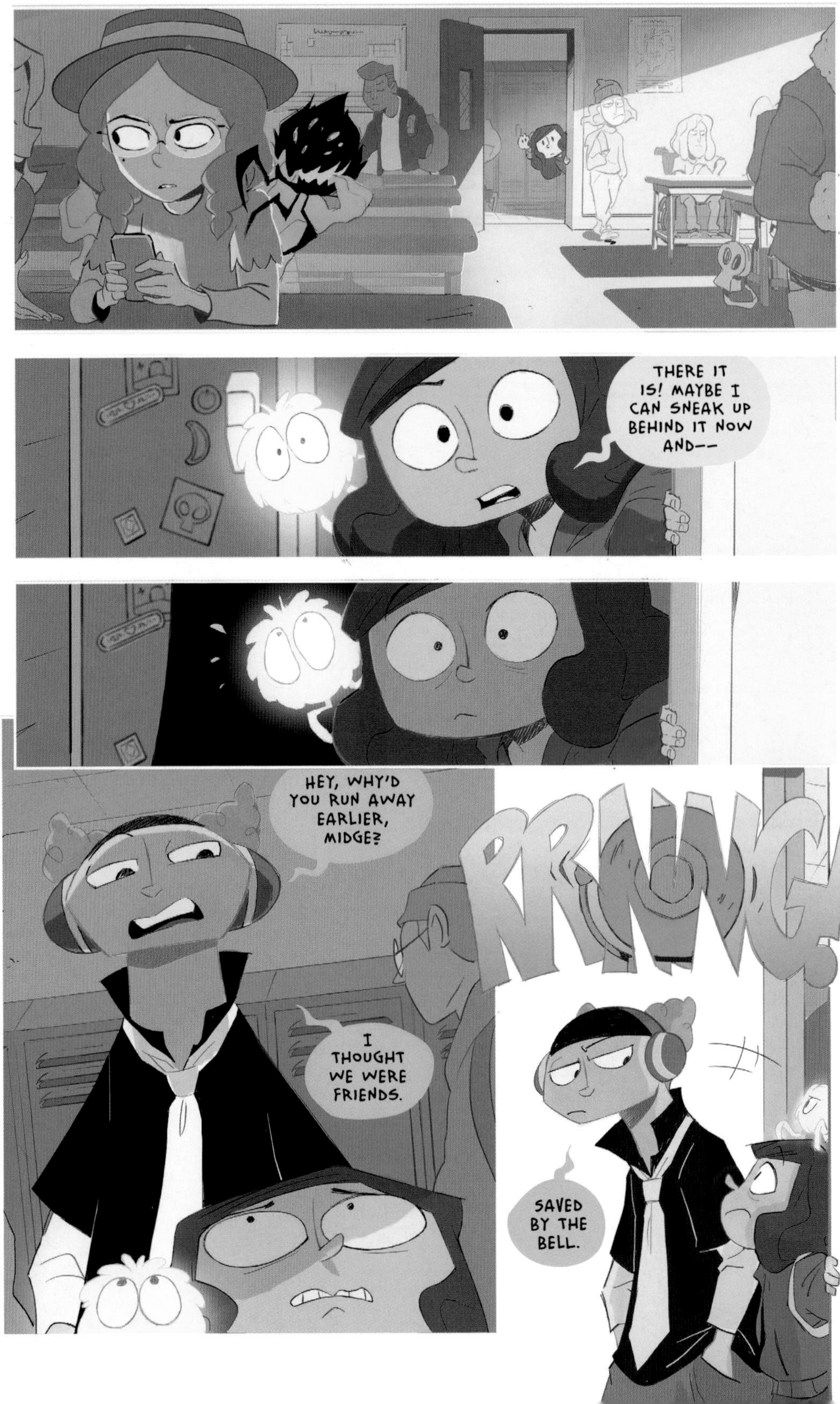
THERE IT IS! MAYBE I CAN SNEAK UP BEHIND IT NOW AND--
HEY, WHY'D YOU RUN AWAY EARLIER, MIDGE?
I THOUGHT WE WERE FRIENDS.
RRIIINNG!
SAVED BY THE BELL.

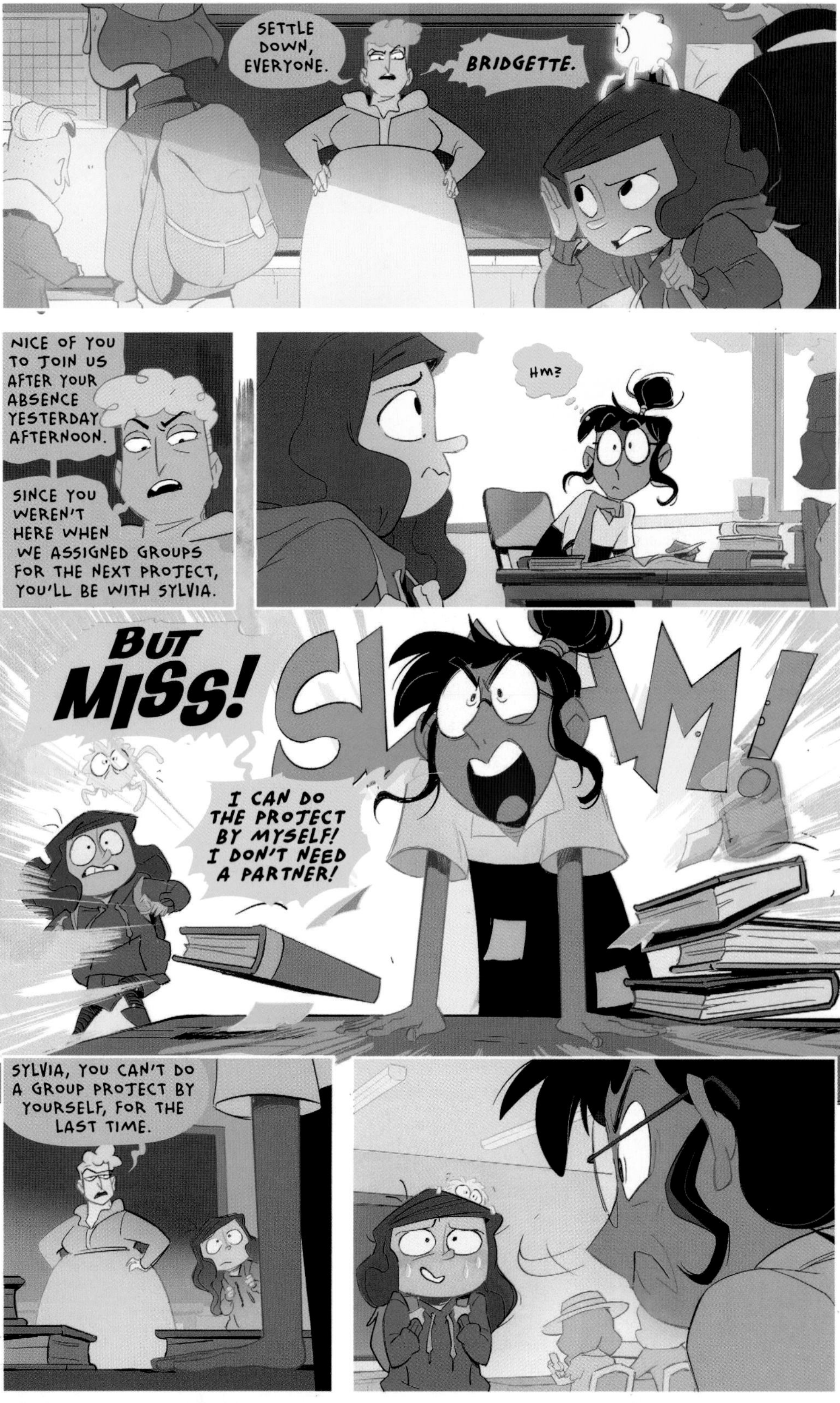
SETTLE DOWN, EVERYONE.
BRIDGETTE.
NICE OF YOU TO JOIN US AFTER YOUR ABSENCE YESTERDAY AFTERNOON.
SINCE YOU WEREN'T HERE WHEN WE ASSIGNED GROUPS FOR THE NEXT PROJECT, YOU'LL BE WITH SYLVIA.
HM?
BUT MISS!
SLAM!
I CAN DO THE PROJECT BY MYSELF! I DON'T NEED A PARTNER!
SYLVIA, YOU CAN'T DO A GROUP PROJECT BY YOURSELF, FOR THE LAST TIME.

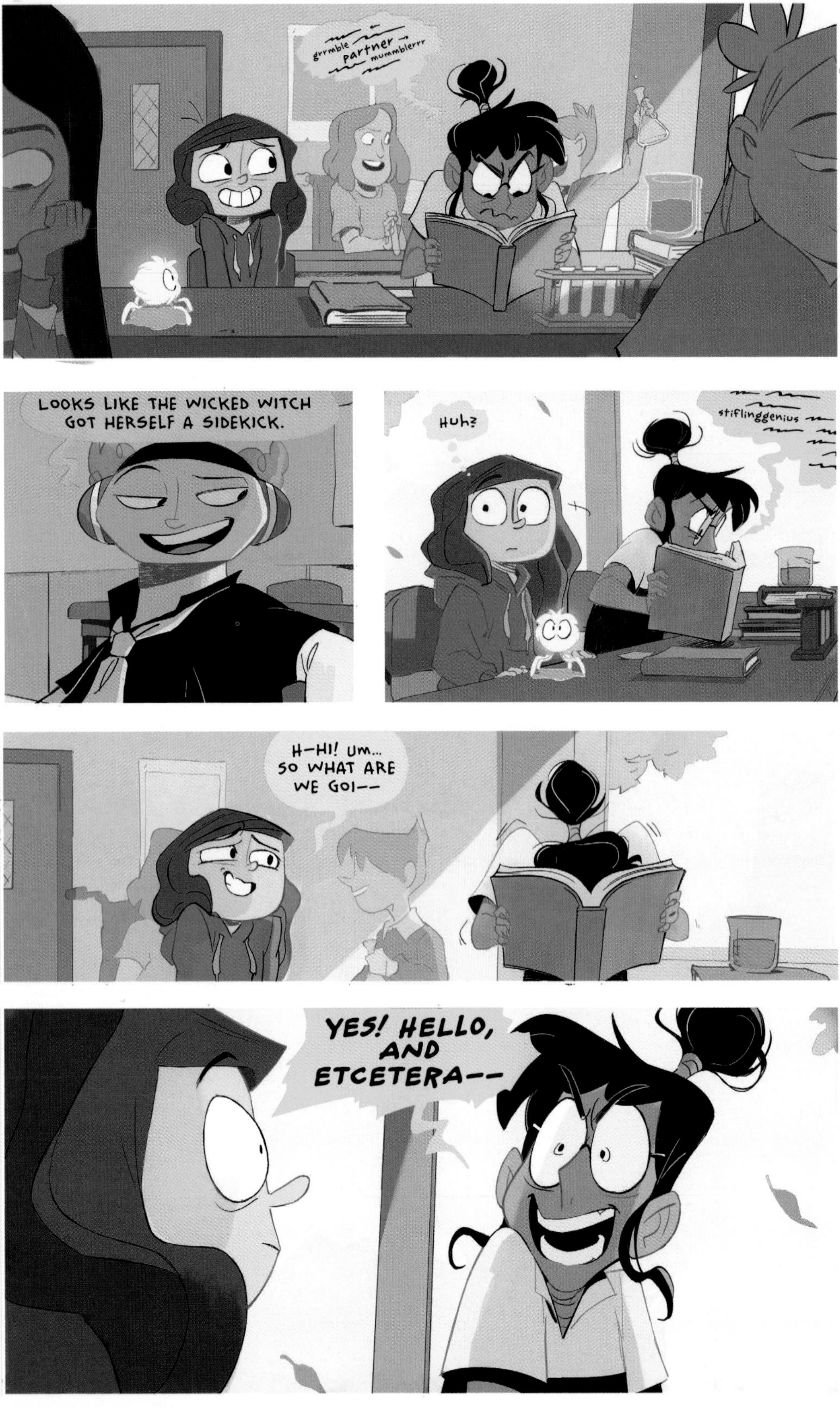
grrmble partner mummblerrr
LOOKS LIKE THE WICKED WITCH GOT HERSELF A SIDEKICK.
Huh?
stiflinggenius
H-HI! UM... SO WHAT ARE WE GOI--
YES! HELLO, AND ETCETERA--

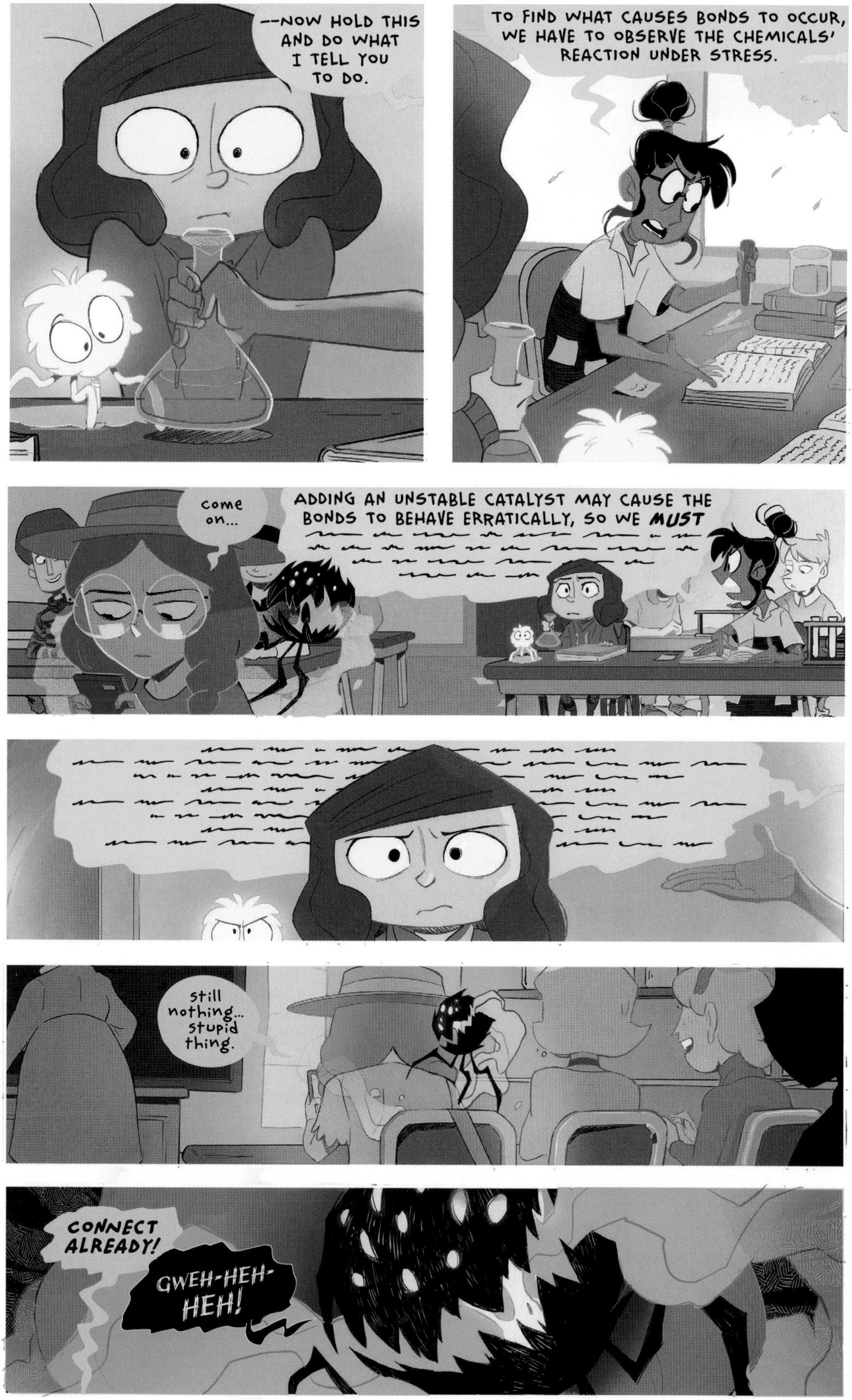
--NOW HOLD THIS AND DO WHAT I TELL YOU TO DO.
TO FIND WHAT CAUSES BONDS TO OCCUR, WE HAVE TO OBSERVE THE CHEMICALS' REACTION UNDER STRESS.
come on...
ADDING AN UNSTABLE CATALYST MAY CAUSE THE BONDS TO BEHAVE ERRATICALLY, SO WE MUST
still nothing... stupid thing.
CONNECT ALREADY!
GWEH-HEH-HEH!

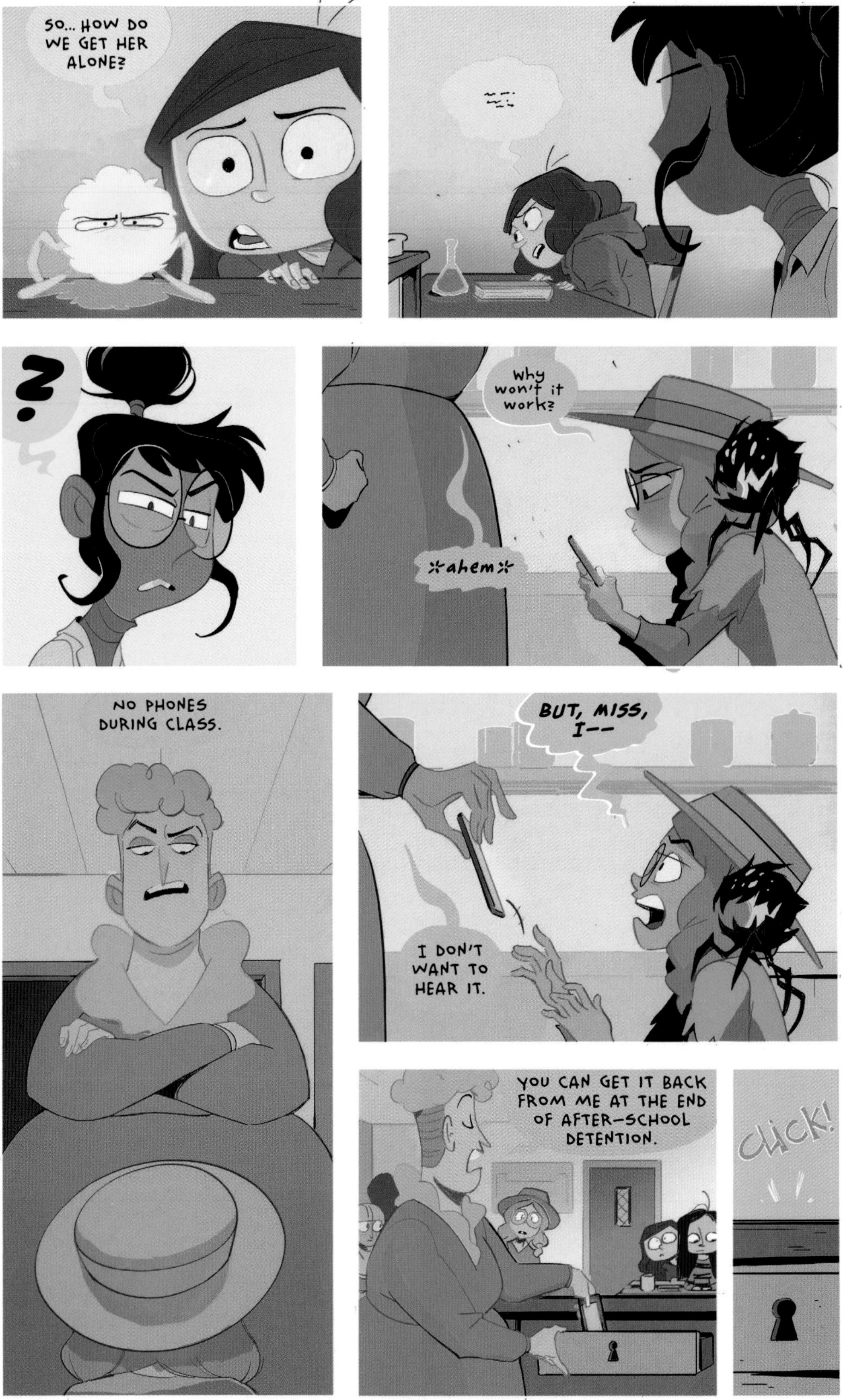
SO... HOW DO WE GET HER ALONE?
Why won't it work?
ahem
NO PHONES DURING CLASS.
BUT, MISS, I--
I DON'T WANT TO HEAR IT.
YOU CAN GET IT BACK FROM ME AT THE END OF AFTER-SCHOOL DETENTION.
CLICK!

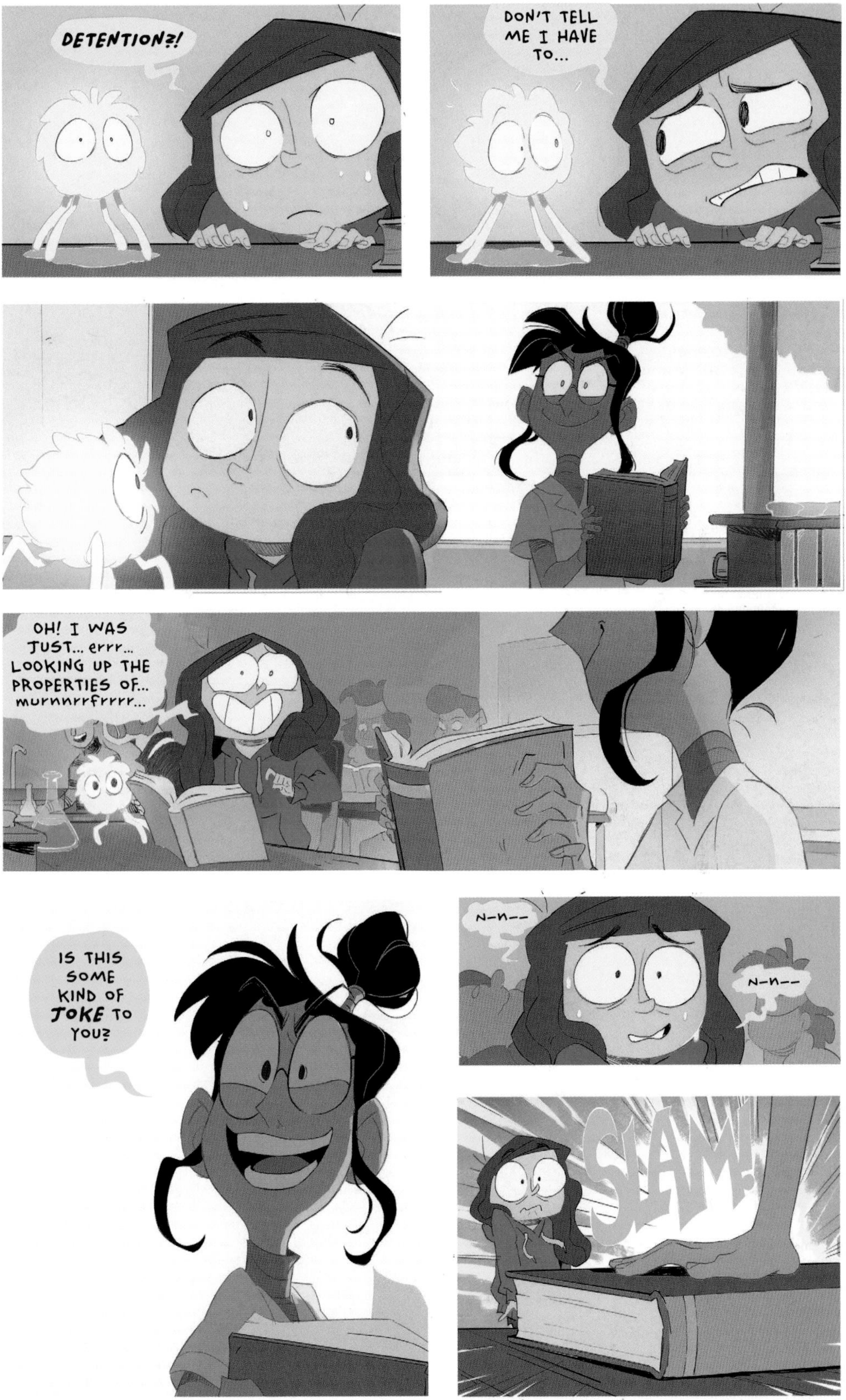
DETENTION?!
DON'T TELL ME I HAVE TO...
OH! I WAS JUST... errr... LOOKING UP THE PROPERTIES OF... murnnrrfrrrr...
IS THIS SOME KIND OF JOKE TO YOU?
N-n--
N-n--
SLAM!

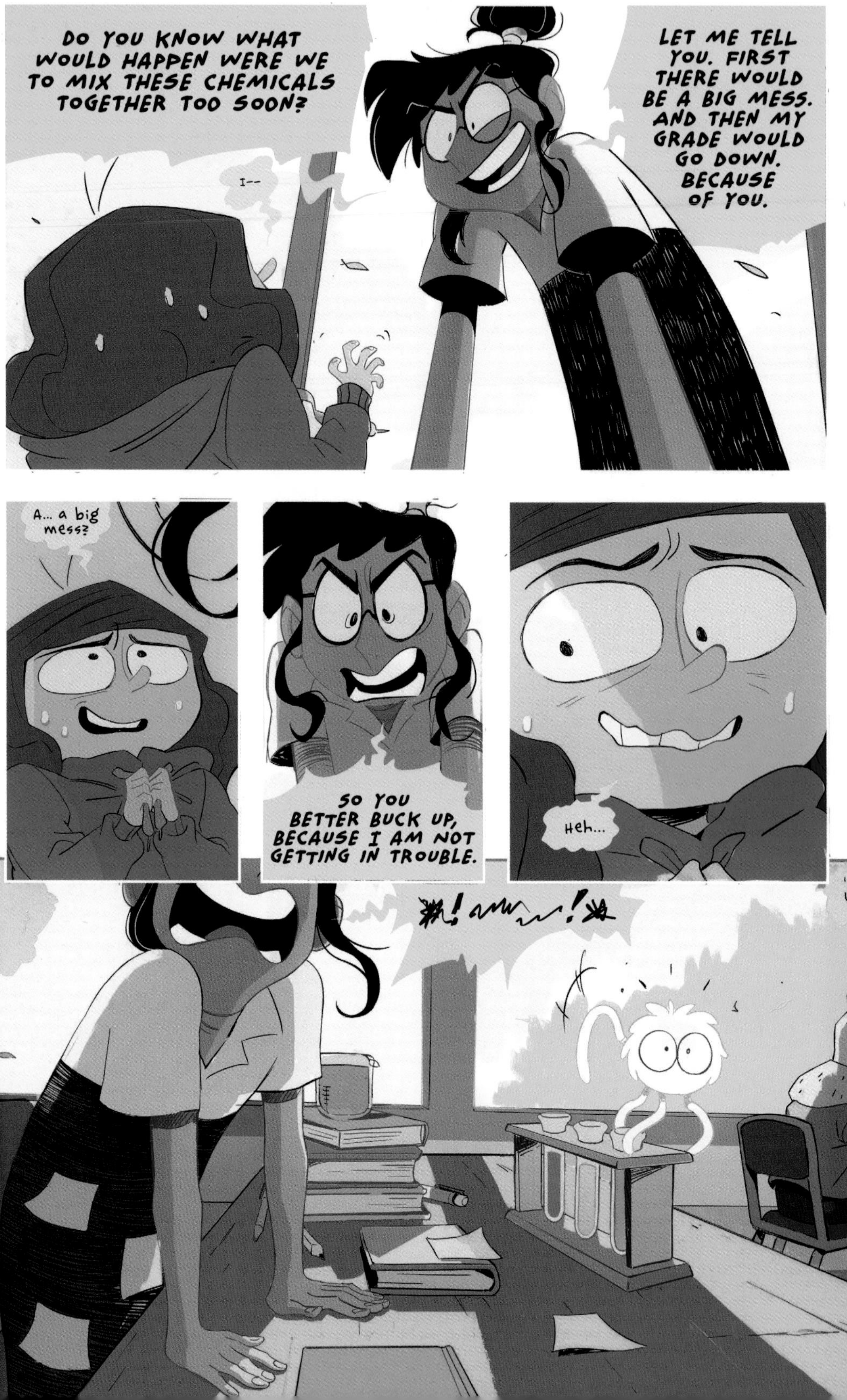
DO YOU KNOW WHAT WOULD HAPPEN WERE WE TO MIX THESE CHEMICALS TOGETHER TOO SOON?
I--
LET ME TELL YOU. FIRST THERE WOULD BE A BIG MESS. AND THEN MY GRADE WOULD GO DOWN. BECAUSE OF YOU.
A... a big mess?
SO YOU BETTER BUCK UP, BECAUSE I AM NOT GETTING IN TROUBLE.
Heh...

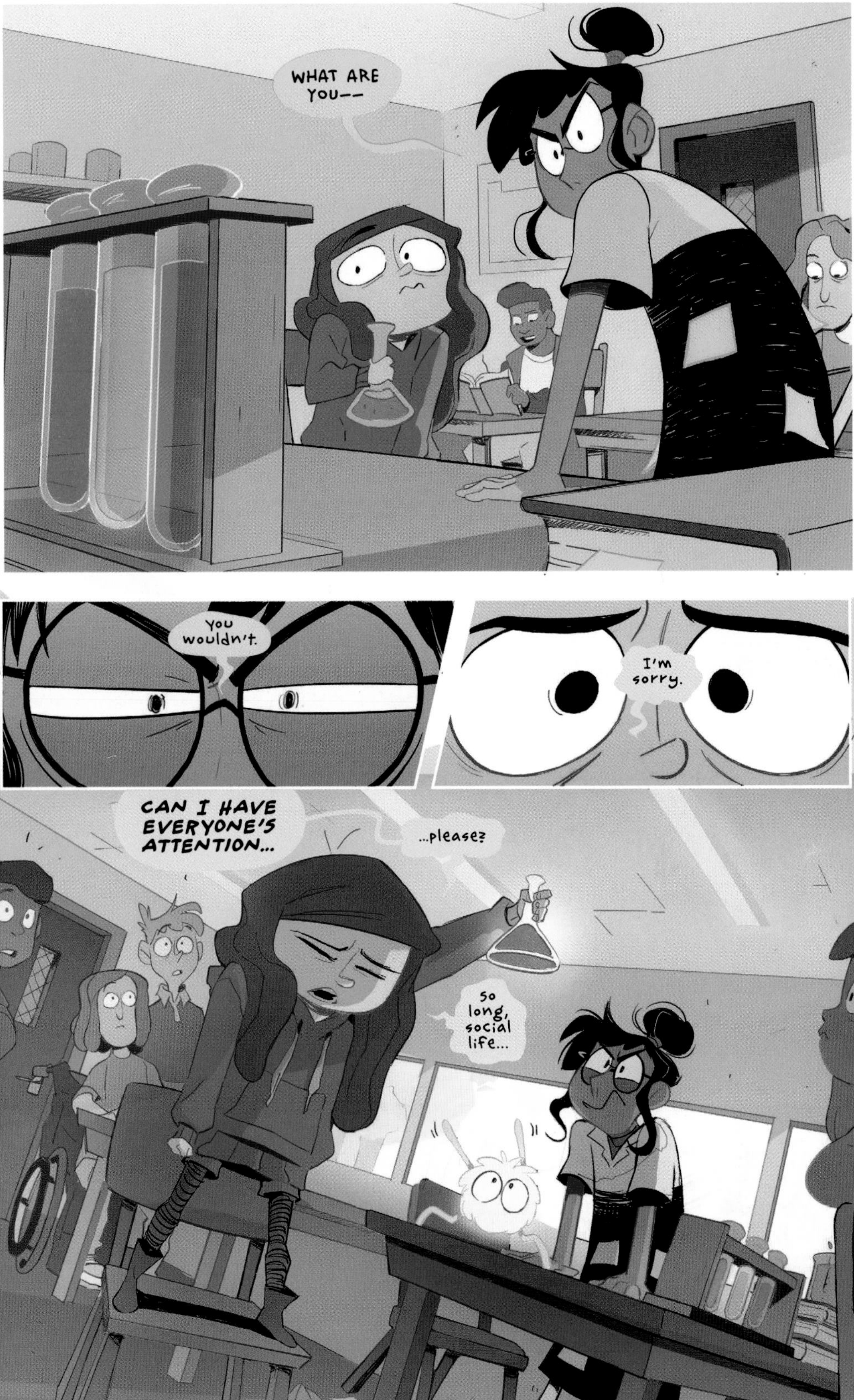
WHAT ARE YOU--
YOU WOULDN'T.
I'M SORRY.
CAN I HAVE EVERYONE'S ATTENTION...
...please?
SO LONG, SOCIAL LIFE...

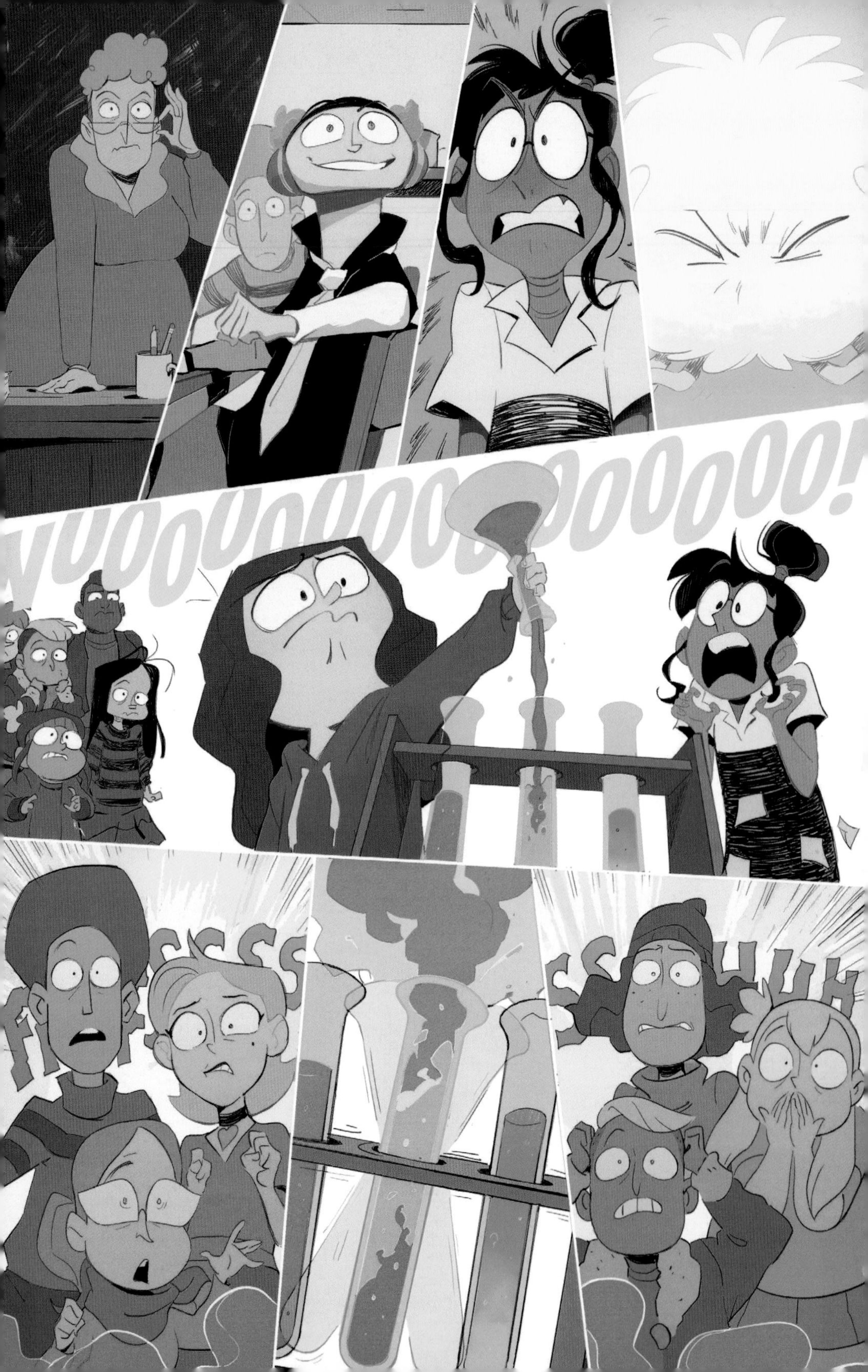

NOOOOOOOOOOOOOOO!
FSSSSS
SSHHH

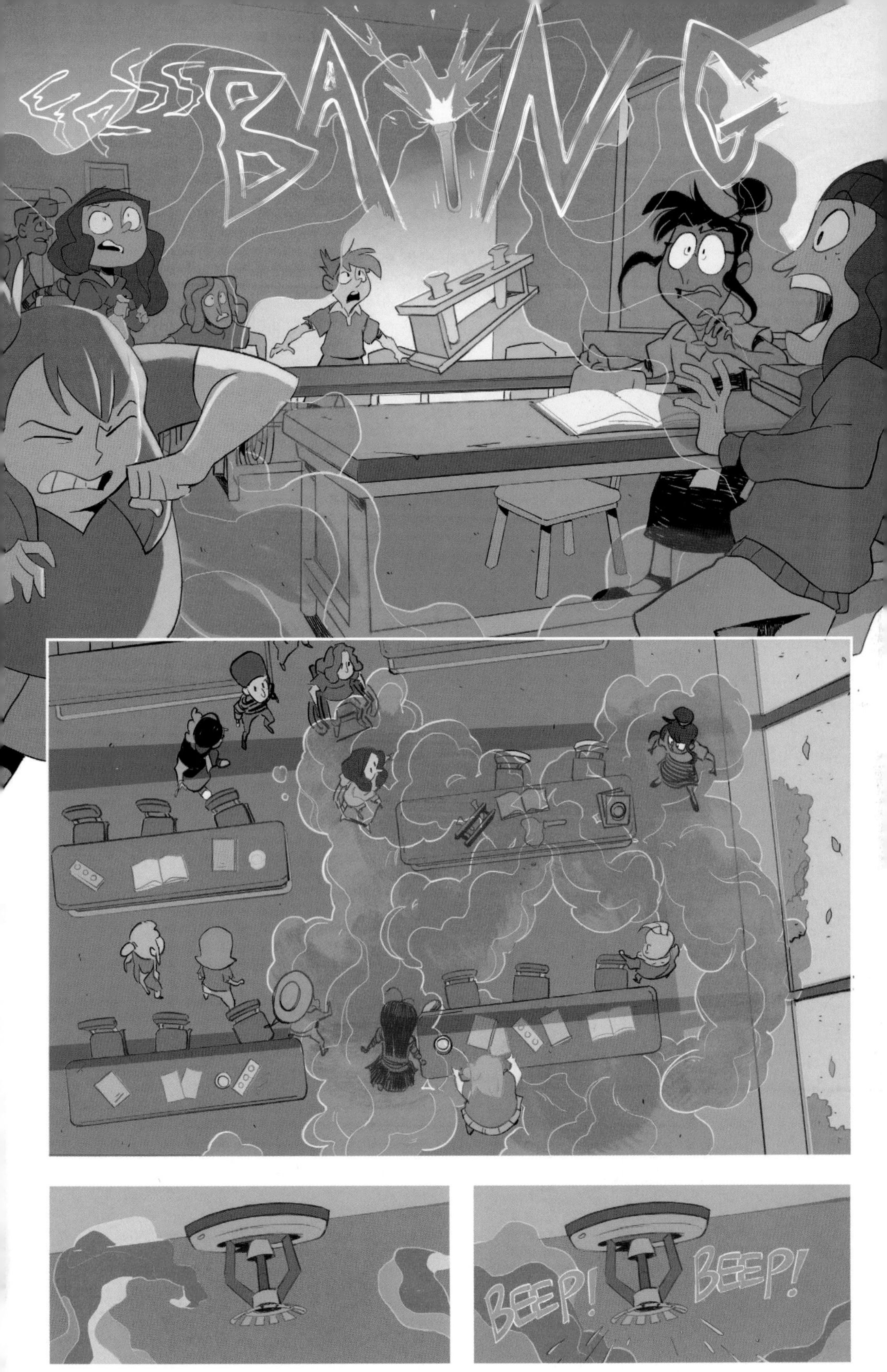
BANG
BEEP! BEEP!

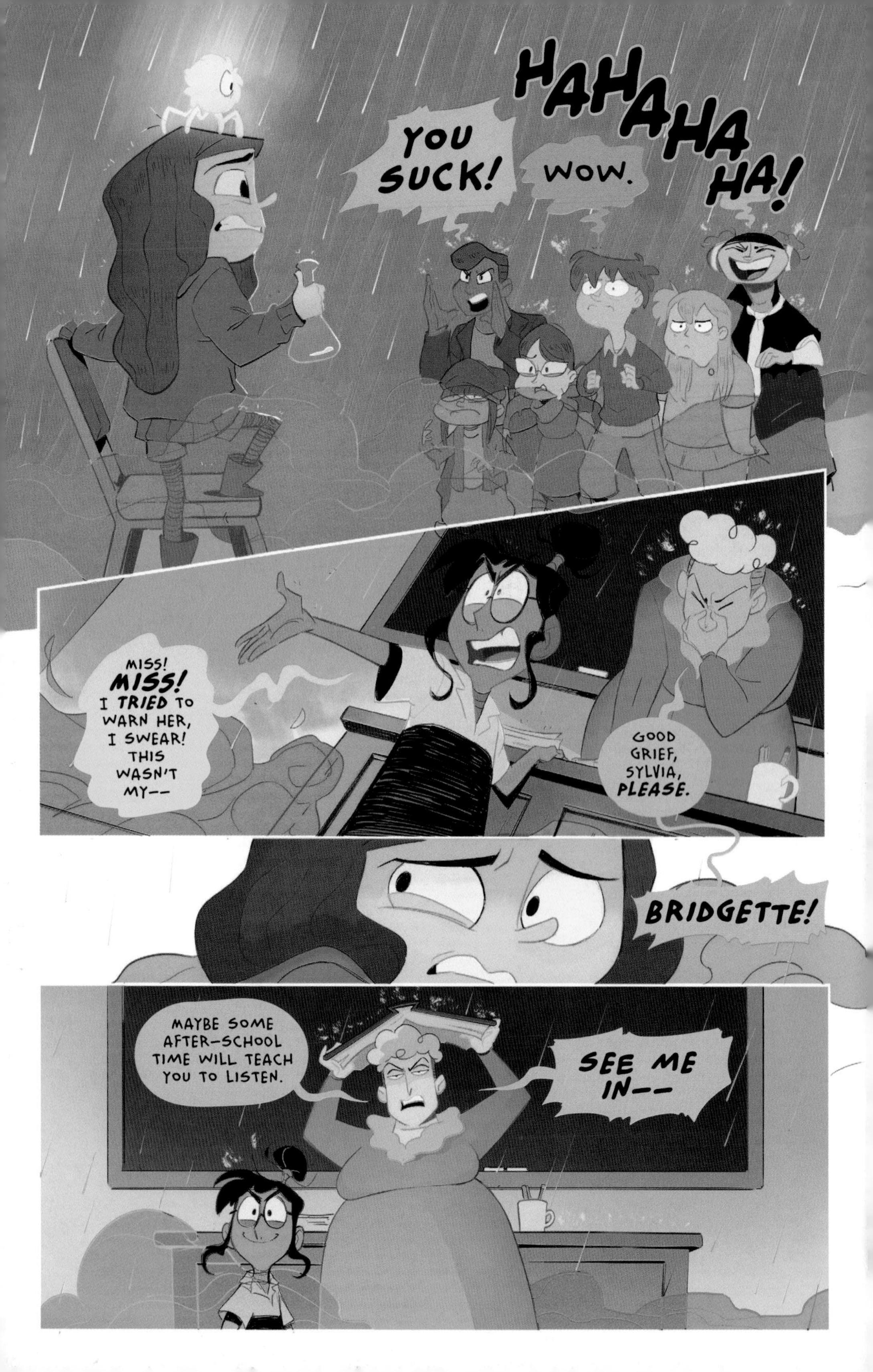
HAHAHAHAHA!
YOU SUCK!
WOW.
MISS! MISS! I TRIED TO WARN HER, I SWEAR! THIS WASN'T MY--
GOOD GRIEF, SYLVIA, PLEASE.
BRIDGETTE!
SEE ME IN--
MAYBE SOME AFTER-SCHOOL TIME WILL TEACH YOU TO LISTEN.

DETENTION

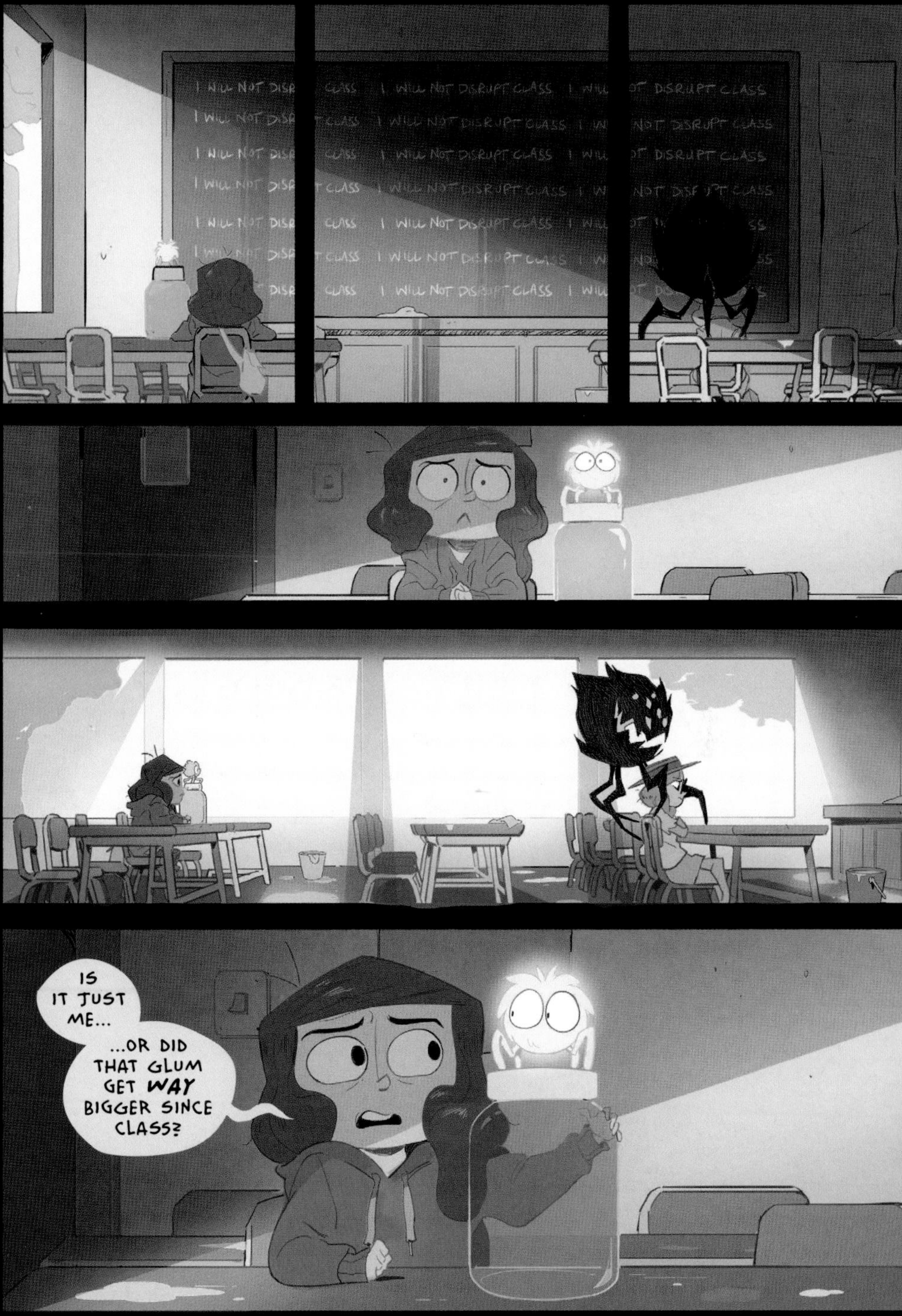

I WILL NOT DISRUPT CLASS
I WILL NOT DISRUPT CLASS
I WILL NOT DISRUPT CLASS
I WILL NOT DISRUPT CLASS
I WILL NOT DISRUPT CLASS
I WILL NOT DISRUPT CLASS
I WILL NOT DISRUPT CLASS
IS IT JUST ME...
...OR DID THAT GLUM GET WAY BIGGER SINCE CLASS?

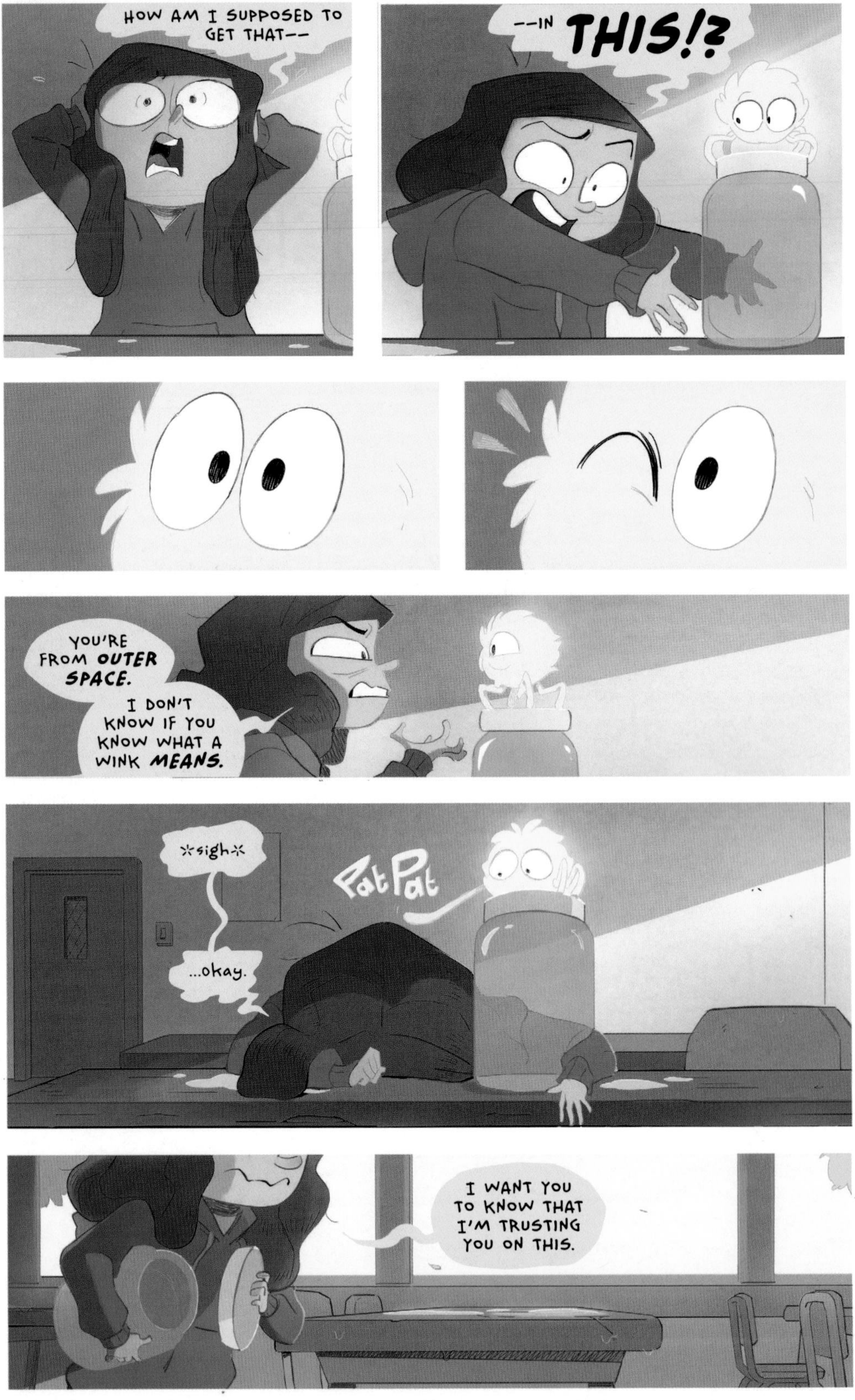
HOW AM I SUPPOSED TO GET THAT--
--IN THIS!?
YOU'RE FROM OUTER SPACE.
I DON'T KNOW IF YOU KNOW WHAT A WINK MEANS.
sigh
...okay.
Pat Pat
I WANT YOU TO KNOW THAT I'M TRUSTING YOU ON THIS.

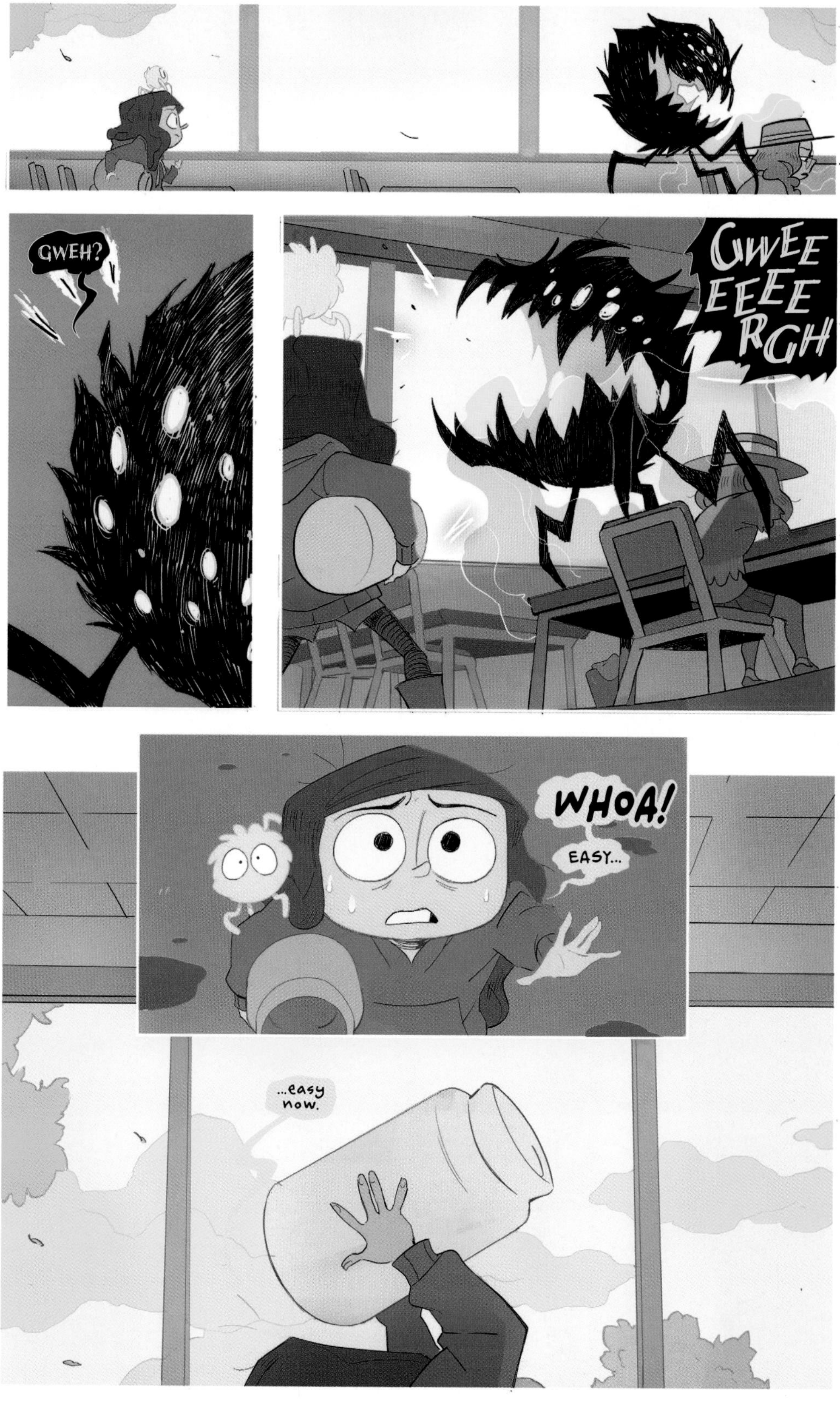
GWEH?
GWEE EEEE RGH
WHOA!
EASY...
...easy now.

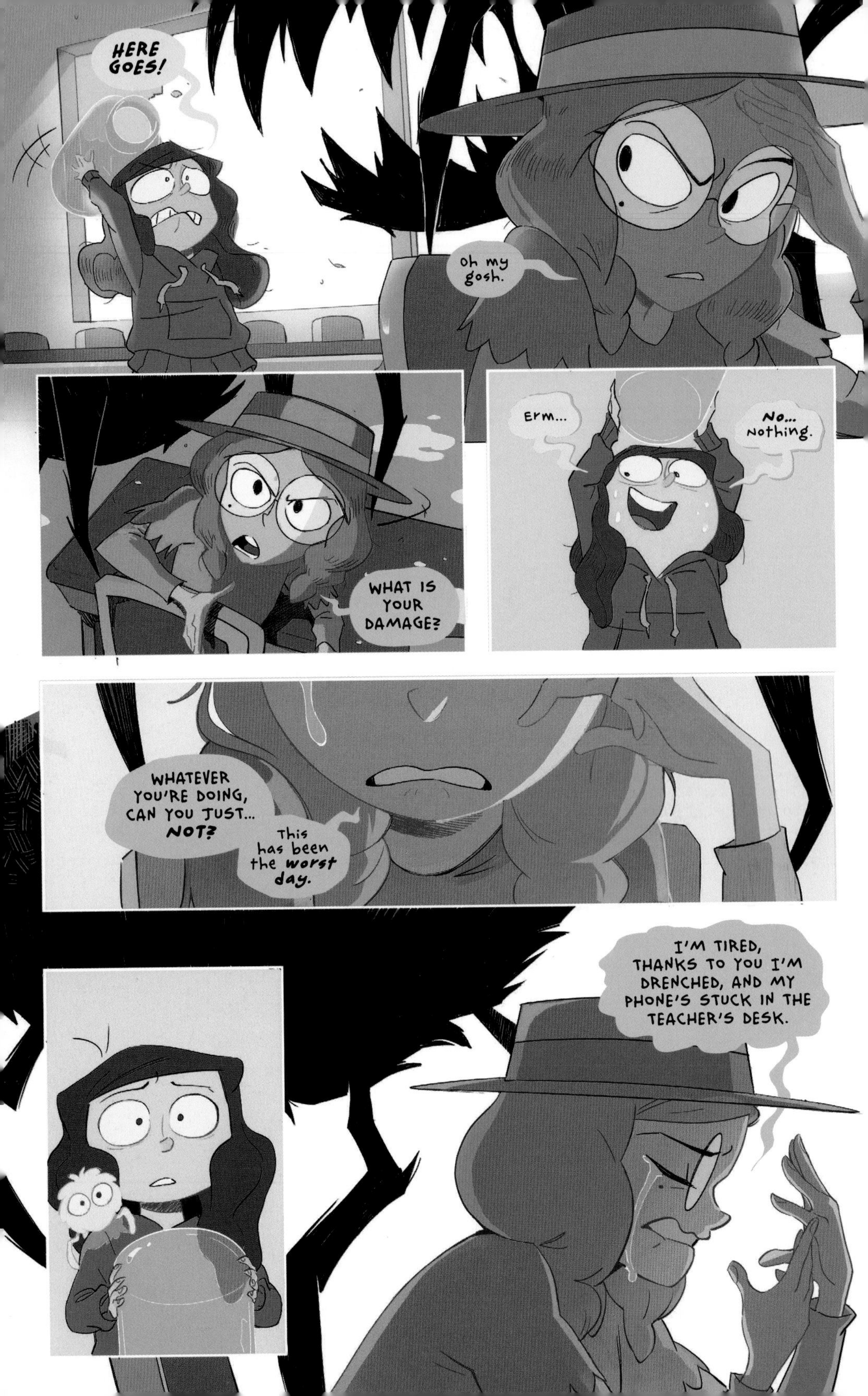
HERE GOES!
oh my gosh.
WHAT IS YOUR DAMAGE?
Erm...
No... Nothing.
WHATEVER YOU'RE DOING, CAN YOU JUST... NOT?
This has been the worst day.
I'M TIRED, THANKS TO YOU I'M DRENCHED, AND MY PHONE'S STUCK IN THE TEACHER'S DESK.

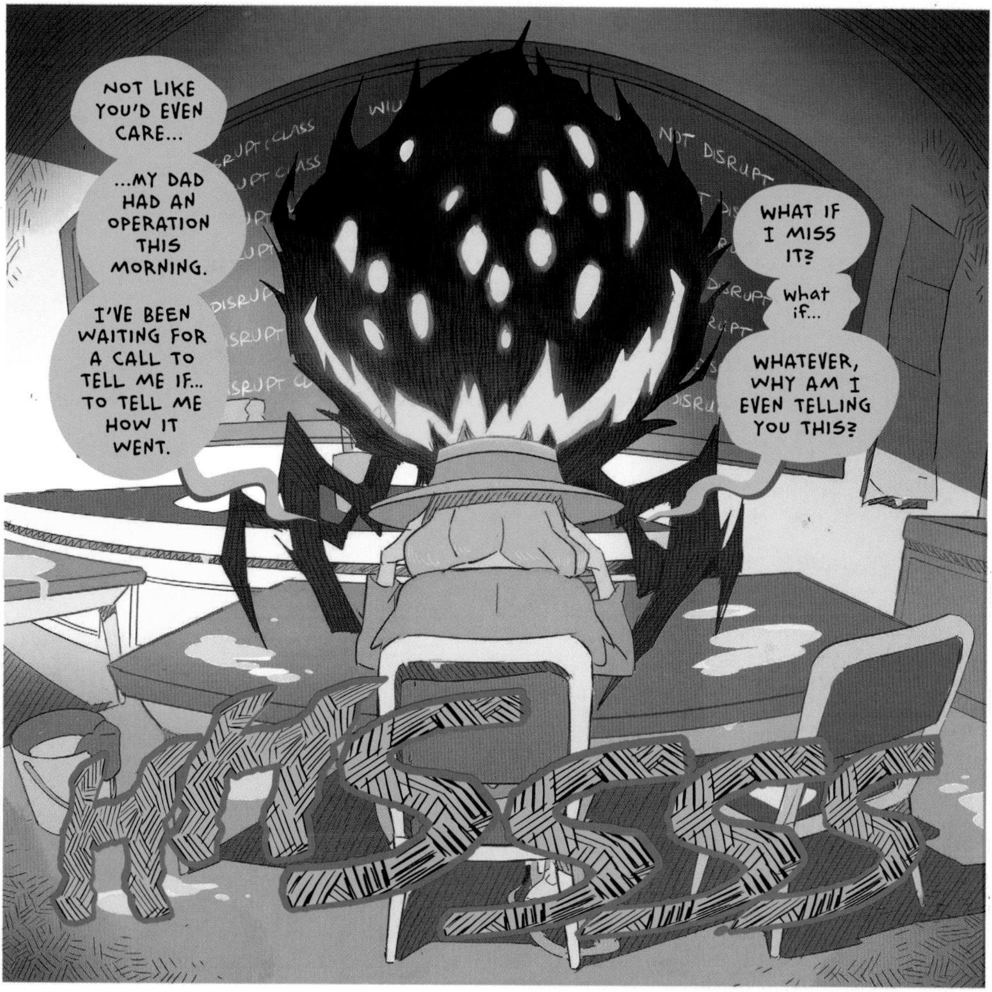
NOT LIKE YOU'D EVEN CARE...
...MY DAD HAD AN OPERATION THIS MORNING.
I'VE BEEN WAITING FOR A CALL TO TELL ME IF... TO TELL ME HOW IT WENT.
WHAT IF I MISS IT?
what if...
WHATEVER, WHY AM I EVEN TELLING YOU THIS?
HHSSSS

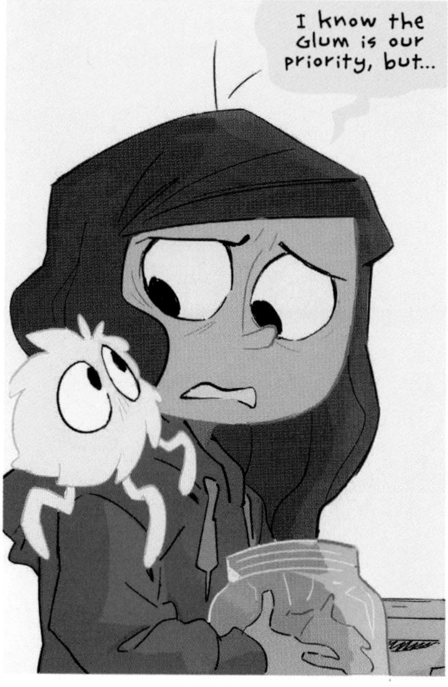
I know the Glum is our priority, but...

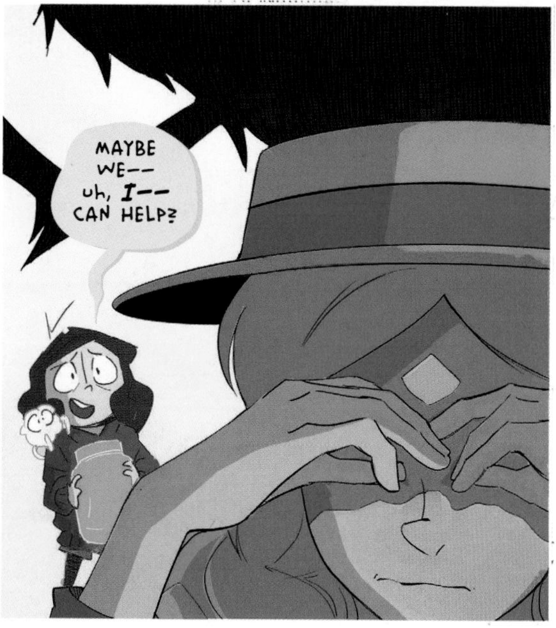
MAYBE WE-- uh, I-- CAN HELP?

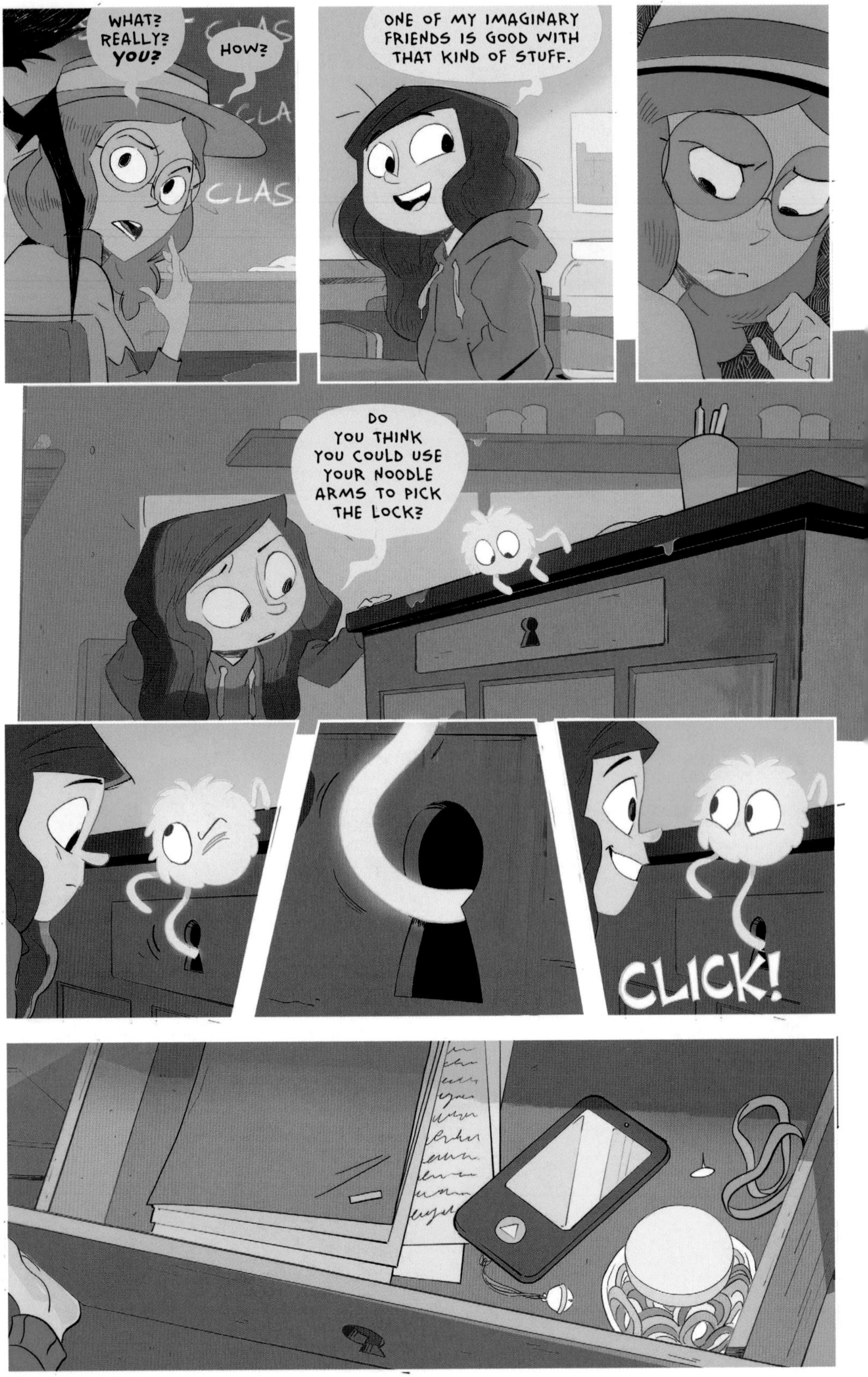
WHAT? REALLY? YOU?
HOW?
CLASS
ONE OF MY IMAGINARY FRIENDS IS GOOD WITH THAT KIND OF STUFF.
DO YOU THINK YOU COULD USE YOUR NOODLE ARMS TO PICK THE LOCK?
CLICK!

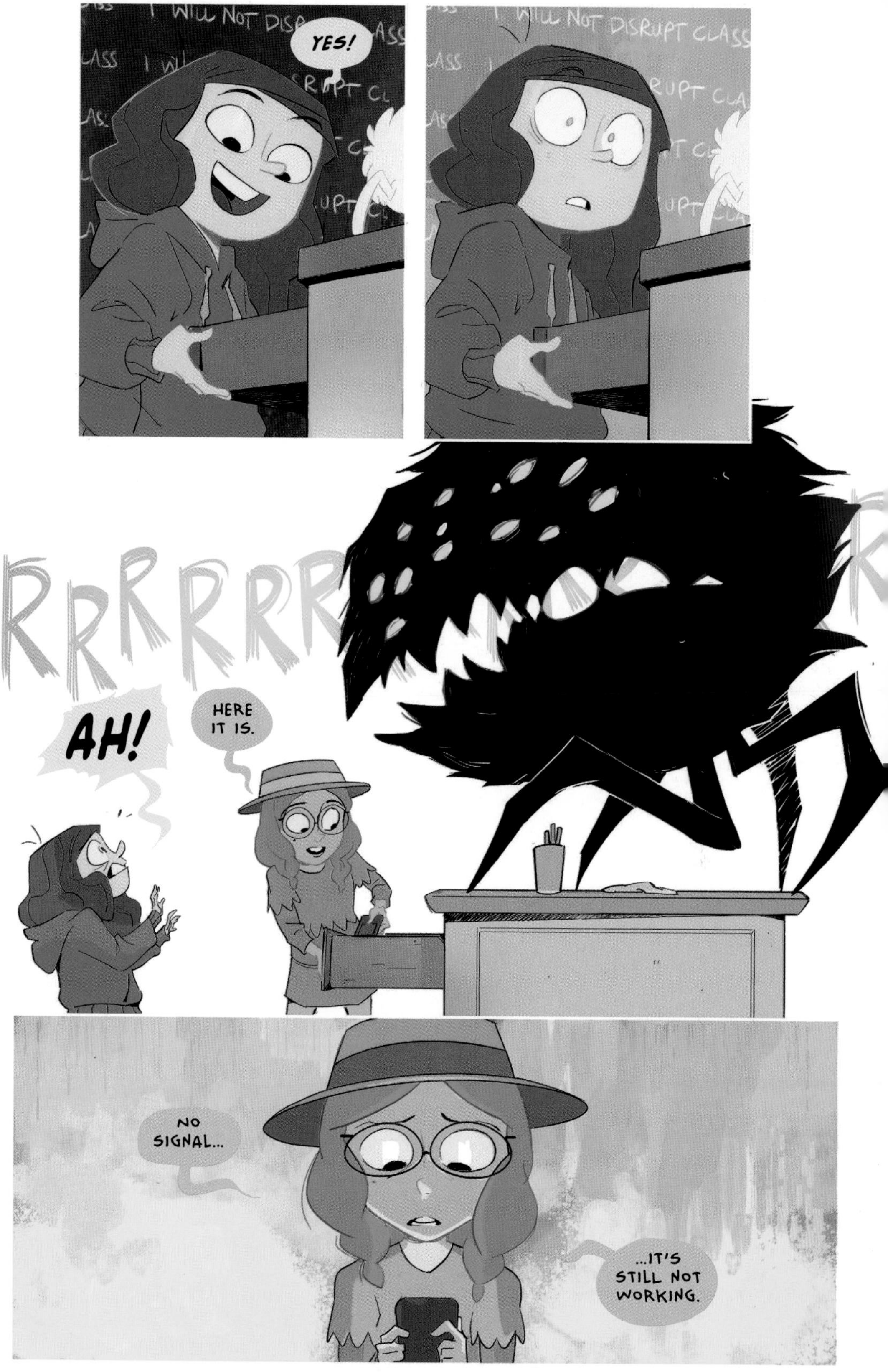
I WILL NOT DISRUPT CLASS
YES!
RRRRRR
AH!
HERE IT IS.
NO SIGNAL...
...IT'S STILL NOT WORKING.

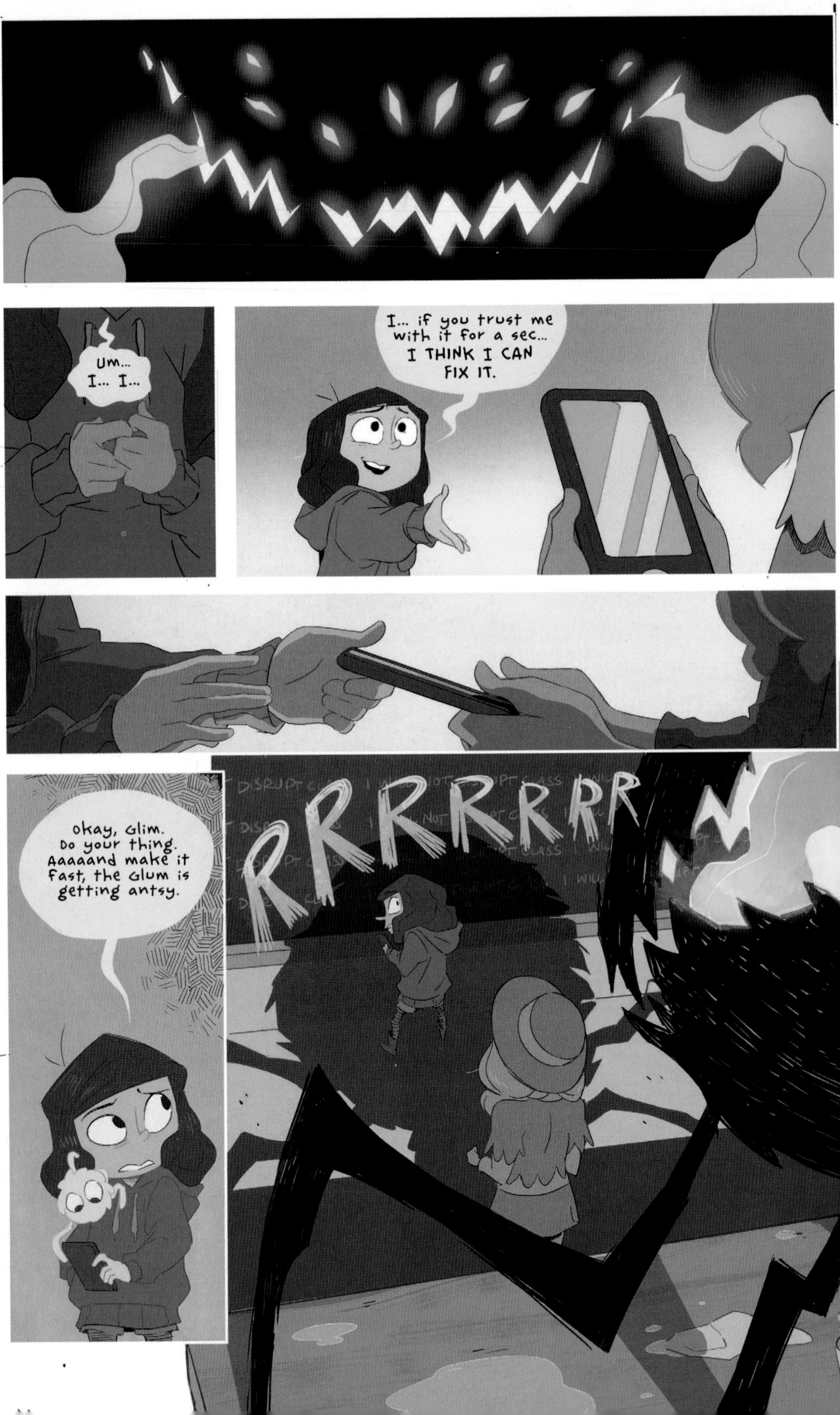
Um... I... I...
I... if you trust me with it for a sec... I THINK I CAN FIX IT.
Okay, Glim. Do your thing. Aaaaand make it fast, the Glum is getting antsy.
RRRRRRRR

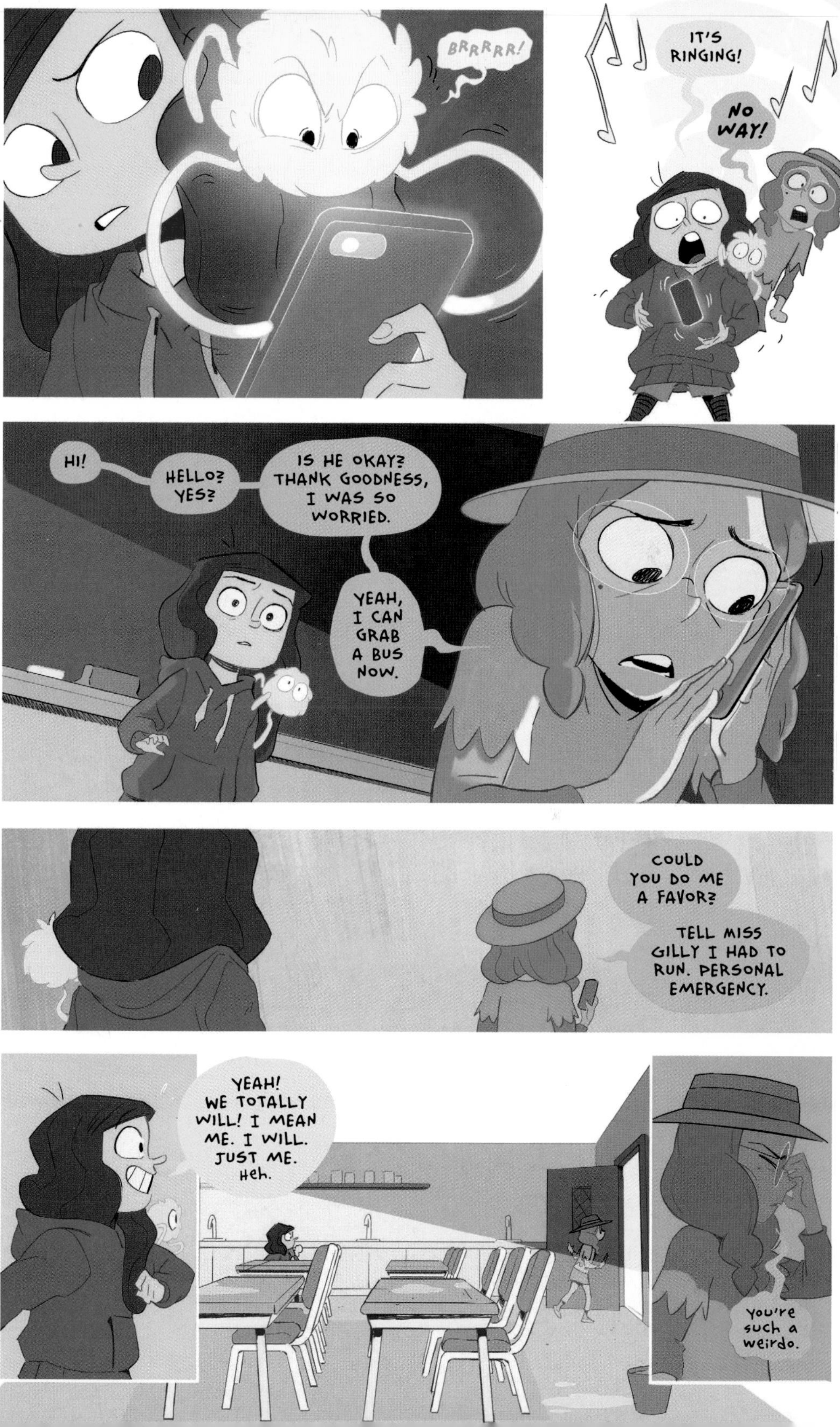
BRRRRR!
IT'S RINGING!
NO WAY!
HI!
HELLO? YES?
IS HE OKAY? THANK GOODNESS, I WAS SO WORRIED.
YEAH, I CAN GRAB A BUS NOW.
COULD YOU DO ME A FAVOR?
TELL MISS GILLY I HAD TO RUN. PERSONAL EMERGENCY.
YEAH! WE TOTALLY WILL! I MEAN ME. I WILL. JUST ME. Heh.
You're such a weirdo.

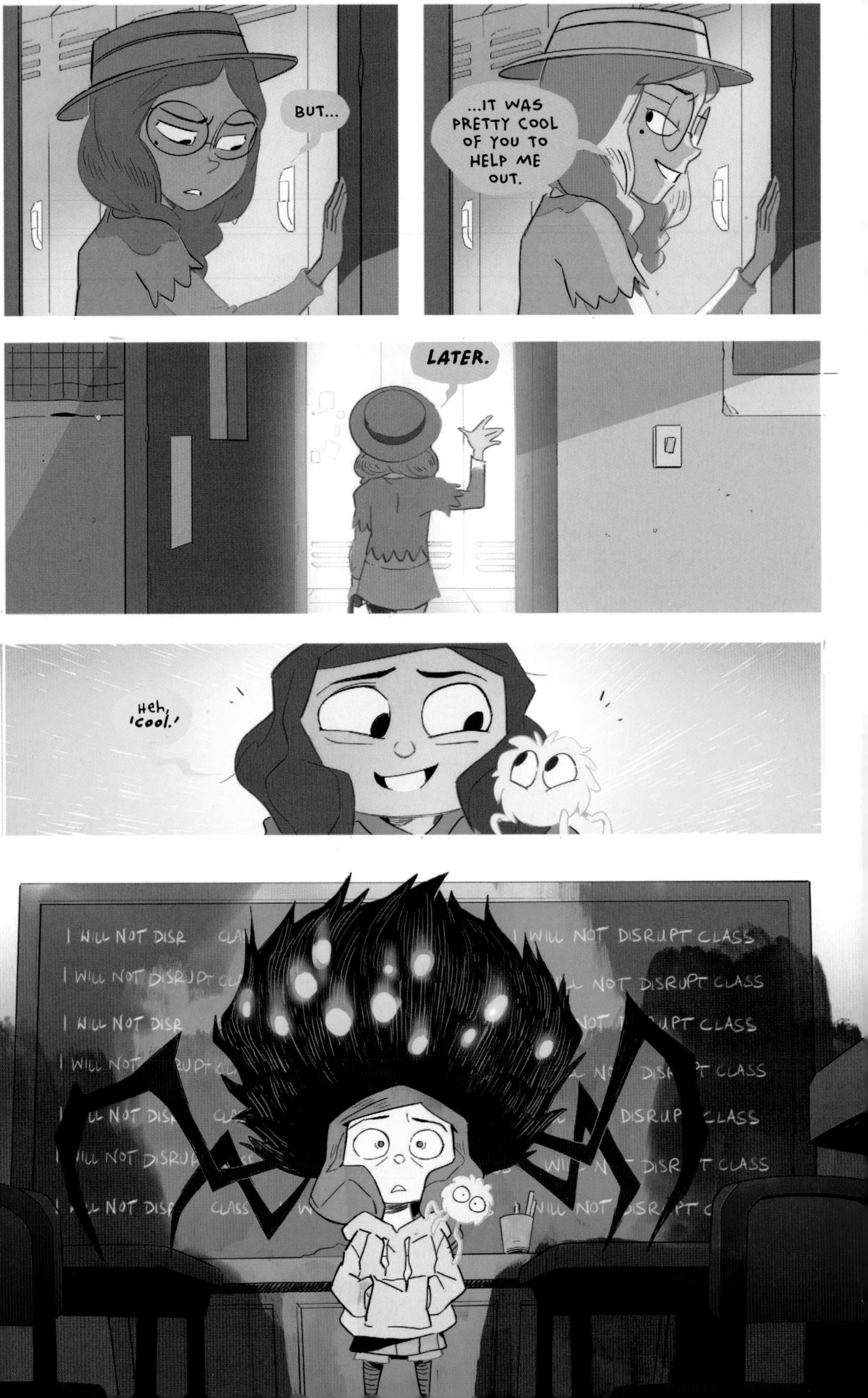
BUT...
...IT WAS PRETTY COOL OF YOU TO HELP ME OUT.
LATER.
Heh, 'cool.'
I WILL NOT DISRUPT CLASS

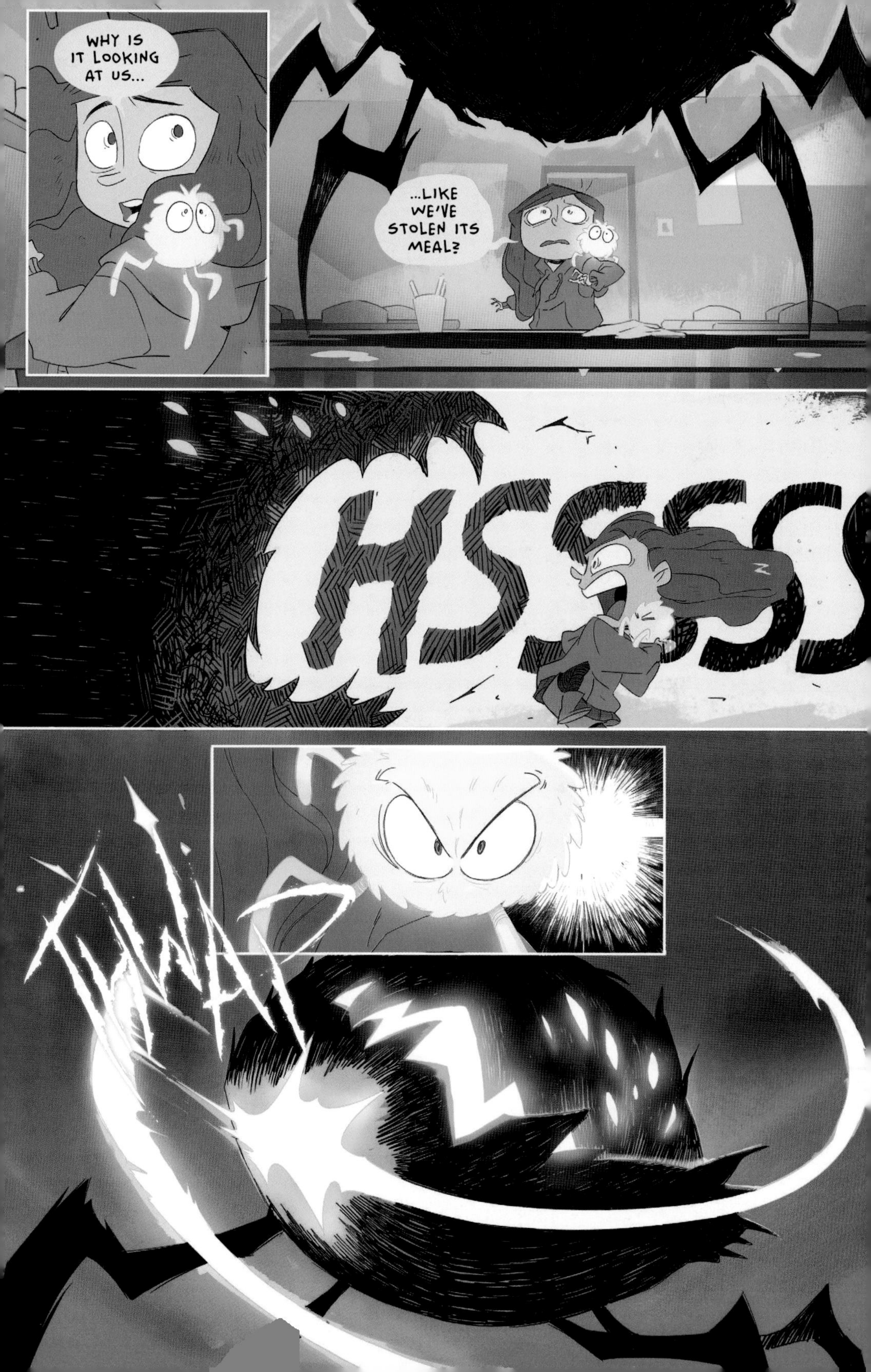
WHY IS IT LOOKING AT US...
...LIKE WE'VE STOLEN ITS MEAL?
HSSSS
THWAP

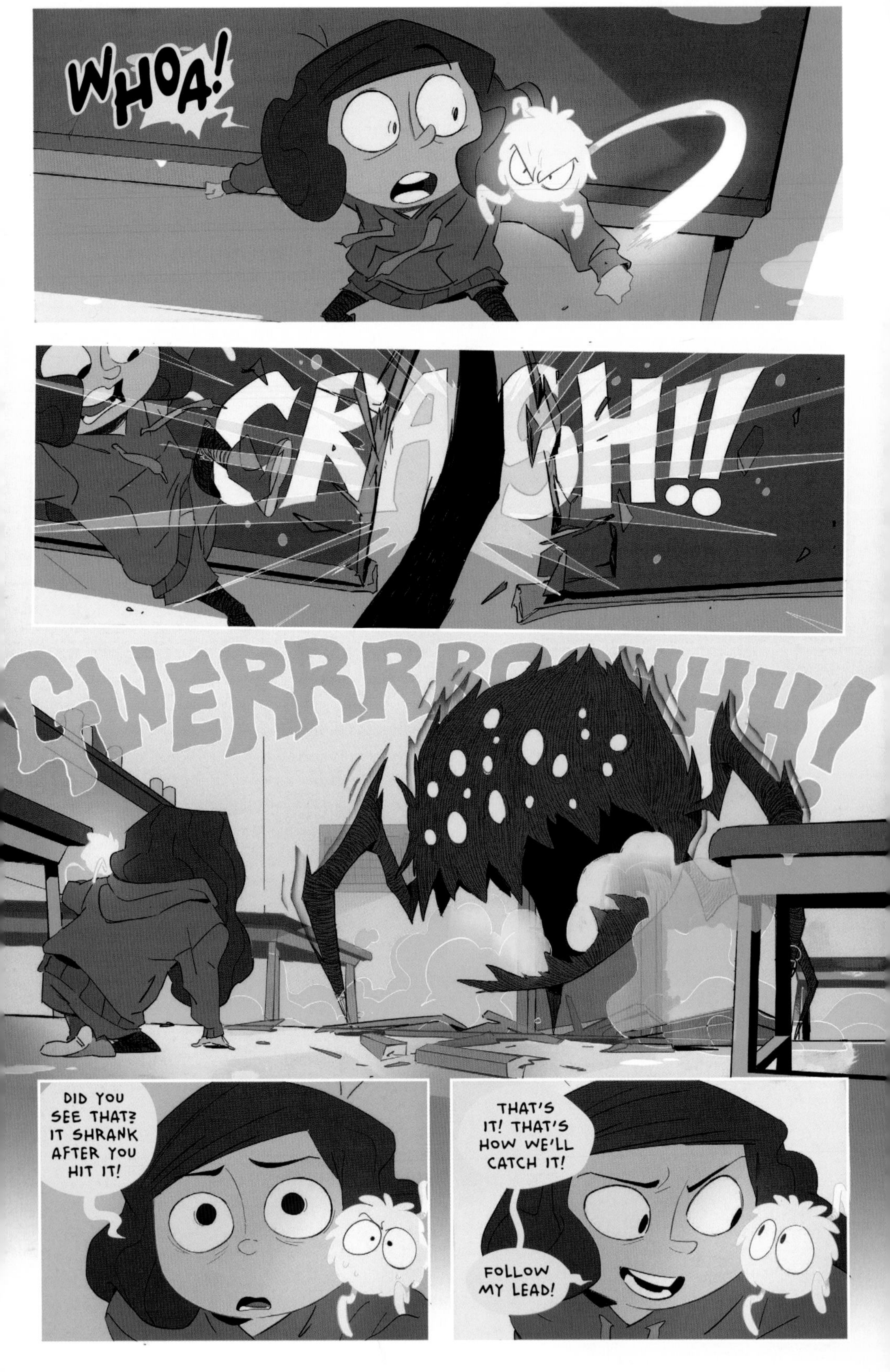
WHOA!
CRASH!!
GWERRRROOHHH!
DID YOU SEE THAT? IT SHRANK AFTER YOU HIT IT!
THAT'S IT! THAT'S HOW WE'LL CATCH IT!
FOLLOW MY LEAD!

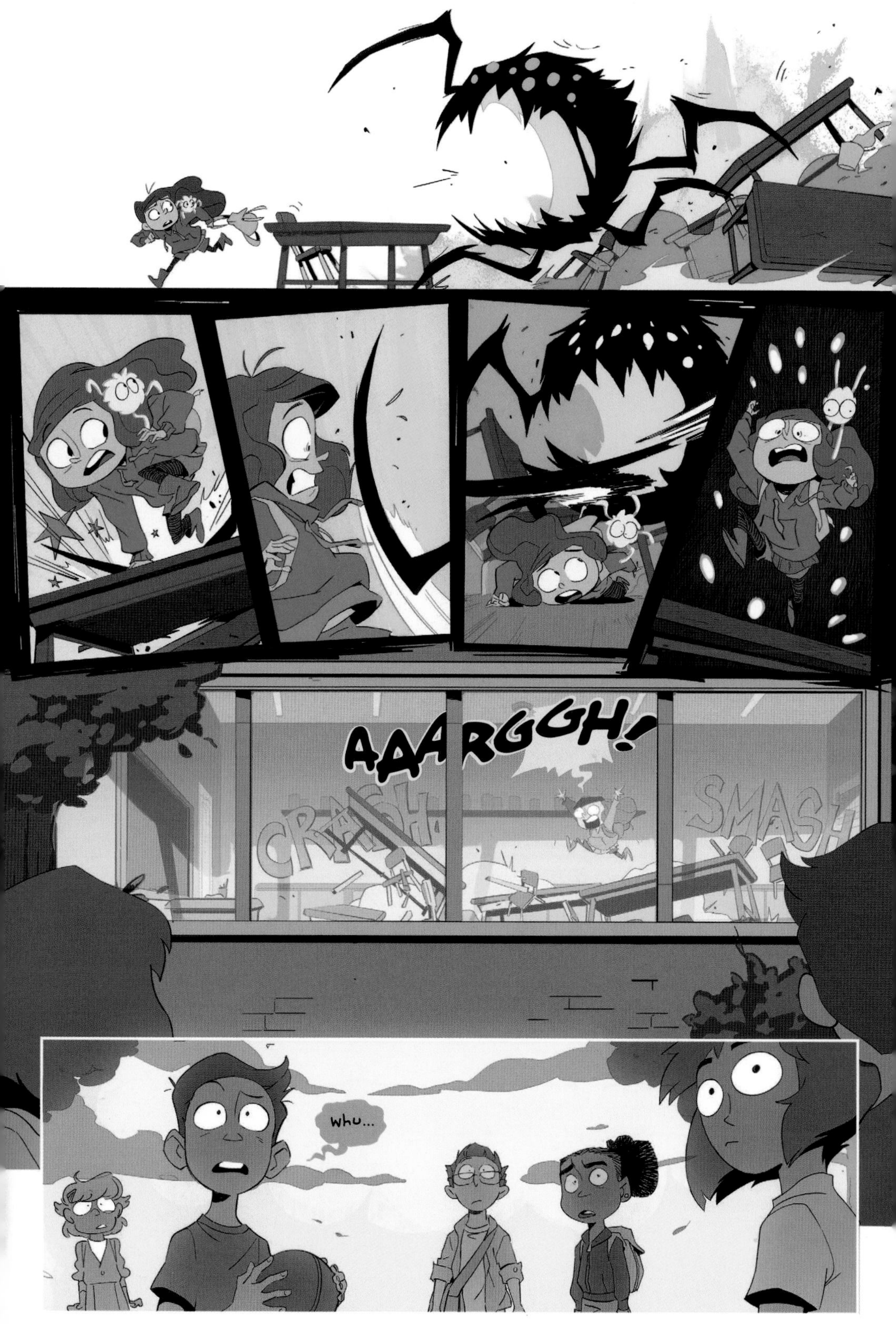
AAARGGH!
CRASH
SMASH
whu...

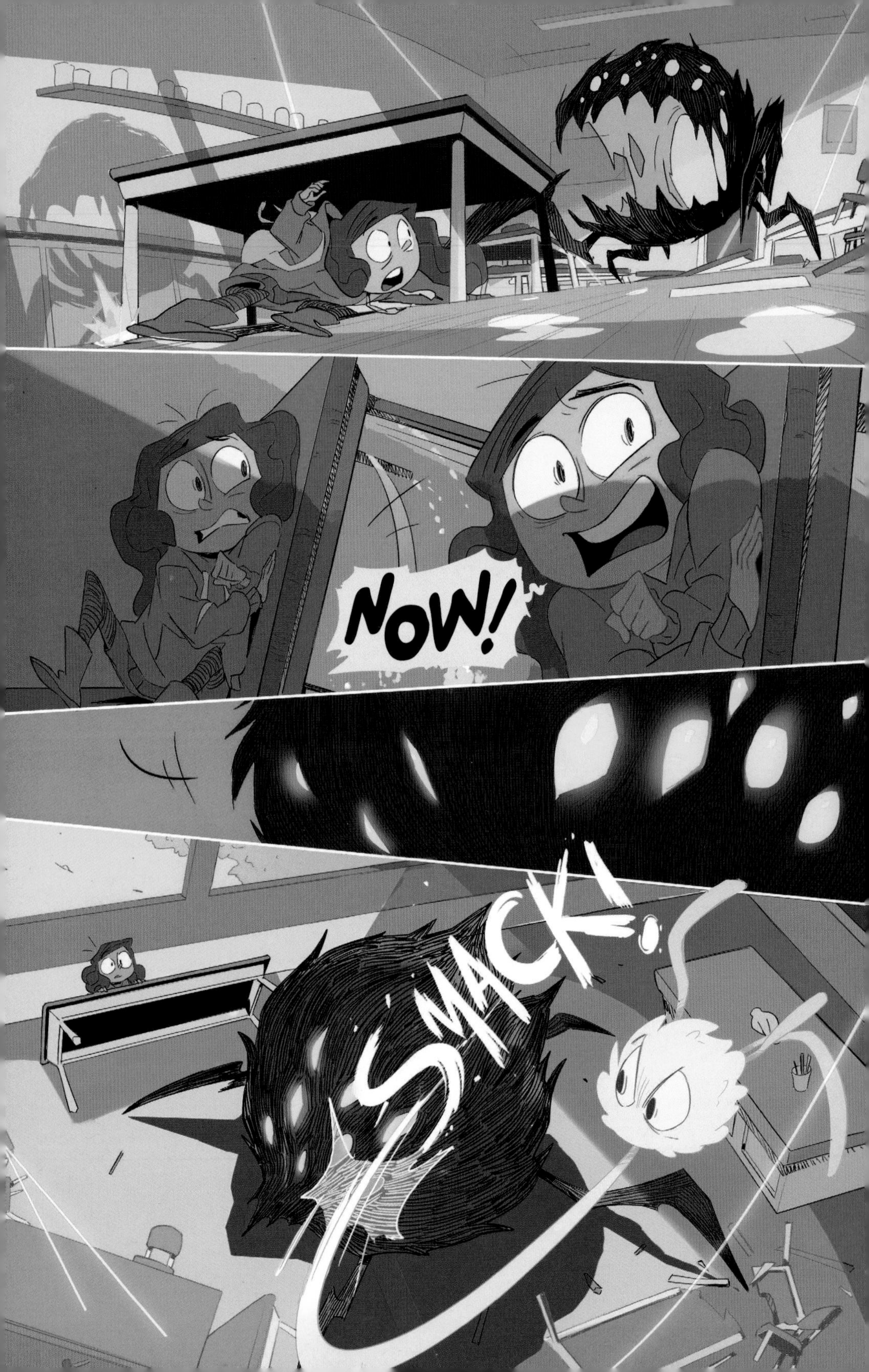
NOW!
SMACK!

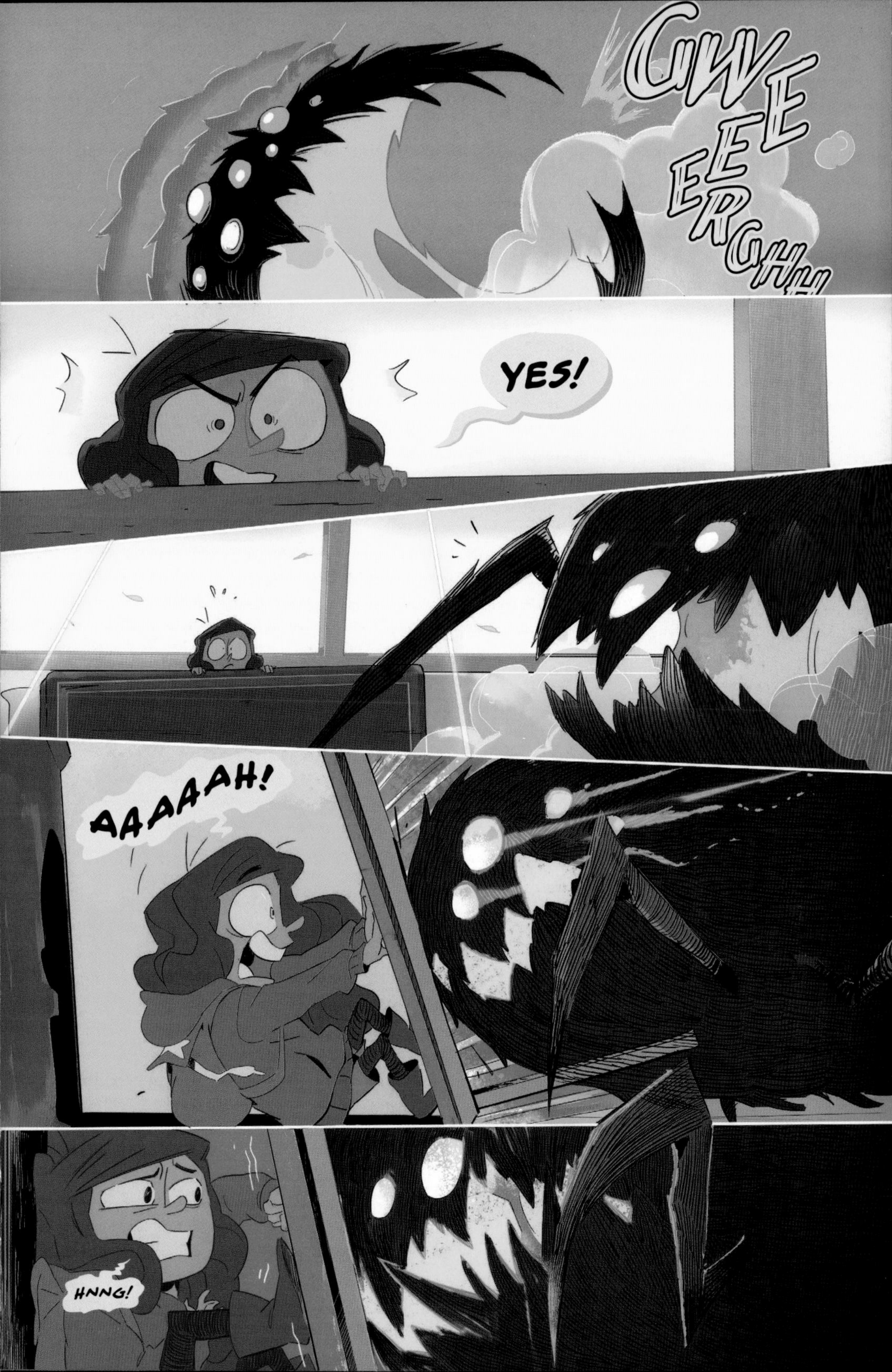
GWEEEERGHH!
YES!
AAAAAH!
HNNG!

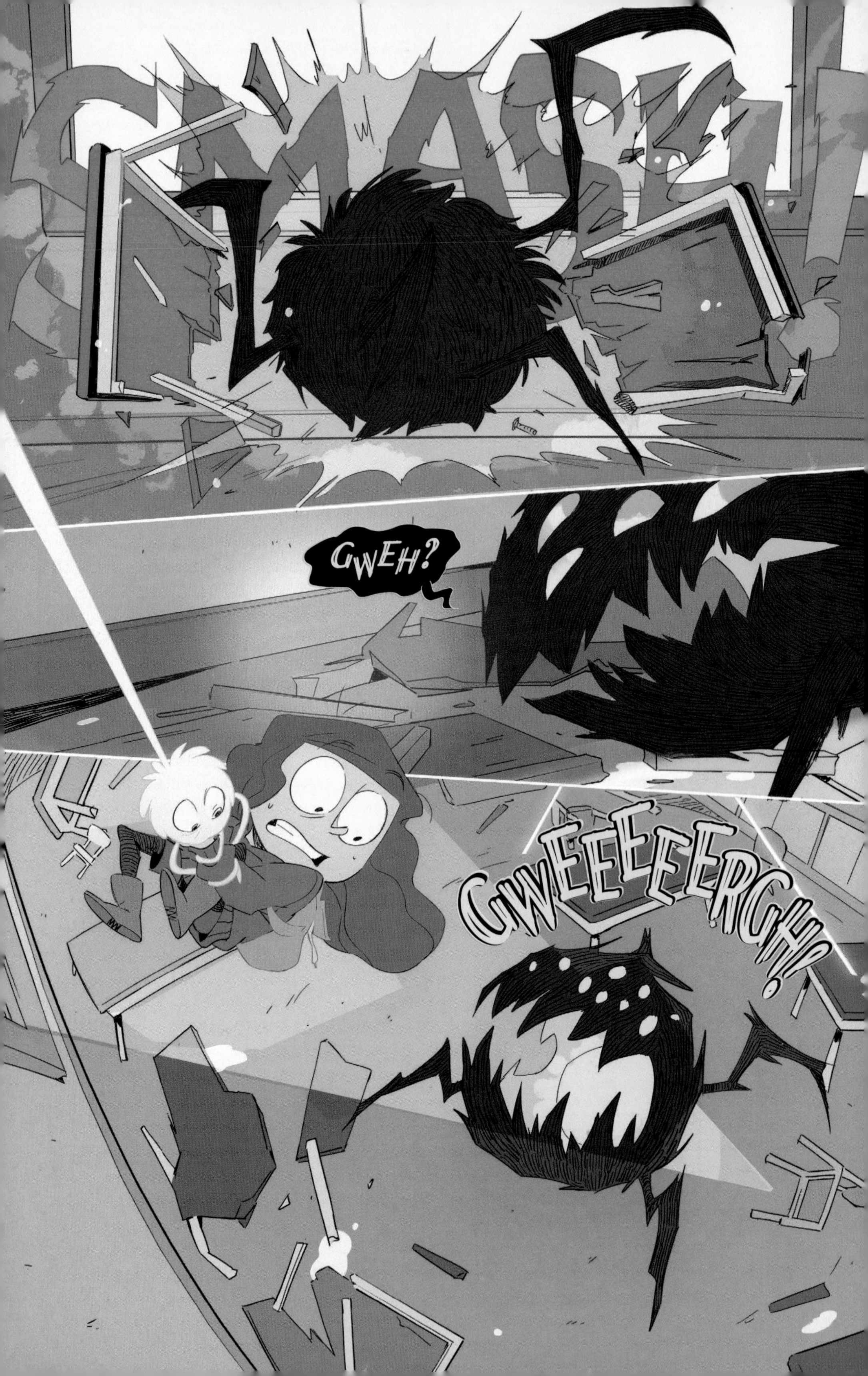
CRASH!
GWEH?
GWEEEEERGH!!

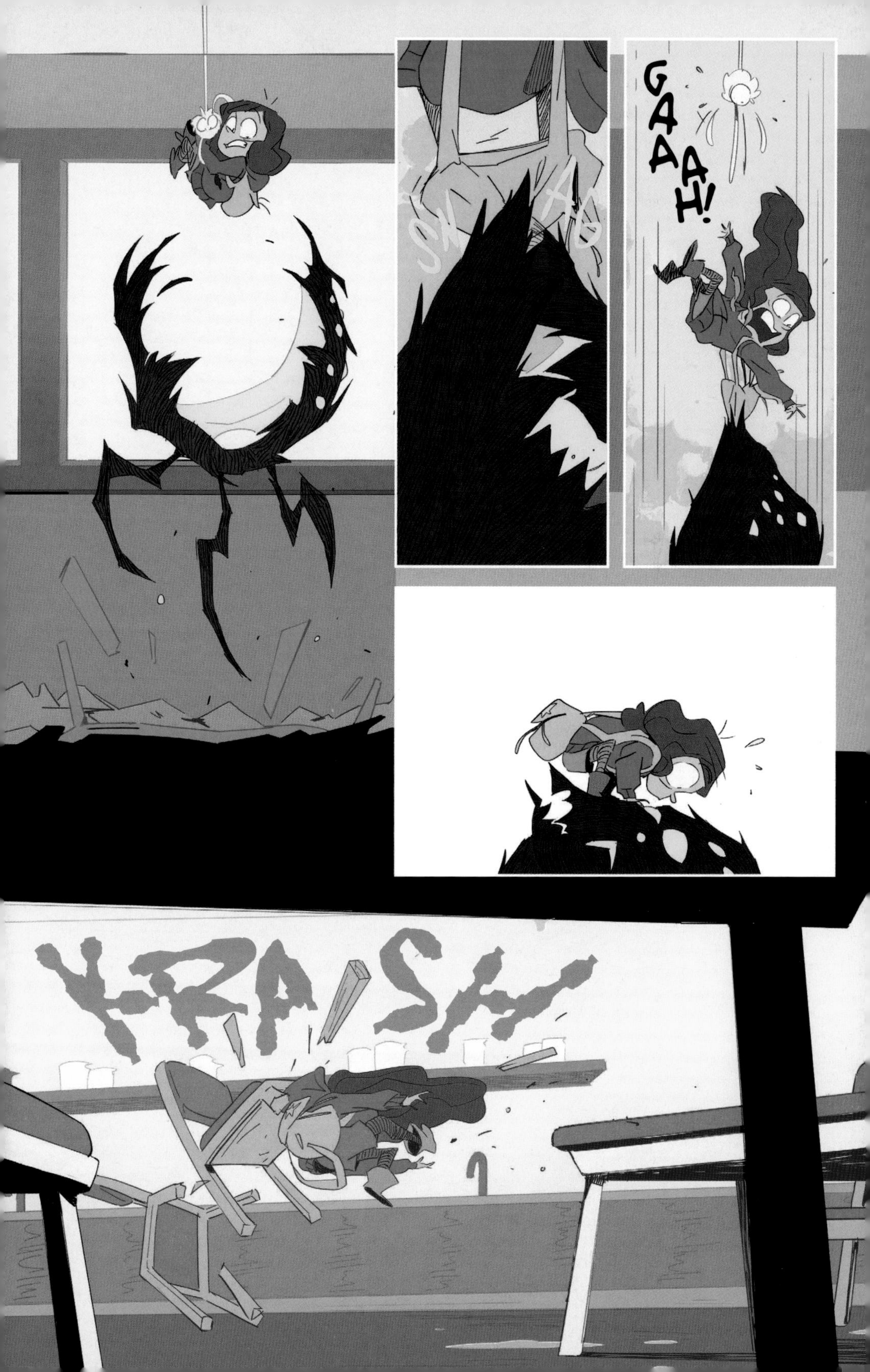
SNAG
GAAAH!
KRASH

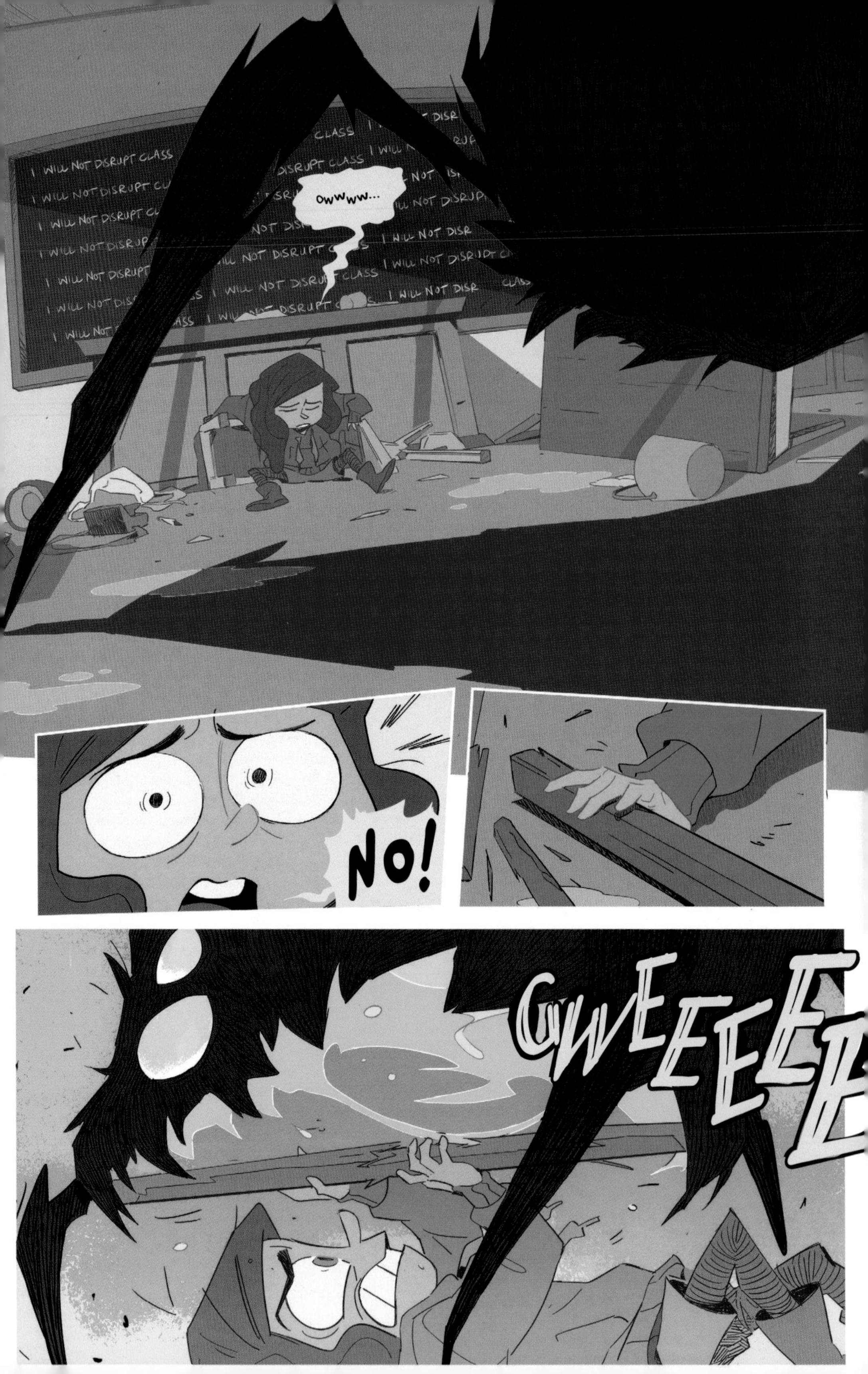
I WILL NOT DISRUPT CLASS
OWWWW...
NO!
GWEEEEE

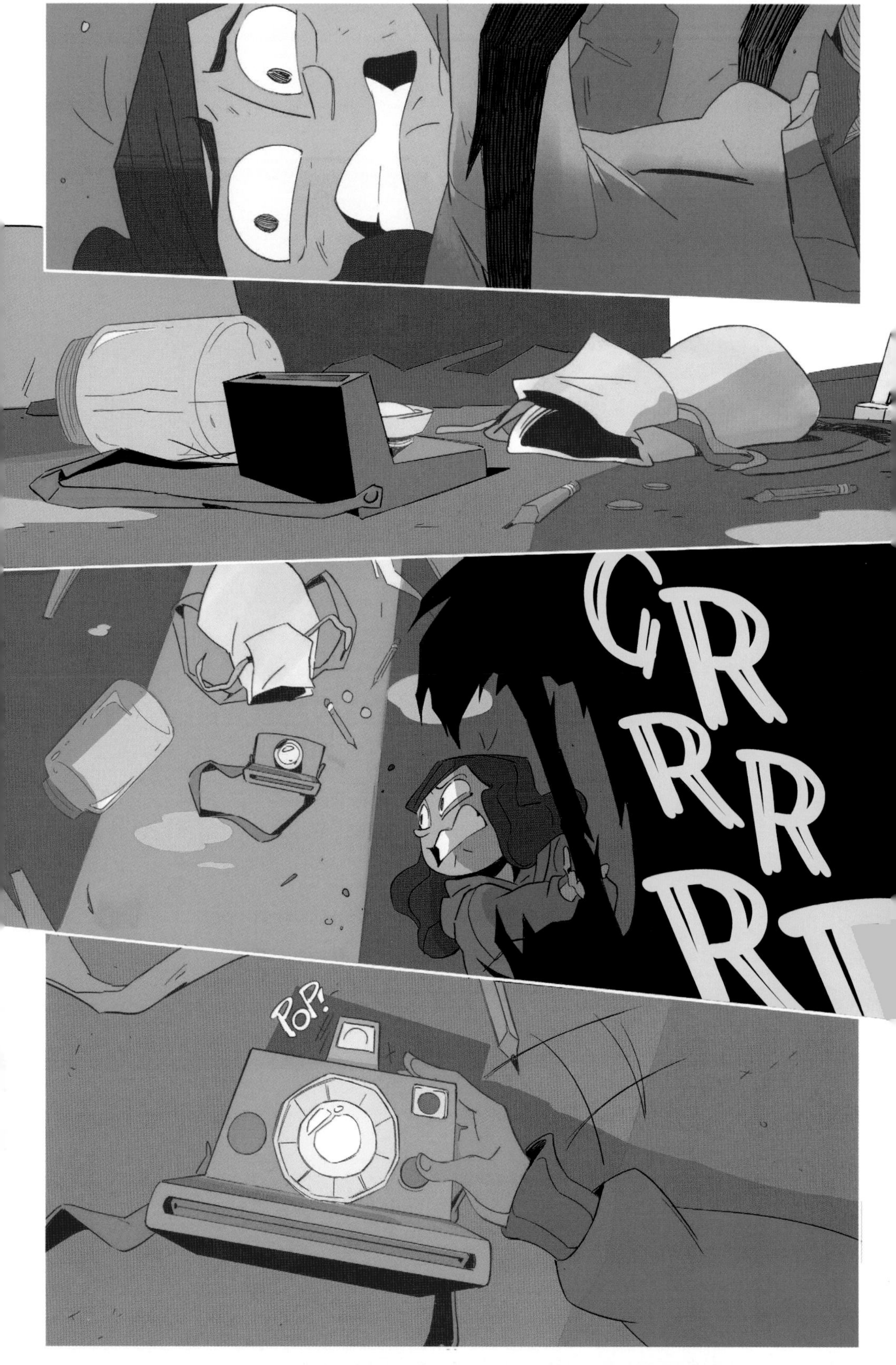
GRRRRT
POP!

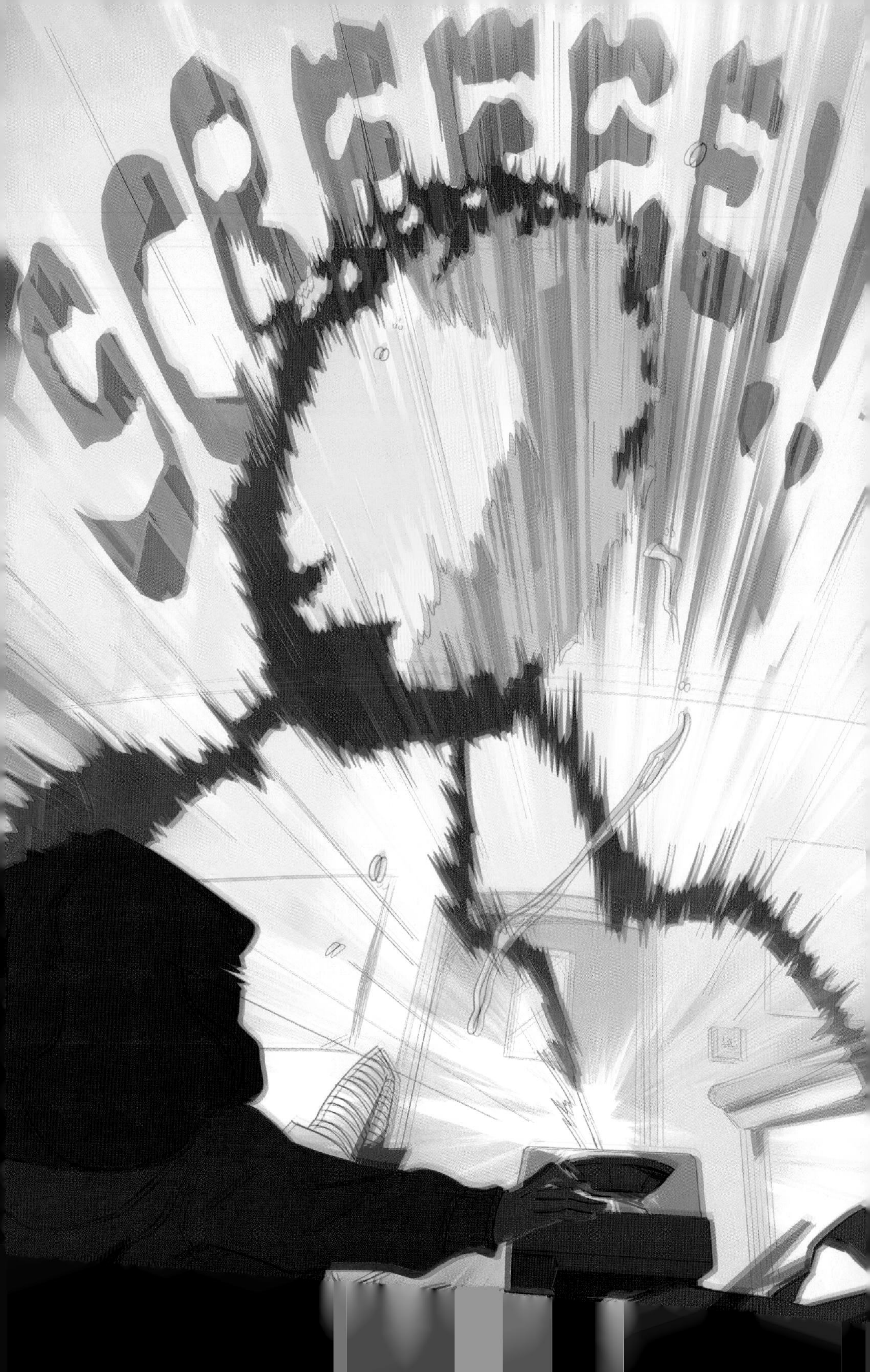

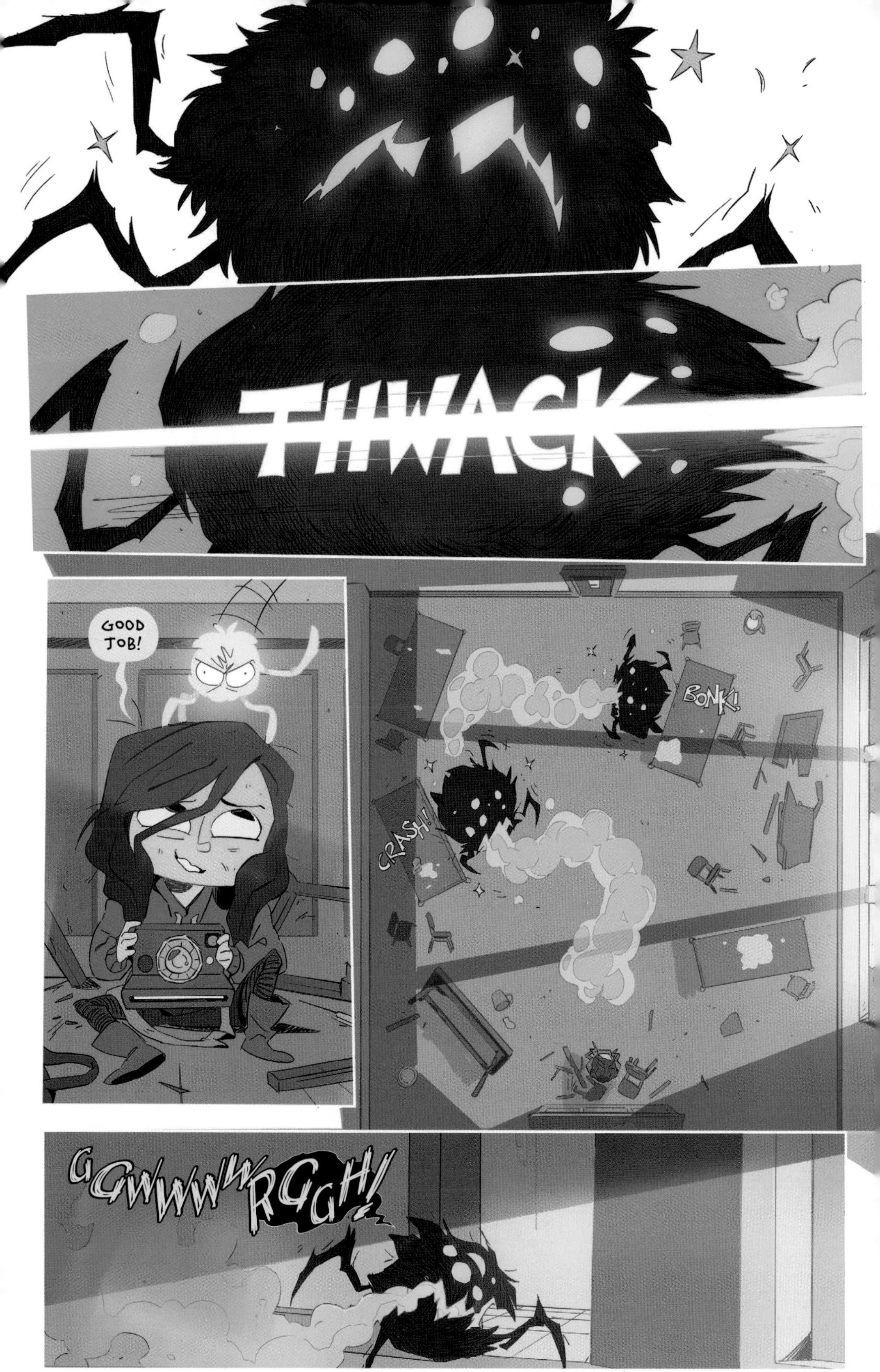
THWACK
GOOD JOB!
BONK!
CRASH!
GGWWWWRGGH!

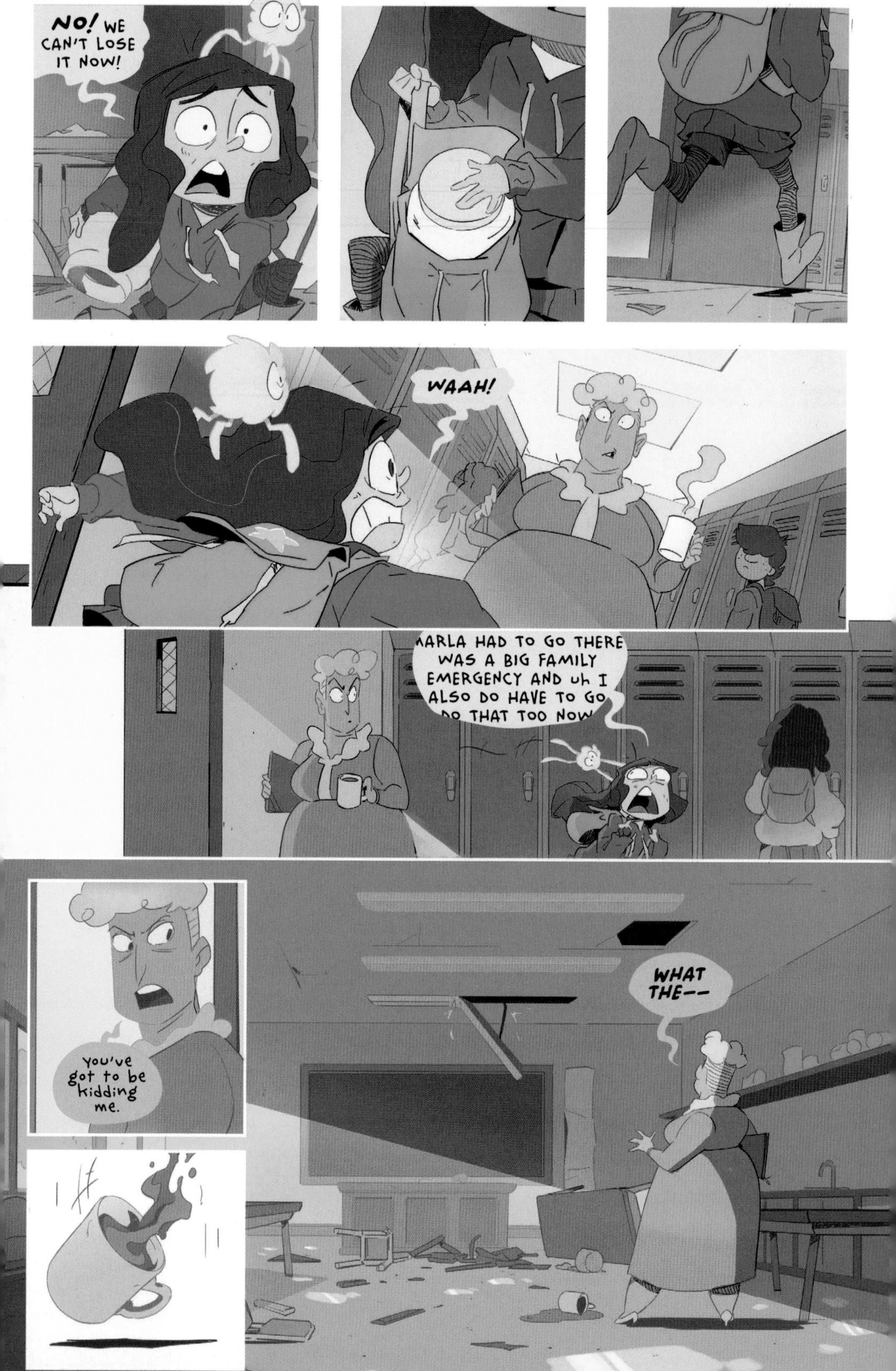
NO! WE CAN'T LOSE IT NOW!
WAAH!
MARLA HAD TO GO THERE WAS A BIG FAMILY EMERGENCY AND uh I ALSO DO HAVE TO GO DO THAT TOO NOW
You've got to be kidding me.
WHAT THE--

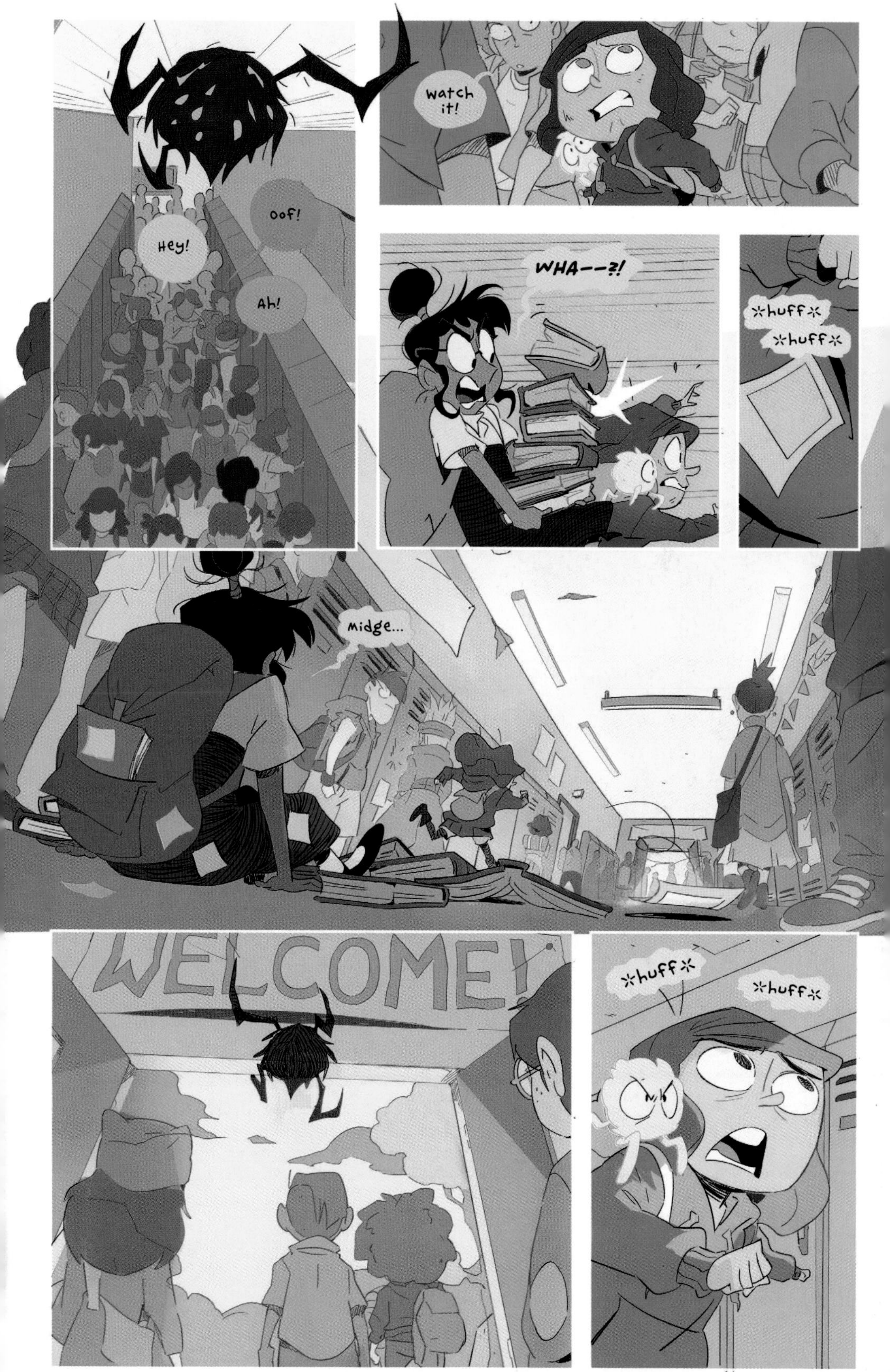

Hey!
Oof!
Ah!
watch it!
WHA--?!
huff
huff
midge...
WELCOME!
huff
huff

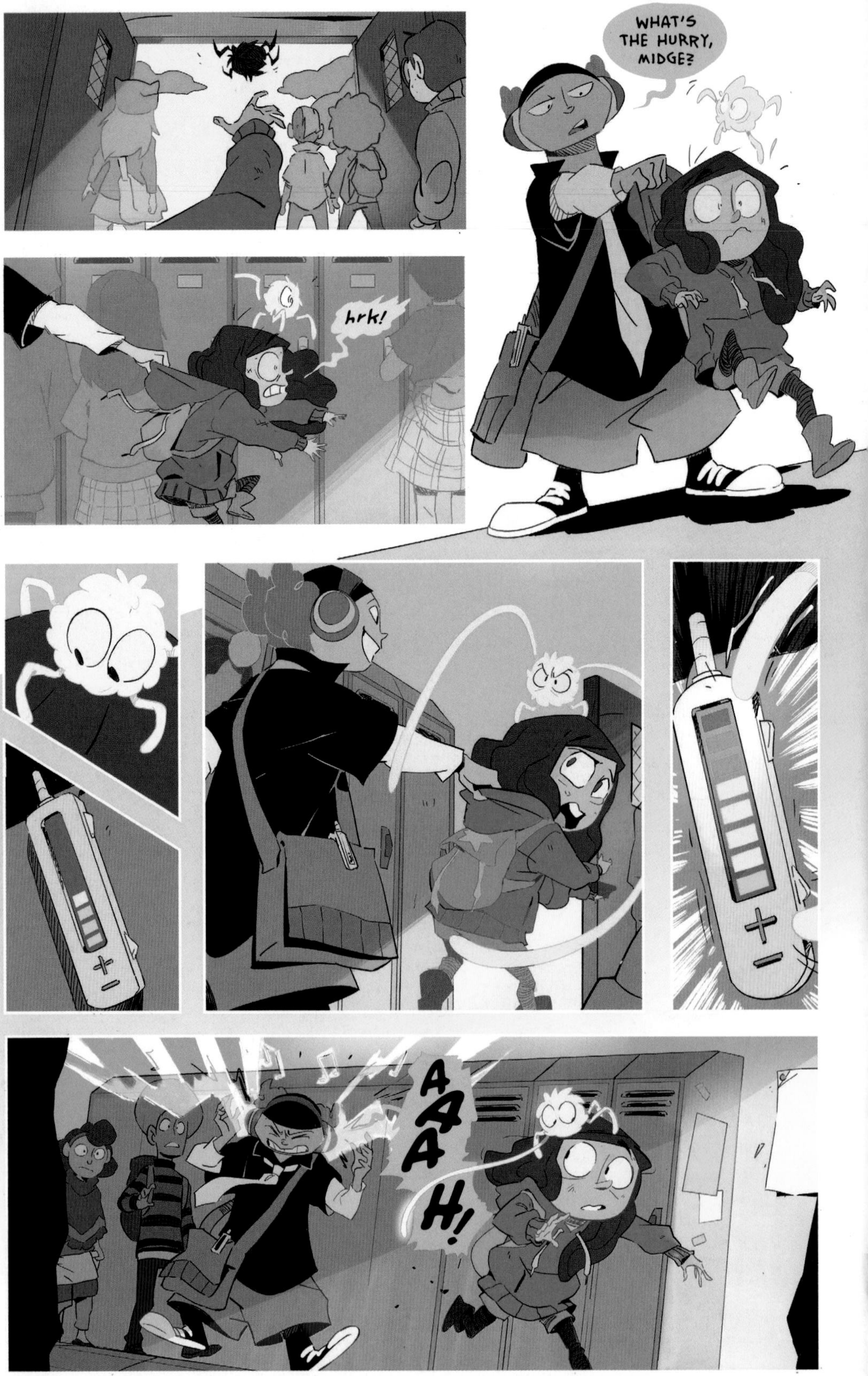
hrk!
WHAT'S THE HURRY, MIDGE?
AAAH!

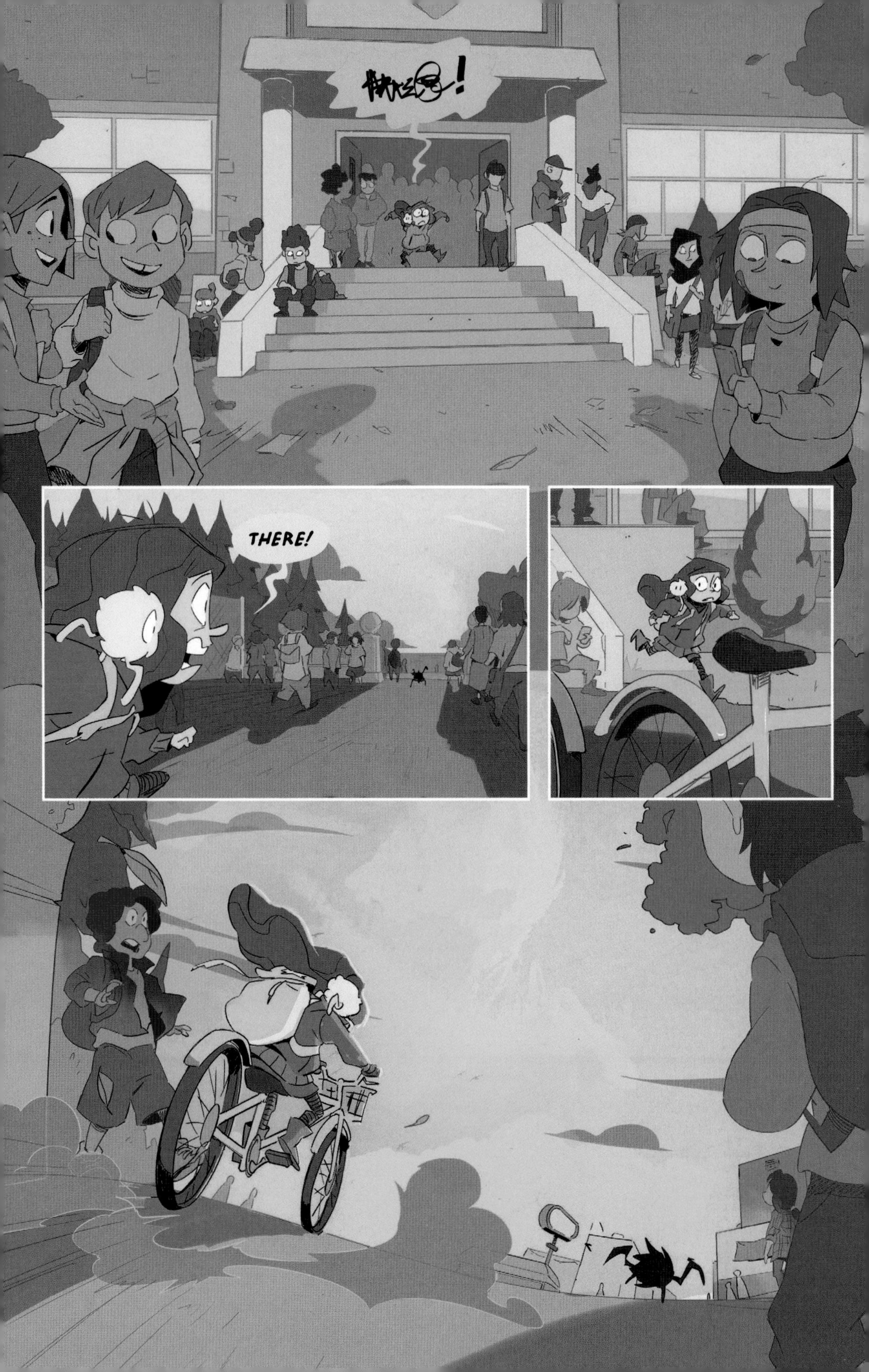
THERE!

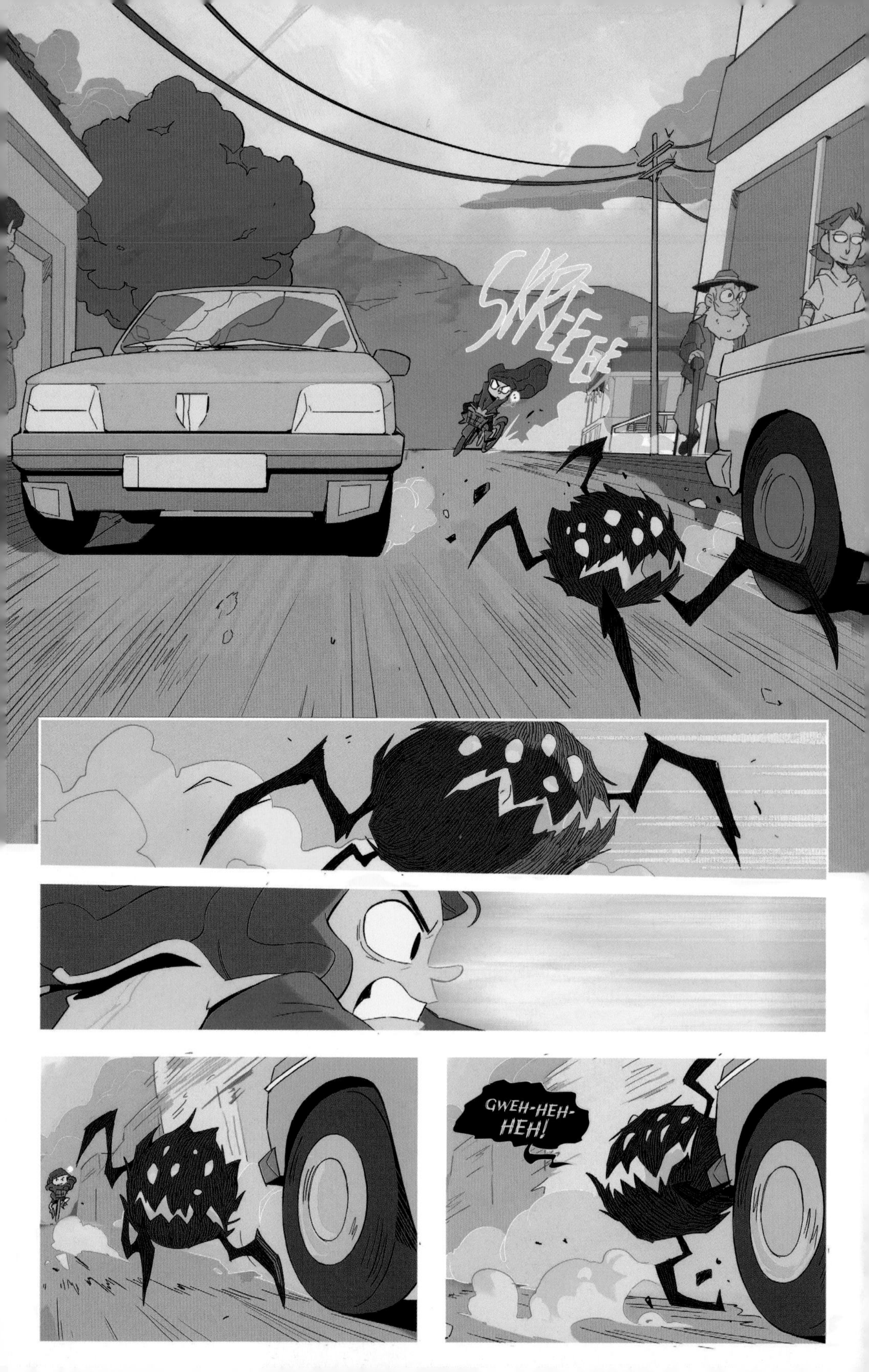
SKREEEEE
GWEH-HEH-HEH!

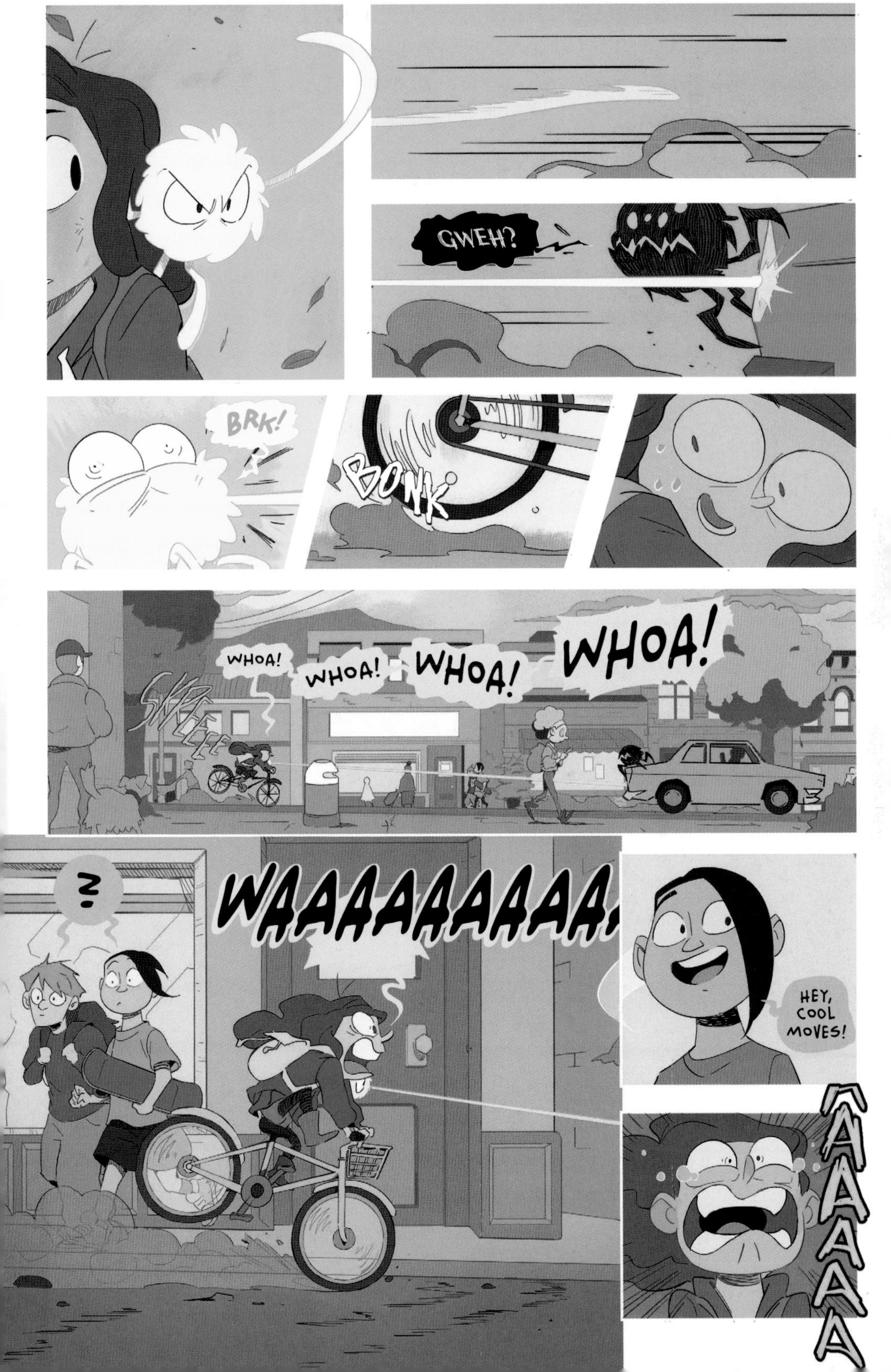
GWEH?
BRK!
BONK
SKREEEE
WHOA!
WHOA!
WHOA!
WHOA!
?
WAAAAAAAAA
HEY, COOL MOVES!
AAAAAA

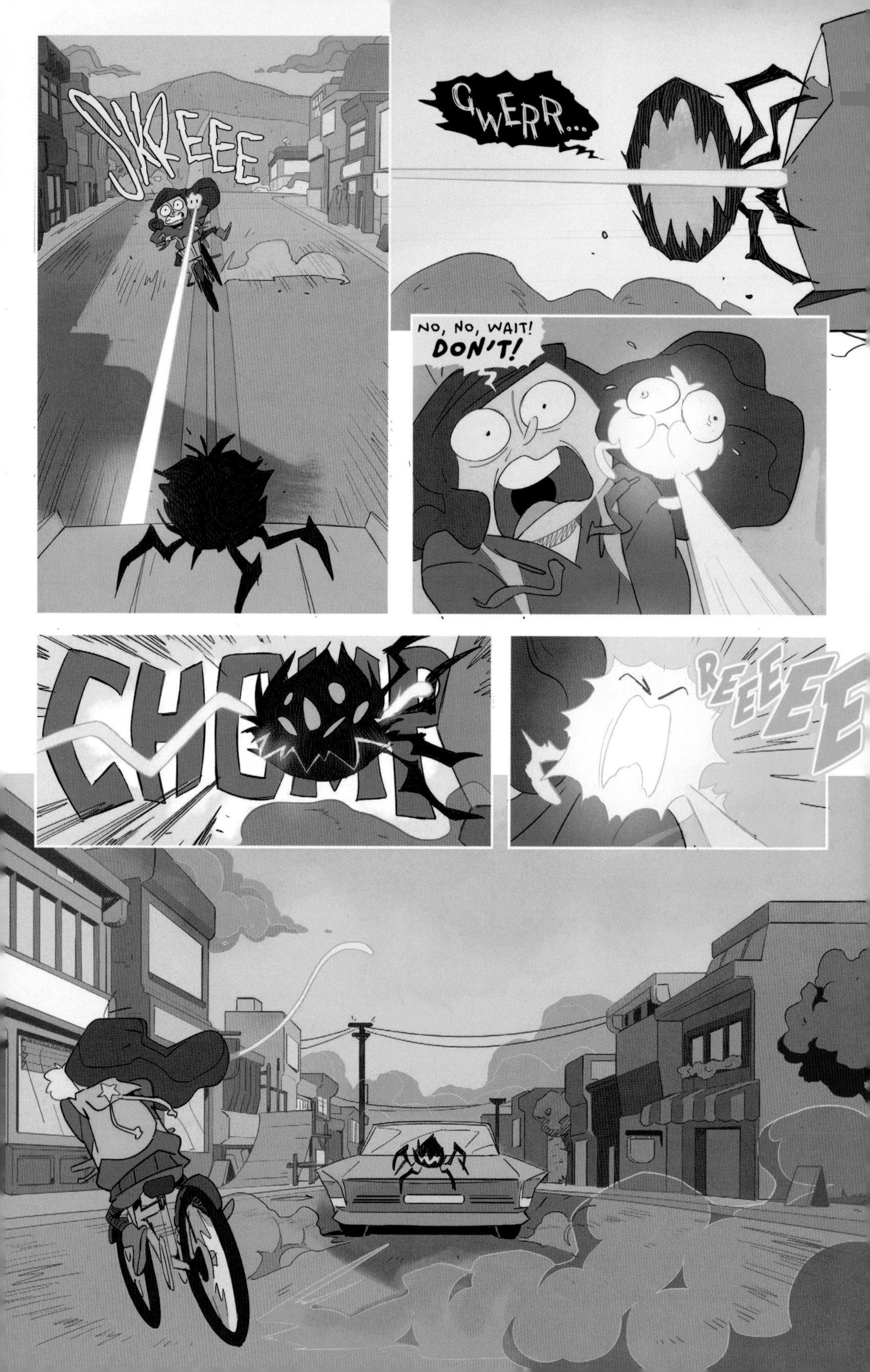
SKREEE
GWERR...
NO, NO, WAIT!
DON'T!
CHOMP
REEEEE

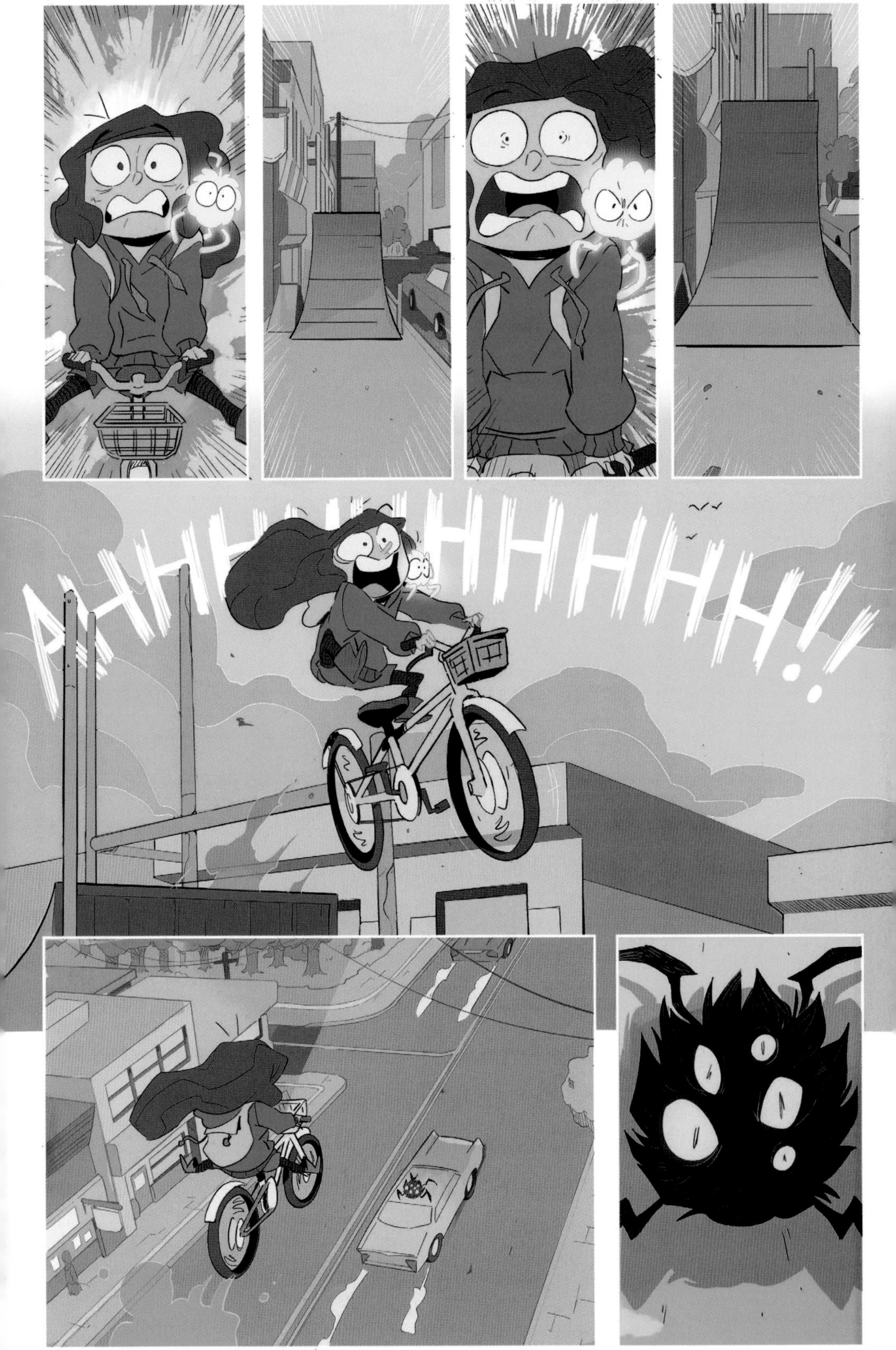
AHHHHHHHHHHH!!

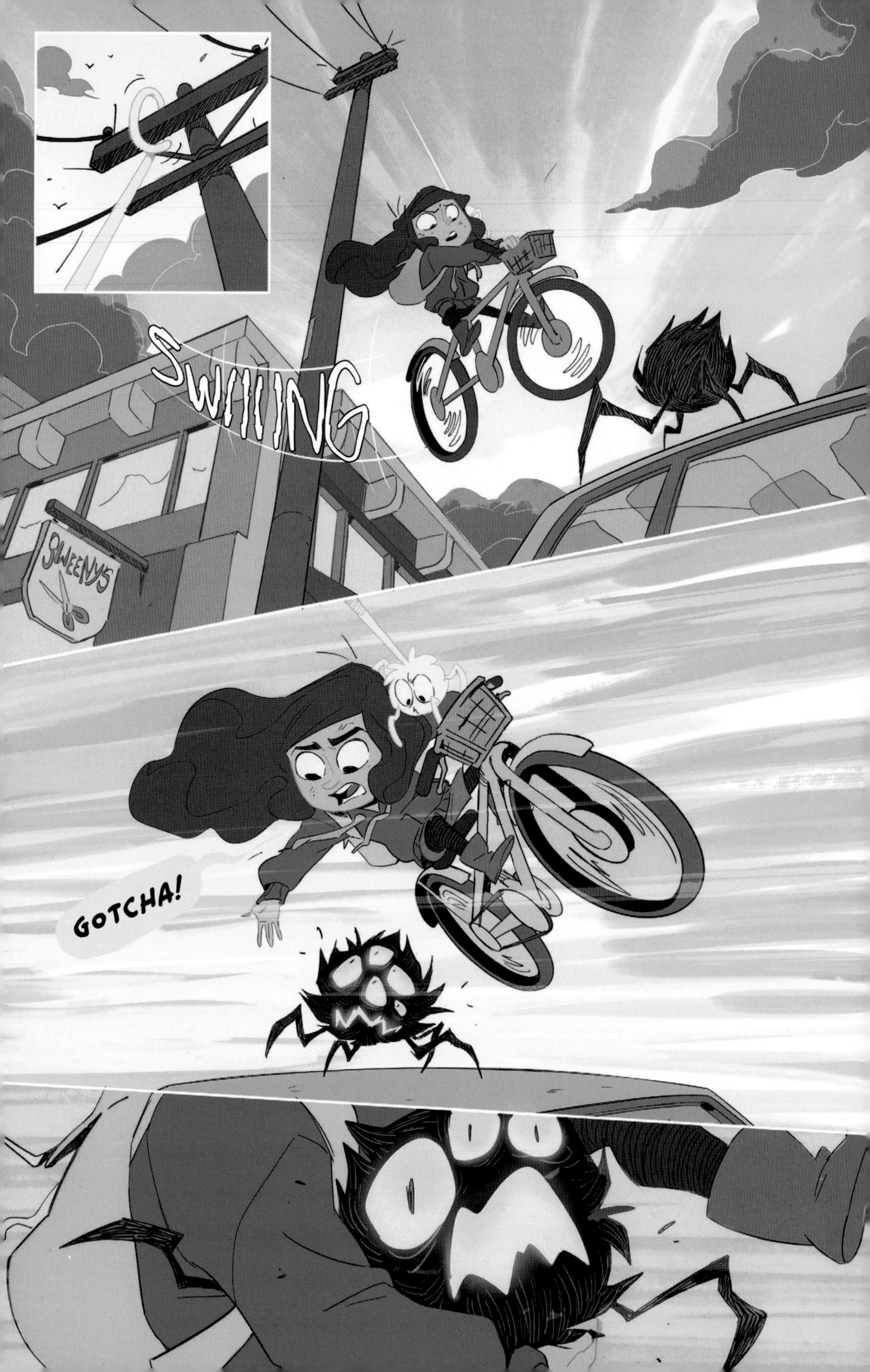
SWIIING
SWEENYS
GOTCHA!

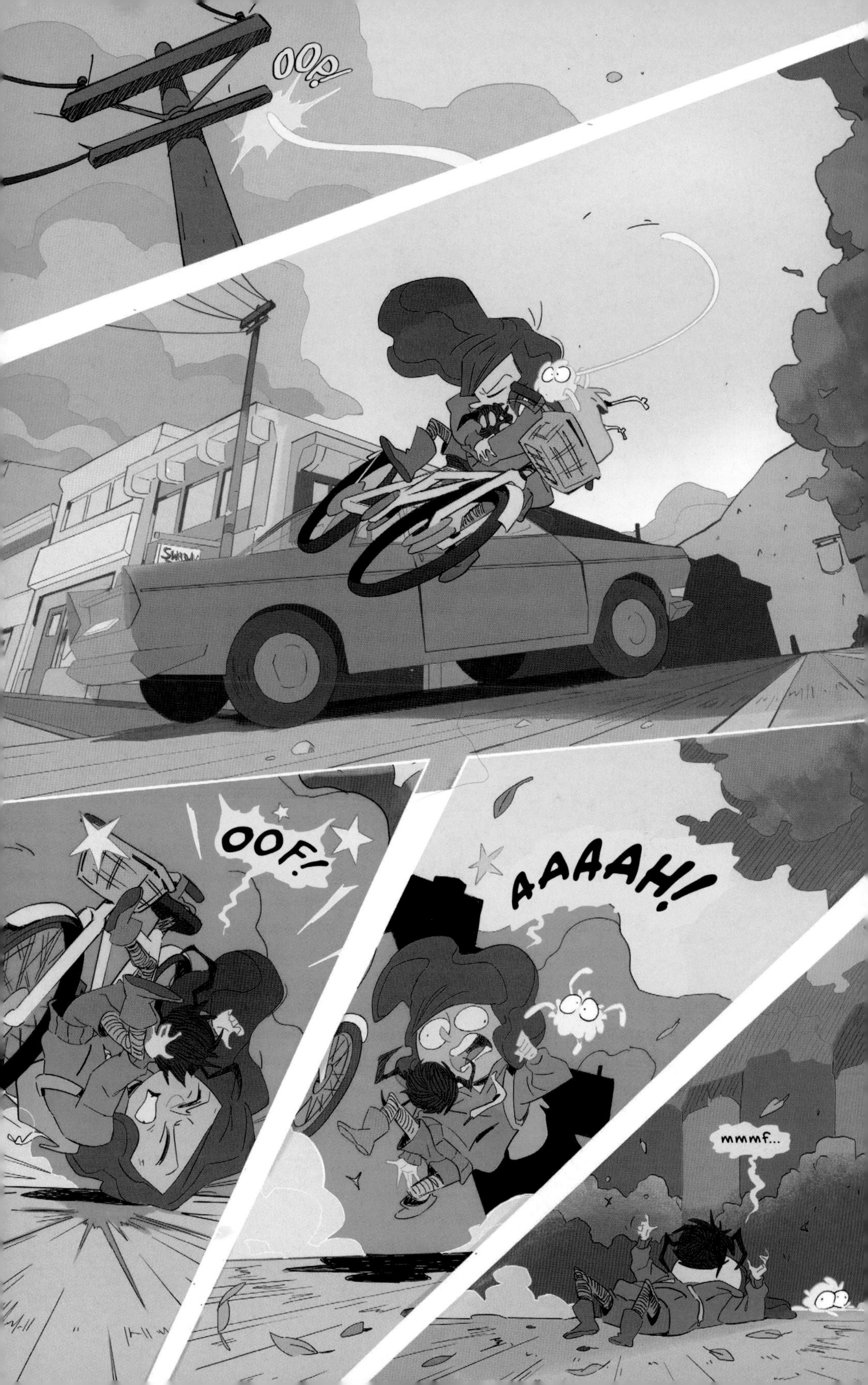
OOP!
OOF!
AAAAH!
mmmf...

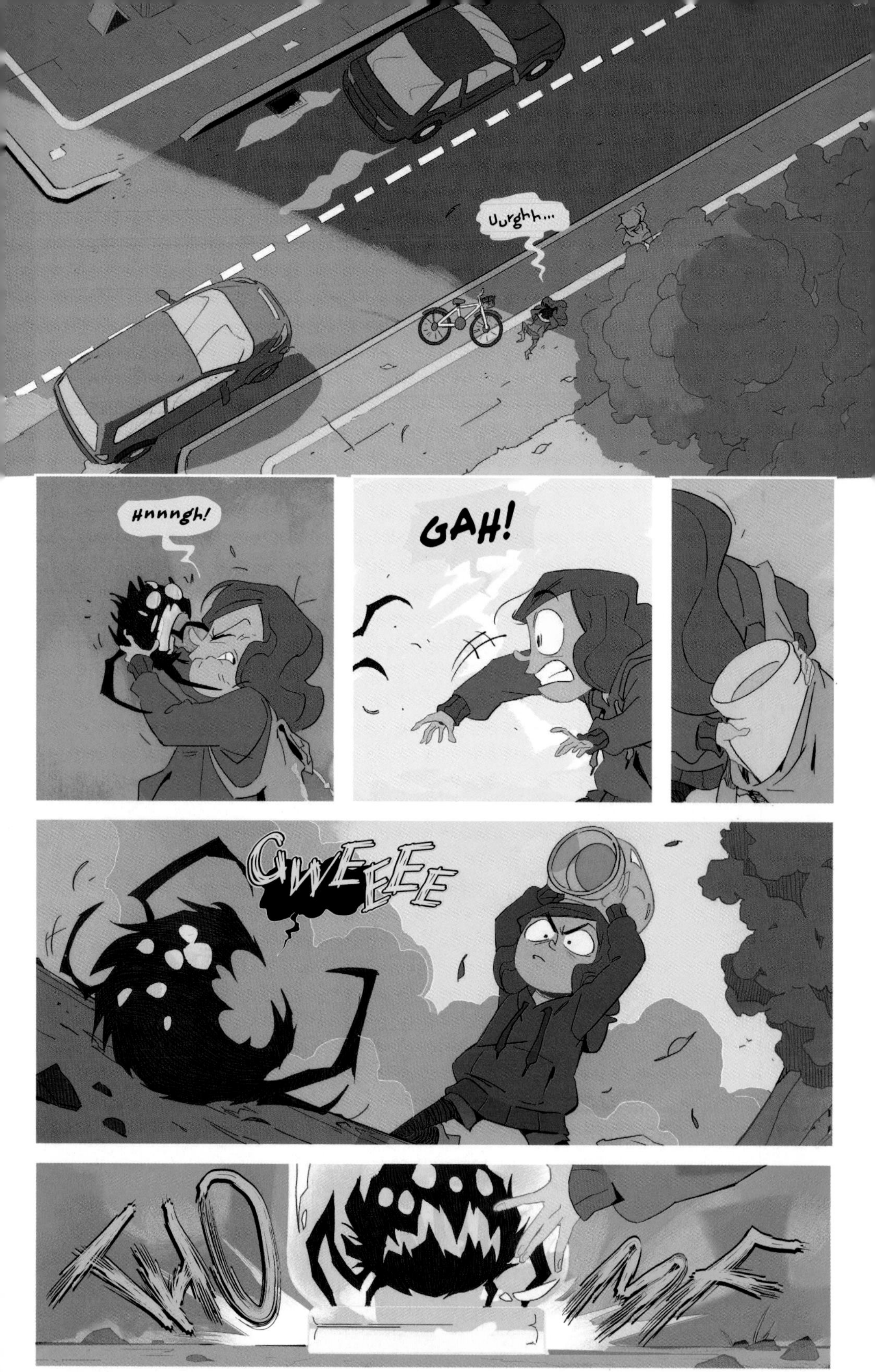

Uurghh...
Hnnngh!
GAH!
GWEEEE
THOMF

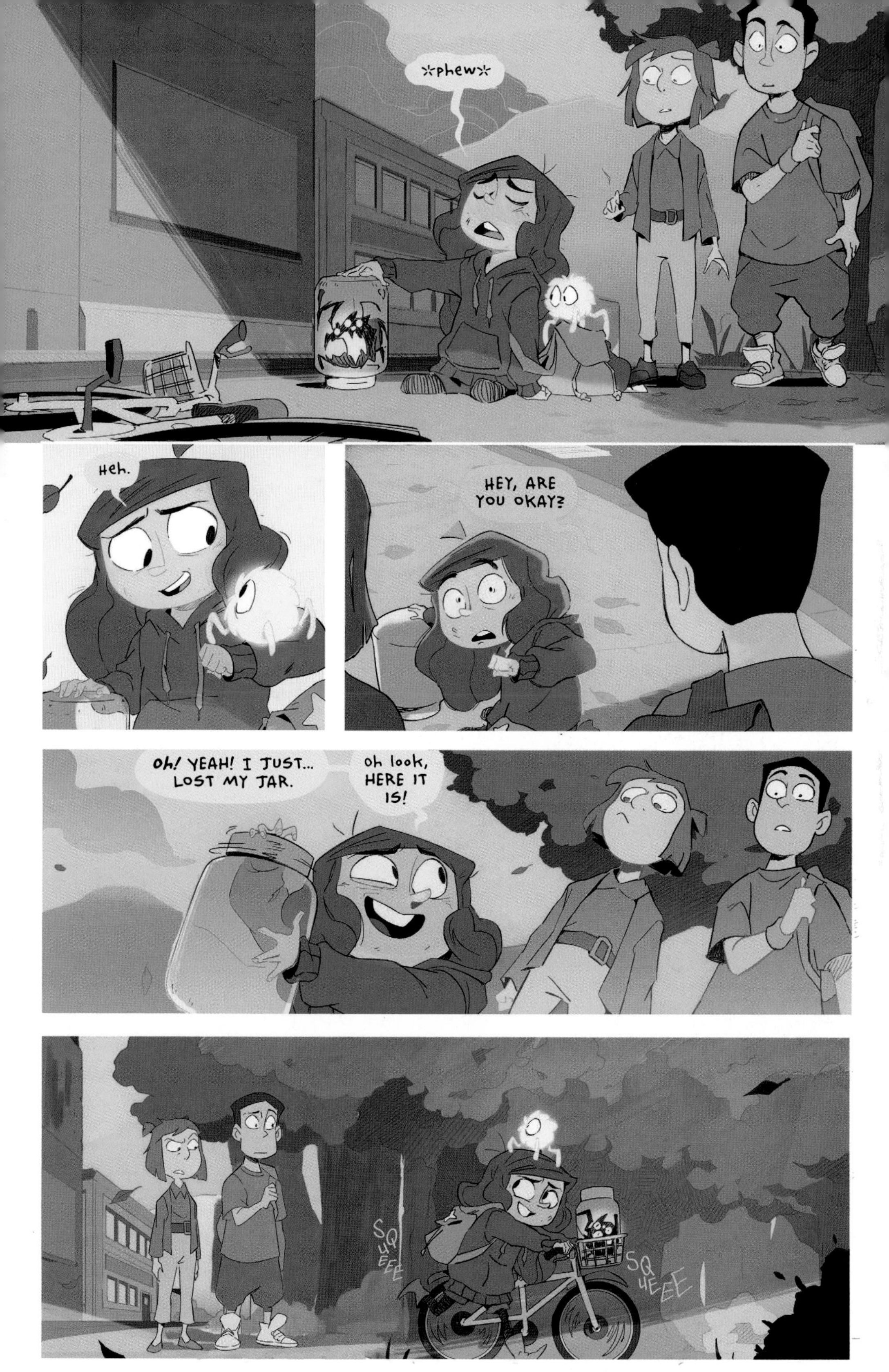
phew
Heh.
HEY, ARE YOU OKAY?
Oh! YEAH! I JUST... LOST MY JAR.
Oh look, HERE IT IS!
SQUEEE
SQUEEE

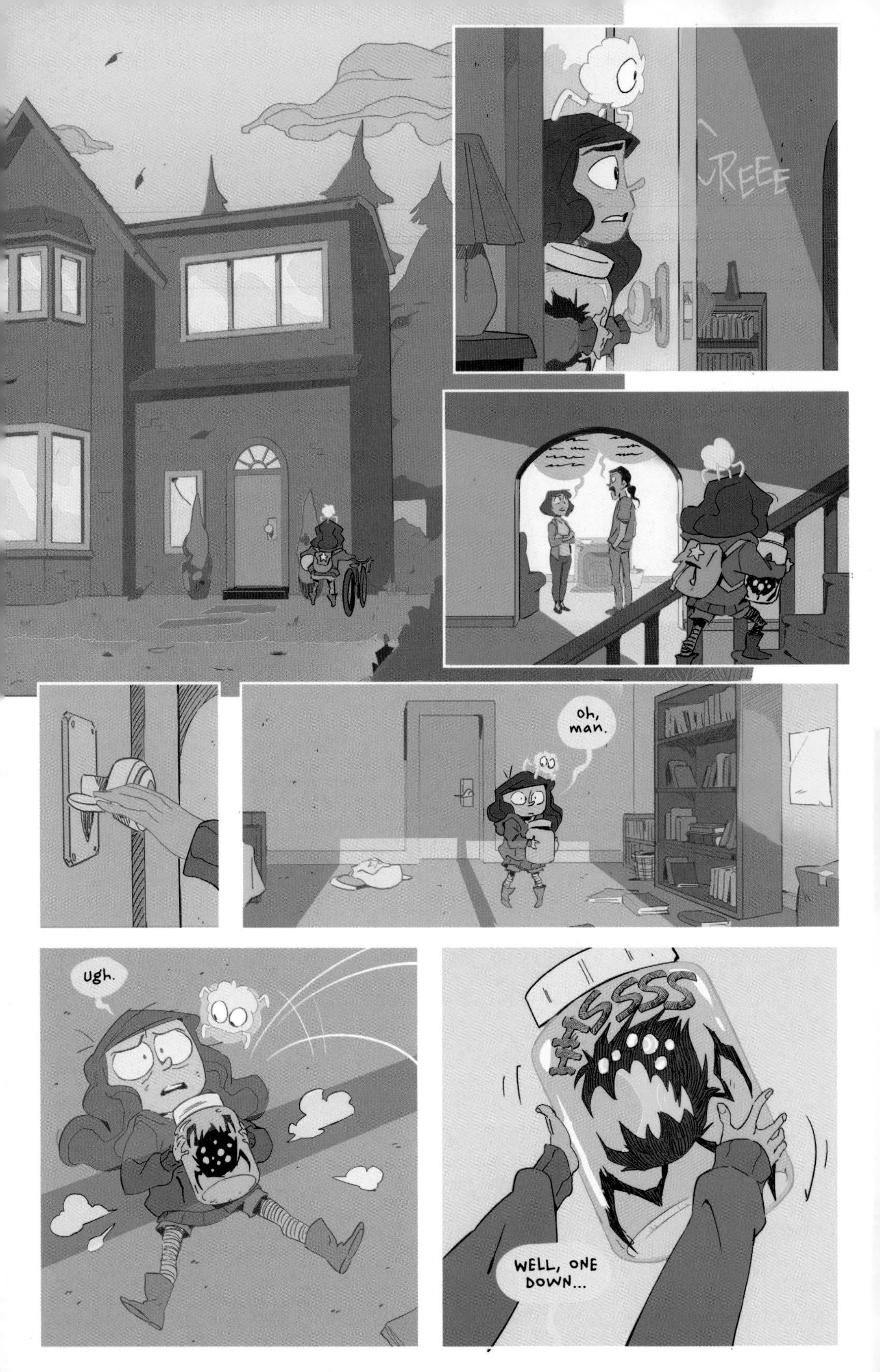
CREEE
oh, man.
Ugh.
HISSSS
WELL, ONE DOWN...

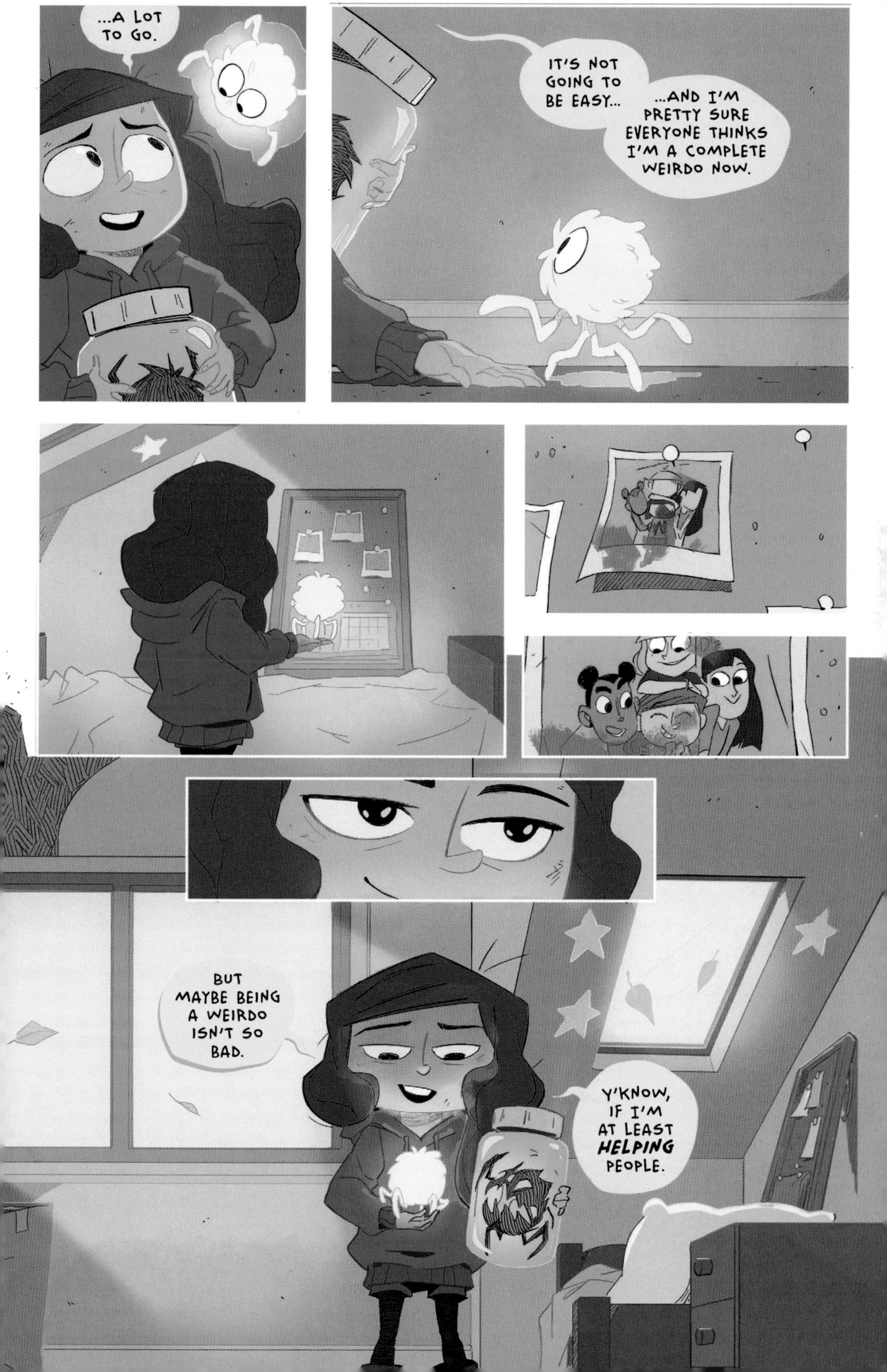
...A LOT TO GO.
IT'S NOT GOING TO BE EASY...
...AND I'M PRETTY SURE EVERYONE THINKS I'M A COMPLETE WEIRDO NOW.
BUT MAYBE BEING A WEIRDO ISN'T SO BAD.
Y'KNOW, IF I'M AT LEAST *HELPING* PEOPLE.

SO...

...WHAT DO WE DO WITH THE GLUM?

I MEAN I CAN'T-- Y'KNOW! BUT I CAN'T JUST **LET IT GO!** BUT CAN I **KEEP IT!?**

I MEAN, DOES IT NEED TO **EAT!?** CAN IT **GET OUT?** WHAT IF IT **ESCAPES?** **WHAT IF--**

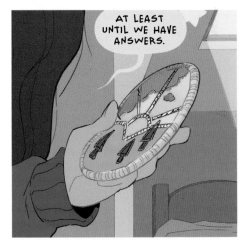

AT LEAST UNTIL WE HAVE ANSWERS.

Heh.

ONE THING AT A TIME.

HERE'S AN IDEA.

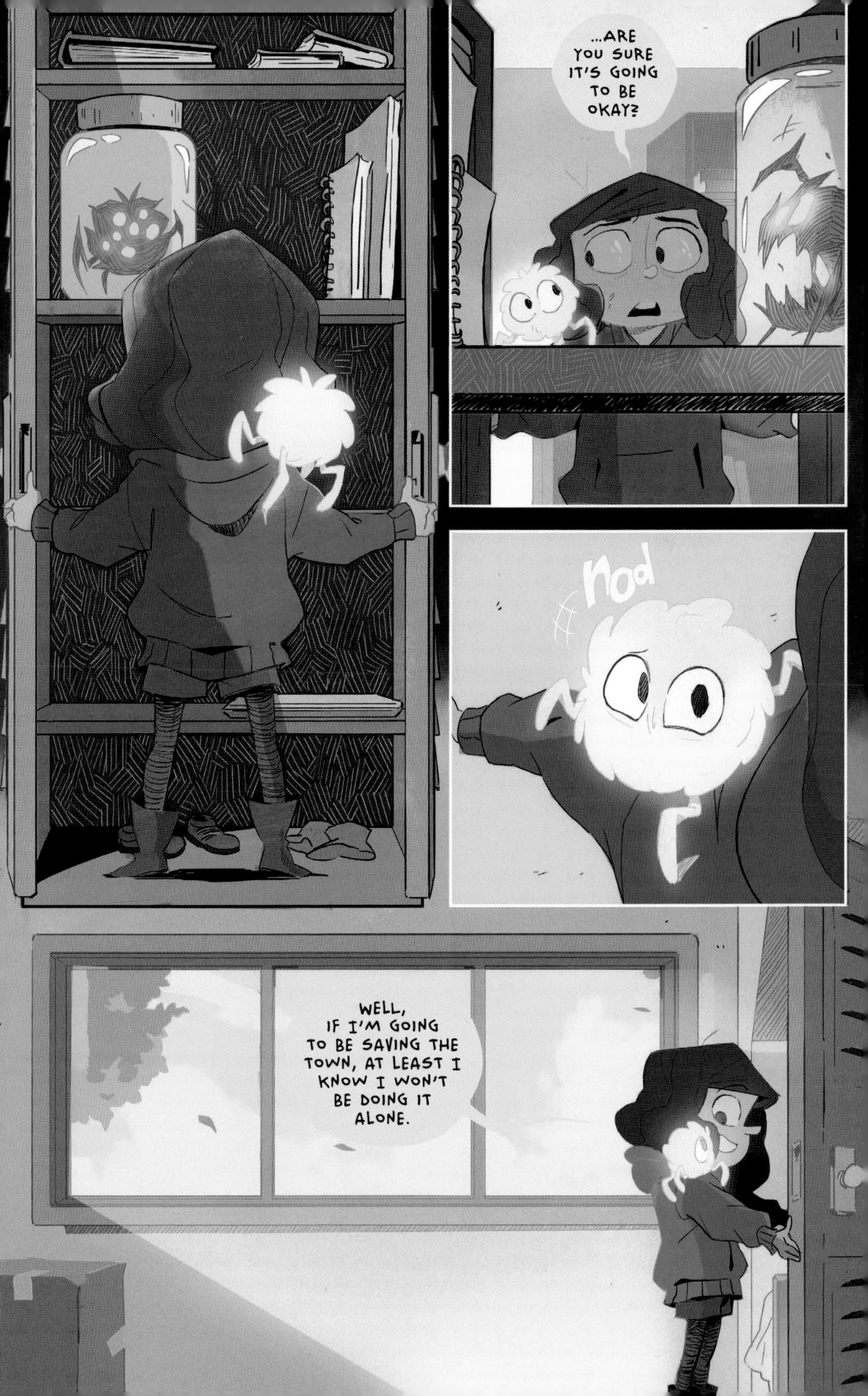
...ARE YOU SURE IT'S GOING TO BE OKAY?
nod
WELL, IF I'M GOING TO BE SAVING THE TOWN, AT LEAST I KNOW I WON'T BE DOING IT ALONE.

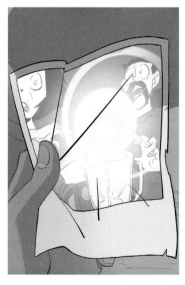

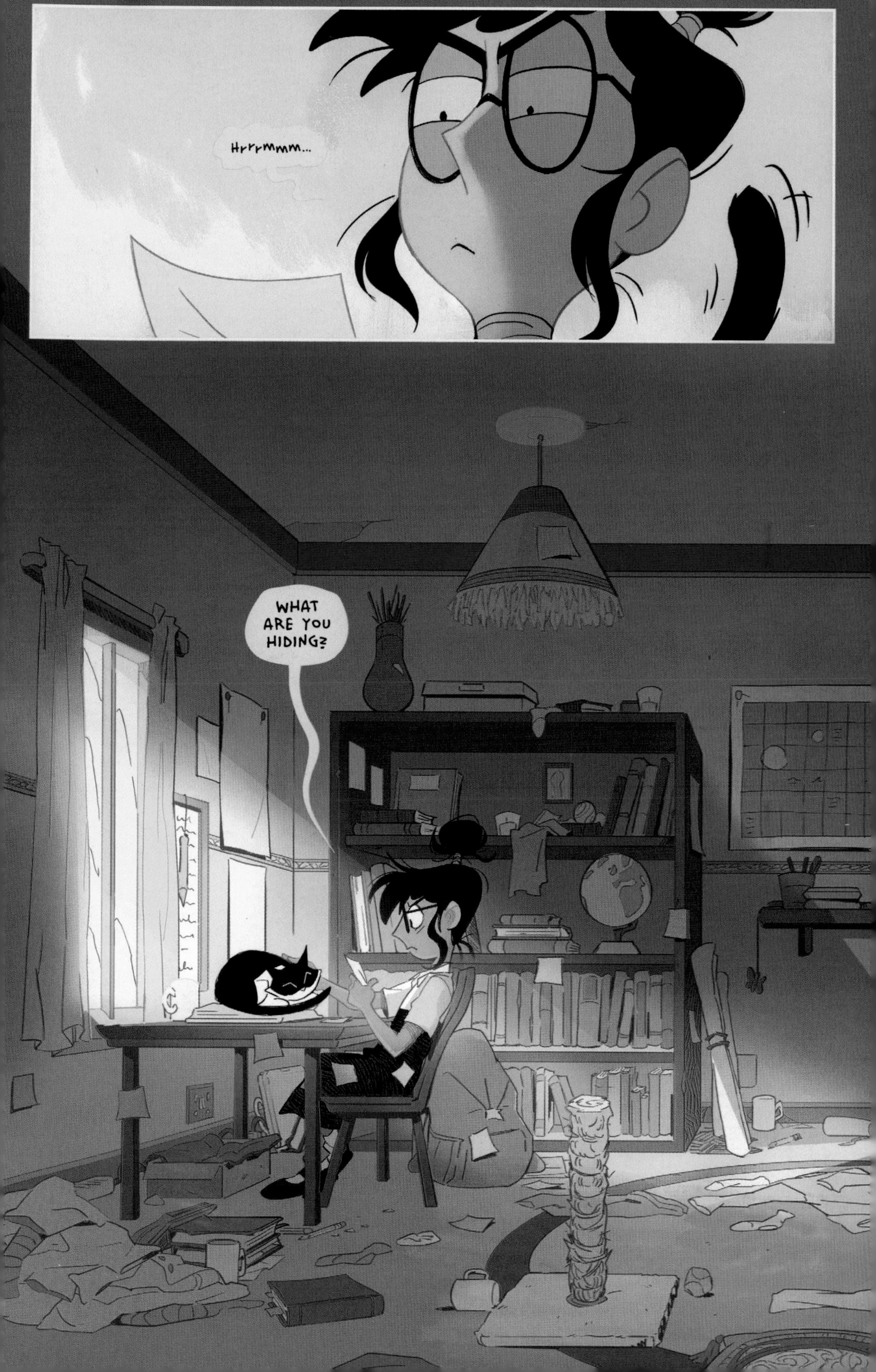
Hrrrmmm...
WHAT ARE YOU HIDING?

India Swift

Animator, sometimes director, story artist, and general ragamuffin. After directing the "Starlight Brigade" music video, India moved on to storyboarding for Nickelodeon's *Rise of the Teenage Mutant Ninja Turtles: The Movie* and, more recently, the *Transformers: Earthspark* series.

Most of all, she wants to create work with a sincerity at its heart that affects and inspires others, leaving a lasting impact and a positive, affirming message.

Michael Doig

Michael is the color wizard of Knights of the Light Table, directing the color design for their "Starlight Brigade" and "Magnum Bullets" animated music videos. In comics, he has assisted Matias Bergara on color for Boom Studios' Eisner-nominated fantasy epic, *Coda*.

He likes cats, and he has a penchant for bears.

You can find them both at **doigswift.com** and discover more about the world they created for Bridgette at **girlandtheglim.com.**